First published in 2017 by Bloodhound Books

www.bloodhoundbooks.com

Print ISBN 978-1-912175-78-9

PRAISE FOR THE RED COBRA

Praise for The Black Hornet

"Wow! It was like a movie in its action packed delivery. I would even go as far to say that it is better than his last bestselling novel, which I gave 5* also."

Abby Jayne Slater-Fairbrother - Anne Bonny Book Reviews

"A fast moving book for fans of spies and subterfuge."

Misfits Farm - Goodreads Reviewer

"There are plenty of twists and turns and quite a few OMG! moments."

Jackie Roche - Goodreads Reviewer

"As I've come to expect from Rob Sinclair, this is a fast moving, well written story with lots of action."

Cathy Ryan - Between The Lines

"Wow! A fantastic read from start to finish."

Helen - Breakaway Reviewers

For My Gran

CHAPTER 1

Lake Maggiore, Italy

Looking out over the edge of the pool to the serenity of the crystal lake below, he could almost believe he was in paradise. Thomas Maddison would defy anyone to spend just a few days at Villa Mariangela and not feel the same way. But underneath the glitz of the lavish setting, the place was far from idyllic, he knew. Scratch the blissful surface, and lies, deceit and blood would ooze from the many cracks and warts.

Maddison pushed the forbidding thoughts aside and swam across the infinity pool to the other side, turned, then went more slowly back the other way. The water seemed to suspend unnaturally in the air, as though conjoined with the glistening blue of the lake below. He grabbed the disguised edge at the far end where the water teasingly cascaded over and down into a small gully, and then he stopped and took a minute to look out across the view as the warm morning sun beat down on his face.

The villa behind him, on the southern tip of the long, winding lake, faced north. Although he couldn't see from his high perch, around the twists and bends in front of him the lake wound its way between the spectacular hills of Lombardy, at the northernmost points of Italy, and on into the alpine scenery of southern Switzerland. Villa Mariangela was not just a beautiful and extravagant home; it was a location of strategic importance for Maddison's employer.

Employer? Was that the right word? It was the simplest way to describe their relationship, Maddison reckoned, though it didn't really explain much.

'Maddison,' came a man's voice.

Maddison spun around in the water, still grasping the edge with one hand as his legs bobbed up and down below. He spotted Clyde approaching the pool. Clyde Montana. The name didn't fit the man at all. To Maddison the name brought with it the image of a nineteenth-century cowboy in the American Old West. Chiselled jaw and stubble and a squint that Clint Eastwood would be proud of. This Clyde, however, was a product of some of England's most expensive educational institutions, which was evident in his stiff manner and old world accent. He was tall, wiry, with closely cropped hair. Always clean-shaven. Always sporting designer and smart casual garb. He basically looked like a rich and weedy geek, inoffensive, and not in the least bit dangerous.

How looks can be deceptive.

'He wants to see you,' Clyde said.

He. Names weren't needed. Not where *he* was concerned.

'Okay, give me five minutes.'

'He's in the guest house.'

Clyde turned and walked off without further elaboration. Maddison let go of the edge and swam back across to the other side of the pool where he pulled himself out. The morning air sent a wave of goose pimples over his wet, tanned brown skin and he grabbed a towel from the pool edge and wrapped it around himself. In front of him was the main villa. The modern pool was a stark contrast to the classical structure which looked like a miniature Renaissance palace. The villa's grounds, rising into the hills behind the lake, extended to over three acres. As well as the main villa, whose history stretched back over three hundred years, there were two other separate living spaces within the grounds: the building Clyde had referred to as the guest house – originally a boat house – and the more modern, glass-rich pool house, which Maddison headed into to get changed.

He slicked back his dark brown hair as he went to the downstairs bathroom then, as he stared at his pile of clothes, he ran his fingers through his speckled grey stubble. No, he'd shave tomorrow. He dressed in the pair of khaki trousers and cotton shirt. He slipped on his loafers then headed back out into the sunshine, across the deep green lawns, through the glorious floral gardens, and finally down the twisting stone steps that led to the lake edge and the guest house.

As he was descending, Maddison saw one of the housekeepers climbing the steps from the bottom, clutching a bundle of white bedsheets. Adriana. She was twenty-three and from one of the local villages. Maddison had taken quite a liking to her since she'd joined the villa's extensive domestic crew some three months previously. He liked that she seemed disinterested in the money and the glamour of the host's lifestyle. He'd seen her spurn advances from some of the men – champagne and rides in fast boats and faster cars didn't seem to appeal to her. He was determined to find out what did.

'*Buon giorno,*' Adriana said as they reached each other and both of them stopped.

'*Buon giorno.*' Maddison gave her a warm smile.

'Another early morning swim,' Adriana said in her thickly accented English.

'Best way to start the day,' Maddison said. Adriana continued past him. 'You should join me sometime.'

She glanced around then looked away coyly. 'Maybe another time.'

'I look forward to it. You have a good day, Adriana.'

'You too. *Ciao.*'

She carried on up the steps and Maddison watched her for a moment before he turned his focus back to the guesthouse. The once-basic wooden structure, which hovered over the edge of the lake, had been converted some ten years earlier when it became too small for its original purpose. Which Maddison understood to mean it wasn't big enough to house the gleaming yacht which was moored alongside it on the purpose built jetty.

The guesthouse was used frequently, but Maddison hadn't realised anyone had been staying there the previous night. Or maybe Adriana was just getting it ready for someone to stay that night? Maddison felt a fleeting pinch of suspicion as he made his way to the front door, but it quickly disappeared. There was no reason to suspect his cover had been blown after all this time.

He stopped at the front door and reached out to knock, but before his knuckle could rap on the thick wood door, it was opened from the inside. Dean, a squat and heavily muscled man, would have looked out of place in any other job but security.

'Morning,' Maddison said.

'He's in the kitchen.'

Maddison carried on through into the expansive open-plan space. There was nothing much classical in the room. Everything was sleek, modern and pricey.

Sure enough his illustrious boss, Draper, was there, standing by the kitchen counter with his back to Maddison.

'You wanted to see me?' Maddison said.

Draper spun around and gave a half smile. He ran a hand through his long silvery slicked-back hair. Together with his sparkling blue eyes, wide toothy smile and prominent cheekbones, he had a face that drew people in. Perhaps a contrast to his plain and casual attire – a pair of scraggy deck shorts, sandals and blue V-neck jumper.

'Damn thing's broken.' Draper turned his attention back to the pristine looking coffee machine and banged it hard on the top. It rattled and gurgled to life. He huffed. 'Can you believe that? Five thousand Euros this thing cost me. It should be faultless, yet it still responds best to a heavy hand.'

Maddison swallowed hard at Draper's offish tone, the first glimmer of doubt fighting to take hold in his mind. He pushed it away.

'You want one?' Draper asked.

'Yeah. An espresso please.'

'Here, you come over and do it.'

Draper grabbed his drink and moved past. Maddison took a small cup from the counter and placed a black capsule into the top of the machine. He looked around the room as the machine gurgled away. No sign of Clyde or anyone else. Maddison and Draper were alone.

'Everything still on for this afternoon?' Maddison asked.

'What? Oh, yeah, that. It is. But I'm not sure I'll need you to come with me.'

'Really?' Maddison pulled the small cup out from under the machine's nozzle. He turned to face Draper who was leaning against a cabinet by the edge of the kitchen area, his head just a couple of inches from the wooden beam above him. At six feet four, he was several inches taller than Maddison.

'That's what I needed to speak to you about,' Draper said. 'Come and take a seat. There's someone I need you to meet.'

Maddison raised an eyebrow but said nothing. He sipped the treacly liquid in his cup and enjoyed the moment as the strong vapour worked through his sinuses. He moved out of the kitchen and across to the oak dining table where he sat down on one of the eight chairs.

Moments later, he heard footsteps coming from the hallway and he turned to see an unfamiliar man walking into the room.

At least, Maddison's first impression was that the man was unfamiliar, but as he stared into his uncaring, knowing eyes, a distant memory tugged away in his mind.

Or was it simple déjà vu?

'So who's this?' Maddison asked, not bothering to hide his agitation. He kept his eyes on the new arrival as he placed his espresso cup down onto the table.

'This is your replacement,' Draper said, looking at the man, who simply smirked. The man came up to Draper's side, both of them remaining a few feet away from Maddison. Maddison said nothing to the statement, despite all of the thoughts that suddenly ballooned in his mind. Draper didn't need to explain further. Maddison understood what was happening. What his confused mind couldn't understand was why.

Had Draper found out?

As Maddison continued to stare at Draper and the man, almost not daring to look away, he heard a creak somewhere behind him. Another person, coming out of the lounge?

So this was how it was going to end. A stab in the back.

Maddison knew in that moment that, for whatever reason, the game was finally over. There was no need to play along anymore. The best course of action was for him to leap up, tackle the man behind him – was it Clyde? – and take whatever weapon he was carrying. Then Maddison would launch himself at Draper and the new arrival. After that, he would attack any other man, woman or beast that got in his way as he made his escape from the secured compound.

He knew the best exit route. Which vehicle to take. Which direction to head. It wasn't as though he hadn't planned for this moment.

But Maddison did none of those things. He couldn't. No matter how much his brain willed him to jump up from the seat and begin the counter-assault, his body felt disconnected. The room was swirling in front of him. Sweat droplets were quickly forming on his head. He felt nauseous and plonked his elbow down onto the table to try to keep from falling off the chair. He stole his eyes from Draper and glanced down to the small cup on the table.

A second later, a leather-gloved hand whipped in front of him from behind, and thrust a metal tent peg into Maddison's hand. He shouted out in pain as a spatter of blood squirted out onto his face. Another gloved hand came forward, clutching a hammer. The head of the tool was slammed down onto the hooked top of the peg, over and over, purposeful strikes that drove the metal further and further through Maddison's hand and securing it firmly to the oak table below. Maddison's hand, arm, his whole body was now shaking in agony.

'It's a muscle relaxant,' Draper said, coming forward toward Maddison, sounding unmoved. 'Clever, isn't it? You can't move a thing right now. But the pain? The pain is still there, raw and strong.'

'What is this?' Maddison tried to shout out, but his words were slurred, his tongue and his jaw barely moving.

'What is this!' the man standing by Draper mocked, deliberately slurring his speech to the point of incomprehension.

Draper gave the man a heartless look before turning his attention back to Maddison.

'Sorry about him,' Draper said. 'He's not like you and me. A bit rough around the edges, you could say. I have to admit, there's a lot about him that I'm not so in tune with. Me and you... we were similar. I think that's why we got along so easily.'

The man grated his teeth, and Maddison could see he'd taken real offence at Draper's words. Not that it helped Maddison's position.

The same sense of déjà vu flashed in Maddison's mind again.

'I know you,' Maddison tried his best to say.

The man narrowed his eyes. Then he moved forward, anger on his face, though Maddison wasn't sure why. He headed past Maddison, then a second later, came back to his side clutching the hammer and another metal rod.

The two gloved hands from the unseen attacker came around Maddison and grabbed at his free arm, pinning his hand to the table. The man at his side, eyes full of menace, held Maddison's stare as he put the metal in position.

'No,' he said. 'You don't know me.'

He brought the hammer down and the metal crunched through flesh and the delicate bones on Maddison's hand. His body spasmed as pain consumed him, but he let out nothing more than a moan. He wouldn't give them the satisfaction.

'You don't know anything about me,' the man spat. He brought his snarling face closer to Maddison's. 'The problem though is that *I* know *you.*'

'Which, I'm sure by now you realise, means that I know everything you've told me about you is a lie,' Draper said, folding his arms. 'Whoever you really are, you won't leave my villa alive. It's up to you how many pieces we take before you talk.'

Draper moved forward and grabbed hold of one of the metal rods sticking out from Maddison's hands. He yanked it back and forth, a squelching sound coming from the stricken hand as the flesh was pushed, pulled and torn. Maddison grimaced and shook in his chair, trying all the tricks he'd been taught many years earlier for channelling away and ignoring the pain.

They didn't work. Not when faced with agony like this.

Draper crouched down. His face was placid, no hint of anger, and when he spoke it was with warmth and comfort that made Maddison, for all his strength and determination, seriously question just what this man was capable of.

'It's time for you talk now, my friend,' Draper said. 'And, one way or another, you can be damn sure you're going to tell me *everything*.'

CHAPTER 2

Undisclosed location, South Pacific

Ryker stared down at the red-stained bones. The colour was not from blood, but from the iron-rich soil in which the bones had lain for several months as the body they once belonged to had slowly decayed. Other than the skeleton there was virtually nothing left of *her*. No flesh, muscle or organs – that had all been eaten away. All that remained was the pile of crumpled bones, teeth, fragments of torn clothing, some thick matted locks of hair and small patches of leathery dried skin that had somehow resisted decay.

Not much that resembled a human being. Nothing that resembled Lisa. But Ryker knew it was her. He clawed away at the thick red soil with his fingertips, exposing more of the remains. He was no pathologist, he had no idea how they'd killed her, how much she'd suffered. He saw no obvious signs of broken bones, no skull fracture, but that didn't mean her death had been quick and pain free.

With the horrific, morbid thoughts crashing through his mind, Ryker clawed more furiously at the earth. He wasn't sure why. Didn't know exactly what he was trying to achieve. His hands, already blistered from digging with the shovel, were becoming swollen and raw. He could feel his fingertips, which were as red as the bones he was uncovering, stinging as the skin was rubbed away with each swipe. He caught his hand on the jagged edge of bone and opened up his skin. Now the dried red soil and bones were joined by his crimson blood, dripping down.

He still didn't stop clawing away. Only when his hands and his arms felt as numb as his mind did he slump back, panting and gasping, against the side of the unevenly dug pit.

He growled in anger. He should have been there for her. He should have protected her. He would never forgive himself. He doubted even revenge – however bloody and nasty he could make it – could ever come close to freeing him of the pain he was feeling.

But he couldn't wallow. Doing so wouldn't help him. It certainly wouldn't help Lisa.

He was about to stand up when a glint of metal among the bones caught his eye. He frowned and reached down with his bloodied hand. He picked away at the soil, ignoring the pain in his fingertips.

When he realised what the metal was, he let out a long, sorrowful sigh and sat back in the pit, the small silvery pendant held tightly in his hand. He and Lisa had never been materialistic, rarely buying each other expensive gifts. This one had been precious, not for its material worth but for what it represented. He'd found the small white gold olive branch, about an inch long, while walking the beach one day. It looked to have snapped off a larger object with a sharp jagged edge of metal at one end. He'd had the piece cleaned up, polished and remounted as a pendant, and had bought a necklace for Lisa to wear it. She'd loved it. Had never taken it off. The olive branch – a symbol of peace going back as far as ancient Greece – had seemed apt at the time, when they'd finally left behind their former chaotic and dangerous lives.

Looking at the pendant, Ryker simply felt naive and stupid to have ever thought they could live a life of peace.

He stuffed the necklace and pendant in his pocket and took one last look at what remained of the only woman he had loved. Then, achingly, he hauled himself back to his feet. He grabbed the shovel and dumped the soil back into place on top of her remains.

When he was finished, he clambered out of the hole and headed across the overgrown grounds to the house. His home. Their home. At least it had been. Now it just resembled a worthless lump of wood and glass.

As Ryker opened the sliding glass doors and stepped inside, there was a hiss and wheeze as tepid air escaped and mixed with the hot dry air on the outside. Either that, or it was the call of the ghost that he was sure now haunted the place.

He couldn't stay there anymore. Not a single night.

Ryker went into the bedroom and grabbed some of his clothes from the wardrobe, ignoring everything else in his path. Then he left the same way he'd come and headed down to the beach to wash himself. There was no running water, no gas, no electricity in the house. He had no idea when the utilities had been turned off.

Down at the frothing shoreline, Ryker stripped off his dirty clothes and plunged into the salty water. He did his best to clean off the red that covered him, only coming out when he was shivering violently.

After wrapping a towel around his goose-pimpled body, he grabbed his clothes from the sand.

He fished in his pocket for the phone he'd bought the day before, when he'd landed back on the island. He frowned when he saw he had a missed call. Only one person had the number. There was also a text message: *Call me.*

No other details, no sign-off, but Ryker knew who it was from, and he thought he knew what it was about.

He hit redial.

She answered on the first ring. 'Ryker.'

'Yeah,' was all he said, his mind too consumed by thoughts of those stained bones to offer up any more.

'I found them. The men you're looking for.'

'Where?' Ryker clenched his fists as anger took hold.

'In Mexico. I–'

'Okay. I'm on my way.'

CHAPTER 3

Four days later

Mérida, Mexico

Ryker was in a taxi heading into the centre of Mérida, the largest city and capital of the state of Yucatan. It was about as far away from Mexico City as Ryker could get while still being in the same country. There were many reasons why he was hesitant to set foot in that part of the world again. Not least because the last time he'd been to Mexico City he'd been ambushed by corrupt police officers, and ended up in jail at the behest of one of the local drugs cartels who'd long held a grudge against him because of his former life. And they still did, most likely.

That was an episode he really was not looking to repeat on this visit. From that mess there had at least been one positive though. Eleanor Willoughby. A field agent for the Joint Intelligence Agency – the JIA, a clandestine agency for which Ryker had worked for many years. Until he'd met Lisa and tried to escape that life for good.

When he'd been imprisoned in Mexico City, Willoughby had turned up at the behest of the JIA to assist him. After being sprung from the jail he'd helped Willoughby and the JIA dismantle a US, Mexico cross-border arms smuggling ring. A quid pro quo, if you like. Yet Willoughby still felt she owed Ryker. He hoped she was about to pay off that debt.

As Ryker stared out of the window, his fingers played with the olive branch pendant around his neck that he'd purchased a thicker, sturdier chain for. The symbol was a constant reminder not just of the life that he and Lisa had tried to find for themselves, but of what he had to do to avenge her death.

Ryker looked out from the taxi to the neat and colourful low-rise buildings, many with prominent stone arches and wrought-iron balconies. From the buildings, it was evident that Mérida was not just far removed from Mexico City in terms of geographic distance, but in culture too. He'd been to the Yucatan Peninsula before, and enjoyed the clash of cultures which still existed in modern times. The majority of the inhabitants in Yucatan were of Mayan rather than European descent. He guessed these were true Mexicans, if there was such a thing.

The taxi driver stopped outside the hotel – a handsome colonial-style stone building – and Ryker paid him a generous tip. The driver rattled off some quick-fire words in heavily accented Spanish, which Ryker just about caught the gist of. He thanked the guy then stepped from the car into the scorching and humid midday heat, lugging his backpack with him.

Ryker waited for the taxi to disappear. He wasn't staying at that hotel. It was an obvious place for a tourist to come to. As distinguishable as Ryker was, given his six foot three height, thick build, and increasingly gnarled face, the taxi driver wouldn't have noticed much out of the ordinary if he was ever asked about the Englishman he'd dropped off there. His destination was a little under a mile away. He'd already memorised the directions from the hotel, and did a quick take up and down the street before he set off on foot.

He'd not been to Mérida before, but as he strolled along through the centre it seemed pleasant enough. Soon though he was moving out of the main commercial area, with its oversized churches and museums and municipal buildings, and into narrower, quieter and quainter streets. Ryker kept his eyes busy as he idled along, past rows of clothes shops and mobile phone stores, cafés and restaurants – the waft of spices and grilled meat filling his nostrils.

It was impossible to know for sure if he'd been followed, but as he continued on, there was nothing to suggest that he had.

Taking a deliberately circuitous route, Ryker came upon the building he was looking for a little over half an hour later.

The five-storey apartment block was inconspicuous in its surroundings. Neither particularly small nor big nor luxurious nor decrepit. Just another building like all the others around it and in a similar state of repair – the yellow-painted render on the outside chipped in places and the paint of many wood shutters peeling.

Ryker headed up to the large entrance door and pressed on the intercom for apartment 4c.

Seconds later, he heard a click. He pushed the door open and stepped into the cool of the high-ceilinged foyer that was finished in mock marble. A staircase was off to the right – no lift.

He headed up the stairs, checking up and down as he went. When he arrived on the fourth floor he saw the door to 4c was already ajar. Ever cautious, he moved with more stealth. He'd arrived in Mexico only a few hours earlier and hadn't had time to arm himself since then, but he would be ready if this meet was some sort of set-up. It wouldn't be the first time, though he couldn't think of any reason why Willoughby would do that. It wasn't that he trusted her one hundred per cent – there wasn't anyone alive he would put in that bracket. He just couldn't figure a scenario where there would be benefit in her deceiving him, like this.

Ryker reached out and pushed the door further open. He peered inside into the box-like apartment and took a small, silent step inside. Then heard movement behind him. Then saw movement off to his left, inside the apartment.

Moving with purpose, Ryker took another step forward, kicked shut the door behind him, spun, and grabbed at the figure to his left, noting the glint of metal in the hand. He twisted around and pushed the figure up against the closed front door, pinning the arm to the wood.

Then he relaxed.

He looked into Willoughby's eyes. Saw the smile. Then he looked at her hand, clutching a silver spatula. He relaxed further and pushed his head forward and looked into the peephole. Out in the corridor, a middle-aged woman was dragging a lapdog out of the apartment opposite.

'All done with your threat assessment?' Willoughby sounded unfazed by Ryker's over-the-top reaction.

Was it over the top though?

'I've never been attacked with a spatula before,' he said. 'So I guess we're good.'

'Believe it or not, it wouldn't be the first time I've used one in anger.'

Ryker raised an eyebrow.

'Perhaps you could let go of me. You're hurting my arm and the eggs are burning.'

Ryker huffed, let go and stepped back. He noticed the reddened flesh on her arm where he'd gripped her. Neither of them said anything more of it. Willoughby moved off into the kitchen area where there was a pan of eggs sizzling away. He watched her for a moment. She was dressed in jeans and a yellow-strapped top. Her loose wavy hair was blonder than he remembered, and reached down into the middle of her back.

'*Huevos revueltos* good for you?' She turned to face him.

'Yeah.'

'I guessed you wouldn't have eaten in a while.'

'You guessed right.'

Ryker glanced about the place. There were two internal doors. One he could see led to a small shower room, the other to the apartment's only bedroom. The kitchen, dining area and lounge were all open plan. The apartment had the basic furniture expected of a home, but no personal ornaments or titbits.

'What is this place?' Ryker asked.

'It's not a designated safe house, if that's what you mean.' Which he'd figured, because it was too basic. 'But you'll be safe enough here. I rented in cash. One week. Less obtrusive you staying here than in a hotel.'

'Thanks.'

'Come on, sit down.' Willoughby spooned the eggs onto two plates and headed to the small, round pine dining table that was heavily scratched and dented.

Ryker went over and sat down, his belly grumbling when his eyes honed in on the food. He took a large forkful. Damn good was the verdict, though he didn't say so. His mind was still too distracted.

'What happened?' Willoughby asked after a few more silent mouthfuls.

'Powell was right. She's dead.'

The words hung in the air. Ryker didn't look up from the plate of food. He didn't want to see the look on Willoughby's face. He didn't want her pity, her emotional support or anything else. He just wanted her help in finding the bastards responsible.

'Powell's dead, you know,' Willoughby said.

Marcus Powell. American agent. Ryker had never quite figured out if he was a good guy or a bad guy. Powell too had been gunning to pull apart the arms smuggling ring that the JIA were investigating in America, and was the man who'd orchestrated Ryker's release from jail. But he'd also tried to set Ryker up. Ryker still didn't know exactly who Powell worked for, yet the man had somehow known not only about Ryker's past, but about Lisa's fate too.

'No. I didn't know he was dead,' Ryker said, not feeling particularly bothered about the fact. Though it did mean he would never get answers from Powell, about who he worked for, and how he knew about Lisa.

'He was in intensive care for weeks after the siege at Camp Joseph, but his injuries were too severe. They turned off his life support.'

'Who was he really?' Ryker asked.

'We still don't know. We believe he was linked to the CIA, but nobody will confirm that officially. Either way he's not a problem anymore.'

They both went silent and Ryker continued scoffing the food.

'You found her?' Willoughby asked.

Ryker shook his head. 'There is no "her" anymore. What I found was a pile of bones, buried right there, where we lived.'

Another silence followed, and it grew more and more uncomfortable.

'The two men you're looking for,' Willoughby said, 'do you really think they did it?'

'If I have to, I'll spill every drop of their blood to find out.'

He could feel Willoughby's gaze on him but he still didn't look up. 'You said you'd found them.'

'I think so.'

When he'd finished the plate of food he put his fork down.

'That was damn good, Willoughby,' he said, finally catching her eye. She smiled at him and he felt a sliver of warmth return inside him. 'But why are you helping me like this?'

She looked put out by his question. She put her fork down on her half-eaten plate of food and stood up.

'You helped me, Ryker. I'm just returning the favour.'

She walked over to the small dresser and opened a drawer. First her hand came out holding a black handgun. An FN Five-Seven. She placed it on the table. 'That's for you. One full magazine already loaded.'

'Good choice,' Ryker said. It wasn't his favourite gun, but it was plenty good enough, renowned for the small calibre, high velocity ammunition that it used. The cartridges of the Five-Seven were capable of penetrating many standard Kevlar vests even at considerable distances.

Next, Willoughby's hand came out holding a manila folder. She sat back down at the table, opened the folder and took out the bundle of papers inside.

'It took quite a bit of searching and calling in of favours to track these two down,' she said. 'I know you think they were involved in Lisa's death, but I'm struggling to see it myself.'

'How do you mean?' he asked. It was searching for these two men that had brought him to Mexico the last time. He hadn't found them then because of the catalogue of events that followed, though was still determined to track them down to find out if and how they were involved in Lisa's murder.

'There's nothing exceptional about them,' Willoughby said. 'They're not trained assassins, Ryker. They don't work for any agency, or even any of the major cartels. They're just regular lowlifes. Thieving, street level drugs, that sort of thing.'

Ryker's brain was whirring. Two everyday scumbags from Mexico had tracked him and Lisa down to their supposedly secret location, and then when Ryker was away they'd managed to get the drop on Lisa? Had then managed to dispose of her body and flee the island leaving such a thin trail of their presence and their movements?

That wasn't possible.

There was something missing. But then the intelligence he'd already found himself several months earlier, when Lisa had first disappeared, was strong. Those two men had been there, on the island. Ryker had worked backward, first identifying that a rented car had been seen outside his house the day Lisa disappeared. He'd tracked back and found where the car had come from, found CCTV images of the men's faces from shops nearby. Had traced their movements back to the local airport, and from pulling in favours found their bogus identities and further traced Mexico City as the origin of their journey. But there the trail had stopped. Ryker believed one hundred per cent they were involved in Lisa's murder, but it seemed increasingly likely that they were simply hired guns. The party responsible for hiring the two men was the real catch. The prey that Ryker would hunt down for as long as he lived.

'Just tell me what you've got,' Ryker said. 'I'll get what I need out of these two.'

'I'm not so sure about that,' Willoughby said.

'Meaning what?'

Willoughby passed a large black and white photograph over the table. The bloodied face of a corpse. Despite the battering his face had taken, Ryker recognised him.

'Apparently it was a bar brawl, though there's no record I can find of anyone else being involved in that fight. Most likely he was beaten to death because of simple gang warfare.'

'And the other guy?'

'He's in jail. In Mexico City.' Ryker felt himself tense. 'And he will be for at least the next two years.'

'I have to speak to him.'

'Are you really sure you want to go down that path? You want to go back *there*?'

'Absolutely sure,' Ryker said.

'Because there may be another way.'

'Another way to what?'

'To get what you need. I said these two are nothing. Even if you could get into that jail to speak to this guy, and even if he decides to tell you what he knows, I don't think it will get you the answers you need.'

'You brought me all the way back out to Mexico just to tell me this? To tell me not to bother searching anymore?'

'No. I said there may be another way.'

'And I said another way to what?'

'To find out who really killed Lisa.'

'Go on then.'

'I think I know who paid those guys, and the answer is right here, in Yucatan.'

CHAPTER 4

Willoughby headed off not long after handing over to Ryker the information she'd uncovered. He didn't ask where she was going. Back to Mexico City, he presumed, where she was still posted by the JIA. Though he wondered whether perhaps she would hang around Mérida in case he needed further assistance. Or simply to spy on him for the JIA.

Really she'd already done more to help him than he could expect of her. Plus, he didn't want her to be part of what was to come next. He liked Willoughby. She was a decent person, and she didn't need the blood on her hands.

The information Willoughby uncovered had added additional layers of intrigue – if that was the right word – to the circumstances of Lisa's murder. One of the two men Ryker had connected to her death through his own investigative work – Diego Tamayo – was now himself dead. He'd been beaten to death, his body found in a back alley. The local police in Mexico City had simply labelled it drug-related violence. No arrests had been made. The fact was the only police time likely spent on his murder was in recording his death.

The other man, Emilio Conesa, was actually American-born, though he held dual nationality. He'd been sentenced to four years for his part in an armed robbery gone wrong. Other than them both residing in Mexico, the two men were seemingly unconnected, as were their fates. But Willoughby had found a connection.

According to informants on the ground in Mexico, both men had recently found themselves with several thousand dollars to splash around. Drugs, booze and prostitutes had been their main choice of spend. Both men had also taken multiple trips to Cancún – the playboy capital of Mexico, and an area renowned for lavish spending and, with it, money laundering.

On the face of it, they were just two young guys partying hard, but there was more to the story. In Cancún, both men had visited the offices of the same real estate business; El Yuca Property. From the little Ryker knew of Tamayo and Conesa, and what could be easily gleaned of El Yuca from open access records, neither man struck him particularly as being interested in, or having the capital, to be involved in the high-end property company.

El Yuca Property was Ryker's next destination. He bought an ageing 900cc Triumph for two hundred dollars in cash from a dealer in Mérida, and early the next morning, he ate at a local café then headed out onto the Carretera Federal 180 which would take him the three hundred kilometres to Cancún.

As he rode out of the city, the scenery around Ryker changed from low-rise apartment blocks to industrial warehouses, to nothing but mile after mile of tropical jungle.

Near to halfway between the two cities, Ryker spotted the turn-off for the world famous Mayan temples of Chichen Itza, and every now and then through the thick trees could see the tops of the grey stone temples. Maybe one day he'd get the chance to visit. But not that day.

It was early afternoon when Ryker arrived in the resort city of Cancún. On the Caribbean coast, the city was a world away from central Mexico, with gleaming new-build high-rise hotels, luxury villas and expensive wine bars aplenty, and miles of white sand beaches. The spot was a favoured haunt of young American partygoers, but there was also money there. Lots of money, as displayed by the variety of five-star hotels and expensive European cars driving about the place.

Ryker wondered though how much of the money floating about – legitimate or otherwise – found its way into the hands of the born and bred locals. Not much of it, was his verdict, given the vast disparity that existed between the obvious tourist areas around the coast and the lagoon – modern and heavily Americanised – and the outer parts of the city which were much more... Mexican. Or was it Mayan?

Ryker parked his motorbike in a small car park outside a cluster of bars and restaurants in downtown Cancún that were still busy with lunchtime customers. He double-checked the GPS map on his phone then walked the short distance through the streets to the offices of El Yuca Property. In his backpack he carried everything he'd brought to Mexico; some spare clothes, a stash of US dollars, a passport in the name of James Ryker, and a small toiletry kit. He wasn't sure where he'd be staying that night, but he'd not left anything behind in Mérida.

The Five-Seven Willoughby had given him was in the waistband of his trousers. He had one full magazine for the gun – twenty bullets. If he could leave Cancún with some answers and with those twenty bullets still inside the magazine, he would be damn satisfied.

Chance would be a fine thing.

The office building Ryker walked up to was a three-storey white-painted unit with large glass windows in blue painted frames. There was a tiny car park adjacent, shared with a number of the other nearby buildings. A quick look suggested five spaces were for El Yuca: three for staff, two for visitors. Just one car was parked there, in a reserved staff space. A near brand new turquoise BMW X6 M with shining alloy wheels – the glare from them in the bright sunshine so vicious it could probably be weaponised. The car was a statement of wealth but little taste, Ryker decided.

He headed to the front door of the office and tried it, but it was locked. He pressed the buzzer and a few seconds later, a female voice crackled out of the little speaker.

'Hello?'

English. At least the language was, though Ryker couldn't place the accent.

'I'm here to see the manager. About some property.'

Ryker didn't feel the need to come up with anything more elaborate than that. He was hardly looking to enter Fort Knox.

Sure enough, the door buzzed a couple of seconds later, and Ryker headed inside.

There was nothing beyond the door other than a small foyer and staircase. Ryker headed up to the next floor and came out into an ultra-modern, sleek office space. The huge floor-to-ceiling windows Ryker had seen from the outside did a good job of bringing life and light to the modest space. A small waiting area was off to his left. On his right, a reception desk. Behind the desk sat a freckled red-haired woman – mid-twenties at most and not at all hard on the eye. She smiled at Ryker though there was a hint of suspicion.

Ryker walked up to her. 'I was hoping to speak to your manager.'

'Yeah. About some property apparently. Do you have an appointment?'

Now he gauged her accent. Irish.

'Where are you from?' he asked.

'Where do you think?'

'Cork?'

He saw the slightest of twitches on her face. 'Closer than I thought you'd get. At least you didn't say Dublin. So do you have an appointment or not? Mr Orrantía is very busy today.'

'Actually I don't. But if he's in I think he might be happy to see me.'

'Is that so? And who should I say is asking for him?'

'James Ryker. Tell him I'm here following up for Diego Tamayo and Emilio Conesa.'

'Who?'

Ryker spelled out the names for her. Either she was a good actress or the names really weren't familiar.

'Okay, give me a minute.'

She got up from her desk and headed over to the right hand of the two closed doors at the other side of the office space. At least Ryker now knew Mateus Orrantía, the registered owner of the business, was in. The secretary disappeared into his office and everything was silent for a few moments.

When she came back out, her face was all smiles. 'Okay, you're in luck. He has half an hour before his next appointment. If you take a seat he'll call you through in a minute.'

Ryker smiled, nodded, and did as he was told.

He studied the secretary as she came back around and grabbed her handbag from the back of the chair. Then she moved around the desk and made her way for the exit.

'Is it something I said?' Ryker asked.

'Lunch break,' was the plain response he got as she moved, head down, across to the stairs.

It wasn't quite two p.m., not far off lunchtime, Ryker thought, but under the circumstances he'd be a fool to believe that was the reason for her quick exit. He also had a damn good idea why Orrantía needed a couple of minutes: he had a call to make. Backup.

That was fine with Ryker. He was actually interested to see who would turn up, and it did at least tell him one thing: there were some answers there. It was a lead worth following.

Perhaps he'd just entered the wolf's lair. The problem for Orrantía was that this time he'd mistakenly believed that Ryker was the prey, and not the hunter he'd always been.

In the apartment building across the street from El Yuca Property, Will Davey reached down into the pocket of his cargo pants and fished out his phone. As he did so he kept one eye on the screen of the camera, mounted on a tripod in front of the window. He dialled the number without looking at the phone and placed the handset to his ear. When the call was answered no formalities or pleasantries were offered or given.

'Orrantía has a visitor,' Davey said.

'And?'

'And something feels off.'

'Feels off how?'

'I don't know. This guy, he just seems... not like the usual customer of El Yuca.'

'Did you get a good face shot?'

'Of course.'

'Send it over. I'll see if we get any hits, though it's going to take a while to do a full search.'

'Is there anyone you can call in for backup? If I need them?'

'Backup for what?'

'I've got an odd feeling about this.'

'Sorry, but I have no agents waiting around enjoying the sun in Cancún today. You're on your own out there for now. If something goes down, do what you can. You can handle that, can't you?'

'Of course. So you're giving me the go ahead to engage?'

'Use your judgment. But yes, if needed then engage. Do whatever's necessary.'

'Got it.'

CHAPTER 5

The office door opened and Ryker looked over the man who stood there. He was short but thick framed, probably once heavily muscled but was now carrying far too much weight on his gut. He wore chinos and a white shirt, the top three buttons opened to reveal wispy grey chest hair. He was bald on top, his skin deeply tanned and leathery – too much time in the sun – and his face was round and puffy. Ryker knew from the information gathered on El Yuca that Orrantía was fifty-one, though he looked older.

The arrogance of the man seeped out of every pore, but then when he saw Ryker he smiled warmly and his face was transformed – a real mixed persona.

'I'm Mateus Orrantía, but call me Mateus. Please, come on in.'

American accent. Ryker headed over and Orrantía extended his hand.

'James Ryker,' he said, giving Orrantía's gargantuan hand a firm shake.

Orrantía stepped to the side and guided Ryker through into the office space. He looked around as Orrantía moved back over to behind his glass-topped desk. Two of the walls in the office were almost entirely glass too, giving a glimpse of the milky water of the Nichupté lagoon beyond. The other walls were sparsely furnished with a single metal and glass bookcase and two large aerial photographs that Ryker guessed were showcasing some of El Yuca's work.

'I understand you want to talk about property.'

'Actually that's not strictly true.' Ryker took a seat opposite Orrantía, who raised an eyebrow at Ryker's response.

'I'm following up on a private matter.'

'Is that right? Siobhan mentioned two names to me, sorry, what were they again?'

'Diego Tamayo and Emilio Conesa.'

Ryker studied Orrantía's reaction to the two names but his face was impassive. After a few moments, he simply shook his head and pursed his lips as if to say 'and?'

'You don't know them?'

'Not that I'm aware of. Who are they?'

Ryker opened up his backpack and took out the bloody picture of Tamayo. He slid it across the desk to Orrantía who looked down then quickly averted his eyes.

'What is this?' he asked, surprise and anger in his voice.

'That's what's left of Tamayo.'

'I've no idea what you're expecting me to say here. You come into my business asking me questions about two Mexicans—'

'I never said they were Mexican.'

'Okay, fine, their names sound Mexican. My point is, why are you here, showing me photographs of dead men?'

'Only one of them's dead actually.'

Orrantía said nothing to that but Ryker could see his host was genuinely uncomfortable with the conversation.

'The thing is, Mateus, I know these two came here—'

Orrantía huffed, exasperated. 'And how exactly do you know that?'

'I just do. I know they came here. I don't know why. What I do know is that those two men were paid to hurt someone very close to me. The only thing I have that links those men to each other is this company.'

'This company? You're talking nonsense!'

'No. I'm not. I'm going to find out who paid them, and why. And I'll—'

'Okay. Okay. I get the picture.' Orrantía held up his hand. 'It's not hard to see what kind of man you are, Mr Ryker, but I'm sorry I really don't know how to help you. I'm just a businessman.'

Outside on the street, Ryker heard a deep rumble as a vehicle pulled into the car park. Orrantía glanced out of the window. The backup had arrived. Pretty promptly too. Ryker heard car doors opening and closing. *Three*, he thought.

'I'm not trying to be unhelpful,' Orrantía said. 'If these men did come here, then it certainly wasn't to see me. But I'm not the only person who works here. I can check with my partner. I think that's her arriving now actually.'

Her. Ryker was thrown slightly. The information Willoughby had given him on El Yuca hadn't suggested Orrantía had any partners. He was listed as the sole owner. And Ryker had expected it to be a bunch of heavies coming after him, not a businesswoman.

Moments later, he heard footsteps coming up the metal staircase. Orrantía got to his feet and headed for his office door. Ryker waited for him to move past before he too stood up. He let his hand brush against the edge of the Five-Seven, making sure he knew exactly where the grip was positioned.

Ryker stayed in the office but slid across slightly to get a good view of the space outside. Orrantía headed over to greet the new arrivals. The first person up the stairs was indeed a woman, mid-forties, dressed in a light grey trouser suit. Her dark brown hair was cut short, her face hard. Two men followed her. One was pale skinned and tall, but not particularly well built. The other was shorter, thicker, with dark skin and a bushy moustache. Both were casually dressed and neither looked particularly ominous. Ryker saw no indication that either they or the woman were carrying any weapons.

The woman stopped by the waiting area and Orrantía struck up a conversation with her, though they were both speaking too quietly for Ryker to hear. The woman glanced over to Ryker intermittently, then, after a few moments she walked over.

'Mr Ryker?'

'Yeah,' Ryker said, coming out of Orrantía's office and giving the woman's outstretched hand a brief shake.

'I'm Helen Collins, Mateus's partner.' Another Irish accent, Ryker noted. 'He says you're asking about two men who came here?'

'Diego Tamayo and Emilio Conesa,' Ryker said, his patience wearing thin.

Collins shrugged. 'Those names don't mean anything to me, I'm afraid. They're certainly not important clients of ours, I'd know. Perhaps if you could be more specific about what it is you need from us?'

This wasn't exactly going how Ryker had expected. He'd thought he was walking into the lion's den. He was well prepared for a fight with a bunch of steroid-fuelled brutes. But Orrantía and Collins? They seemed like everyday office workers.

Yet Collins did have the two lumps with her. Plus Willoughby's intel had been so clear-cut. CCTV shots of Tamayo and Conesa outside the door of the building, on more than one occasion. Having said that, those two men had assumed several aliases, Ryker knew, when they'd travelled to Ryker and Lisa's home. So was it the names that had thrown Orrantía and Collins?

Ryker hauled his backpack around and as he did so the tall man, who was standing off to Collins's right, flinched, as though he thought Ryker was about to make a move. His edginess gave him away. Despite the polite, business-like approach of Orrantía and Collins, these guys were prepped and ready to try to take on Ryker, if they were given the nod.

Okay, so maybe Ryker hadn't misread the situation.

Ryker pulled out some more pictures of the two Mexican men. Not the one of the corpse this time. He handed the snaps to Collins. She took only a couple of seconds to leaf through the photos before handing them back.

'No, I don't remember ever seeing them here before.'

Ryker studied her for a few moments but her face gave nothing away. Both Collins and Orrantía were staring intently at Ryker, waiting to see if he had anywhere else to take the stilted conversation.

He didn't.

'Must be my mistake then,' Ryker said.

No one said anything to that, though Collins did look surprised at his abrupt change of heart. Ryker packed the pictures away then slung the bag over his shoulder.

'Sorry we weren't able to help,' Orrantía said, standing aside.

'I'm sure you are. You all have a good day,' Ryker said.

He moved forward, first giving the tall man the eye, then the shorter guy. Both held Ryker's gaze. Ryker moved to his right slightly as he passed the short guy, coming to within inches of him. The guy held his ground. When he was level with him, Ryker quickly reached out with his hand and used the tip of his finger to deftly lift up the bottom of the man's loose shirt. Just a quick in and out. Not a hostile move. Ryker stared down. Sure enough, he caught a glimpse of the butt of a handgun as the shirt wafted down into place.

Ryker jumped back, holding his hands up in the air in apology. The short guy's face creased with anger but he didn't make a move for the weapon.

'Didn't know it was normal to carry guns in the real estate business,' Ryker said, glancing back at Orrantía and Collins.

Neither said anything. Ryker lowered his hands and continued toward the stairs, not fully turning his back on the foursome at any point.

He quickly made his way down and then out onto the street.

When he was outside, he scanned the area. There were a few pedestrians meandering about but they all looked like tourists. Ryker scanned over to the car park. He guessed the shining white Ford SUV was the car Collins and crew had just arrived in. But that wasn't all that caught Ryker's eye. As he walked away, still surveying the streets and the buildings all around, his gaze fixed onto the third floor window of an apartment building about a hundred yards away. He was sure he'd seen a glint in the window.

What could he say? Ryker had a naturally suspicious mind, and he'd been on stakeouts plenty of times – he was good at spotting them.

Ryker continued to stare for a few moments longer as he carried on toward his bike, but he saw nothing more in the window, and soon he'd passed by the building. Yet he couldn't shake the feeling that eyes were on him.

There were definitely unspoken secrets about El Yuca. Ryker was determined to find out what those secrets were.

'Shit!' Davey said, falling back and grabbing the tripod as he went. The camera clattered down onto the floor next to him.

The guy had just looked right at him.

He had, hadn't he?

Davey sat on the floor for a few seconds, clutching the tripod in his hands. He then edged up to look out of the window.

No, he was gone.

Then a thought struck him. Davey dropped the tripod, stood up and grabbed the Glock handgun from the side table. He moved over to the door, feeling his heart accelerating in his chest. He heard movement outside the door. Someone moving up the staircase. He peered into the spyhole. No sign of the guy there. No sign of anyone, though Davey could still hear the soft footfalls on the stone steps.

Then his phone blared and Davey almost jumped out of his skin. He cursed under his breath and grabbed the phone from his pocket. He accepted the call but then for a couple of seconds he listened silently for any more sounds from outside. There was nothing.

'Yeah?' Davey said, pulling the phone to his ear, one eye still on the spyhole.

'Update?'

'This is weird, man. Collins and her boys turned up, but barely a minute later this guy just casually walks out of there. No fuss, no trouble.'

'Really? And he came out alone?'

'Yeah. Odd, isn't it? Have you found anything on him?'

'Nothing on regular databases. Extending the searches now.'

'I don't like it. We need to know who he is, otherwise what am I supposed to do?'

'Just sit tight.'

'He clocked me. When he was leaving. I'm sure of it.'

Silence.

'Did you hear what I said?'

'Yes. I heard. How could he have clocked you?'

'I don't know! It's like he knew.'

More silence. Davey didn't like that. He could feel it was his own performance that was being judged harshly here, but he'd done nothing wrong.

'What do you want me to do?' he asked.

'Stay put. This could be nothing. Until we find out more, stay vigilant.'

'Okay.'

The call went dead.

Davey shoved the phone back in his pocket.

Outside in the corridor, all was quiet and still.

CHAPTER 6

London, England

'Sorry,' Winter said, pushing two fingers hard against his temple until he could feel a stabbing pain in his brain. 'Explain this to me again.'

His assistant, Rod Flowers, was sitting across the opposite side of Winter's desk. Winter's desk. Strange. It wasn't that long before that Mackie had sat where Winter was, rubbing his temple in frustration and disbelief as he listened to the most recent news of the messy existence of Carl Logan – aka James Ryker.

How long before Winter himself was gone, and Flowers was sitting in the chair? Ryker, undoubtedly, would carry on forever.

Winter had assumed the role of commander at the JIA three years earlier when Mackie, his former boss, had been gunned down outside a café in the Russian city of Omsk. It seemed Ryker's life had moved from one chaotic mess to another ever since. It hadn't escaped Winter's attention that nearly all of the problems and twists and turns that had taken place – not to mention Mackie's death itself – involved James Ryker.

Not that Ryker, a former agent of Mackie's, was *entirely* to blame for everything that had happened. Yet he sure as hell had a way of continually attracting and causing destruction.

Despite all that, and despite the impossibility of reining in the ex-operative, Winter still felt loyal to Ryker. The man had saved Winter's life. Which was one of many reasons why Winter had agreed that Ryker could retire from the game. That was the sensible choice to make, under the circumstances. Once a great asset for the JIA, Ryker was a highly trained agent who hadn't lost any of his raw talent – his combat and investigative skills were still as strong as ever, for example – but he had lost his head.

He was no longer the cool and collected spy who could make rational judgements based on big picture reasoning. He was too... emotional. Keeping him on as an agent would have backfired – sooner, rather than later – and neither Winter nor Ryker had wanted it.

Instead, Winter had set up a new life – new identities – for Ryker and his girlfriend, Lisa. That hadn't lasted long. The two of them had done a runner, moving to a different, even more remote location, taking on new names, ever fearful that even having Winter – Ryker's only ally – know of their whereabouts was too big a risk to take.

Their extreme caution was ultimately proved right, in the worst possible way. Someone from Ryker's – or Lisa's – past had hunted them down. Lisa was dead and Ryker was on a mission to get revenge.

Winter knew there would be blood.

Although the JIA would never officially sanction any help for Ryker, privately Winter would offer the ex-asset assistance in his mission, if he could. He still felt he owed it to him.

That was the reason Winter still kept careful watch over Ryker, from afar.

James Ryker had no official profile in the JIA records, nor did any official profile of him exist on any other agency or law enforcement database or watch list. Ryker, as an identity, was a ghost. Winter had, however, set up a far-reaching alert that tripped any time Ryker's identity – his name and those of his aliases, his face, his fingerprints, his DNA – was passed through any of the law enforcement or intelligence agency systems that the JIA had access to. Anyone searching for Ryker would find nothing, but Winter would be alerted that the search had taken place.

As had happened not long earlier when Ryker had been hauled into a Mexican jail for a murder he didn't commit. Winter had barely finished picking up the pieces of that one, and now another alert had come in.

Why the hell were the US Drug Enforcement Administration interested in finding out about Ryker?

'The DEA are passing a snapshot of Ryker through every system they have access to, trying to identify him,' Flowers said.

Winter sighed. 'I know, you said that already, but what exactly is happening?'

'I really don't know. The search was initiated by a senior member of staff in the US, but it seems the intel was referred from a man they have on the ground in Cancún. I'm still digging into it but haven't yet been able to find out who it is or what the DEA are doing there.'

'Flowers, it doesn't take a genius to figure that one out.'

Flowers raised an eyebrow. 'The DEA are investigating a Mexican gang who're smuggling drugs into the US, most likely. But what I meant was I don't know *who* they're investigating, or why. Or how on earth Ryker's got himself caught in the middle.'

'No, but I know someone who might.'

Winter tapped on his computer's keyboard, then when he'd found what he was looking for he pressed a button on the phone and the dial tone blared out of the speaker. He dialled the number then, as the call rang through, he checked his watch, calculating what the local time would be.

'Hello,' the woman said. Her single word greeting sounded questioning and suspicious. Likely because she'd seen the caller ID and realised it was a JIA number calling her. But not her boss's.

'This is Peter Winter.'

Silence for a few seconds. 'How can I help you?' Eleanor Willoughby sounded almost amenable.

'It seems our good friend is back in Mexico. You wouldn't happen to know anything about that, would you?'

'I'm not sure what it would have to do with you either way.'

Winter gritted his teeth but quickly calmed himself. 'Really. Okay, well how about this, Willoughby. You might not report to me but how about I go and find your commander. I think she's in today, actually. Her office is just down the corridor from where I'm sitting. I know this is a siloed organisation, but believe me, the closer you get to the top and the more of it you see, the more power you have over those like you, who work on the periphery. So how about I explain to your boss how you've been using your time and resources providing assistance to James Ryker, without her authority, and how that assistance has wound up with Ryker jeopardising an important DEA investigation. That's the DEA, who, you probably know, we work very closely with on occasion.'

Winter looked over at Flowers and noticed him raising his eyebrows again. Winter shrugged. So his words had included some leaps of deduction, and quite a lot of embellishment. *Sorry, Flowers, but that's the game.* And what Winter had said wasn't so outlandish, knowing Ryker as well as he did.

Willoughby didn't try to correct any of his points.

'But I'm not going to do that, Willoughby,' Winter said. 'Ryker has obviously taken a shine to you, and you to him...' Winter thought he heard her scoff but she didn't say a word '... and I want to help him as much as you do.'

'Is that so?'

'Yes. Where are you?'

'Mexico City. Where I'm supposed to be.'

'And why is Ryker in Cancún?'

'If you know so much about him, then how do you not know the answer to that?'

'I'm not playing here, Willoughby. Who is he looking for?'

'I honestly don't know.'

'I honestly believe you're lying to me. But okay. This is what you'll do. You need to get to Cancún. I'll clear your movements at this end. By the time you get there hopefully we'll have figured out who it is from the DEA that has Ryker on their radar, and why. You'll need to speak to them and find out what they know, and make sure they're not going to cause an explosion by trying to stop him. But, most importantly, you need to find Ryker, and what exactly he's up to. Get him to call me. Before this spirals out of control.'

'I can't drop everything here just like that–'

'If you really want to help Ryker, and if you want to save your JIA career, then that's exactly what you'll do.'

'How am I supposed to explain–?'

'Just do it.'

Winter hit the button to end the call then sat back in his chair and let out a long sigh. He stared over to Flowers whose face was a combination of confused and awestruck.

'That told her,' he said.

Winter held his assistant's gaze but said nothing. Flowers had worked for the JIA for less than twelve months. He was only twenty-seven but had a resume far longer than Winter's; a bachelor's degree in politics, a master's degree in international diplomacy, a PhD in political science, his dissertation on irregular warfare, counterinsurgency and counterterrorism having been widely praised in the intelligence arena. He'd spent two years as an advisor at NATO before being headhunted for the JIA. Intellectually, he was probably the brightest person Winter had ever met. If Flowers could rein in that intellect, and develop some real-world skills, he would make a fine commander at the JIA in the years to come. *If.* The problem was, no matter how good you were at the theory, it was never the same in real life. Winter was still reserving judgment on the likely longevity of Flowers' JIA career.

'So what now?' Flowers asked after a few moments. 'You want me to get back onto the DEA?'

'Yes. We need to know more. I don't want them going after Ryker; he'll only fight back and who knows where that'll end. But I need to know who it is we're dealing with before we try to explain the situation.'

'Explain the situation. Which is what exactly?'

Winter detected the slightest hostility in Flowers's tone. But then the youngster had never met Ryker, nor had he spent a day on the frontline in the field, so he couldn't possibly understand why Winter was prepared to stick his neck out so far.

'The situation is that I'm asking you to do something, and you're going to do it.'

Flowers humphed. 'Yeah, okay, I get it.'

Just then there was a knock on the door. Both men turned around.

'Come in!' Winter shouted. The door inched open and Winter caught a glimpse of a young lady on the other side. He recognised the face though didn't know her name. It seemed she wasn't after him anyway.

'Er, sorry to interrupt,' she said to Winter before turning her focus to Flowers. 'You might want to see this.'

Flowers looked to Winter, who nodded. The assistant got to his feet and headed to the door where he had a brief and hushed conversation before the woman scuttled off. Flowers shut the door, holding some papers.

'And that was?'

'Jenny Whitehall. A new analyst downstairs.'

'You two seemed very cosy together.'

Flowers said nothing to that.

'And?' Winter prompted for an explanation when none was forthcoming.

'And this.'

Flowers moved over to the desk and dropped the papers. On the top was a candid photograph of a man. A man Winter recognised.

'That's—'

'I know exactly who that is, Flowers.'

Winter reached forward and grabbed the photo, turning it over to look at the date stamp. He shook his head. His eyes scanned to the papers below. He saw the location name, but he wasn't quite ready to believe it.

'What the hell is going on?' Winter asked. 'Who took this?'

'You asked me to find out what the DEA are doing in Cancún,' Flowers said. 'This is what I got back. *This* is who they're looking for.'

CHAPTER 7

Cancún, Mexico

Following the frustrating trip to El Yuca, Ryker determined it was best to stay put in the area for the night, and he found a cheap hotel a few hundred yards away from the more expensive properties that lined the city's coast. The place did at least have Wi-Fi, and having purchased some much-needed supplies, including a second-hand tablet computer, he planned his next steps.

His trip to El Yuca hadn't been entirely fruitless, he'd decided, despite the initial annoyance at having come away from the office with no information of use. He did know for sure that Collins and Orrantía were hiding something. Why else would Collins have armed guards? And Tamayo and Conesa had definitely been there.

At nightfall, after doing some research on the tablet, Ryker took the opportunity to get some rest. He wasn't sleeping right through until morning though. He set his alarm for midnight, and when it blared Ryker got up from the bed and within minutes, backpack over his shoulders, he was out on the street. He'd taken most of his belongings from the backpack, storing the cash and passport in the room's small safe so that he was only carrying what he needed, with the Five-Seven back in his waistband.

Ryker headed on foot through the streets of Cancún, intermittently walking along roads that were unlit and deserted, and others which were awash with lights, noise and people partying in the bars and clubs. The road El Yuca was on, with most of the nearby buildings either offices or apartments, was one of the quieter streets at the late hour. Ryker headed along it, never spending too much time in the thin illumination coming from the sporadic streetlights. He glanced up at the building across the road from El Yuca to the same window. He spotted nothing this time, though he firmly believed he could still feel eyes on him, somewhere in the darkness.

Ryker didn't let it faze him. He reached El Yuca's building and scooted into a dark recess by a fire exit of the neighbouring office. He had to do this next part quickly and smoothly. When he'd been in the office earlier, he'd paid close attention to the security; a quite standard wireless alarm system that used infra-red sensors in each room and magnetic contacts on the external doors. A brief search on the internet had confirmed Ryker's initial guess; that the sensors and contacts relied on radio frequencies to transmit data. He took out the radio transceiver he'd bought earlier and paired to the app on his phone, allowing him to analyse the frequencies of the sensors.

It only took a couple of minutes for the app to log everything, and then he manually entered the frequencies into the transceiver and hit the transmit button. The jamming signals sent by the transceiver would stop the alarm's control panel picking up the signals from the individual sensors that he was about to trip.

He performed one last take up and down the street to check everything was quiet. It was. Then Ryker peeled away from the darkness and up to the entrance door for El Yuca. He took out the pins and small torsion wrench from his backpack and worked the lock on the door for a few seconds before he heard it release.

The door, as expected, didn't open though. The lock was just an added security measure for when the office was empty. During the day, a simple magnetic lock was utilised, opened by swipe cards and attached to the integrated intercom. That lock was still engaged.

Not for long. Ryker took out the security card he'd pilfered from Orrantía's desk earlier – when Orrantía had headed out to greet his partner. Ryker was gambling on Orrantía having not yet realised, or at worst having noticed the missing card but not thought it suspicious.

Ryker swiped the card against the small pad and sure enough he heard the click as the magnets released and he pushed the door open. He paused for a second, waiting to see if there were any bleeps from the security system because of the broken door contact.

There was nothing. As far as the system was concerned, all was good. There was always the possibility that although the control panel was silent, the local security company who'd set up the system would receive a notification that the front door contact had been broken, but regardless no alarm was blaring inside, and that was the main thing.

Now, Ryker had a window of opportunity. He needed to be quick – he gave himself three minutes. He stepped through and closed the door behind him then quickly moved up the stairs.

First he plugged a small thumb drive into the desktop computer under the reception desk. The red light blinked to show the device – pre-loaded with auto-imaging software – was downloading the contents of the hard drive.

He checked the drawers by the desk. Each was unlocked but there was nothing of interest inside. Ryker quickly headed over to Orrantía's office. He'd noticed earlier that Orrantía had a laptop, but the device was nowhere to be seen. Ryker dashed to the desk drawers. They were locked. But the locks looked so flimsy they weren't even worth picking. Ryker yanked hard on the handle of the top drawer and after two tugs it came free in his hand. Nothing in there. He did the same with the next and found two plain-labelled DVDs and two thumb drives. He took both. The third drawer down was empty.

Ryker looked at his watch. One and a half minutes gone already. He rushed out of Orrantía's office and into Collins's. Again, no computer, though there was a large filing cabinet, the doors on it locked shut. Ryker headed over and took the small crowbar from his backpack. He quickly jimmied the doors open.

He almost smiled when he looked inside. There, right at the bottom, was a small safe, about a foot square, its walls and door nearly an inch thick. Much like the one in the cupboard in his hotel room where he'd put his own things. It was an electronic safe, which needed a code to release the lock. He didn't have time to crack the safe there and then. He didn't need to. He was taking it with him.

He wedged the crowbar underneath it and hauled downward as hard as he could, letting out a loud grunt as he did so. There was cracking and splintering as the thick screws holding the safe in place failed. Ryker yanked, tugged and pulled the heavy box free. Out of breath, he lifted up the box and managed to squeeze it into the backpack. He looked at his watch again. Nearly four minutes gone. He wouldn't stay any longer, however much he wanted to.

Ryker pulled the now weighty backpack over his shoulder and was heading back out to the reception desk when he heard it; the grumble of car engines. The vehicles were pulling up outside.

CHAPTER 8

Ryker didn't bother to look out the window to see who had just arrived. He hadn't heard sirens or seen any flashing lights, which narrowed down the options somewhat. Ryker rushed back over to the reception desk and pulled the thumb drive from the desktop. More than likely it wouldn't have had time to download everything from the hard drive, but he had to hope there was something of use.

He was at the head of the stairs when he heard hushed voices and soft footsteps down below. He stopped. He held back, out of view, and listened. There was no other exit route from where he was. He had to get down there somehow.

The next second, the lights in the whole building flicked on and Ryker was bathed in white. Realising his shadow was leaping out across the top of the stairs, he jerked back and pulled up against the wall by the waiting area.

Moments later, he heard creaks as someone came up the stairs. They were moving quietly. Certainly not the police. Whoever it was though, they could do nothing about the natural strains echoing from the staircase.

Then he heard a creak from much closer by. They were already at the top of the stairs, just a few yards from where Ryker was standing. He looked over to his left. Spotted the panel of five light switches. He had no idea which switch worked which light.

He reached his hand up, slowly and carefully, trying not to make any sound. With his other hand, he reached around and grabbed the handgun from his waistband. His eyes darted up and down as he waited for someone to appear through the doorway.

After a number of seconds of silence, he spotted the outline of a shoe – a white trainer – edging into view. He didn't hesitate another moment. He flipped all five switches.

All of the lights in the reception area and in Orrantía and Collins's offices went out. So too did the one on the landing. But the office wasn't quite plunged into darkness; light still seeped in from further down the stairway and from the streetlights outside. Nonetheless, the move had the desired effect, and gave Ryker an upper hand again.

The man the trainer belonged to moved forward with purpose, clearly sensing he was about to be attacked. He wasn't wrong. As he rushed into the office he couldn't do a thing as Ryker lashed out from behind and smacked the heel of his hand into the back of the guy's neck. He went down in a heap as Ryker darted out into the open.

Another man was there, at the top of the stairs. Ryker didn't get chance to take stock of who it was, or whether he was armed. He just launched himself forward.

His knee crashed into the man's groin. The man exhaled and bent down, and Ryker delivered another blow to the back of his neck, once again hitting the pressure point of nerves to send the guy to the floor.

Ryker wouldn't get to the third man quite so easily, though: he'd spotted the outline of him at the bottom of the stairs, several yards away. Rather than retreat to safety, Ryker opted to keep on the front foot. He quickly pulled the gun around and fired two shots. Both were intended to miss; both did, though the second bullet came within a couple of inches of the man's foot, lodging in the polished concrete floor in front of him.

The booming shots and the near misses did the trick. The man, panicked, flung himself out of the firing line, moving across the floor and out of view. Ryker bounded down the stairs, two, three at a time, gun at the ready. His eyes remained busy as he surveyed for other people, and also the man he'd shot at. Was he armed? Ryker hadn't spotted a gun, but as he hurtled downward he let off two more shots in the direction of where the man was hiding, hoping it would be enough to deter him from countering.

It was. Ryker sprinted out onto the street. He glanced left and right, but saw no sign of anyone. He turned left and carried on running, putting distance between himself and the office. He still didn't know who he'd just attacked. He hadn't recognised the three men, all casually dressed, or the car that they'd arrived in – a dark estate, no branding; he wasn't sure of the model.

Ryker was more than fifty yards away when he slowed, the heavy backpack making a hasty escape difficult. Whoever those guys were, they hadn't yet come out of the office, and if they did, he felt he could easily lose them at this distance. He turned the corner onto a quieter and darker street. Then he walked more casually along, looking behind him every now and then. Still no sign of anyone. But Ryker wouldn't feel relief so soon. Not until he was well away.

Sure enough, as Ryker was about to take another turn, he was certain he spotted the outline of a head, sticking out from around the corner he'd come from. One of the guys he'd attacked? Or someone else entirely?

He couldn't be sure, though he was surprised at how close the person was. Probably only twenty or thirty yards. Ryker increased his pace and took a quick-fire route back toward the busier streets. It would be far easier to lose a tail on busy streets, and there was far less chance of whoever it was engaging Ryker in a firefight that way.

Within a couple of minutes, Ryker was on a small strip where several late-night bars were clustered together. The mostly young revellers were spilling out from the courtyards of the bars and onto the road, and although it was noisy, the atmosphere wasn't too raucous.

Ryker hadn't seen any further sign of the tail. One option was to keep moving, putting distance between himself and whoever was following – if there'd been anyone.

But Ryker didn't want to play safe. He wanted to be sure.

He darted across the street, slid off his jacket, and dumped it into a bin. He moved into a bar and quickly edged into the crowd of drinkers milling about. He dropped the backpack down and it clunked on the ground, eliciting one or two curious stares from the other punters, but no one said anything. Ryker grabbed a half-finished beer from an empty table and edged closer to a small group of twenty-somethings: two men, four women.

'Evening,' Ryker said, lifting up the drink. One of the guys nodded but said nothing. The other, along with three of the girls, looked away. The remaining girl gave him a suspicious look.

'Nice place,' Ryker said to her, keeping one eye on the street he'd just come from.

'Yeah,' the girl said, peeling a half-step away from her friends, closer to Ryker. 'Drinking on your own? Did she stand you up or something?'

Her accent was American.

'No,' Ryker said. 'There is no she. Not yet.'

He smiled as he said it and the girl laughed, though it was a slightly uncomfortable laugh like she wasn't sure what to make of the comment.

'You're English,' the girl said.

'How did you know?' Ryker tried his best to act happy and carefree. 'Before you ask, no, I don't know Prince William. But I can do a decent impression.'

Then Ryker saw him. Coming out from around the corner. The guy moved cautiously but purposefully. He wasn't making himself too obvious, not to any old passer-by at least. But Ryker knew this guy was on his tail. He was tall, with light skin and short-cut wavy dark hair. European. Or North American. He wore jeans and a buttoned shirt. Everything about him was quite unassuming. He just... blended.

Except to Ryker he stuck out like a sore thumb for that exact reason.

Ryker was pretty sure it wasn't one of the three guys from the office. So who was he?

Ryker took off his cap and dropped it to the ground. Losing the cap and jacket wasn't the most extravagant transformation, but it would have to do for now.

'What do you say I buy you and your friends a round of drinks,' Ryker said to the girl. 'Your choice.'

The others in the group took notice at the offer.

'I'm James,' Ryker said, holding out his hand to the girl.

'Charlie,' the girl said, giving his hand a gentle shake. 'We wouldn't say no to some Jägerbombs.'

She looked over to her friends for confirmation and several of them nodded and smiled, suddenly a little more interested in the stranger, but probably only until they had their drinks.

'And why would you when they're free,' Ryker said. 'Come on then, can you give me a hand?'

'Of course.'

'Let me just grab my money,' Ryker said.

He kneeled down to the ground, opened up the backpack, and took his time as he fished for some notes. From the ground, he caught a glimpse of the legs of the man on the street, moving slowly along as he gauged the people in the bars. Once he had moved past, Ryker straightened up. The group were giving him suspicious looks once again. Ryker ignored them and looked to the street. The guy was still milling. He must have known Ryker was in among the crowds somewhere – where else could he have gone?

Ryker had a choice to make. He could head back out and try to lose the guy. Or he could go ahead and confront him, find out who he was. Ryker's immediate instinct was for the latter, though he'd prefer to do that away from two hundred witnesses.

'Sorry,' Ryker said, turning to Charlie again. 'Change of plans. I need to go, but this should cover the drinks.'

Ryker slapped the money in Charlie's hand, and she murmured something not very nice under her breath as her friends gawked. Ryker couldn't care less. He picked up his backpack, which thunked down onto his shoulder. The guy was facing away as Ryker headed back to the street, still mulling over his two choices.

CHAPTER 9

Ryker couldn't help himself. He followed the guy. The hunted becoming the hunter. Ryker's natural instinct had seldom been to run when he could instead confront his problems head on, other than the time he and Lisa had headed off to live in a far-flung location in secret. Look at how that had turned out. Ryker was much better on the front foot than he was on the back.

Following the guy wasn't hard either. He simply wasn't that good at noticing his surroundings, wasn't looking around enough, kept to the same pace all the time, and took a straight route back to his base. The way he moved, the way he looked, suggested he was some sort of agent. Undercover police, FBI, CIA. No doubt he'd been trained in surveillance and tracking, but he was raw, likely had spent too long in a classroom learning the theory rather than out in the real world where life generally had a way of screwing up people's well-laid plans by throwing them into unfamiliar situations that could never be taught from a book.

Having said that, there was always the slim possibility that the guy was playing Ryker – deliberately appearing poorly skilled to make Ryker underestimate him and lure Ryker into a trap. Even that thought didn't particularly worry Ryker. It wasn't because of a lack of confidence that he'd led the life he had.

After following the guy for nearly thirty minutes, Ryker eventually wound up back where he had started, near to the El Yuca office. That was when Ryker decided to call it a night, because parked up outside the office was a police car, lights flashing. The guy he was following headed in through the entrance of the apartment block down the road. The one where Ryker had previously thought he'd seen a watcher.

It looked like he'd been right about that then.

Ryker would be back – he wanted to know who the man was, who he worked for, and whether he was a threat or a potential ally. But not that night. He was still lugging all of the items he'd taken from El Yuca, including the not exactly lightweight safe box. The guy could wait. For whatever reason he was on a stakeout at El Yuca, and Ryker didn't think he'd be disappearing in a hurry.

It was gone three a.m. when Ryker finally stepped into his hotel room and shut and locked the door. However much he needed sleep, he wasn't going to bed yet. He still had work to do. First, Ryker took out the safe from his backpack and put it down onto the room's battered and scratched desk. The safe required the input of a six-digit code. Ryker had no idea what the code was, and he hoped he wouldn't need it. He knew there were several common types of safes like the one in front of him. Some had manual overrides – to allow hotel staff to unlock them if a customer forgot their code, for example – but others didn't. Where an override was in place, some were sequence based, while others made use of physical keys that fitted into discreetly placed locks. They were the easiest to break, and Ryker hoped that was what he was looking at.

He grabbed his multi-tool from his pocket and unscrewed the small company nameplate on the front of the safe. If there was a manual keyhole, it was most likely to be either there, or behind the keypad. Ryker prised off the little metal plate. No luck. He was just staring at solid metal.

Next, Ryker slowly pulled away the cover of the keypad by wedging the tip of a flathead screwdriver behind the outer casing. He had to be careful not to disturb the unit too much, or to pull out any wires, which could trigger an anti-tamper locking mechanism.

Still no luck. There was no keyhole anywhere. The only way to get into the safe was to read the code from the electronic unit that controlled the lock. Ryker knew how to do it, but he'd have to take a trip to an electronics store to find the right equipment, and he couldn't do that at three a.m.

Frustrated, Ryker slapped his tools down on top of the safe and went back to his bag. He still had his own thumb drive, plus the items he'd found in Orrantía's desk. It took Ryker an hour to download all of the files from each of the data sources onto an external hard drive connected to his tablet. It took him another hour to set up the keyword searches that would run over the files and hopefully spit out some data that he could use. Evidence of Tamayo and Conesa having been at El Yuca. Evidence of *why*, and who had paid them – emails, meeting logs, maybe payments from El Yuca to the men.

The keyword searches resulted in thousands of initial hits, but Ryker was weary; he didn't have the stamina or the will to review all of those documents just then – doing so properly would take days. Notable though was that there were zero direct hits across the many thousands of files for each of the names Tamayo and Conesa.

Ryker grunted in frustration, though he really shouldn't have expected it to be so easy.

What did catch his eye though were several spreadsheet files, all with similar titles, only differentiated by their numerical dates. He opened several of the files and scanned through, quickly determining that the files detailed payments into and out of the El Yuca business.

Ryker was no accounting expert, but he'd had to analyse company accounts probably hundreds of times in his JIA career, whether the case had related to terrorism or money laundering or drug dealing or weapons smuggling. Sometimes it was all of those on one job. There were common methods of recording – and hiding – illegitimate transactions within business records that were consistently similar regardless of the nefarious activity being undertaken, or the parties involved. Even criminals wanted to know how much money they were making – they needed to keep a record of their income somehow. And high-level criminals rarely dealt exclusively in cash – they needed bank accounts. Bank accounts left paper trails.

What Ryker was looking at was a classic; two sets of books. One set of properly detailed records for the official company accounts – the ones that El Yuca would file with the Mexican authorities. Plus a whole set of alternative accounts showing the true position of the company – the many millions of dollars coming into and out of the businesses, both in cash and through its bank accounts. Those records were held on spreadsheets that were much more spuriously titled, and where the transaction descriptions were vague to say the least.

Ryker didn't know exactly what side business El Yuca was running, but he was convinced it was illegal, and that among those transactions were the answers he was looking for.

Among the vague transaction descriptions, the initials SW cropped up over and over. They meant nothing to Ryker, but he felt it could be something. It was by far the most frequent description.

Ryker performed a standalone search for SW, whole words only so that he didn't pull up hits for any old word that contained those two letters. He found several further spreadsheets that repeatedly included SW in transaction descriptions. Others were labelled SW Inv. Plus two references to SW Investments. A company? But there were also a small number of emails where SW seemed to refer not to an investment company, but to a person.

Taking one last shot before he crashed out from exhaustion, Ryker further refined the search so that it pulled up all documents where the text contained a capital S and a capital W at the start of adjacent words.

Just two hits. But Ryker smiled when he saw both hits contained the same words. In one, the reference was to Silver Wolf Investments. In the other, Silver Wolf was referring to a person.

Ryker had no idea who or what that was, but he knew he had another lead.

CHAPTER 10

Lake Maggiore, Italy

Of the many roles that Lawrence Draper had in life, this had to be the one that he enjoyed the most, which gave him the most genuine pleasure and satisfaction, even if it wasn't the one that necessarily came to him most naturally.

He loved early mornings like these, particularly at Lake Maggiore. The sun was peeking up over the hills across the lake, the thick rays touching everything with orange warmth. Draper was on his haunches, his eyes twitching back and forth between the stopwatch and Angelica who was hurtling toward him, her long, wavy blonde hair flapping wildly behind her.

When she was a yard away, she flung herself forward, an excited giggle escaping her lips. Draper tapped on the stopwatch then wrapped his arms around his daughter as she bundled into his chest, nearly knocking him backward onto the grass.

'How fast?' Angelica asked, panting. He could feel her little heart racing at what felt like a thousand beats a minute.

'Twenty-one point two. A new record.'

He brushed the hair away from her face and saw her wide smile had disappeared.

'What's the matter, honey?' he asked.

'I wanted it to be faster.'

She looked genuinely devastated, as though running a loop of the lawn as quickly as possible was the most important thing in life. At least she had his drive to succeed.

'I'm going to do it again,' she said, pulling herself away.

'Just one more. You must be getting tired. And hungry.'

'Okay. Tell me when.'

'Three, two, one... go!'

He waited a beat then hit the stopwatch as he watched Angelica dart off barefoot across the lawn, her lilac dress flapping about and hardly helping her sporting endeavours. Draper smiled, straightened up and checked his watch. Nearly eight a.m. He should still have some more time with her before the others showed their ugly faces. He didn't have to leave the villa until midday so he guessed no one would be up particularly early.

Angelica had just reached the far end of the lawn when Draper noticed someone approaching from the house.

'Mr Draper,' Estella called in her thick accent. 'Your breakfast is ready.'

'Thanks, we're coming now.'

'Daddy!' he heard Angelica scream in frustration, and he looked down to see her a couple of yards away from him. Somewhat off guard, he managed to catch her in his arms and did his best to stop the clock at the same time.

'So?'

'You did it! Twenty point nine.'

'Yes!'

'Come on, let's go and eat.'

'Oaahhh.'

'We can come back out later.'

She grumbled and moaned but he hauled her onto his shoulders, and she then giggled as he bounced his way up the steps to the villa.

Inside, he lifted her down onto one of the six chairs at the farmhouse style oak table in the kitchen. The table could easily sit ten and would be big in most houses, but in here it looked small in the enormous space, and Angelica was tiny sitting there all on her own.

'What would you like, my dear?' Estella asked Angelica.

'Eggs please.'

'No sausage, bacon?'

'Just lots of eggs. Daddy said it will make me strong.'

'You're a sweet girl,' Estella said, ruffling Angelica's hair.

In her fifties, Estella was short and plump and matronly. Natasha, Draper's ex-wife, had chosen her mainly because of her unassuming looks. That bitch had never trusted Draper. Estella had worked for him for more than ten years, and she was as near to part of the family as she could be. She was much more than the head housekeeper; she was a thoughtful and loving carer for Draper's only child too.

'And for you?' she asked Draper.

'Whatever you've made.'

'Take a seat,' she said with a smile.

Moments later, Draper and his daughter were tucking in to the hearty breakfasts. It wasn't every day they did that, eating together only the two of them. In fact, they didn't do it often enough.

Estella was cleaning in the kitchen and Draper noticed Angelica wasn't eating much, just pushing some egg around her plate with a fork.

'What's the matter?' he asked.

'I was just thinking...' she said before trailing off.

She always started sentences like that when she was going to ask for something she knew would likely get a 'no', or when she was going to say something that she knew would be difficult.

'Go on.'

'I was thinking... do you think I'll ever have a mummy again?'

Draper took a well-timed big mouthful of food to give himself a few seconds to compose his answer.

'Honey, you have me. And you have Estella and everyone else here who looks after you. We're your family.'

'But I want a real mummy. Everyone else at school has one.'

Draper sighed. Life had certainly been easier before Angelica had started school, that was for sure. On the plus side, she was getting a top-notch education. She was already fluent in both English and Italian, and clearly had natural intelligence that the teachers at her school would no doubt be able to foster. On the downside, now that she was out in the real world, away from the confines of the villa, it felt like he no longer had full control over her. It was incredible how quickly she was becoming her own person with her own views and outlook on life, regardless of his careful influence.

'You have a mummy too,' Draper said. 'She's just not here anymore.'

'I wish she was.'

'Me too. You'll see her again one day.'

'You mean when I'm dead too?'

Draper took another mouthful of food rather than respond to that one. He noticed Estella looking over, her ears no doubt pricking at the awkward conversation, but she knew better than to say a word.

'It's just that Vito at school, he's had two daddies already, and I'm five months older than he is. When the first one went away they got another one. So why can't I have another mummy?'

Draper reached out and put his hand onto hers. 'You don't need another mummy,' he said. 'Your mummy will always be here, watching over you. You just can't see her.'

She still didn't look convinced by that. He studied her perfect features for a few seconds. Angelica. They'd chosen the name because, quite simply, she looked like an angel. She'd always been a good kid too. Angelic. At seven years old, he could already see the cracks appearing though, and he often wondered who she'd turn out more like; him or Natasha. Certainly neither of *them* was angelic. Which was one of the big reasons why, ultimately, Natasha had to go. The house, the family was better – more stable – without her. He could only hope his daughter hadn't picked up too much from her mother.

Draper heard footsteps on the marble out in the hallway and he turned to see Clyde coming in, smartly dressed as always, walking tall and stiff as though he had metal rods inserted in his socks that stretched up through his trousers and shirt to his neck.

'Sorry to disturb you,' he said, 'have you got a minute?'

Draper huffed and looked over to his daughter. She had her head down, but he could see that she was now uncomfortable. She was always like that around Clyde. Draper could understand why. For all of Clyde's undoubted positives, his social skills were severely lacking, and he had no way with children.

'I think you'll want to hear this,' Clyde added.

'Okay, give me a minute,' Draper said. Clyde padded off. 'We'll try to break that record again later, yeah?'

'Maybe,' Angelica said.

Draper wanted to stay, but got to his feet and headed out through the villa. Clyde hadn't said exactly where to go, but Draper could already hear voices coming from the drawing room at the front of the house. He walked in and saw Clyde standing by the window, looking out. Sitting at the stool by the grand piano was Henderson. What a contrast the two men made.

Draper had known Clyde for years, since Clyde was a messed-up teenager. Many people assumed he was Draper's son, which always made Draper feel uneasy – because he *knew* Clyde. He knew what kind of man he was. Yes, on the outside he was handsome but unassuming, hair always neatly parted, clean-shaven, his smart clothes tailored for his thin frame. What lay inside though... Draper didn't know how to describe *that*. Was Clyde a product of Draper's very deliberate nurturing, or was he just an oddity of life? Regardless, he had some real talents, that *was* for sure. Look at what he'd done to Maddison...

Henderson couldn't have been more different. He was older and looked it; his face gnarled and scarred. He wasn't tall but he was thick framed and muscular. He had a look in his eye that told everyone what he was about. He was ex-army. Special Forces, to be precise, and he carried an arrogance about him that made even Draper look mild and meek.

Both of the men performed useful roles for Draper, though they were also quite screwed up in the head. There wouldn't be much joy hanging out with them down the pub, but Draper would bet on them to save his life. Clyde was just... odd. Not exactly a conversationalist. Henderson was loud and brash, full of self-confidence. Actually, thinking about it, Draper could share beers with Henderson. He at least had social skills, once you got over that arrogance, self-importance, and his general hatred of the world and almost everything in it.

'You wanted me?' Draper folded his arms.

Both men looked over.

'We've had a development,' Henderson said. He plonked a thick finger down onto a key on the piano. Somehow he made that one note sound grating and obtrusive.

'And?' Draper said.

'A problem in Mexico,' Clyde added.

Henderson hit some more keys, eliciting an ominous tune – a not too bad attempt at the death march.

'Can you just tell me?' Draper said.

'The DEA are crawling all over operations in Cancún,' Clyde said.

'How the fuck did that happen?'

'I don't know. But I think we need to shut them down. For good this time.'

Draper sighed but he didn't need to mull it over long. A risk was a risk, and there was nothing and no one over there worth jeopardising the bigger picture for.

'Fine,' he said. 'Do it.'

'And Orrantía?' Clyde asked.

'Destroy everything. If we're closing it down then what's his use now?'

'I couldn't agree more,' Henderson added. 'But the problem isn't just in Cancún, is it?'

'Meaning…'

'Meaning why do you think they're looking there at all?'

'Maddison?'

'Exactly.'

'So what are you suggesting?' Draper asked.

'When you said destroy *everything*, what about the trail that Maddison left behind? That must be why the DEA are there in the first place.'

'I know,' Draper said, not hiding the fact that he was agitated not just with the situation, but with Henderson challenging him. 'We've discussed this. How do we get to *that* trail and destroy it without everything blowing back in my face? And yours too?'

'For every problem, there's a solution,' Henderson said, giving a menacing grin. 'And for this problem, I think I know the solution.'

Draper looked over to Clyde who shrugged. That at least suggested some sort of affirmation, otherwise Clyde would have argued vehemently. Henderson hadn't been on the scene there long but it was already clear that Clyde detested him. Draper didn't exactly like the older guy either, but he knew their interests were closely aligned, even if their motives were quite different. Draper's drivers in life were and always had been power and money. Henderson, on the other hand, was a man who'd been badly burned by life. You didn't need to see his scars to know that. He was a man on a long-running and blood-filled mission of vengeance, and he'd already shown Draper that he had powerful connections that could make things happen. Bad things.

'Okay,' Draper said. 'Tell me what you're planning. We'll eliminate every risk that we can.'

CHAPTER 11

Cancún, Mexico

The next morning, Davey was feeling a combination of tired, angry and frustrated. He'd been sleeping on the sofa when the motion sensor connected to his camera had beeped incessantly. That was almost one a.m. He knew something was up. Why was anyone going into El Yuca's office at that time?

He'd groggily pulled himself over to the camera to which he'd already attached a night vision scope. When he'd looked at the green and black screen, he'd seen nothing for a few moments and wondered whether it was a false alarm. Then he saw him. Despite the green colouring of the image, and even though he had a cap pulled low over his face, Davey had known it was the same guy again – the one who'd visited earlier in the day.

He'd watched, impressed by how quickly the man broke into El Yuca, though equally worried by exactly what was unfolding in front of him.

When Orrantía's backup had arrived, Davey made the decision to head out there. He'd been given the go ahead to engage if necessary, though Davey's instinct was to remain in the shadows as long as he could. Several gunshots were fired before the guy made a purposeful escape, and Davey put his recent surveillance training to good use in tailing the man as he made his getaway, lugging what looked like a damn heavy backpack through the streets of Cancún.

But then the guy had simply disappeared.

Davey could do nothing. The only option had been to head back to the apartment.

Once back there, he'd sat by the camera a couple of hours more, until the police had finally headed away from El Yuca empty-handed. Davey was surprised they'd been called at all. Most likely it was a resident who'd heard the gunshots who had called the cops, rather than Orrantía's crew. It would be interesting to know how they'd explained to the police what had happened.

After that, Davey had conked out on the sofa, exhausted. It was nearly midday when he'd stirred and he headed back to his spy position. He noted the cars in the car park – both Collins's and Orrantía's. The van of a local maintenance company was also parked outside; no doubt they'd been hired to rectify whatever damage the previous night's intruder had caused.

When Davey's phone buzzed, he groaned. He'd given his boss the briefest of briefs in the night, when he'd arrived back at the apartment. The conversation had lasted only a couple of minutes – his boss unhappy at being woken, and Davey not wanting to dwell on the frustration of having no idea what was happening. Even in that short time, he'd sensed that his performance was now under serious scrutiny. But it was a new day, and even though he didn't really want to speak to him again so soon, Davey was determined to pull the situation around.

He picked up the phone and answered it.

'Anything going down today?'

'Nothing yet,' Davey said. 'Any luck identifying our new arrival?'

He heard his boss humph. 'No. I've had the team search everywhere we have access to. He's not on any criminal database or any agency watch list. And he's not law enforcement or intelligence as far as I can see – not FBI, CIA, MI6, FSB, or any other damn three letter acronym you can think of.'

'That makes no sense.'

'Why not?'

'He's not some average Joe who's turned up in Cancún for the weather and cheap beer.'

'Maybe, maybe not. If you'd managed to keep on his tail last night than perhaps you could have found out more.'

Davey gritted his teeth but said nothing.

'Next time you see him, don't lose him. Do whatever you need to do to find out who he is and whether he poses a threat to our operation.'

Whatever you need to do. Davey briefly thought about those words.

'Got it,' Davey said. 'Is that all?'

'No. I told you I was sending someone else out there.'

Actually Davey had asked for backup. The way his boss was talking, it sounded more like a replacement.

'Who?'

'Eric Quintero.' Davey knew him. He was an okay guy. They were peers, had been in the organisation for almost the same amount of time. Was that a good thing that he was being sent to help? Or was he being sent to take over? 'He's on his way to you, should be there before evening. He'll call you when he hits the city.'

The line went dead.

Davey grunted in frustration then got up, headed back to the camera and pressed the record button. He needed a break. He left the apartment and, feeling more apprehensive than normal following the previous night's events, walked to a local café where he was seriously tempted to order a beer or two with his tacos to help him relax. He didn't.

After finishing the food, he made his way to the apartment. Once again he felt uneasy. Rather than going straight back, he took a more circuitous route, doing his best to appear calm and relaxed, but at the same time keenly surveying all around him for anyone following.

He saw nothing. He was just being paranoid.

It was three p.m. when he arrived back at the apartment block. The seals he'd placed on the door and frame were still there. He opened the door and quickly gave the apartment a once over, confirming that nothing was untoward. Then, having checked the recording on the camera and satisfied himself that nothing of note had taken place, Davey slumped back down on the sofa and waited.

A few minutes later, there was a soft knock on the apartment door.

Who the hell was that? Davey looked over but didn't make a move to get up. In the two weeks he'd been in Cancún, he'd never once had anyone come to the apartment. Could it be Quintero?

Davey sat in silence for a few moments, debating what to do. The soft knocks came again. Quintero was supposed to phone. And if that were him standing out there wouldn't he call out?

Davey carefully pulled himself up from the sofa, making as little noise as possible. He slipped off his shoes then slid silently across the wooden floor, grabbing his Glock from the side table as he went. He pulled up against the wall next to the door. The spyhole was there, just inches from where Davey was standing, but there was no chance he was putting his face up against that. He hadn't needed any training from the DEA to know how that could go wrong.

The knocks came again. Davey pressed his ear to the wall then stood motionless. With his ear against the plasterboard he could hear the thudding of blood pumping around his body – a little quicker than he would have liked. He could hear nothing of who was outside. No voices, no footsteps, no breathing.

No more knocks came, and Davey stood there, waiting, thinking. He barely moved for nearly thirty minutes. Then he heard footsteps out on the stairs. They didn't seem to be particularly disguised. Someone coming home, most likely. The steps got louder as the person headed upward, finally arriving on Davey's floor, then quieter again as they carried on further up. Davey heaved a sigh of relief, only then realising he'd been holding his breath as he listened.

There'd been no hesitation in the footsteps. Nothing to indicate that the person walking up the stairs had encountered an unexpected lurker when they'd reached Davey's floor. No pleasantries or anything like that. And he certainly hadn't heard anyone outside the door suddenly moving away to hide when the new arrival passed.

This was getting ridiculous, he told himself. Deciding he couldn't stand there all day like a schmuck, Davey finally put his eye to the spyhole, pressing the barrel of the Glock up against the door. He saw no one out there. His hand reached down to the handle. He turned it.

The door was flung open and smashed Davey in the face. He reeled back and instinctively lifted up the gun. He never got a shot off. The man – that same damn man! – came barrelling in. With the element of surprise in his favour, the man kicked shut the door behind him, turned Davey's arm outward and pushed the wrist back to the point of breaking. Davey had no choice but to drop the gun.

But he wasn't beaten just like that. He was trained for this shit. Davey ducked and spun out of the hold and launched a hook toward the guy's temple. He was no slouch – in training, hand-to-hand combat had been his favourite, and his best subject.

The guy blocked the shot, but Davey wasn't finished. He sidestepped and went for the guy again. A roundhouse kick, followed by a straight punch, then, with his front leg to the side of the man, Davey would haul him over his outstretched leg.

But the guy blocked all Davey's moves, and countered with venom. Davey quickly realised this wasn't training, and the guy was something else. Whatever Davey did to block or attack, the man had an answer and more. He was like a robot, moving in steady rhythm, anticipating everything.

Within a few seconds of increasingly desperate attempts, Davey found himself hurtling to the floor, his legs taken out from under him. The back of his head smacked painfully off the wood boards and Davey's vision jumped and blurred.

The next second, the guy was on top of Davey, pinning him down. His face was impassive; he wasn't even out of breath.

'Who the fuck are–' were the only words Davey managed to get out before the man's fist connected with Davey's head, and he was out cold.

CHAPTER 12

Davey's eyes sprang open and his body jerked in shock. It took him a few seconds to recalibrate and realise both where he was – the apartment – and what had so vigorously roused him from unconsciousness – cold water. The icy liquid covered his head and was dripping down his brow, down his cheeks, onto his torso, which he now realised was naked. He could hear droplets pattering off him onto the wood floor. In front of him, the man was standing, impassive expression still intact, an empty plastic bowl in his hand.

Davey tried to move but couldn't. He was on a wooden dining chair, his hands secured behind the back, each ankle fixed against a chair leg.

'Nice of you to re-join me,' the man said. His accent was English. He spoke calmly. No aggression or anger there. Yet Davey sensed the danger in the man, not least because of his overbearing size and the scars on his hands, arms and face. Whoever he was, this guy had been in some serious scrapes. He was a warrior. A serious fighter. Hell, Davey had just been witness to that.

The guy placed the bowl down onto the table and picked up something, concealing it behind his back. Davey's brain whirred as ominous visions bored into his mind.

What's in his hand?

'I'm going to make this really simple for you,' the man said. 'I tell you something, you tell me something. An exchange of information. Does that sound fair to you?'

Davey said nothing, tried not to show a reaction, as he scoped out what he could do to escape. He could see neither his hands nor his ankles, but when he wriggled his joints, it felt as though the restraints were thin and flexible – cable ties, rather than rope or cuffs? And the chair wasn't secured to the floor.

'My name's James Ryker,' the man said, before pausing for a few seconds.

Davey was confused. Why tell him that? What did that mean?

'I'm not the bad guy here,' Ryker said. 'You might not believe that, right now, but it's the truth.'

'Then why did you attack me? Why am I tied up?'

'I'm the one asking the questions. But let me finish first. I know you're with the good guys too. We've crossed paths here. But it doesn't have to end badly. We can both walk away from this and carry on. But only if you help me. Got it?'

Davey didn't respond.

'I think you got it. So first question. I told you my name, what's yours?'

Davey pursed his lips and Ryker let out a long, almost mocking sigh. Davey tensed as Ryker's hand came from around his back, but he quickly relaxed when he saw Ryker wasn't holding any kind of weapon, but two passports.

The relief was short-lived though. Two? Davey had carefully hidden one of them. How had Ryker found that so quickly? What else did he already know?

'Under the floorboard. Classic. But I'm curious. Am I talking to Greg Tyler the American, or Richard Blake, the Canadian?'

Davey looked away, trying to stay strong, to *not* think about how hard Ryker could make this situation if he really wanted to. But then he'd said he was a good guy. Could Davey trust him?

No, absolutely not. He had to stick to protocol.

'Actually,' Ryker said, 'my guess is you're neither. So what's your real name?'

Davey still said nothing.

'Why are you in Mexico?'

Davey didn't answer.

'Why are you spying on El Yuca? And on me?'

No response.

'Who do you work for?'

Davey stayed silent.

'CIA? ATF? DEA? No, not CIA. You're not good enough. DEA is my guess.'

Davey tried his best not to react but Ryker smirked as though he'd seen a tell, looking pleased with himself both for his correct deduction but also for the slight about Davey's aptitude.

'So you think El Yuca are running drugs?'

When he got no answer, Ryker moved over to the window and looked out across the street. Davey squirmed and tried working on the restraints. There had to be a way to break through these things. But even after a few seconds, the thin plastic cut into his flesh and the pain was too severe to carry on.

Ryker was messing with the camera, but he was facing the window so Davey couldn't see exactly what he was doing. Davey knew there was only the day's footage still on there. He transferred the data to his laptop and deleted the camera's memory card every day.

The laptop. Shit. It had all of the footage Davey had taken, but that was probably the least noteworthy data on there. Davey also had all of his logs, the background information on the case – profiles, suspects – plus his email account. The laptop was at least locked though, and it needed both a six-digit PIN and Davey's thumbprint to unlock it.

A gruesome thought crashed through Davey's mind and he gulped loudly.

'Bloody hell, you must be bored shitless doing this day in, day out. How much are they paying you for this crap?' Ryker dropped the camera and it clanked on the floor. He then moved over to the laptop and lifted the lid. He craned his neck to look back over to Davey, a grin on his face. He reached into his trouser pocket and came out with a pair of pliers.

'I thought these might come in handy today,' Ryker said, clicking the pliers together.

'No, please,' Davey said, before he could stop himself.

'Or...'

He put the pliers down, picked up the laptop, moved over to Davey, and crouched down at his side. Davey balled his fist but Ryker was able to quickly prise the thumb away, and after a couple of seconds, Davey heard the blip which told him the fingerprint had been accepted.

'That was easy,' Ryker said, straightening up, his eyes on the laptop screen. 'So now I just need your code.'

He turned back to Davey, who simply gave a slight shake of his head. Ryker sighed again. He put down the laptop and fished again into his pocket. Davey tensed once more, but was then confused when Ryker's hand came out holding on to a small, black square object.

Ryker held the object up in the air nonchalantly, then dropped his hand and slid the device into a USB slot on the laptop. Davey saw a little red light flicker on the device.

'Who needs passwords, eh?' Ryker turned back to Davey. 'That'll take a few minutes. Don't worry about encryption, it'll crack all that for me too. So how about we go back to the beginning here. What's your real name?'

Davey still didn't say a word, and the look of nonchalance on Ryker's face slowly melted away. First, the impassive look reappeared. But that quickly fell away too, leaving something quite different. Anger. That wasn't good.

'Fine. It looks like we'll have to do this the old-fashioned way.'

Ryker stormed toward Davey, who winced as the bulky figure loomed over him. But Ryker simply strode past, out of sight. Davey twisted his head, shuffling in his seat, trying to get a look at where Ryker was.

For what seemed like minutes, he could see and hear nothing. Where the hell was he!

Davey thought about shouting out. Calling for help...

Or should he push back on the chair and send it crashing over. Maybe it would smash and at least he'd be able to manoeuvre then.

But before he could move, there was a thudding sound as something hard hit him in the back of his head, which sprang forward and recoiled violently. His vision blurred from the force of the blow.

After a few moments, as it was coming back into focus, he was hit again on the back of the head.

'What the hell!' he slurred, his world spinning.

An arm was thrust around his neck, and Davey and his chair were lifted off the ground as Ryker squeezed hard with his thick arm. Davey gargled and gasped, trying to breathe, but nothing was coming in or out.

Davey struggled as much as he could against his ties, but he could barely move. Why hadn't he spoken? Was the sparse information he had on El Yuca really worth dying for?

With no way of escape, and with the life being choked out of him, Davey's eyes drooped, and the world began to fade.

Then, suddenly, the arm was released.

Davey inhaled so deeply that he thought his lungs were going to explode, and he continued to wheeze and pant as his body recovered.

'Wh... Why!'

'Tell me why you're here,' Ryker said. 'What do you have on El Yuca?'

A thought tugged at Davey's mind. This Ryker guy, he certainly wasn't an ally of Orrantía or any of the others at El Yuca. Davey had no clue who he worked for, but Ryker wasn't one of *them*. Was the best course here to talk? He said he was with the good guys.

'Let me make this really clear for you,' Ryker said. 'I *will* get the information I need, and I will do anything necessary. Do you understand?'

'What information?' Davey managed to choke out.

'Great. You got your voice back. Two men came here. Mexicans. Tamayo and Conesa.' Ryker went over and fished in his backpack then came back holding two photos which he held out. Davey stared at the faces but he didn't recognise either.

'You don't know them,' Ryker said.

Davey thought it was more of a statement than a question – had his reaction to the photos given that away?

'You're not the first person around here to deny knowing them,' Ryker said. 'But they did come to El Yuca. They were paid by someone – I don't know who – to hurt someone very close to me. They killed her. And I'm going to kill anyone who was involved.'

Davey's brain was whirring with a thousand thoughts.

'I know nothing about that!'

Ryker dropped the photos onto the floor and scooted back around Davey. The arm came forward again and Davey, sensing what was coming, shouted out before the grip became too tight. 'No! No!'

It worked. The arm was there, but it wasn't choking him yet.

'Tell me what you know,' Ryker said.

The grip became tighter again, and Davey gasped and struggled uselessly.

'Tell me what you know,' Ryker repeated, calm and assured. 'What are Orrantía and Collins involved in?'

'I ca... can't.'

'Who's pulling the strings?'

This time Davey didn't say a word, his brain was too confused to think of a response.

The grip around his neck tightened further. Davey's feeble protests went unheeded, and he could do nothing as Ryker slowly squeezed the life out of him.

Everything had begun to turn black when Ryker once again took his arm away. It was like a shot of adrenaline delivered right to Davey's heart, the panicked organ thudding ferociously in his chest.

'Tell me now,' Ryker said, as Davey panted and wheezed. 'I can keep doing this all day. It hurts like hell, doesn't it? Feels like your lungs are being burned from the inside out? It'll only get worse each time I do it. Sooner or later, I might not stop in time.

Might even break your scrawny little neck by mistake. Nobody's perfect you know.'

Ryker paused. Davey's head was in such a mess that he wasn't even sure what Ryker's last question had been. Was Ryker waiting for an answer still?

'Who's the Silver Wolf?' Ryker asked, breaking the uneasy silence.

After a few seconds without an answer, something dug into the back of Davey's neck – a small blunt object, knuckleduster maybe. Not a terrible pain, not at first at least, but as it was pushed deeper and deeper into the tissue in his neck, grinding against the vast bundle of nerves there, the pain grew by the second, shooting down his back and into his arms and legs.

'I don't know who it is!' Davey screamed. 'That's the whole reason I'm here. To find out more. But the Silver Wolf hasn't been seen for months. Not once since I've been here.'

'Who is he!' Ryker shouted, no calmness in his voice. Just anger. He hit Davey hard in his right ear. 'Tell me his name!'

Davey was beginning to feel delirious, his ears ringing, his head in a spin.

'Give me something and I'll stop. We can go back to talking. Give me a name. Anything to help me.'

Davey wracked his brain but he said nothing. Soon, he couldn't. The arm came back around and choked him again. Davey was too weak now, and it felt like there was nothing he could do to stop Ryker. His lungs, heart and brain were all starved of oxygen, and the world was quickly fading away once again.

Then a shrill noise filled Davey's ears, sending a shot of clarity to his brain. A phone. His phone.

Ryker released Davey's neck. Davey coughed, spluttered and wheezed as he quickly replenished his starved body with oxygen. The sudden surge sent his heart into a heightened panic. Somehow he managed to remain conscious.

When focus returned to his vision, he realised Ryker was kneeling down in front of him, holding the phone up for Davey to see. He could read the details of the missed call on the screen. He recognised the number. His boss had sent it to him earlier.

Relief enveloped him. Davey wasn't going to die. It was Eric Quintero. He was here.

CHAPTER 13

'It's my boss,' Davey lied, his voice was raspy, a stinging pain in his throat with every word he spoke.

'What does he want?' Ryker asked.

'I don't know. I didn't answer the call, did I?' Davey saw the glint in Ryker's eye, and he worried for a second that his more confident tone might not have been the wisest of moves. 'I have to check in at set times. If I don't, he'll know something's up.'

'And then what?'

'And then they'll send a team to check on me.'

'From where? America? That could take the best part of a day. I've been here for a few minutes. Imagine what I could do to you in a few hours.'

Davey gulped. 'He'll call the police. They'd be here within minutes.'

Ryker seemed to mull that prospect over. He glanced behind him, back over to the laptop. Davey noticed that the small thumb drive had a green light blinking. When Ryker turned, there was the slightest grin again.

'I'll call him back,' Ryker said. 'You tell him everything's okay. Yeah?'

Davey nodded. Ryker looked at the phone and pressed the screen a couple of times before holding the handset up to Davey.

After a few seconds, he heard the dial tone, loud and clear on the phone's speaker. But then he realised that the sound seemed to be echoing, and when Ryker looked over to the front door, Davey realised why.

The call was answered.

'Davey, I'm right outside,' came Quintero's voice in stereo.

'Red two!' Davey shouted, more to the door than to the phone. Red two. A pre-arranged duress code for their operation. Davey hoped it would be enough. But would Quintero barge in to save him or just run off for help?

The call immediately dropped. Ryker shot upright and Davey caught sight of the elbow, arcing toward his face. The pointed joint crashed into the side of Davey's head, and a second later, he was out cold once more.

No, this wasn't déjà vu. That would have been much better, because it would have meant this was the first time Davey was waking from unconsciousness to find himself tied to a chair in a room with the madman James Ryker.

This second time was noticeably different, though, Davey quickly realised. There was now a third man in the room. Eric Quintero. The agent, head bowed, was a few feet in front of Davey. His tall, thick frame looked odd and oversized on the simple wooden chair he was tied to.

'Quite a party now,' Ryker said to Davey.

'You're going to pay for this,' Davey said through gritted teeth.

'This was your choice. I only wanted to talk to you.'

'He's hurt,' Davey said, noticing the droplets of blood falling from Quintero's head. 'He needs a doctor.'

'He'll be fine.'

Ryker kneeled down to Quintero and lifted up his head. Davey could see there was a gash above his left eye, which was swollen almost shut.

'Wakey, wakey,' Ryker said, shaking Quintero and slapping his cheeks.

After a few moments, Quintero managed to hold his head up, and he slowly opened his flickering eyelids.

'What the...'

'So what's *your* name?' Ryker asked him. Quintero seemed too out of it to answer. 'Okay. This is dragging on too much. We need to speed this up.'

Ryker moved over and grabbed a small hunting blade that was on the table next to the laptop. Davey noticed the thumb drive was no longer there. Ryker leaned against the table and used the tip of the knife to pick at his fingernails.

'Come on, I'm not being unreasonable here. I know you're the good guys, which is why I'm *trying* to be nice. We can help each other. I don't want to hurt you two.'

'Don't want to hurt us?' Davey shouted. 'You nearly choked me to death! And look at *him*!'

Ryker shook his head. 'I already told you I'll do whatever's necessary to get the information I need.'

Ryker walked up to Quintero, who was looking more lucid – and panicked. Ryker grabbed Quintero's ankle and pulled off his leather boot and sock, and grabbed his big toe. Quintero's eyes widened and he bucked on the seat.

'There're a lot of fingers and toes at my disposal. Forty, right? That equals a long time to hold out. Let's see how many it takes.'

'Please,' Quintero begged, showing none of the steel that Davey was feeling. But was that because Davey wasn't the one who was about to have his toes sliced off?

'Who's the Silver Wolf?' Ryker asked.

Quintero was bubbling and spluttering. Ryker pushed the blade of the knife against the skin on Quintero's toe.

'Who is the Silver Wolf? Tell me what you know. A name. A location. Something.'

'Don't say a word,' Davey said to Quintero who was looking at him pleadingly.

'It's not your fucking toe!' Quintero screamed.

Davey saw Ryker push the knife down and the blade cut into Quintero's skin. Thick red blood oozed out onto the silvery metal.

'Okay!' Quintero said. 'We're from the DEA!'

'I know that already,' Ryker said, looking up at Davey. 'He told me.'

'What? No—'

'Tell me about the Silver Wolf.'

'El Yuca is a front for the Silver Wolf,' Quintero gabbled. 'The company is used to launder money from drug sales in Mexico and South America.'

'And? What else?'

'There're plenty more companies like it. El Yuca's just a tiny part of a huge operation. It's nothing. *We're* nothing!'

'What about Orrantía and Collins?'

'Orrantía made his money smuggling drugs,' Quintero said, his voice becoming more panicked when Ryker pushed the knife further still. 'Collins is legit. As legit as she could be, anyway.'

'Quintero, shut your goddamn mouth!'

'No! I'm not dying over this.'

'Tell me what you know and I'll be gone,' Ryker said, finally taking the knife away. Both Davey and Quintero slumped in relief. 'Who's the Silver Wolf? What's his name?'

'That's the thing. He hasn't been seen for months,' Quintero said. 'We don't even know his real name. Just aliases. Diaz, Draper, Edwards... Henderson.'

'What am I supposed to do with that?' Ryker asked.

'That's all we know!' Quintero said. 'Why do you think we're here? We were sent to find out more. To stake out El Yuca. To hopefully see the Silver Wolf coming here.'

'We don't know anything about the two men you're looking for,' Davey said. 'That's nothing to do with us.'

Ryker straightened up.

'But you do know what he looks like?' Ryker asked. 'The Silver Wolf?'

Davey shut his eyes and nodded.

'So?'

'There's a picture in my files. I'm guessing your nifty little device captured all that already.'

Ryker held Davey's stare as though waiting for more.

'I guess we're done here then,' Ryker said.

Davey wasn't about to argue with that. He watched as Ryker picked up his few belongings. Davey just wanted him to go but then he caught a glimpse of the butt of a handgun sticking out of Ryker's waistband and he froze. Ryker caught Davey's eye.

He wouldn't. Would he?

Ryker's eyes narrowed. He took a step toward Davey, then another. His hand reached behind him...

Then he simply carried on, right past.

A moment later, Davey heard Ryker pull down on the door handle.

'I'm sorry I had to hurt you both,' he said. Davey huffed at the strange gesture. Quintero said nothing. 'I'm sure you'll figure a way to free yourselves. If not, your boss will no doubt raise the alarm soon enough. You'll be fine.'

The next moment, Ryker opened the door and was gone.

CHAPTER 14

London, England

Just another day at work. That's what she had to keep reminding herself. That night she'd leave the office, go home, eat tea, watch TV, go to bed, and in the morning everything would be just the same as it always was.

Almost the same, anyway. Except for the money.

Ffion Brady wasn't greedy. No more than most people, anyway. Was she materialistic? Of course. The whole world was materialistic. So yes, it was the money that had swayed her. Or, more correctly, it was her *need* for the money, the desire for a better life for her and Andre.

She finished pinning her strawberry blonde hair into a bun and looked at her freckled features in the mirror for a few seconds, willing herself to get up from the chair and get on with it.

'Okay, honey,' she said, turning from the mirror and looking down at Andre, lying in the bed. 'I'll see you tonight.'

'You look amazing,' he said with genuine admiration, though she saw the sadness behind his grey-blue eyes – that ever present sadness.

Why had life been so cruel to them?

She felt her face tighten as a wave of anger rushed through her. There really was no explanation as to *why*. *Who* on the other hand... Which was the other big reason why she'd been so easily swayed. This wasn't just about the money they needed, and deserved, it was about something much more primal; vengeance.

Ffion moved over, running her hands across the creases of her tight grey skirt, then bent down and gave her husband a soft kiss on his lips. She wished she felt more when she kissed him, like she used to. She straightened up and squeezed his hand. As ever, there was no response to the gesture, his bony fingers and palm remaining lifeless.

'I shouldn't be late,' Ffion said, turning to Clarissa who was sitting in the armchair by Andre's side, her short plump form filling out most of the chair.

'Do you want me to make some food for you?' Clarissa asked, in her Caribbean twang.

'No. I can sort something out. I'll see you both later.'

'You have a good day,' Clarissa said with a warm smile.

Andre said nothing.

Ffion turned and walked out of the room, angry for the lump she felt in her throat.

Things will get better, she tried to convince herself. *The money will make everything better for us again. A new life, a new start.*

But then would the money really make a difference for *Andre* now? Wouldn't the best thing be for her to take the money and run? Start a new life on her own. Andre would be happy for her, if she was happy. He'd always said that, hadn't he?

Those thoughts bounced around in her mind, but by the time Ffion made it out onto the busy Islington street where their apartment was located, her forehead was creased in anger again.

What a selfish, callous bitch you can be sometimes.

The money was for both of them. That was the whole damn point. Why else would she be putting herself through this?

She headed down the high street toward Angel tube station, walking as fast as she could in her heels, past the rows of trendy cafés, bars and restaurants – most either closed or getting set up for the breakfast rush – with offerings from a multitude of different countries and cultures, like a mini-gastronomic world tour over just a few hundred yards. Usually on a weekday, she headed in the opposite direction from home, to Highbury and Islington, and took the Victoria line to Vauxhall. She wasn't heading to the JIA office first thing. She had an errand to run.

An errand? High treason more like.

It was just gone eight when she reached the platform which was already rammed with commuters. She managed to squeeze onto the first train that came through, but had to settle for standing room only. When wasn't that the case in the morning? The train had come from Euston and then King's Cross.

The train slowly emptied with each stop that went by, and there were soon plenty of seats spare, but Ffion's mind was too busy to notice.

When the doors whizzed open at Borough a few minutes later, Ffion headed out onto the platform. She made her way up and out of the station, and was soon walking through the already buzzing and bustling Borough Market. Some of the traders were calling out the varieties and prices of their fresh goods with thick Cockney accents. Did they really need to do that, or was it just for the tourists? As focused as she was, Ffion couldn't help but eyeball some of the delights at more than one cake stall. She didn't stop though, to try any of the offerings. Maybe afterward she would.

At the edge of the market, Ffion turned and headed under one of the many grand arches underneath the railway line. She came out onto an alley where a looming redbrick building stood adjacent to the railway. The old structure – a former factory with row upon row of elegant sash windows on each of its five storeys – had recently been restored and renovated, and the upper floors were now offices for various small, trendy businesses; architects, a design studio, a software company. On the ground level was a line of similarly trendy retail outlets; a fashion boutique, a hair salon, nail bar, an estate agents.

It was to the least noticeable of the establishments – a delicatessen with minimalist branding – that Ffion headed. She opened the door and there was a tinkle on the bell above it as she stepped inside. She stood in the small space and looked around at the wide array of unusual gourmet goods – mostly bottled or canned, but there was also a large counter with fresh cheeses and meats and other delicacies that, as always, smelled amazing.

Moments later, a bearded, barrel-chested man came out from the back, wiping his hands on a tea towel. He initially had a welcoming smile, but then when he saw Ffion standing there, alone, the smile disappeared, replaced with a much more stoic and business-like look.

The man looked past Ffion, checking outside, then stepped to his left and lifted up the hatch in the counter.

'Come on then,' he said.

'Thanks.' Ffion double-checked behind her before she moved through and into the back of the shop.

She walked along the narrow brick passageway, past the shop's storeroom, and onward to the stairs that led to the basement level. She looked behind her again. The man hadn't followed. She often wondered about him. About who he really was and what he knew. Was he just an ageing shopkeeper or actually some super-trained and inconspicuous agent? Neither scenario would surprise her that much.

Ffion stopped at a thick steel door at the bottom of the stairs. She knocked on the door and looked up at the small CCTV camera above it. The underground space was dimly lit by flickering overhead bulbs, but still Ffion thought she could see the lens in the camera widening and constricting as whoever was manning the system zoomed in and out. After a few seconds, a small panel in the wall next to the door slid open and a touchscreen pad glided out. Ffion lifted her hand and placed it, open-palmed, onto the pad. The pad lit up green and whirred back out of sight, and a moment later she heard the sound of heavy locks disengaging. The metal door opened inward an inch. Ffion pushed it open further and stepped through into the corridor that looked much like the one she'd just been in. She walked along, noting the cameras above her to her left and right, eventually coming to a plain-looking frosted glass door. She turned the handle and it opened.

It was like stepping into a different world. Beyond this door the space opened out, the bright white lights, floors, walls, ceiling –

bright white everything – giving a truly futuristic look. Ffion moved across the polished floor up to the desk, behind which sat another stoic looking man, wearing what looked like a bog-standard navy blue security uniform. He knew Ffion. At least, he should have done given how many times she'd been there, yet there was never any recognition in his face. No small talk, or even much by way of pleasantries.

Ffion smiled at him, took out her ID card from her handbag and placed it onto the desk. The man took the card and placed it under the scanner. There was a bleeping noise which Ffion recognised as meaning her ID card had passed its test.

'Authorisation?' the man said.

Ffion was already digging in her handbag. She found the folded piece of paper, took it out and handed it to the man. It always amazed her that despite how high-tech this place was in almost every way, the key authorisation for her presence here took the form of a piece of paper signed and dated by her boss.

The man took the paper, unfolded it, inspected it for a few seconds, and then placed it under a different scanner. This time, Ffion held her breath. She'd been practising that signature for weeks. She thought she'd pulled it off. To the naked eye, the signature looked legitimate enough, but she knew the scanner was looking for both similarities and differences that the human eye couldn't pick up.

No blips came and the man took out the paper, frowned, looked at it again, smoothed it over a little bit with his chubby fingers. He looked up to Ffion and smiled casually, though she could feel her nerves rapidly building.

Just as well they didn't have sensors that could monitor her stress levels: heart rate, perspiration – she'd certainly fail.

Or maybe they did?

The man put the paper back under the scanner and this time the welcome sound came almost straight away. The man pulled the paper out, took one more look at it, then handed it back to Ffion.

'Room four, bay twelve, server XCV1,' he said, handing her a small printout with those same details.

'Thanks.'

He pressed a button under the desk and the door beyond him wheezed open and Ffion moved through. On the other side was another brightly lit but quite barren room, and she was greeted by a similarly uniformed female who was standing behind another desk. Next to this one was a walk-through X-ray scanner. Ffion, her body now stiff with nerves, moved over to the desk, took her handbag off her shoulder and handed it to the woman, who Ffion didn't recognise.

'Morning,' Ffion said.

'Any metal or electronic devices on you?' the woman asked.

'No. I put all my jewellery in my bag already. My phone's in there too.'

'Okay, please move through.'

The woman went to take the bag away, but Ffion reached out and grabbed it.

'Sorry, can I check the location again? I've forgotten the server number.'

The woman frowned but Ffion pulled on the bag's strap. It toppled over, sending her belongings across the counter and onto the floor behind the woman.

'Oh, bloody hell. I'm so sorry.' Ffion quickly scooped up items.

She hunched down in front of the desk, to pick up a lipstick and an eyeliner that had rolled on the floor.

'Ma'am, please remain where I can see you!' the woman called, her voice stern.

Ffion reached under her skirt, pulled off the sticky tab that was stuck to her leg and quickly flung it forward, through the small gap between the X-ray machine and the desk. There was a tiny clunk as it landed in place and stuck to the underside of the lip on the desk.

'Ma'am!' the lady shouted, leaning right over the top of the desk, her face creased in anger.

Ffion stood tall and plonked the make-up onto the desk. She realised she was blushing. That was a good reaction, wasn't it? An innocent reaction. She smoothed over her clothes, pulling down her ridden-up skirt.

'I'm sorry,' Ffion said. 'I'm so clumsy.'

'It's fine. Is that everything?'

'Yes.'

The woman grabbed the handbag forcibly and stashed it under the desk, out of Ffion's sight.

'Please go into the centre when you're ready.'

Ffion moved into the middle of the X-ray machine.

'Facing me,' the woman said, staring at a screen on the desk. 'Arms and legs apart.'

Ffion followed the orders.

'Turn to the left ninety degrees,' the woman said after a couple of seconds.

Ffion did so and the lady repeated the request two more times, Ffion calmly following the orders each time.

'Okay, thank you,' the woman said, looking back up. 'Please walk through to the other side.'

Ffion did so and headed up to the desk on the other side. As the woman was searching in a drawer, Ffion discreetly snatched the tab off the underside of the desk and stuck it back on her leg.

'Use this for any files you need to download,' the woman said, handing Ffion a small thumb drive.

'Thanks,' Ffion said, taking the device and clutching it in her hand. 'Shouldn't be long.'

Ffion smiled. The woman didn't. Ffion moved over to the security door and waited a few seconds for the woman to unlock it. When she did, the door swung open automatically, and Ffion took a deep breath.

Then she moved forward into the depths of the Hive.

CHAPTER 15

Ffion had been to the Hive many times before. In fact, her role as a data analyst for the JIA meant she was probably one of its more frequent visitors. The heavily disguised high-security facility was used to store all electronic data related to past JIA investigations. Ffion guessed in years gone by the Hive, or some other equivalent facility, would have been a big old, dusty industrial warehouse, with rows upon rows of shelves crammed with boxes and paper files. There were no paper files. Everything that hadn't been destroyed already following their routine data retention protocols, was stored electronically on dedicated servers.

Ffion walked along the corridor, past closed doors that led into each of the server rooms. While the reception area was bathed in bright light, in the depths of the Hive it was dark and quite ominous. Black floor, ceiling, walls, doors. Soft LED lighting in green and blue and red maintained the futuristic look.

Ffion reached the door for room four and turned the handle and walked through. The temperature drop was noticeable, as was the persistent whirr and buzz of the servers and the fans required to keep them cool. The room consisted of three rows of cabinets, each one with numerous servers stacked side by side along the length, and one on top of the other from the floor, reaching over seven feet high. Signposts sticking out of the cabinets denoted the bay numbers. Looking at the signs, Ffion could see that bay twelve was on the far side and she headed off to the right.

She nearly jumped out of her skin when she reached the end of the aisle and realised there was already a man there, quietly typing away at the terminal of bay nine. She let out a nervous gasp, and he looked over and gave her a sheepish smile. She didn't recognise him.

'Morning,' was all he said, before turning his attention back to his screen.

'Morning,' Ffion said, moving forward and past him until she reached bay twelve.

She pressed on the button and the glass on the bay slid out of sight. The screen behind it lit up and a keyboard tray skated out.

Ffion looked over to the man again. He caught her gaze and simply nodded. She smiled and turned her attention back to the screen. She was still clasping the thumb drive in her hand, but it was the much smaller drive that was stuck to her leg that she really needed to use.

She looked over at the man again. He was turned away, busy typing on his terminal. Ffion quickly took the drive from her leg and slotted it into the USB slot on her terminal. She inputted her security details and connected not to server XCV1 but to the one she really needed: XCV2.

She didn't know how long this would take. There'd been no dress rehearsal. She'd been told minutes, but how many? Five? Five thousand?

With the software on the drive busy doing its job, bypassing the Hive's security and systematically destroying every last file on XCV2, Ffion simply stood and waited. Every few seconds, she gently tapped on the keyboard, pretending to type, trying not to arouse suspicion in either the man standing across the way, or whoever was watching her on the CCTV cameras which were undoubtedly filming her every move.

A flicker of doubt wormed into her mind as the seconds and then minutes dragged on. No, it was more than a flicker.

How much could she really trust that this little device was working exactly as she'd been told it would? She wasn't an IT expert – far from it. She'd been assured no alarms would be raised as the deletion began, that no marker of her presence would be left on the server, that a fatal system glitch would ultimately be blamed, that no one would even notice the missing data until the next time an analyst came to view files on XCV2. Was *any* of that true? Or was Ffion going to find herself on the wrong side of the all-powerful JIA before she even left the building?

If that were the case would she even leave the damn place alive or would they put a bullet in her head right there? Or, worse, ship her off to some horrific underground site and let the JIA's field agents take turns in extracting information from her?

After a few minutes, she noticed the man to her left shuffling and she turned to see he was finishing up.

'See you around,' he said to her.

'Probably not,' Ffion said. 'You know how it is.'

He winked at her then turned and walked out of sight. Ffion let out a sigh of relief. She looked at the thumb drive, wondering exactly what secrets would now be forever lost.

Less than a minute later, a message popped up on the terminal screen. *Remove device now.*

It only stayed on screen for a second. Ffion reached forward and pulled it free, and in the same move placed in the drive that the security woman had given her. She then connected to XCV1 and began a brief search through the documents on there, pulling off a small number at random. As she typed away on the keyboard, she realised her hands were clammy, the keys becoming slippery under her touch. She could feel moisture on her back, on her forehead too, despite the cool temperature.

She wanted to get out, into the fresh air of central London.

Now there was a first.

She carried on for only another couple of minutes before she wrapped things up and took out the thumb drive. She had no further use for the one that had earlier been stuck to her leg. She needed to discard it. Ffion pushed the keyboard tray and it slid away and then she moved back to the door and into the corridor. She headed for the single cubicle unisex toilet, locked the door, hitched her skirt up, her knickers down and sat on the toilet. She glanced up and around the small space. Would there be a camera in the toilet too? It wouldn't surprise her. Which was why she was going through the motions. She squeezed what she could out of her bladder, stood, then as she reached down to pull up her knickers she flicked the thumb drive into the toilet before turning and quickly flushing.

She sighed in relief a couple of seconds later when she saw the drive was gone.

She washed her hands, and was soon walking back along the dark corridor toward the exit.

When she reached the security desk, the woman wasn't in sight, and Ffion once again felt her nerves building. Had she been found out? Was the SWAT team on its way already?

Or had the woman disappeared because any second a deadly nerve agent was about to seep through the air conditioning vents, a silent killer that would render Ffion lifeless within minutes through irreversible paralysis?

She gulped, but then let out a long, gentle sigh when the woman came into view, holding Ffion's bag.

'If you give me the thumb drive then walk through to the other side, please.'

Ffion handed her the legitimate drive then turned and walked through the scanner. She emerged the other side without any alarms blaring and she moved up to the desk.

'Here you go,' the woman said, handing Ffion both her bag and the thumb drive. 'Enjoy the rest of the day, Mrs Brady.'

'Thanks, you too.'

'Oh, I will. It's a real ball down here,' the woman said, not smiling at her joke.

It was a joke, wasn't it?

Ffion turned and was soon in the first white room and walking past the security man.

'Bye,' Ffion said.

The guy nodded then watched, eagle-eyed, as Ffion made her way to the door.

Almost there.

Out in the brick corridor, Ffion could feel her heart racing faster with each step she took. Nerves, but also anticipation. In her head, she was imagining the sense of relief she would feel when she stepped out into the street.

She moved up the stairs to the deli. The shopkeeper was there, behind the counter. No punters were in. He lifted the hatch on the counter and Ffion walked through and was halfway to the door...

'Mrs Brady! Stop!'

Ffion didn't. It was the security man from the white room. *Keep going*, she told herself. The door was right there, two yards away. If she made it to the street she could make a run for it. She'd head straight for the market, get lost in the crowds.

'Mrs Brady!'

Ffion reached out for the door handle...

An arm shot in front of her, blocking her path.

Startled, Ffion stopped. Her heart lurched in her chest as she turned to see the shopkeeper standing next to her, glaring. Behind him, the security man was rushing over from behind the counter, out of breath.

Ffion's whole body was tensed. Should she attack, make the first move? These two pot-bellied louts surely wouldn't be able to stop her, would they?

'Mrs Brady,' the security guard said. 'Gayle said you dropped this earlier. It was under her desk.'

Ffion felt faint, such was the power of the relief that washed over her. She was surprised she managed to stay on her feet. The security man handed her the phone that had dropped from her bag. *The* phone. Bloody hell, if she'd left that behind! She took it and thanked the man, and he actually smiled. She looked back to the shopkeeper who was still glaring at her suspiciously.

Did *he* know? How could he?

The shopkeeper reached out, and Ffion was a split second from delivering a blow to his throat that would likely be fatal.

But he simply opened the door for her. A breeze wafted in and the smell of smog filled Ffion's lungs, and it was like a taste of heaven.

'Have a good day, Miss,' the shopkeeper said.

'Thank you.'

The phone grasped in her hand, she walked out of the shop and along the cobbles. Her legs felt unsteady as she hurried. She looked behind her twice as she went, but no one had followed her out.

When she reached the end of the road, she ducked back through the railway arch and was soon weaving her way through the crowds in the market. She looked at the prepaid phone in her hand, unlocked it, and dialled the number she'd memorised.

'It's me,' she said when it was answered with silence.

'And?' came the husky voice.

'It's done.'

'The money will be with you by the end of the day.'

The line went dead and Ffion stuffed the phone in her bag.

CHAPTER 16

Playa del Carmen, Mexico

Ryker didn't really feel bad for what he'd done to the two DEA agents – needs must. The two guys had their chance at talking freely, but one had passed on it. At least the other had opened his mouth before things got out of hand. Ryker had meant what he said. He'd do anything to find out who was responsible for Lisa's death.

Even before the second guy had decided to speak, Ryker's assumption was that the two of them worked for the US Drug Enforcement Agency – the DEA. That belief had been fully confirmed when Ryker surveyed the data he'd captured from Davey's laptop, which he did from the safety of a new hotel in the nearby town of Playa del Carmen – a shrunken version of its larger neighbour that was filled with trendy boutique hotels and bars. He was finished in Cancún, and having held hostage two DEA agents there, it wouldn't have been wise to hang around unnecessarily.

Ryker wasn't finished in Yucatan though. It was clear there was much more to El Yuca than met the eye. Orrantía was a bad apple. His business was a front for the mysterious Silver Wolf. Did Orrantía really know nothing about the Mexicans who'd tracked down Ryker and Lisa? Maybe, maybe not. There was only one way to find out.

Although he hadn't had anywhere near enough time to properly search through the vast quantities of electronic data he'd stolen over the last twenty-four hours, Ryker had managed to uncover a grainy picture of the man dubbed the Silver Wolf on Davey's laptop data. The black and white image wasn't the best quality but it gave Ryker another angle to pursue, if Orrantía proved to be a dead end.

First, Ryker was determined to push Orrantía as hard as he could. The shady businessman was now Ryker's best bet for answers in this country. He knew the end game wasn't in Mexico. He hoped Orrantía would provide the next connection. The next lead and location.

But Ryker had to resist the urge to rush off after Orrantía all guns blazing. He could feel he was being pulled deeper into a dark world and he needed to move with some caution. He couldn't find the answers he needed with a bullet in his head.

So he spent that evening scoping out Orrantía's home from a safe distance. He lived in a lavish mansion directly off a white sand beach flanked by palm trees, a short distance from the small town of Puerto Morelos. Ryker had found photos and the address of the property in Davey's data.

Satisfied from his recon that he had the lay of the land, Ryker spent the night in the hotel in Playa del Carmen, getting some much-needed sleep.

The next day he continued to scan through the data he'd acquired, though, frustratingly, came away with nothing new of note – other than further evidence of El Yuca's laundering of large quantities of US dollars of unknown origin.

Two hours before dusk, Ryker set off on his motorbike for Puerto Morelos once more. He stopped a mile short of the property and hid the bike in a small clearing in the jungle on the opposite side of the road to the coastline. Once satisfied the bike was out of sight from the road, he made his way to the beach and then along the sand to Orrantía's home.

He'd determined the previous day that the beach provided the easiest access to the mansion. At the front of the property was a large gate and wraparound wall, some seven feet high. He'd spotted four CCTV cameras dotted about there. On the beach side, though, there was no fence, no wall, no gate. The whole point of an exclusive beachfront property was that it opened out directly onto the sand.

There were still cameras to contend with coming in from that angle, within the property's garden, though that didn't deter Ryker. Orrantía was a rich and security-conscious man, but there was nothing to suggest he was overly paranoid. There was no indication of permanent armed guards at the property or anything else as elaborate as that, and Ryker assumed the CCTV was a deterrent, rather than Orrantía having someone sitting and monitoring live feeds around the clock.

And if Ryker's assumptions were wrong, he'd deal with it.

As he walked along the beach, he looked out across the calm Caribbean Sea. There were numerous specks dotted along the water – faraway yachts and sailing boats of the rich and famous. One, though, was much closer by, about two hundred yards back from the frothing waves. Ryker didn't know boats too well, but the yacht was big – and likely expensive – and its bright white finish glistened with almost surreal intensity. It wasn't moving, and Ryker thought he could see the silvery chains of an anchor dangling from the side of the boat, into the water.

The yacht hadn't been there the day before, and Ryker wondered if it was Orrantía's, or perhaps belonged to a guest of his. There were other villas spread along the secluded beach but that yacht was right in front of Orrantía's home. And as Ryker got closer to the villa, he spotted a small dingy with an outboard motor pulled up onto the sand. Yep, definitely someone to do with Orrantía then.

The Silver Wolf?

Whoever the boat belonged to, it looked like someone was home.

Ryker moved with more caution as the villa came into view from around the surrounding palm trees.

At first, all seemed quiet on the outside of the property, which included a large swimming pool just yards from the sand. But then, as Ryker crept closer, he spotted a dark clad figure coming out from an open patio door. He was dressed in military-like fatigues with combat trousers, a tooled-up utility belt and a bulletproof vest. In his hand he was casually holding an assault rifle, the strap dangling off his shoulder. He had a hard helmet on though the visor was pulled up over his face to reveal his olive skin.

There was no insignia on his uniform, but Ryker seriously doubted this was Orrantía's private security detail. The guy was kitted out in heavy-duty gear, and there'd certainly been no such manpower the previous day. It was possible he was from the Mexican Policia Federal, but it was equally possible he was a mercenary.

Why on earth would that be the case though?

When Ryker's eyes scanned over from the man to the patio doors next to him, he realised the glass on one of the doors was cracked around the handle. The lock had been forced, splintering the double-glazed window in the process.

Ryker didn't know what was happening, and was in two minds whether it was really something he wanted to be involved in. He darted over to his left toward a row of palm trees, gaining cover from the house, while his mind raced with which choice he should take. It would be easy to retrace his steps and head back to Playa del Carmen. But then he'd come away from this trip with nothing.

The biggest problem, other than not knowing who the armed man was, was that Ryker didn't know how many more men he would face on Orrantía's property.

The reality, though, was that whoever they were, they were up to no good. This wasn't a police raid – there were no sirens, no flashing lights, no cars or helicopters, only that yacht. Hardly the type of craft law enforcement would use.

A piercing scream of agony filled the air. It sounded like a man. Ryker pulled away and peered back over to the house. The man on the outside was still strolling around casually, as if oblivious to the noise.

That was it. Ryker made up his mind. He didn't care for Orrantía, didn't really know anything about what sort of man he was, but Orrantía might have answers that Ryker needed. Whatever was happening, Ryker couldn't walk away. He might never get to speak to Orrantía again.

He pulled out his gun and moved off for the house.

CHAPTER 17

Ryker glided along the soft sand, his gaze moving back and forth between the man in black and the yacht out at sea. There was a chance someone was still on that boat. Someone with binoculars or even a sniper rifle who was closely monitoring the beach and Orrantía's house. Regardless, Ryker kept moving, believing the element of surprise would work in his favour against both seen and unseen adversaries.

Staying low and using tree trunks and bushes as cover, he climbed up the small sandbank and into Orrantía's manicured garden. The man in black was still there, casually patrolling the outside of the house. When the man turned away, Ryker darted silently forward and came to a stop behind a wood and brick poolside bar. There was no sign of anyone else out in the garden. No wife, kids, gardener, or anything like that. Just the armed sentry.

Ryker held back for a minute as the man in black turned and retraced his steps in Ryker's direction. Ryker had his gun in his hand and a knife sheathed by his side, but firing the gun would be too noisy, and the knife too messy. Plus, he didn't even know who the man was, so he wasn't going to just kill him. When the man was about ten yards from him, he again turned and sauntered away.

Ryker leaped out and burst forward. He lifted his hand and smashed the gun into the side of the man's head. There was a horrendous a crack at impact and Ryker expected the man would be heading for the ground in an instant. But he didn't. His brain and his nervous system battled to stay conscious. Pure survival mode. He wobbled from the blow, but then turned and drew up his rifle. Ryker readied his own gun again, prepared to smash the guy a second time in the skull – though he knew that another blow like that could very possibly finish him for good.

Both men were mid-arc with their weapons. The guy had an angry snarl and was growling... Then his legs suddenly gave way, his eyes rolled and he plummeted toward the poolside slabs.

Skull on stone – another potentially fatal blow. Ryker was feeling kind, and reached out and caught the man's sinking mass, and helped him safely and quietly to the ground. He was out cold, two thick lines of blood dribbling down his face from where Ryker had pistol-whipped him. Ryker grabbed underneath the shoulders of the Kevlar vest and dragged the man back over to the poolside bar so they were out of sight of the back of the house.

Before moving away, Ryker quickly checked the man's belongings. As well as the rifle, he had a Glock handgun, a ceramic hunting knife, a pocketknife, binoculars, a radio and plastic cable ties. Ryker took three sets of ties and hog-tied the unconscious man. He didn't want the risk of him springing back up and re-joining the fight. Ryker also pocketed the knife, Glock and binoculars, and quickly pulled off the Kevlar vest for himself.

Then he moved away and pulled up against the wall of the house, right by the open patio doors. He listened for noises from inside. Heard nothing. He looked out to the sea, but from his position there was no sign of the yacht; it was hidden by the sporadic palm trees that dotted Orrantía's garden.

Or had whoever was on the yacht already scarpered when they saw Ryker arrive and take down one of their men? The man he'd felled was carrying a radio, so all the men he was facing were likely connected. He had to move fast to retain the upper hand and keep his stealthy approach going.

Then Ryker heard movement inside, heavy feet on a hard floor. A muffled scream. It sounded like a woman this time. Ryker craned his head to get a look through the patio window but he couldn't see past the glare of the sun reflecting on the broken glass.

Ryker waited until everything went quiet again before he jumped out from his position and into the open doorway, gun held out, ready to shoot. He found himself standing in the entrance to an expansive kitchen. He saw no threats, but quickly moved forward, trying to keep his feet light as he moved. He could do nothing about the broken glass underfoot though, and he gritted his teeth as he crunched forward. He ducked down behind a marble-topped breakfast bar and waited.

No sound of footsteps. No voices. It looked like his arrival was still unnoticed, for now.

Then Ryker spotted something that changed his course of action. A pool of blood on the sparkling tiles next to him. Large red footprints trailed past where Ryker was crouched, heading out of sight, over to an archway that led into a hall.

He followed the red prints the other way and there, slumped against the kitchen counter, was the source of all that blood. A young local woman. Probably early twenties at most. She wore a maid's outfit, the dress hitched up around her hips. Her limbs were twisted at awkward angles from the way her body had fallen into a heap. Her head was hanging unnaturally on one shoulder because of the deep slash that went across her neck. Her glazed eyes were staring at Ryker.

He clenched his fists, feeling anger bubbling inside. He still didn't know what was happening, who was attacking Orrantía or why, but they weren't the good guys, that was for sure. Ryker felt no need to hold back any longer – sod his rarely seen kindness.

Then Ryker heard the crackle of a radio outside. From the guy he'd moments earlier floored. When his colleagues got no response, the alarm would surely be raised.

Ryker moved quickly back on his haunches, staying in cover as long as he could. He got to the edge of the breakfast bar and peeped over to the archway. He could see a glimpse of the hall beyond. All seemed quiet and still out there.

Then, from his new position, Ryker spotted the legs of another person on the floor, near to the door – one shoe on, one shoe off.

He moved his head forward to complete the picture. The man – dressed in casual clothing – was on his side. Three patches of red were spreading out on his light blue shirt. He was dead, no doubt about it. Ryker recognised him. One of the men who'd come to El Yuca the night he'd broken in.

So where were Orrantía's other henchmen?

Another scream sounded out. A woman again. Still muffled, but more distant. Coming from upstairs?

Ryker glanced one more time to the archway. Still no signs of movement out there. He rushed out of his cover and moved out into the hallway without breaking stride. Several open doorways led to more rooms, but it was to the grand, central staircase that Ryker headed.

At least, that was, before he spotted the figure off to his right. The guy was emerging from another of the downstairs rooms and was dressed in identical black clothing to the man outside. He hadn't been hiding there, waiting to pounce, but was likely patrolling the downstairs.

Ryker lifted the knife from its sheath and flung it forward. The knife span through the air and Ryker darted forward right behind it. The blade sank into the man's Kevlar, but Ryker knew the vest would save him from a life-threatening wound. Which was why he was moving forward with such speed.

As the man twisted his arms to bring up his rifle, Ryker hurled himself through the air and lifted his foot and thudded it into the man's chest, sending him to the floor. He landed on top and grabbed the man's head and smashed it off the wooden floorboards, three times in quick succession. There was a sickening squelch on the third blow and Ryker let go. His hands were covered in blood. The man wasn't moving. Ryker wasn't sure that he ever would, and he didn't particularly care. He wiped his hands on the man's vest then pulled out his knife and sheathed it.

The next moment, he was heading for the stairs, gun held out and pointed upward. He was halfway up the twisting staircase when he heard more muffled cries above. He could pinpoint the sounds as coming from a room at the far end of the upstairs landing.

Then he heard radio crackle, from the opposite side.

Then fast moving feet. Two sets?

Ryker had to assume whoever was left knew of his presence. He moved with more caution.

Up ahead, the stairs opened out on a large carpeted landing. In the centre, huge thick-framed canvases hung either side of a large stained glass window. There were several doors, most were closed. Two were open.

Ryker span around when he heard noise above and behind him. The next second rapid gunfire echoed through the house and bullets raked along the stairs and the bannister, spitting splinters of wood into the air. Ryker leaped up two, three steps at a time. As he did so, he quickly turned and fired off several shots, sending the shooter scurrying back into the room he'd come from.

Ryker didn't stop to hide. He carried on moving, reached the top of the staircase and sped along the landing to the doorway where the shooter had gone. Rays of sunshine seeped in through the stained glass, lighting up the landing in swathes of blue, red, yellow and green. A long shadow reached out from one of the adjacent doorways, across from where Ryker was. He span, sinking down and lifting the gun. His eyes followed the shadow and Ryker fired into the doorway the shadow was coming from before his eyes had even properly locked on to the target.

The bullet hit the man just below his left eye. He went down in a heap, never getting off a single shot from his rifle. Ryker didn't hesitate; he carried on moving back to where the original shooter was now hiding. The smallest sliver of the barrel of his rifle poked out from the doorway in front of Ryker, who could see nothing of the man who was holding it.

He didn't need to. Orrantía's home was massive, and lavish too, but it was also a modern construction. Ryker had already figured the internal walls were plasterboard stud. He pulled on the trigger of his gun, and he kept pulling as he moved forward. Five shots, six.

The man shouted out. The rifle barrel disappeared back into the room.

Ryker kept moving. The man likely had a Kevlar vest, like his accomplices. The plasterboard too would significantly slow down the bullets. Ryker wanted a clean shot – he wanted this man out of the game for good, giving him no chance to retaliate.

Ryker reached the doorway and saw the man on his backside, scrambling back, his black fatigues covered in white plaster dust. Ryker fired off one more shot, and this bullet hit the man in his neck. Gargling and spluttering, he crumpled in a heap. His finger twitched on the trigger of his rifle as he fell, letting off just one bullet which sailed harmlessly into the ceiling.

Ryker, eyes on the dead man, quickly realised they weren't alone in the room. He adjusted his aim.

But didn't fire.

His gun was now pointing to the centre mass of a woman at the other side of the lavish master bedroom. Streaks of blood and tears wormed down her face. A barely visible figure standing by her was holding a knife against her throat, and lines of blood ran down her floral dress. At her feet, on the floor, was another man – Orrantía. His hands were cable-tied behind his back, his ankles too were secured together. He, like the woman, was staring at Ryker pleadingly.

'I'll kill her,' the man with the knife said, in Spanish. 'Put your gun down.'

Ryker didn't even know who *she* was. Orrantía's wife? Did it matter?

A distorted voice burst out from the man's radio. Ryker wouldn't give him a chance to respond. He looked into the desperate eyes of the woman.

'Sorry,' he said to her, then pulled the trigger.

CHAPTER 18

Lake Maggiore, Italy

Draper looked at his watch again. Nearly eight p.m. The last update from Henderson was that his crew was heading to the shore and the operation would be over within minutes. That was over half an hour earlier, so what on earth was happening? And where the hell was Henderson anyway? He'd buggered off to the toilet more than ten minutes earlier.

'Daddy, I'm stuck,' Angelica said, her voice meek.

Draper looked away from the window and down to his daughter, sitting on the thick carpet of her bedroom floor. His face softened in an instant as he put himself back into Daddy-mode, but the uneasy look Angelica gave suggested she wasn't quite buying it.

He often wondered how old she'd be when she came to know of the *other* side of him. Would it be down to him telling her? Unlikely. Would someone else tell her? Or would she catch him in the act, so to speak? That was perhaps his biggest fear. He wanted to protect his daughter, and that meant shielding her from the horrors that he at times had to witness. Witness? Not quite the right word.

If it were down to him, he'd have Angelica live in her little bubble of wealth and sunshine forever, however unlikely it would be to achieve that.

'Sorry, sweetie, show me.' He kneeled down next to her.

'It's too hard,' she said, staring at the pile of jigsaw pieces.

She'd managed to fit together just two of the one hundred and twenty pieces. The bigger picture was a princess's party – the two pieces she'd put together were the shining jewels of a tiara.

'Why don't you start at the edges,' he said, picking up one of the corners. 'Find all the pieces with a straight edge.'

'Okay... but can you help me?'

Draper sighed. He knew she was pining for his attention because he'd been distracted. He'd seen her breeze through much harder puzzles without any help. He'd only come to her room to give her a goodnight kiss though, and it was way past her bedtime.

He looked at his watch again. Angelica had her head bowed, and Draper could see that her bottom lip was protruding in a sullen pout.

'Find the straight ones first – it'll make it much easier. I'll come and take a look in a few minutes, yeah?'

'Stupid things!' Angelica yelled, swiping the pieces with her hand and sending them clattering across the floor.

'Perhaps you should get into bed, sweetie,' he said. 'It'll be easier when you're not so tired.'

'No!' she shouted, her face screwing up. 'I want to do it now, but you won't help me!'

She wailed at the top of her voice. An overreaction, but not one that was particularly out of the norm for her.

Estella came scuttling into the room, and on seeing Angelica writhing about in tears on the floor, she gave Draper a withering look as though he'd done something terribly wrong.

He was opening his mouth to speak when Henderson stuck his head around the door.

'A word?' he said.

'Yeah.' Draper bent down and kissed Angelica on the cheek, but she took no comfort in the gesture. 'Goodnight, darling. I love you.'

Estella could deal with the little mite. Draper headed out and followed Henderson across to the wood-panelled study.

'So,' he said, when they were both inside and the door was pushed shut.

Henderson reached out and picked up the phone that was on the desk. It was crackling with noise – a live call.

'They're in the house,' Henderson said. 'They have Orrantía and his girlfriend.'

'Have them? Just kill them!'

Henderson scoffed, as though Draper was being an idiot. 'My guys have to make sure they have everything first. But there's a problem.'

'What problem?' Draper asked, already pissed off. Did he really have to hold Henderson's hand through this?

'Another guy turned up.'

'Stick a bullet in him as well then,' Draper said, to which Henderson simply glared and said nothing. 'Who is he?'

'Not police. Possibly intelligence services. He's fought his way inside. He's killed at least two of my men.'

'Just one guy?'

'Just one guy.'

'Then what are you waiting for?'

'It's going to cause quite the scene.'

'Finish this! I already said destroy everything. Get it done.'

'That's what I expected you'd say. Thought it better to check. You're the boss.'

The way he said it made it sound like Draper was anything but.

'Tell me when it's over,' Draper said.

He turned and stormed out, back along the corridor to Angelica's room. He stopped a few yards short. He could hear her giggling away as Estella told her a made-up story about slimy monsters and a schoolgirl wizard.

Draper sighed. No point in disturbing them, but he'd had enough of Henderson for that night too. Draper turned and went the other way, to the head of the stairs. A strong drink. That's what he needed.

CHAPTER 19

Puerto Morelos, Mexico

Ryker had had no clean shot on the man holding the woman, and with the knife at her throat he knew that any move he made carried a risk. But then if Ryker hadn't been there, the woman would surely have suffered far more.

The bullet had caught her in the shoulder. At such close range, Ryker knew the high velocity of the projectile from the Five-Seven would go straight through her. He'd aimed right at the edge of her shoulder, for the spot of unprotected flesh to the side of the Kevlar vest of the man standing behind her. He could only hope the guy's reaction on being shot wouldn't be to open up the woman's neck.

It wasn't.

The woman screamed in pain. So did the man. After that, it was hard to figure what caused what. Ryker wasn't quite sure if the woman pulled herself free, or if the man let go, but the next second, her body separated from her captor's, just enough for his face to become visible.

Ryker fired again. This time, the bullet hit the man in his eye, and a mess of blood and brain sprayed out over the wall behind him. His body keeled over, somehow taking the woman with him.

They landed in a tangled mess on the floor, and Ryker rushed over. The woman was screaming hysterically as Ryker pulled her free of the dead man. She kicked and screamed and he heard Orrantía shouting out too.

'It's okay,' Ryker said, 'It's okay.'

She was covered in blood. How much of it was hers and how much was the man's, Ryker didn't know. He let go of her and held up his hands. 'It's okay.'

She looked into his eyes and seemed to believe him. Then she flung herself toward Orrantía who was trying to prop himself up against the side of the low sitting king-sized bed. She cradled him and sobbed uncontrollably as Ryker scoped out the rest of the room; the doorway to an en-suite across the other side of the bed, the large French doors off to his right that led onto a small balcony that looked out over the sea. To that yacht. He got no sense of any remaining threat on the inside. But out there?

'You shot her!' Orrantía shouted.

'I saved her life,' Ryker said, bringing his attention back to Orrantía and the woman.

'She's bleeding. She needs a doctor.'

Ryker saw the spark of recognition in Orrantía's eyes.

'You?' Orrantía said. 'What the fuck is going on here!'

'You tell me.'

Ryker moved to them, crouched, and grabbed the woman's arm to pull her back. She squirmed and resisted but when Ryker increased the pressure on her arm she relented.

'Let me take a look,' Ryker said to her and she relaxed some more. He inspected the wound. 'It doesn't look that bad. If you have a first aid kit I can bandage it up. If not, an old shirt will do for now.'

Orrantía and the woman looked at each other. Then he nodded and she got to her feet. She never made it more than two steps. The first Ryker knew was when he heard the crack of breaking glass. Then a dull thunking sound. The woman was halfway to the floor when Ryker realised she'd been shot.

A sniper.

Ryker slumped further to the floor and looked over to the French doors where one of the glass panes now had a bullet-sized hole with cracks reaching a few inches all around it. On the floor, they were out of view of the yacht, where the bullet must have come from, but Ryker knew they had to move to stay safe.

Orrantía was staring over at the body of the dead woman, a series of unintelligible words coming from his quivering lips.

'You need to focus,' Ryker said to him.

Orrantía didn't seem to take any notice.

'She's your wife?' Ryker asked.

Orrantía shook his head as tears rolled down his cheeks. He didn't provide any further clarification of his answer. A mistress perhaps? For Ryker it wasn't the most important point right then.

He grabbed hold of Orrantía by the shoulders. 'Focus, Orrantía! Or we're both dead.'

After a few seconds, Orrantía seemed to come around to that realisation. Resolve showed on his face.

'Who's trying to kill you?' Ryker asked.

'I don't fucking know!'

Ryker quickly looked around the bedroom again. His eye was caught by a two-foot-high cubbyhole in the wall, behind a dresser that had been pulled forward. 'You've got a panic room?'

'I was in there. But Josefina... they would have killed her.'

'Did you call anyone?' Ryker asked. 'The police?'

'Not the police,' was Orrantía's response, which Ryker took to mean he *had* made a call to someone.

Orrantía's backup was on the way. Ryker would rather not be around when they arrived. He'd come here to question Orrantía, to interrogate him forcibly if need be. Quite unexpectedly he'd turned into Orrantía's saviour, but he wasn't intending on that remaining the case. He still needed answers, so still needed time with the man, uninterrupted. He wasn't going to get far with a sniper out there ready to put a bullet into anything that moved, and with Orrantía's own heavies descending any minute.

'I'm going to get you out of here,' Ryker said. 'We'll take a car.'

'Why?' Orrantía asked.

'Why what?'

'What do you want from me?'

'I think you know.'

Ryker took the knife from his side and cut off Orrantía's cable ties. He pulled Orrantía up into a crouch.

'We need to stay out of view of the back windows.'

Ryker grabbed Orrantía's arm and pulled him along, and they both stayed low as they moved toward the bedroom doorway.

'I can't believe she's gone,' Orrantía blubbered as they passed the lifeless body of Josefina.

'Is there anyone else home?' Ryker asked. 'Wife, kids, maids?'

'I don't know,' Orrantía said, shaking his head, confused by the simple question. Ryker wasn't going to get much out of him. They had to get away.

They moved out onto the landing, Ryker's eyes darting left and right and up and down. He saw no more threats, though remained crouched low as they moved cautiously toward the stairs.

'Why are *you* here?' Orrantía asked, suddenly sounding more with it.

'Because you lied to me,' Ryker said, glaring at Orrantía. 'Someone very close to me was murdered. The only two men I can link to her death both had a connection to El Yuca. I came here to find out what you know.'

'About those two Mexicans?' Orrantía's anger took over. 'I already said I have no idea who they are.'

'And what about the Silver Wolf? Does *he* know who they are?'

Orrantía snatched his arm away from Ryker and stood straight. 'You have no idea what you're getting involved in here.'

'Actually I just might, and I could say the same to you. Without me here, exactly what do you think would have happened to you? I'd say I'm more suited to this world than you.'

Orrantía opened his mouth to speak.

That was when the back of the house exploded.

CHAPTER 20

Ryker was lying flat on his face. A high-pitched ringing noise bounced inside his brain. He wasn't sure how long he'd been lying there, disorientated. Five seconds. A minute, two? When the ringing died down, the noise that took over was a much lower-pitched rumble. Or was it a roar? It took Ryker a short while to process the sound.

Fire.

Ryker pushed himself up off the carpet, onto his knees. He coughed and spluttered, removing dust and debris from his throat and mouth. His dizzy mind tried to take in his surroundings. He was still on the landing, the head of the stairs just a few yards in front of him. He turned, looking behind. A fire was raging in the destruction at the back of the house which had moments earlier been the master bedroom. No longer framed by those tall French windows, this was now a real sea view – a gaping hole some twenty feet wide blown open by the force of the blast.

'Orrantía?' Ryker called. His voice was coarse and quiet. He cleared his throat and tried a second time, more forcibly. 'Orrantía!'

Louder this time, though still drowned out by the sound of the fire and the ringing in his ears. He heard no answer.

Dizzy, Ryker staggered to his feet. Other than being disorientated he was unhurt. Just then, there was a crunching sound above, and Ryker looked up to see the fire was spreading across the ceiling. A louder crack echoed through the mess of Orrantía's mansion and the ceiling above Ryker opened up. He dived to the side, closer to the stairs, just as two thick wooden beams came crashing down onto the landing where he'd been.

Ryker scrambled back further. 'Orrantía!' he shouted out again.

Still nothing in response.

Ryker got back to his feet. Through the wide view out to sea, Ryker could make out the shape of the yacht, framed by orange flames. It was only at that point that he thought about what had caused the explosion that had decimated the master bedroom. Planted explosives? No, an RPG – a rocket-propelled grenade – was the most likely answer. He already knew there was a sniper out on that boat, so it wasn't unthinkable they – who the fuck were *they?* – had a mini-arsenal out there. Having dispatched Josefina with the long-range rifle, they'd taken to a more brutal and indiscriminate means to eliminate anyone else who was still alive in the house.

Where the hell was Orrantía?

Ryker's eyes moved from the yacht to the bobbing mass on the calm waves, just in front of it. A dingy. At first, Ryker thought it was the same one he'd seen earlier, heading back to the yacht. One or more of the black-clad men escaping. But then, when the flames were fanned by the sea breeze, he clearly saw the trail of frothy white water leading from the dingy back to the yacht. The boat was coming to the house. Whoever was on it was likely coming to finish off the job they'd started.

Ryker's brain was ticking away, trying to figure out what he should do next, when his eye was caught by a flash of orange on the deck of the yacht. Then the trail of smoke. Another grenade.

Ryker turned and flung himself toward the stairs, a second before the explosion sent him hurtling forward. He somersaulted, bounced and crashed down the stairs, out of control. Not exactly elegant, and only luck meant that he didn't break any bones, but the downward tumble likely saved his life.

He crashed onto the marble-floored hallway, skidding along the tiles several feet.

Up above, in what was left of the upper floor of Orrantía's mansion, there was a series of further cracks, creaks and bangs as the inner structure of the house faltered under the heat of the flames and the weight of debris. Ryker had to get out before the whole thing collapsed. And with that boat heading for shore, and the yacht and its armed combatants still out there, Ryker sure as hell wasn't going to take to the beach this time.

Ignoring the aching in his bruised and beaten body, Ryker hauled himself to his feet and through the building smoke tried to find the doorway out to the front. That was when he noticed the glistening pool of red, a few feet away. Then he saw the hand, covered in dust and filth, sticking out from under a beam of wood that had fallen from the upper floor all the way down into the hall. Ryker darted over, crouched down and stared into the wide-open eyes of Orrantía. Ryker could only assume the force of that first blast had catapulted Orrantía right over the banister and down into the hallway below, the wood landing on top of him only adding insult to fatal injury. A broken back. A snapped neck. Cracked skull. Take your pick from any one or a combination of those deadly injuries. Either way, Orrantía was dead.

Ryker fought through the smoke and the heat to the front door. There was another huge creak from above. Ryker half-turned and saw the movement out of the corner of his eye. He flung himself to the side as another flaming beam of wood came crashing down from the roof, into the hallway, spitting out glowing splinters as it landed. Further rumbles came from the bowels of the fire up above. Although the front of the house was still intact, the heat from the rapidly growing fire at the back was becoming debilitating. It wasn't just the heat that was the problem, either, it was the build-up of carbon dioxide as the fire ate away at the oxygen around it.

Ryker got back to his feet and made a final dash for the door. He flung it open and raced outside, taking huge lungfuls of fresh air. Out at the front of the property, Ryker could be forgiven for thinking it was just another sunny day at Puerto Morelos; that there hadn't already been two massive explosions at the back of Orrantía's house, and there weren't several dead bodies inside.

Four cars were parked on the in-and-out driveway – two sports cars, two SUVs – but Ryker wasn't going searching for keys.

A second later, there was an almighty crash behind him as roof tiles, beams, bricks and glass crumbled away from the top of the mansion. So much for the damage only being at the back end.

Ryker ran as fast as he could for the front gates as debris crashed down all around him. A chunk of brick – or something else similarly hard – smacked into Ryker's back and caused him to lose his footing. He stumbled on the gravel drive and landed flat on his face, his elbow, knee and chin scraping on the rough surface.

Then, above the hiss and rumble of the fire, piercing sirens cut through the air. Hardly surprising, given the chaos taking place. Whether it was the fire service, an ambulance or the police, or even all three, he had no clue, nor did he want to be meeting them head-on as he made his escape from the property.

Ryker dashed forward and clambered up and over the front gates, landing on the dirt track that led away from what was left of Orrantía's mansion and back to the coastal road.

A whizzing sound flashed past Ryker's ear. He knew what it was. He dashed for cover in the trees, glancing behind momentarily to see the black-clad figure beyond the bars of the gates, rifle held up close to his face.

The sirens were getting louder, but there was still no sign of any vehicles. Then Ryker heard the rumble of an engine. He carried on moving forward at speed, heading further into the dense treeline beside the property.

A few seconds later, he caught a glimpse of the approaching vehicle. It looked to be the same one he'd seen outside El Yuca before. Orrantía's backup. With the rifleman hunting Ryker down behind him, it was the exact distraction he needed at that moment. Within seconds, whoever was in that car would become embroiled in a battle with the remaining assailants while they tried in vain to find Orrantía and rescue him alive.

Ryker waited for the vehicle to flash past on the road.

Seconds later, he heard screeching tyres. Heard doors opening. Shouting. Then echoing gunfire.

It was time to make himself scarce.

Ryker moved off from his position and headed west, keeping within the trees as he trudged away from Orrantía's mansion.

After a couple of hundred yards, he changed course so that he'd close the gap to the coastal road. A mini convoy of fire engines and police cars whizzed past, but after that it was all quiet. No sounds of explosions or gunfire or anything else except for Ryker's thumping heart, his heavy breaths and the cracking of his feet on the twigs underfoot.

Before long, Ryker had retraced his steps back to his motorbike. He fished in his pockets for the key, relieved when he finally grabbed it. The key was about the only thing he still had left on him. The gun and the knife had been lost somewhere along the way.

Ryker rolled the bike back to the road, cautiously looking up and down the tarmac as far as the eye could see. Nothing untoward. He turned the key in the ignition, the engine roared to life and he was soon heading along the smooth tarmac back to Playa del Carmen.

CHAPTER 21

Ryker was angry, frustrated. He'd gone to Orrantía's home looking for answers to Lisa's death, but he'd come away with nothing but his life. Orrantía was dead. Where Ryker went next, he really didn't know. It was dark by the time he made it back to Playa del Carmen. There'd been no hint of trouble on the way back from Puerto Morelos, but Ryker's mind had been swimming with thoughts as to exactly what had happened there. Who had come after Orrantía and why? And was Ryker, having witnessed the assault and escaped it, now on the hit list too? He really didn't need any more enemies, but he had to assume he was now a target.

Which was why he parked his motorbike a half mile from the hotel and went the rest of his way on foot, keeping to the busier streets of the town that were lined with tourist-friendly bars and restaurants. He saw no signs that anyone was following him, but after the events of the last few days, he was taking nothing for granted.

When he arrived outside his hotel room door, Ryker did a quick check and was satisfied that the seals he'd placed were still there, and hadn't been tampered with, then he headed inside. He wasn't staying though. He quickly gathered his few belongings into the backpack. Then he stood and stared at the bag, on the bed, and back over to the safe, on the table. He'd still not had time to buy the equipment to crack the safe. Was there likely anything of use in there anyway? Probably not. Probably just more spurious accounting data and bland references to the Silver Wolf. Was that really going to get him much further?

There was always Collins. Would she have any useful information? The DEA agents in Cancún had suggested she was a legitimate business partner of Orrantía's, but Ryker would bet on her having at least an inkling of El Yuca's side business, or even some involvement in it. That still didn't mean she'd know anything about what happened to Lisa, but Ryker was in Mexico, and tracking Collins down had to be worth a try. It wasn't as though he was inundated with other potential leads to follow.

He opted to take the safe. Yes it was heavy and cumbersome to carry, but he didn't like the idea of leaving it – and the information it contained – behind. If anything, the damn thing could even come in useful as an impromptu weapon, Ryker thought with a wry smile.

After showering and tending to his cuts and scrapes, he dressed in fresh clothes – jeans and a plain black T-shirt – before lugging the heavy backpack out onto the street, retracing his steps to where he'd left the bike. He was only a few minutes into the walk though, when his instincts screamed at him. He'd turned a corner and was sure he'd seen a figure behind dart out of sight. Ryker moved more quickly and took a series of turns so that he was eventually heading back on himself, hoping he would either lose the follower or come up on them from behind.

But he spotted no further signs of anyone out of the ordinary either in front or behind him.

Not satisfied, he nonetheless headed back closer to his bike. The streets he was walking down weren't exactly quiet, with plenty of people out and about eating and drinking, which made spotting a tail harder, but it was safer that way, and less likely that anyone would confront him.

Then Ryker saw it again, when he turned to look behind him; just the shadow of a person darting out of view behind a parked car, maybe as much as fifty yards away.

No more games, no more guessing, it was time to draw them out.

Ryker took a turn onto a quieter street and then after a few yards, another turn onto an alley that led behind the parallel row of bars. The alley was open at both ends but was unlit and filled with bins. Ryker could see little reason why anyone would come down there – unless they were following him. He pulled up alongside a crumbling brick wall and took the backpack off his shoulders, holding it at the ready.

One clonk around the head with that safe and he could quite easily kill a person. And he probably would only get one shot, because the weight of the safe on the fabric of the bag would likely rip it open at the first swipe.

Although a kill shot wasn't his primary aim, he decided.

Ryker strained his ears. The sounds of chatter from the nearby bars was still audible, though faint. Ryker tried to filter through the noise: talking, giggling, plates banging in a kitchen, glasses clinking. Footsteps.

Slow and soft, but definitely footsteps. Ryker's hands tensed around the bag's straps. He was only two yards away from the edge of the alley. At the first sign of a person turning that corner, he'd spring his attack. He wouldn't aim for the head. He just wanted to subdue whoever was after him.

The footsteps were slowing, getting closer. Then another noise grabbed Ryker's attention. Much quicker and more deliberate footsteps. More than one set. Shouting and laughing too. Ryker pulled back a couple of steps, moving into the darkest shadows of the alley.

Seconds later, he spotted three young men coming into sight on the adjacent street. They were drunk, one of them with his arm around his friend's shoulder. The man on the left looked up and Ryker wasn't sure if he'd been spotted...

They carried on walking past and were soon out of sight.

But the watcher was out there still.

'Alright, mate,' he heard one of the drunk men call out. He was English. 'Bit too much to drink, eh?'

Ryker knew exactly who they were speaking to. Laughter followed, and then the men's footsteps and chatter faded and merged with the noise coming from the bars. Ryker stood and waited. At first he heard nothing more. Had the watcher already gone? But then those same soft but deliberate footsteps came again. Ryker readied himself once more.

His heart then burst in his chest and his body flinched, ready to attack, when a door, just five yards from where he was standing, was suddenly flung open. Rays of light swept through the alley and a man with a large white apron came out of the doorway lugging two filled black bin bags. Ryker pressed his body up against the wall as the man headed to a bin and threw the bags in. He turned and glanced in Ryker's direction but then simply moved back to the open door and slammed it shut behind him, plunging the alley into darkness once more.

Ryker's heart rate and breathing calmed again, and he remained still for minutes as he listened for the sounds of the stalker. He heard no more footsteps though. Whoever had followed him had been spooked.

Or were they hiding in wait, like Ryker?

After close to ten minutes, Ryker finally peeled away from the wall, moved across the alley and pushed himself up against the building on the opposite side. He edged closer and closer to the end of the alley, his view of the street he'd come from, and where the stalker had been, widening all the time.

The street was empty.

Without further hesitation, Ryker moved away and walked quickly down the street in the opposite direction, keeping his senses on high alert.

When he finally reached his bike, Ryker jumped on and pushed his key into the ignition. He fired up the engine and wound the bike out onto the road. He pulled gently on the throttle and accelerated away.

Then a van came out of nowhere, hurtling toward him. He knew the driver was aiming for him. Ryker was caught in a moment of doubt – accelerate away, or brake to avoid the collision.

In the end, he did a bit of both. He twisted the throttle, initially hoping he could swerve past the van. The bike surged forward, but then he realised he'd never make it. The van was already too close. He braked hard and the bike wobbled, and the van still kept racing straight for him. Then its brakes screeched and it slid to a stop and Ryker, battling to control the wobbling bike, did his best to avoid a shattering impact.

The van clipped the front of the bike, and the impact was enough to turn it over and fling Ryker off and to the side. The straps of the backpack snapped on his shoulders and he heard the safe clunking across the street as he thumped down onto the tarmac.

Losing the safe was the least of Ryker's concerns though. The back doors of the van sprang open. At the same time, Ryker heard the front doors opening. As he hauled himself to his feet, he realised he was staring into the barrel of a shotgun, poking out of the back of the van.

The man holding the gun was in darkness, but when Ryker edged forward, he caught a glimpse of his face. It was the DEA agent. Then Ryker saw movement either side of the guy. His eyes darted left and right as he took in the faces of the two people who'd emerged from the front of the van. One was the other DEA agent. Perhaps not a surprise, given his colleague's appearance. He too was armed, gun barrel pointed at Ryker's chest.

The third figure was a surprise though. Not a DEA agent, and not a man.

It was Eleanor Willoughby.

'Get in the van,' she said.

CHAPTER 22

'Where are we going?' Ryker asked Willoughby.

She was sitting in the back of the van, on the opposite side to Ryker, both of them on simple metal benches attached to the van's floor. Davey was next to her, the shotgun on his lap. The other DEA Agent, Quintero, was driving.

'Away from Playa del Carmen,' Willoughby answered. 'Before you really get yourself in the shit.'

Ryker studied her as best he could for a few moments. They had no lights in the back, but the orange streetlights came and went in flashes and every now and then the bright white beams of a passing vehicle lit them up fully for a few seconds. He didn't think Willoughby was armed. She was dressed in a pair of jeans and a tight-fitting top. He saw no unusual bulges.

Despite the extreme nature of her arrival, as soon as he'd seen her face he'd relaxed. Before that he'd been well prepared to attempt an unlikely attack on Davey and Quintero to get away from them.

Although he'd got in the van with her, Ryker still had no idea why Willoughby was there – why she was teamed up with the DEA agents. He hadn't sensed a threat from her, but he could tell she was pissed off with him. Because of what Ryker was doing out there, or because her boss had for some reason dragged her away from Mexico City to get involved?

'How did you find me?' Ryker asked.

Willoughby turned to Davey but said nothing.

'I'm not a complete idiot,' Davey said. 'I know how to surveil.'

'The DEA have been keeping a close eye on Orrantía for months,' Willoughby said.

'I know,' Ryker said. 'Because of the Silver Wolf.'

Ryker tried to gauge whether that name meant anything to her, but in the darkness he couldn't be sure of her reaction.

'We're heading back to Merida,' Willoughby said. 'When we get there, there's someone you need to speak to.'

Ryker didn't say anything, though the truth was he was angry. He didn't like being told what to do, or the thought that the JIA were about to hamper his mission to find Lisa's killers. He wanted to stay near Cancún and put pressure on Collins. The DEA and the JIA, between them, were trying to take that prospect away from him. Why?

'Why are you here, Willoughby?' Ryker asked. 'And how have you ended up alongside these guys?'

'This was *our* investigation,' Davey said, his bitterness clear. Ryker just glared at him.

'It's a long story,' Willoughby said. 'I've been trying to reach you for days.'

'I've got a new phone,' Ryker said.

'I figured. Just as well I had these two to help me track you down then.'

'Yeah, I'm really glad about that.'

'Oh, you should be,' Davey said. 'If it weren't for your old outfit coming onto the scene I'm not sure we'd be sitting having a conversation like this.'

'You mean because I'd have kicked your arse and gotten away?'

'Okay, boys,' Willoughby said. 'Enough macho bullshit.'

Ryker again saw that Davey was glaring at him but neither man said anything more.

When they eventually reached Merida, Willoughby and Ryker got out of the van and he realised they were outside the apartment block that the two of them had met at some days earlier, at the start of Ryker's trip to Yucatan.

'You're leaving your new friends behind?'

'For now,' was Willoughby's bland response.

'Maybe we'll see you around,' Davey said, sounding way more cocky than he had any right to be.

Ryker said nothing. Gave him nothing. Just walked off with Willoughby. He knew those two wouldn't be going far. It was clear the JIA wanted Ryker in their sights, and somehow they'd persuaded the DEA to help out with that.

When he and Willoughby were inside the apartment, she took out a mobile phone and dialled a number and turned away from Ryker. She began a brief and quiet conversation with whoever was on the other end of the line, then, after a minute or so, she turned back to Ryker, pressed a button on the phone's screen, and set the device down onto the glass coffee table.

'Ryker?' came the man's voice from the phone's speaker.

It was Peter Winter. Ryker sighed. It seemed that no matter what he did in life, Peter Winter and the JIA were always one step away from treading on his toes.

'Yes,' Ryker said. 'And to what do I owe this pleasure? Shouldn't you be in bed?'

'Cocksure as always, I see. And I *was* in bed. Unfortunately for me, *you* ruined my sleep. You know, Ryker, just because I consider you a close ally, that doesn't mean I can always be there to save you when you start running amok in a foreign country.'

'Who said I needed saving?'

'From what I understand you've forcibly interrogated two DEA agents out there, not to mention getting involved in what looks like a mini-war at Mateus Orrantía's mansion. Or what's left of it. You know he's at the centre of an official DEA investigation, right? That means we'll soon have all manner of US government departments hounding us by the hour. Multiple bodies found out at Orrantía's place, I hear. Without my help they'd put you away for life!'

'That doesn't mean I need your help,' Ryker said. He looked over to Willoughby, feeling a flash of betrayal. Had she spilled the beans of his movements in Mexico to the JIA from day one?

'It doesn't matter either way now, Ryker,' Winter said. 'The fact is you've found yourself neck deep in something out there, and I'm pulling you out before you drown.'

'No you're not,' Ryker said.

'Yes. I. Am.' Winter's voice raised, his tone flinty.

Every time Ryker spoke to Winter, the young commander reminded Ryker more and more of Mackie – Ryker's long time boss and mentor. He was certainly growing comfortable in his new position of authority now that the old dog was dead.

'I simply can't have you annihilating parties to a DEA investigation to satisfy your own need for revenge. That's not how the JIA works—'

'Actually it is the way it works when that's what you want,' Ryker said. 'Since when did you give a shit about the DEA or any other agency?'

'Since their interests align with the JIA.'

'Meaning what?'

'Meaning the JIA *do* have an interest in the DEA's work out there.'

It didn't take Ryker long to figure out what that might mean. 'The Silver Wolf?'

Silence on the other end. Ryker looked over to Willoughby but her face remained impassive. In fact she looked almost disinterested in the conversation, as if this was all just an inconvenience for her. But then Ryker knew from experience that she was a great actress.

'Winter, tell me straight,' Ryker said. 'Do you know who the Silver Wolf is?'

'I don't know what you're talking about.'

'You're lying. You told me you know about the DEA's investigation here. So surely you know the man they're after is called the Silver Wolf. Not exactly John Smith, is it?'

'It's not relevant to you what I do and don't know.'

'Yes it is. Don't forget what happened to Lisa. I'm going to find out who did that and why. At the moment the trail is leading me to some guy called the Silver Wolf. But every time I mention that name everyone clams up.'

'Doesn't that tell you something?' Willoughby said. 'That perhaps this is something you'd better stay away from?'

Ryker shook his head. 'Willoughby, you know me better than that. So tell me the truth, Winter, do you know about the Silver Wolf?'

More silence. Then a long sigh. 'Yes, Ryker, we know of him.'

'I need to find him.'

'I can't help you with that.'

'Yes, you can.'

'Okay, then I *won't* help you.'

'I thought you said the interests of the DEA were aligned with yours–'

'I know what I said–'

'I have a picture.'

Winter said nothing straight away. 'A picture? Of the Silver Wolf?'

'Of the man the DEA believes to be the Silver Wolf, yes.'

More silence. Ryker could only guess that Winter's response meant that this was news to him. Clearly the DEA hadn't been entirely forthcoming with their findings.

'Send it to me,' Winter said.

'Why?'

'Just do it.'

'What's in it for me?'

'I'll continue being hospitable with you and won't hand you over to the Mexican police or the Americans.'

'Hospitable? I was basically kidnapped tonight.'

'Send it to me,' Winter repeated. 'I'm not joking, Ryker. What you've stumbled into here is far more significant than you realise.'

More significant than finding Lisa's killers? Ryker wasn't so sure about that. Regardless, he relented. As much as he preferred acting as a sole operator, he'd also taken on board Winter's words of warning about the DEA and the Americans, even if he wouldn't openly admit it. He could do with keeping Winter on his side, if possible.

He moved over to his broken backpack and grabbed the tablet from inside. The glass front was cracked from when the bag had fallen off his shoulders, but the screen underneath was still working fine. Ryker quickly went through the documents until he found the grainy image of the Silver Wolf. Willoughby stood over his shoulder the whole time. With the picture on the screen, he turned to her. She simply pursed her lips and shrugged to indicate the picture – the man in it – was of no significance to her.

'Where shall I send it to?' Ryker asked.

Winter gave him brief instructions. A secure file drop service on an encrypted website so that no trail was left in cyberspace. It took Ryker a couple of minutes to gain access to the site and upload the file. Winter remained on the line the whole time though no one said a word.

'You should have it now,' Ryker said when he was done.

Still Winter didn't speak.

'Have you got it?' Ryker asked.

'Yes,' Winter said eventually.

'And?'

'And you're saying that's who the DEA are looking for? The Silver Wolf?'

'That's what I'm saying. Is there a problem with that?'

'Actually yes there is. A big problem.'

'Which is?'

'Which is that whatever you've been led to believe, I'm having a hard time understanding how that man can possibly be a criminal mastermind.'

'And why's that?'

'Because that man is a JIA agent.'

CHAPTER 23

Lake Maggiore, Italy

Draper was sitting in the garden room at the back of Villa Mariangela with a pot of strong coffee. The weather was magnificent, as was the view, but Draper was distracted. He checked his watch again. Was he the only person in the world who cared about being on time? They should have arrived by nine-thirty. The flight had landed bang on time, some three hours earlier – Clyde had already confirmed that. So where the hell were they? Draper wasn't worried about the lateness, he didn't think there was a problem, he was simply aggrieved that his visitors felt it wasn't important to keep to the agreed schedule. As though he would just sit around happily all day waiting for them to turn up.

Then Draper heard it. The rumbling of powerful car engines. This had to be them. Finally.

He downed the rest of his coffee then got up and made his way through the house. He stepped out the open front door.

'Morning,' called one of the two men stationed outside the house. Draper couldn't remember his name. Or that of his companion. Derek? Daniel?

'Morning,' Draper said.

The second guy, across the other side, nodded. Both were dressed casually, but Draper knew the men, highly trained in combat, were also carrying. Discreet. This was his home. He didn't want guys wielding AK-47s wandering about – at least not all the time.

The first car to park up on the gravel driveway was a black BMW X5 – Clyde's car – that had been shiny the day before, sitting on the driveway, but was now covered in a thin film of yellow dust from the journey. Clyde emerged first, from the front passenger side, immaculately dressed as always. He was followed by three more of Draper's men. Clyde came straight over.

'All good?' Draper asked.

Clyde nodded then stood by Draper's side.

Three other cars pulled up in a line behind the X5 – the limousines that Draper had arranged for the guests. Men emerged from the vehicles. Most were dressed smartly in cream suits, though one or two wore white, ankle-length thawbs with keffiyeh over their heads – traditional Arab dress. Draper focused on the bearded faces of those men. But he couldn't see the one he was looking for. He looked over to Clyde and gave him a questioning look.

Then he heard the roar of a high-revving car engine. Certainly not a limo. Draper looked back over and gnashed his teeth when he saw the bright purple Lamborghini crunching to a stop behind the limos. The driver revved the engine, letting out a few more ear-splitting howls and pops, before shutting it down. The gull-wing doors slid upward elegantly – if that was the right word for the ostentatious vehicle – and two more men in Arab dress stepped out.

'Subtle,' Draper said to Clyde.

Clyde said nothing.

The two men from the Lamborghini strutted over while their entourage milled about.

'Sheik Falah,' Draper said, holding his hand out to the taller of the two men, whose face was fresh and youthful, his beard neatly trimmed. His dark eyes were kind and innocent, and all in all, minus the garb, he looked more like a well-groomed film star rather than a ruthless multibillionaire tycoon.

'Mr Andrews,' the Sheik said, referring to Draper by one of his many cover names. Even when dealing with people as important as the Sheik, Draper rarely went by his real name. Why create unnecessary noise if any of their communications or dealings were somehow intercepted?

'Please, it's Syed to you,' the Sheik said, giving Draper's hand a gentle shake.

'Peter,' Draper said.

'It's a wonderful villa you have,' Falah said, looking beyond Draper. His English was perfect, but then he'd been educated in ridiculously expensive international schools his whole childhood before studying at Cambridge.

'Thank you,' Draper said. 'I'm sure it's nothing compared to the royal palaces you live in.'

Draper meant the words tongue in cheek, but the knowing look Falah gave him suggested he really did live in monstrous palace complexes the size of small towns with hundreds of eager staff on hand.

'You didn't like the transport I arranged?' Draper said.

'I'm in Italy, Peter. I couldn't resist.'

'Fair enough. But you could have asked me, so I could arrange it for you. You can never be too careful.'

'I think I know what you mean. I can assure you the source of the car is bona fide. Nothing to worry about.'

Draper mulled that over for a few seconds. He wasn't happy with the unexpected turn. It wouldn't have escaped the authorities' attention that the Sheik was in the country. He was mega rich and high profile. Riding around in that purple monstrosity, he was hardly inconspicuous, and if he'd been lax in how he'd arranged the damn car then for all Draper knew, the authorities had tracked it or bugged it and would be all over this meeting.

But Falah was hardly the type of man Draper could berate. He needed this deal to go through smoothly. Falah had no loyalty to Draper, and both men knew they weren't equals. Falah was calling the shots, however superior Draper felt. He'd worked for his position in life. Falah had been born into money, and his family had simply been lucky that they were there on the scene when the oil boom started. They were among the richest people in the world, yet a generation before and all the Sheik's ancestors were probably just sheep farmers.

'It's a lovely day,' Draper said, 'the sun's out and you've probably been stuck inside planes and cars far too long already, so

I've had breakfast laid out in the garden for you. The rest of your crew will be shown into the house.'

'Wonderful,' Falah said. 'Show me the way.'

Draper moved off and Falah followed by his side. Clyde and one of Draper's bodyguards followed too, along with two other of Falah's crew. The rest of his many men stayed put. Draper wasn't giving them all his best hospitality. What were they, anyway? Security? Manicurists? Hair stylists? Rent boys? Draper wasn't sure, and he didn't care to ask about the whims and habits of the Sheik. He'd simply been told the party arriving would consist of twenty men and he'd made provisions as such.

They moved around the side of the house, the view of the lake widening with each step. Draper waited for the wow moment...

Falah stopped and took a deep intake of breath.

'Incredible,' Falah said, to murmurs of assent from his companions.

Draper smiled. *Gets them every time.* 'Thanks. I've lived here for ten years. I can't imagine ever leaving this place, not when I wake up to that.'

'And why would you?'

'But I hope you appreciate that it's not every day I bring my business partners here, Syed. This is my family home.'

'I understand. I'm grateful. And I'll return the favour to you soon, have no doubt.'

'I look forward to it.'

The lie sounded genuine enough. The truth was that Draper had rarely enjoyed travelling to the Arab peninsula, and the thought of spending time in Falah's native Qatar – however luxurious the trip undoubtedly would be – felt more like a chore than a draw. Despite the gleaming glass high rises and the ridiculous amounts of money floating about that place, as far as Draper was concerned it remained a backward society and a breeding ground of religious extremism that wreaked havoc across the world.

Still, extremists needed guns and bombs, and if not from Draper, the terrorists and the militias would find them somewhere else.

They arrived at the main pool. Two large tables, in the shade under the huge gazebo, were crammed with a selection of local delicacies – meats, seafood, cheeses, bread, pastries, juices, champagne. Two of the kitchen staff were there – dressed up in their white-tie outfits.

'It looks wonderful,' Falah said.

'Help yourselves,' Draper said.

The men, remaining standing, huddled together by the food and Draper let them tuck in for a few minutes, the kitchen staff dutifully filling glasses with juice and champagne, and cups with coffee. Draper took a few titbits then gave Falah the opportunity to enjoy the moment, though really he could feel himself getting more tense by the minute. He wanted to get down to business and get the ball rolling on the negotiations.

'You certainly know how to treat your guests,' Falah said.

'Of course.'

Then the Sheik's face hardened somewhat and he looked around edgily. 'Shall we talk?'

'Over here,' Draper said, pointing the way. Falah went to put his plate down. 'It's fine, bring it with you. Some more champagne?'

Falah nodded, and within a second a waiter was refilling the glass, then Draper and the Sheik headed off across the lawn. Draper looked behind him. Clyde was happy enough keeping the others in line, it seemed. The man was odd indeed, but he was perfectly okay at striking up banal conversation to keep guests entertained.

Draper and Falah walked on through the gardens, past immaculate flowerbeds and shrubberies and rockeries, up and down steps until they reached Draper's favourite spot of the entire property. In front of them, a small lawn gave way to jagged rocks, and a cliff face that plummeted to the lake below. A single olive tree jutted out over the edge at more than a forty-five degree angle, its trunk and branches suspended over the water creating a spectacular frame.

'Just when I thought it couldn't get any better,' Falah said. 'Please, take a seat.'

Draper indicated to the wooden bench by the olive tree, and the two of them sat and stared out over the glistening lake.

'I have to ask, Peter, why is it we've never dealt with each other before? I can see from your home that you're not new to business.'

'The world never stops turning, Syed. I've been doing this for a long time, but I'm always looking for new contacts. I can only assume that the fact you're sitting here means I passed whatever checks you performed on my background.'

'You did pass. But here's the thing. You really do have quite a muddled history, don't you?'

Draper took that to mean Falah hadn't been able to figure out *exactly* who he was dealing with, or his full potted history, likely because Draper used so many aliases, not to mention substitutes – men like Clyde and Henderson, who acted on his behalf and in his name, so he didn't even need to show his face. Draper could only conclude that the Sheik was comfortable enough with what he'd found to decide that Draper was the real deal, and that he was worth the risk.

Money talks.

'You're obviously a very careful man,' the Sheik said. He paused and stared at Draper. 'I like that.'

'Careful has got me to where I am today. Did you like the first shipment?'

'It was impressive. But of course that was just a taster. You know I need more.'

'I'm glad to hear it.'

'You're undercutting your competitors by a significant amount though. I do wonder how you're able to do that.'

'You let me worry about that.'

'Oh, I'm not worried. Curious, that's all. Like I'm still curious as to how I came to be here at all.'

Draper looked away from Falah's dark eyes. He hadn't liked the way Falah had said that, a slight suspicion in his tone.

'If you want to ask me something, then ask.'

'Our mutual friend. Thomas Maddison. What happened to him?'

Maddison. Why couldn't the world forget about Thomas fucking Maddison? Though the simple fact was that it was only through Maddison that the Sheik was there at all.

'Actually Maddison's here, with me,' Draper said.

Falah looked unsure. 'Here? But...'

'But?'

Falah didn't say anything else. Draper could practically see the cogs turning behind the Sheik's eyes.

'He's here?' Falah asked after a few seconds.

'You're finished with your food?'

'Yes, I–'

'Why don't you leave the plate and the glass there. Someone will clear it up.' Draper got to his feet. 'Come on, I've got something else to show you.'

Falah looked uncertain but he got to his feet and the two of them meandered back through the gardens in silence, eventually finding the stone steps that led down to the water and the guesthouse.

'This is yours as well?' Falah asked when they were halfway down the steps.

'Yes. Everything you see here is mine.'

They reached the bottom and walked past the guesthouse and onto the jetty.

'We're going on the boat?' Falah still sounded unsure.

'Not yet. Maybe later, if you want to?'

Falah didn't answer. They walked along the jetty, the crystal blue waters on their right shimmering in the sun. Off to the left the cliff face rose up sharply into the sky. They came to the point where the rock opened up into a natural cave eight feet tall, six wide at its opening.

'In here?' Falah asked.

Draper nodded. 'After you.'

Falah stopped and looked behind him. Draper wondered whether he was looking for his bodyguards.

'There's nothing to worry about,' Draper assured him.

'Why would there be?' Falah edged forward into the black space.

Draper followed and pulled out his phone and turned on the torchlight. His and Falah's footsteps echoed in the cold, dank space. They came to a stop at the door in front of them, built into the rock, and Draper took the thick key from his pocket, sank it into the lock and turned.

He pressed down on the handle and pushed the heavy door open, then stood to the side so Falah could get a look. He reached out and shone the beam from his phone ahead so it lit up the small space inside. The shrivelled mess in the corner looked nothing more than a pile of dirtied fabrics. Nothing identifiable as a human. Not anymore.

But then it moved. There was a faint, guttural noise.

Falah gasped and muttered under his breath. Draper's Arabic wasn't great but he'd understood some of the words. A prayer to Allah, he believed. But it was another word, uttered in horror, that stuck in Draper's head. *Iblis*. Devil.

Draper looked over to Falah. He couldn't see the Sheik's face clearly in the darkness, but he could see enough to know that Falah was genuinely horrified.

'You did *this*?' Falah said. And then that word again. 'Devil'.

Draper said nothing as his hard face slowly broke out into a smile.

CHAPTER 24

It was gone two a.m. when Falah and his crew finally left Villa
Mariangela. Draper had plenty of beds to accommodate them,
but the plan had always been for them to stay elsewhere. The
Sheik would be in Italy for a few days while they ironed out the
terms of their agreement, and he also had wider plans for his
trip to Europe, largely involving casinos, fast cars and prostitutes
apparently. Draper had no interest in being part of that. He'd
just have to be patient – if he could. If all went to plan, the deal
would net him in excess of one hundred million dollars – the
biggest single deal of his life. He felt sure that if Maddison kept
producing, kept giving up what he knew, he'd even trump that
soon enough.

'Here you go,' Draper said, handing Clyde one of two
tumblers, before taking a seat on a cream sofa opposite.

They were in one of the main villa's three lounges, the glass
each of them held containing a not particularly generous measure
of a thirty-year-old Speyside single malt. It wasn't Draper's
favourite, but it was damn expensive.

It was only the second alcoholic drink either of them had
touched all day, the other being a small glass of champagne to
toast the Sheik's arrival in Italy. Despite the copious amounts of
champagne and other drinks on offer through the day and night,
Draper had held firm, wanting to be bright and alert for the Sheik
and for any negotiations or awkward questions.

Draper had noticed that Clyde had similarly refused the many
offers from the waiters, but then he wasn't a big drinker. Draper
had only seen the man drunk one time. He wasn't a happy drunk,
Draper had concluded. That night had come to a close with a lot

of blood and two dead bodies. Far too much cleaning up to do to justify a few beers.

What harm could a nightcap do though?

'So what do you make of it all?' Clyde asked.

'How do you mean?'

'You think it's worth the risk?'

'For a hundred million dollars? Yes, I do.' Draper took a sip of his drink and studied the younger man for a few moments as he worked the liquor around his gums. 'I'm sensing you're not as sure as I am.'

'How did you guess?'

'So what gives? You don't trust Falah?'

'It's not about trusting him. Look at what happened today, with that car, and all his crew. I just think he's a bit... noisy. And perhaps this deal is too big.'

'Too big?'

'If you ask me, ten smaller deals is better than one big one.'

'But I didn't ask you. Ten smaller deals means ten negotiations, multiple partners, more time and effort to put all the elements together, and less overall profit because of it.'

Clyde looked away, his body language clear that he was frustrated.

'But I get what you're saying about the noise,' Draper said. 'I need you to keep an eye on that for me. I agree with you that the deal isn't so big it's worth jeopardising everything else. If there's any hint of heat because of what we're setting up here, we'll pull out. I need you to make sure the stopgaps are in place to do that, and that the trail never comes back here.'

'Of course,' Clyde said.

Draper finished the rest of his drink and set the empty tumbler down onto the lamp table next to him.

'You took him to the cave?' Clyde asked.

'Why do you ask?'

'Just interested to know how he reacted.'

'He said it was the work of the devil,' Draper said, straight-faced.

Clyde's face flickered. Draper was sure he spotted a glint of pride behind his eyes as though he took the words as a compliment on his handiwork.

The look soon disappeared though and Clyde swirled the whisky around his glass. He looked as though he was still hanging on to something.

'Talk to me,' Draper said.

Clyde screwed his face as if contemplating whether he should open up or not.

'It's about Henderson, isn't it?' Draper asked, and the surprised look on Clyde's face told him his hunch was right.

'Have you spoken to him today?' Clyde asked.

'Yes. Everything's in hand now.'

'Sure about that?'

'What's that supposed to mean?'

'Come on, that was a complete cock-up over in Mexico. What happened to slipping in and taking people out quietly? I mean... fucking rocket launchers!'

Draper said nothing to that, though he did have to agree. Yes, Henderson had gotten the job done, he'd eliminated Orrantía and anything that could come back to them from El Yuca was destroyed. But at what price? Plus there was also the issue of the mystery man Henderson was blaming for all that destruction. Who the hell was he?

'Don't you get the feeling that it's all a bit too convenient with Henderson?'

'Convenient how?'

'Look at what happened with Maddison too.'

Draper clenched his fists at the mention of the name. Why did everything always come back to Maddison?

'What are you trying to say?'

'How does Henderson know so much?'

'Are you saying Henderson is a–'

'No, I'm sure he is what we think he is.'

'Which is what?'

'A thug. A thug with contacts, yes, but at heart he wants to wreak havoc.'

Draper wouldn't have described Henderson quite so bluntly, but he did understand where Clyde was coming from.

'Henderson won't do anything without me telling him to,' Draper said, 'He knows exactly what will happen if he does.'

'I'm not so sure. I get the feeling he's not told you everything. Just what you wanted to hear.'

'And you're basing that on what?'

'A hunch.'

'And you want me to do what, exactly, based on your hunch? If Henderson came to me with a hunch about you, would–'

'I get it. I'm not saying you need to cut ties or anything like that. Only that I think there's more to the story than he's told. He's not in this for the money, like you. He's after something. Or maybe someone.'

'Someone?'

Clyde threw back his glass and drained the Scotch, then got up from his sofa.

'Forget it. My paranoid side talking.' Clyde put his glass down on the cabinet next to the whisky bottle and headed for the door. 'See you in the morning.'

'Yeah.' Draper waited until Clyde's footsteps faded away, then got up and headed for the bottle and poured himself a much larger measure. Draper took a large mouthful then sat back in his chair, Clyde's words still sloshing in his head. He had to admit there was more than one thing he didn't like about recent events. Maybe Henderson *was* playing him, though Draper didn't know why.

But, if the worst came to the worst, there was plenty of room for one more in the cave.

CHAPTER 25

London, England

The simple fact was, under the circumstances, it would have been stupid for Ryker to reject the offer of assistance. Wouldn't it? Yes, he felt like on his own he was getting closer to the answers he needed, but there was no doubt he was also creating a lot of noise in the process. He was hardly entirely to blame for that though. It just so happened that the answers he needed about Lisa's death had led him into the midst of a DEA investigation. Had led him to a real estate business in Mexico that was a front for money-launderers, and where the boss of the business had got on the wrong side of a gang of armed mercenaries of as yet unknown identity or origin.

Typical Ryker.

So yes, perhaps given the spiralling problems he was involved in, it was time to accept Winter's olive branch. The mere thought made Ryker touch Lisa's pendant.

Offer of assistance. That was the term Peter Winter had used, though the reality was that the situation was more 'you scratch my back and I'll scratch yours'.

As long as it achieved the same aim – catching Lisa's killers – that was okay by Ryker. Which was why he'd agreed to head to London.

He strolled along the bank of the Thames, the brick tower of the Oxo building prominent across the other side of the river on the heavily revamped waterfront, the London Eye looming in the near distance. Water rippled around the wide tour boats that jostled for position on the water, all crammed with camera-happy tourists from around the world.

Ryker wondered what it was like to be one of those people who had never seen the dark side of humanity, who had regular jobs and homes and families and friends and who went on holidays, took pictures and kept photo albums of happy times.

In the past he'd felt pity for them, because their closed mentalities were so far removed from the reality of the world he saw. They were all so oblivious. Now he felt pity for himself. He wished he were just one of the billions of ignorant people, living in their little cocoons. Ignorance is bliss.

Ryker spotted Winter sitting on a bench looking out over the Thames, the red and white painted wrought iron arches of Blackfriars Bridge in the near distance. He was staring into space, not paying attention to the world around him. Now there was a man comfortable in his surroundings. Someone who felt safe, protected.

Or was that all an act?

Ryker, on the other hand, had been busy scanning the street, the road, the water, the buildings. Looking for anyone or anything out of place. Maybe Winter didn't need to do that. Maybe he *was* protected. A sniper or two hidden somewhere. Not that Ryker had spotted anything or anyone untoward. The only thing that didn't belong in the scene was him.

Winter looked up when Ryker was a few yards away and he gave a half smile. He didn't get up from the bench and Ryker sat down next to him.

'Welcome home,' Winter said.

Ryker huffed. England was his country of birth, and London was where he'd been based for the near twenty years he'd worked for the JIA (though really much of that had been spent abroad, sometimes for years at a time). Regardless, he'd never seen London as his home, just a place where he slept occasionally. And he didn't miss it. Until two days earlier, he'd never seen himself returning, either to the country or to the city.

'No problems in immigration?' Winter asked.

'No,' Ryker said, unsure why Winter had bothered to ask. Winter had needed to prearrange all of Ryker's travel documents;

otherwise he couldn't have entered the country on a standard commercial flight.

'I'm glad you came,' Winter said.

'Of course you are. You're always happy when you have people on hand to do your dirty work for you.'

Ryker had meant the words partly in jest, though he realised they'd come out with a hard edge.

The look on Winter's face suggested he wasn't impressed with the slight. 'I'm helping you here as well, remember.'

'I remember. Shall we cut the small talk?'

Winter reached to his side and pulled a printed photograph out of his brown leather satchel. He handed it to Ryker, who tensed when he saw the face of the man. The Silver Wolf. He folded the paper and passed it back.

'Thomas Maddison was last seen in Morocco nearly two years ago,' Winter said. 'That's him, on CCTV, walking out from Marrakech Menara Airport. After that he simply disappeared.'

'Why did he go to Morocco?'

'I don't know.'

Ryker waited for Winter to expand. He didn't.

'On JIA business?' Ryker asked.

'No.'

'He was your agent?'

'No.'

'Then whose?'

'Victoria Cameron's.'

The name was vaguely familiar to Ryker. She was a commander at the JIA, like Winter, though he didn't think he'd ever met her. 'Then what does she say about him going there?'

'I don't know. She's dead.'

Ryker raised an eyebrow at Winter. The agency man's face remained impassive as he looked toward the river.

'How and when did she die?' Ryker asked.

'Not long before Maddison disappeared. Cameron suffered a heart attack at home, alone.'

'And?'

'And that's it. No drugs or alcohol in her system. Toxicology was clean, so there was certainly no identifiable poison. No evidence of foul play was the official verdict.'

'And you bought that?'

'There was no evidence to think otherwise.'

'No one thought her death followed by the disappearance of her agent soon after was suspicious?'

Winter turned to Ryker, his face now hard. 'Of course we think it's suspicious, and believe me we spent a great deal of time and effort trying to figure out who killed her and why. But we came up with nothing. Was her death connected to Maddison's disappearance? In all likelihood, yes. Do we know why? No.'

'So you have no answers? Either on who killed her or where Maddison went? Do you think it was him?'

'I simply don't know. We've followed leads, yes. We've had plenty of spurious sightings of Maddison, but all have turned out to be dead ends. Until you found that picture of him in Cancún. Which was dated when?'

'It wasn't that recent, over a year ago.'

'But still some time after he went missing. Which means you're now holding more up-to-date information on him than anyone else.'

'Technically it was the DEA's information.'

'Finders keepers, I say. Where's the rest of it anyway?'

By *it,* Ryker guessed that Winter meant all of the information he'd 'acquired' from El Yuca and the DEA agents in Cancún. Before leaving Mexico, he'd finally had the chance to crack that safe as well. He hadn't wanted to be lugging the damn thing on a transatlantic flight.

Inside the safe, he'd found rolls of US dollars, paperwork for an upcoming property development in Cancún, plus various DVDs, thumb drives, and a two-terabyte external hard drive.

'It's all right here,' Ryker said, tapping the backpack he'd purchased in Mexico that was by his side on the bench. He picked it up and handed it over to Winter.

'You keep a copy of anything?' Winter asked.

'Why would I do that?'

Winter shrugged.

'You want me to sign anything?' Ryker asked. 'A chain of custody form perhaps?'

'Very funny.'

'But you will let me know what you find.'

'That was the deal.'

Ryker had to leave it to trust Winter to uphold that deal. He knew that alone it would take him weeks or even months to properly sift through the vast quantities of data he'd taken. And he might not even find a single piece of useful information in the process. At least, not useful information related to Lisa or her killers. The JIA, on the other hand, could devote entire teams of analysts to searching and evaluating and cataloguing the data. They'd almost certainly find something of use for their own purposes. The DEA were crawling all over El Yuca because of their illegal activities, now the JIA would find out exactly why that was.

Ryker knew though that the real catch for Winter was Thomas Maddison – the Silver Wolf? – and figuring out where he'd gone and why.

'So you think Maddison went rogue?' Ryker asked.

'Hard to say. We've come across references to the Silver Wolf before but never had enough evidence to start a full investigation. If Maddison is actually the Silver Wolf... I'm really not sure what that means. But we need to know.'

Given the life he'd led, Ryker could understand how easy it was for an agent to go rogue. Not only were JIA agents trained to be evasive, to live under the radar, but their lives put them on a collision course with all sorts of bad guys and nefarious activities. Any JIA agent would have a whole host of contacts in the criminal underworld that they could readily exploit for personal gain if they wanted.

But why would they want that?

'Was there anything in Victoria Cameron's case files to suggest what Maddison had been working on before he disappeared?' Ryker asked.

'That's the thing,' Winter said. 'There was nothing. Maddison hadn't been on a sanctioned case for more than twelve months before he went missing. I've had people piece together his movements in that time, but it's not been easy. Like you, he used numerous aliases. Some official, some not.'

'That might say a lot then,' Ryker said.

'How do you mean?'

'I don't think he was sitting on his hands for that twelve months. Either he was working on something so top secret that no official record was kept within the JIA files, or he was already working against us at that point. Cameron too perhaps.'

'Both are theories that have been toyed with, but we really don't know.'

'There must be something,' Ryker said. 'What about at the Hive?'

'All of Cameron's case files are stored there. But we checked those already and found nothing. I told you, Maddison hadn't been on a sanctioned case for months before we lost contact with him.'

'You checked everything of hers? And his? Personal email files, mobile phones, home computers?'

'Everything, Ryker.'

'And it's all stored at the Hive?'

'Of course.'

'But I bet you didn't check for references to the Silver Wolf?'

'Not against their files, no. We had no reason to at the time.'

'And I'm betting you didn't check every single server down there, probably just the obvious places. If Maddison and Cameron were running an unsanctioned gig then it's possible there's still some kind of record somewhere, deeply hidden, of what they were up to, even if it was only recorded accidentally without them knowing.'

'It's possible, but we can't search the entirety of the Hive data in one go. Each individual server needs to be accessed and searched separately. We've never had cause to do that in this case.'

'One dead commander and one missing agent wasn't good enough cause?'

'I think you're underestimating just how much data we store there, and how little information we have to work with here. Needle in haystack doesn't even come close.'

'Maybe. But I think that's where I'll start anyway.'

'*You*,' Winter said with a hint of disdain. 'You want me to let *you* into the Hive?'

'I know what I'm looking for.'

'Do you?'

'What have you got to lose?'

'By letting you, an ex-agent who's well known for causing shit storms wherever he goes, have unfettered access to every piece of electronic data related to any historic JIA case, agent or informant ever? Ryker, I couldn't possibly imagine what could go wrong with that.'

'So you agree then?'

Winter sighed. 'Give me a few hours.'

CHAPTER 26

Ffion typed in the web address for Banque DPS and hit enter, then input her security details for the tenth time that morning. Or was it eleven? Once again, when the account information opened up, Ffion stared in horror at the account balance. Nil. Nothing. Zilch.

What the hell was going on?

She heard footsteps behind her and quickly slammed shut the laptop lid then turned to see Clarissa standing in the doorway.

'You sure you don't want a sandwich or anything before you go?' she asked.

'No, really, we'll be fine, thank you.'

'And you can cope without me?'

Ffion knew Clarissa was only being sweet by asking – again – but actually it made Ffion kind of mad. Of course she could bloody cope with spending time alone with her own husband.

'We'll be fine,' Ffion said. 'You probably need the break as much as we do.'

Clarissa humphed then padded out of sight. Ffion sat back in the swivel chair and let out a long sigh. What should she do? She'd thought countless times about calling the number and asking where the money was. Was it an innocent mistake? Had they paid the money into the wrong numbered account in error? Or given her the wrong account details? Had they paid the money to her normal account rather than the specifically set up Swiss one?

No, she'd checked her current account many times already. It was riding close to zero, like it nearly always was toward the end of a month.

So where was the money? *Her* money?

She hadn't made the call though. She was too scared.

Perhaps, instead, it was time to come clean with the JIA about what she'd done. They would protect her, wouldn't they, if she told them everything? Yes, doing that was a risk, but wasn't the risk better than just running away and hiding and hoping everything would sort itself out, which was the plan she was about to follow through on?

Ffion grunted in frustration, and grabbed the laptop from the desk then stuffed it into her bag. She headed out of the office-cum-spare-bedroom and across the hall into the master bedroom.

'You ready?' Ffion asked Andre. He was sitting in the wheelchair, his wasted-away body slumped awkwardly, his limbs all over the place. Clarissa was busy trying to make him look more presentable.

'Ready,' he said. 'Though I'm not sure why we're going, really?'

Ffion couldn't help but be hurt by that, even though she had a massive ulterior motive for their impromptu getaway. 'You've not been out of the house for ages. Except to the damn hospital. I thought you'd enjoy going away. And I need it, Andre.'

He pursed his lips. 'Of course.'

'Where are you two going again?' Clarissa asked.

'To Wales,' Ffion lied. 'Aberdovey. It was one of the first places we went away to together.'

Ffion smiled at Andre and he smiled back and she hoped he was reminiscing fondly about the time they'd spent there back then, when everything in life had been so simple and full of promise still.

'Sounds wonderful,' Clarissa said. 'Come on, you, let's get you to the car.'

'It's okay, really,' Ffion said. 'Let me.'

Clarissa looked put out as Ffion moved over and grabbed the handles of the wheelchair off her.

'I'll just tidy up here then before I go,' Clarissa said.

Ffion nodded then wheeled Andre out of the bedroom and through the apartment to the front door.

'So what's really going on?' he asked.

'How do you mean?'

'Why are we going away like this, out of the blue?'

'I thought you'd want to.'

'No, that's not it. Please don't forget my mind is still the same as it always was. I'm not dumb. Something's wrong. You're scared. But of what?'

'I've just had a hard time at work. I need a break.'

'And you want me to come too? It's hardly going to be a relaxing time for you.'

'You're my husband.'

'I'm an invalid who holds you down.'

'Don't say that,' Ffion said, feeling her eyes well with tears. What did he feel when he said things like that?

'I wish you'd open up to me. Tell me what's really going on in your head.'

Ffion said nothing to that, though she wished the same thing. But then that was the way their relationship had always been, even before the accident. Andre had no idea what her real job was. He didn't know about the JIA, who they were or what they did. He simply believed she was a data analyst working for the government. So how could she possibly tell him what was really going on in her head? Where would she start? Their whole life together was based on lies.

Ffion opened the front door and did a quick take up and down the street. What threat was she looking for exactly? She saw nothing, so guided the wheelchair over the ridge outside the front door and Andre's limp body jolted, his head lolling to the side. She lifted his head up and pushed the chair down the ramp and toward the street.

When Andre had the accident they'd been living in an apartment on the second floor of a town house just a few streets away. The local council had at first insisted the best option was to make that place more accessible. They'd wanted to build ramps, handrails, a stair lift inside. It was ridiculous. Ffion had searched for weeks before finding their ground floor apartment that was already wheelchair accessible by original design, with no steps – a highly unusual find in the area where the architects of the largely Georgian houses had clearly had a passion for stairs here, there and everywhere.

Back then, finding the apartment had seemed like a blessing. Three years on and it had never felt like a home for Ffion. Perhaps, given the shit she was in, she should take the opportunity to leave it for good.

Ffion turned left out on the street and pushed the chair toward her Citroen Berlingo, an unusual shaped car that looked quite hideous really, but that was specifically designed for holding wheelchairs, allowing her to push Andre directly into the back of it. She put the brake on the wheelchair and unlocked the car then set up the ramp.

She heard a car door opening nearby. Then another. Her senses still on high alert, Ffion looked around again and spotted the black saloon parked a few cars down. She didn't recognise it. Two men had got out and were walking toward her. Both were average height and build, perhaps forties, dressed in smart casual clothing – quite innocuous really. She didn't recognise the man who'd stepped from the driver's side. But the other one... He had a hard, weathered face, square jaw, deep-set eyes and a sweeping brow that may or may not have been because he was heavily receding. Ffion knew him.

What was *he* doing here?

Ffion straightened up and realised her legs were shaking. Both men walked with their hands in their jacket pockets. Were they armed?

She could make a run for it. Jump into the car, drive off and keep on driving until she was far away from this place.

And leave Andre there for the lions?

'Do you have a minute?' asked the man Ffion knew only as Henderson.

She realised Andre was looking at her and she tried her best to appear relaxed and unfazed. She smiled at Henderson. 'We were getting ready to go out.'

'Really? Glad we caught you before you headed off.' He turned to Andre. 'Could I borrow your wife for a minute? We have some pressing government business to discuss.'

'I've never been one to stand in the way of government business,' Andre said, his tone not overly friendly.

Henderson smiled, amused, though Ffion didn't understand why. 'Shall we go inside?' he said to Ffion.

She really didn't want to, she'd much rather remain out in the open, but she also didn't feel in a position to say no. The fact was these people, Henderson in particular, terrified her. 'Sure,' she said, still trying her hardest to sound calm. 'But this needs to be quick. I want to hit the road before the traffic gets too bad.'

'Just a couple of minutes.'

'Okay, come on then.'

Ffion bent down and kissed Andre on the cheek. Thoughts cascaded in her mind as she did so. She imagined herself saying 'goodbye'. Or 'sorry', and then legging it, leaving Andre behind for good.

What she really wanted to say to him was 'run'. 'Get away from here'. If he hadn't been stuck in that chair, would she have done that?

Instead she said nothing to him. She turned and walked back toward the apartment leaving Andre with the other man. Henderson, hands still in his pockets, walked by her side.

'Not so easy to run away when your husband's a cripple,' Henderson mocked.

Ffion cringed in anger – she hated that word – and also because she'd been found out.

'Running away?' she asked. 'I'm not sure what you mean. We're going to Wales for a few days. We've not had a holiday since... I can't even remember.'

'Good for you.'

They walked up the path to the still open front door. Clarissa emerged, jacket on. When she spotted Ffion, she first looked quizzical, then downright suspicious when she clocked Henderson.

'Everything okay?' Clarissa asked. 'Where's Andre?'

'Don't worry,' Henderson said. 'He's having a chat with Peter. I need Ffion for a couple of minutes. Work stuff.'

'You head off,' Ffion said to Clarissa. 'We'll see you in a couple of days.'

Clarissa looked unsure but said nothing of it.

'No problem,' she said before heading on past.

Henderson followed Ffion into the apartment and she shut the door and moved into the lounge, over to the sash window so she could see Andre out on the street. He was in a conversation with the man Henderson had called Peter. He looked relaxed and happy. What on earth were they talking about?

'You're probably wondering where the money is,' Henderson said, coming and standing next to Ffion by the window.

'What do you think?'

'I think you're scared and might do something stupid.'

'I was thinking maybe I already did.'

'No, you did good, Ffion. You really did.'

'Why are you here?'

'We still need your help. That's why you haven't been paid yet.'

'That's a strange way to buy loyalty.'

Henderson shrugged.

'You're the right person for this next job,' he said. 'You've already shown you're capable.'

'I need the money,' Ffion said.

'I know. Why else would you be in this position? After this next task you'll get it. Double what we agreed.'

Double. Two million pounds. That wasn't exactly pocket change. It would transform her and Andre's lives. They could move out of the city, buy a place suited to them both, and have a fresh start.

'How do I know you won't screw me over? How do I know you haven't already?'

Henderson once again had that smug, amused look on his face. Ffion detested him, even though she knew virtually nothing about him.

'I can have two hundred thousand pounds in your account within an hour. Would that convince you?'

Ffion said nothing. Just nodded.

'But you're not going on your little road trip. You need to stay here.'

'Where you can keep an eye on me, right?'

'Something like that. I don't want you going getting silly ideas in your head that you can disappear without upholding your end of the bargain. Believe me, that won't end well for you, or your hubby. We would find you, wherever you run to. We're good at that sort of thing. And I'm sure you can imagine we're good at hurting people too.'

Ffion looked out to Andre again. God, he was so vulnerable. What would they do to him, to her, if she said no? And he had no way whatsoever of fighting back.

She felt her eyes filling with tears again, but really she was angry. At herself. She'd put them both in this situation. What was wrong with her?

But she'd done it for good reasons. It wasn't just about the money. *They* deserved to be punished. That had to be her main driving force through all this. She wasn't greedy, she wanted revenge.

'Tell me what you want me to do first,' Ffion said. 'Then I'll decide.'

'Decide?' Henderson snorted. 'Sorry, but at what point did I say anything about you having a choice?'

CHAPTER 27

A t nine the next morning, the sun was alone up in the sky as Ffion walked along the Thames, though despite the warm rays there was a slight chill in the air. She shivered. She didn't have a coat, or even a jacket on, having deliberately dressed light. She knew only too well one of her reactions to nerves was to overheat and get flushed. However anxious she was, she had to do everything she could to appear calm and... normal.

After this, life would never be the same again. But she had to see it through. Firstly, it really was time to get her own back. The money would help her and Andre to run and set up a new life. Secondly, the risk of not seeing this through – to her, to Andre – was simply too great. Henderson had made that very clear.

As she walked along, her mind took her back to the apartment. Henderson standing by her side as they looked out at Andre on the street.

'You studied philosophy at university, didn't you?' Henderson had said to her, his tone measured though an ominous glint remained in his eye.

'Yes, why?'

'You must have heard of the runaway train problem then?'

Ffion nodded. 'A runaway train is heading down a track. Five people are tied to the track and will be killed by the train. But you have the ability to pull the switch and divert the train to another track, where only one person is tied.'

'Sacrificing one person to save five,' Henderson said. 'It's a classic conundrum in ethics. That's the situation you're in now, Ffion.'

'How?' Ffion said, not quite understanding the similarity, and not liking where the conversation was going.

'What would you do faced with that situation?' Henderson asked. 'Would you pull that switch? Sacrifice one to save five?'

'Some people say doing so constitutes murder. That the one person's life has been taken away because of your direct action.'

'Yet morally it makes perfect sense, doesn't it?'

'That's the generally accepted response.'

'I'm going to make this very clear for you,' Henderson said. 'People will die because of what you have to do.' Ffion's heart leaped about wildly. 'But more people will be saved because of your actions. And you will save Andre. Do you understand?'

As Ffion reached the revolving glass doors to the JIA offices, her mind snapped back to the present. She moved through into the reception area that looked like any other modern office block; an expansive atrium several storeys tall, mock-marble floors, a shining wood and chrome reception desk where several receptionists sat with flat-screens, a waiting area with designer black leather sofas. Simple swipe cards were used to get through the glass security barriers, with the main checks – including X-ray scanning – taking place further inside, out of sight of the street entrance.

Ffion looked over at one of the uniformed guards standing by the row of gates. He caught Ffion's eye and smiled.

'Morning,' he said.

Ffion just smiled as she held her card up against the keypad. The gate opened. As she walked through, Henderson's words swam in her head again: *Do you understand?*

Yes, Ffion did understand. The money was important. Even more important was getting her own back, but there was also a bigger, more fundamental moral rationale – or was it just an excuse? – for what she was about to do. People would die, but more would be saved. She *had* to do this.

For nearly a week, Ryker had been sitting in the server rooms at the Hive, day in, day out, searching through the data for any mention of the Silver Wolf. He didn't have the time to manually review and search every single file on every single server – he was there to cherry-pick. Using the master directory list, he'd honed in on those servers most likely to yield results; those containing case files related to Maddison and Cameron, or that otherwise appeared to contain miscellaneous, uncatalogued data.

So far, though, he'd found nothing concrete. Which tied in with what Winter had said. Little was known about the Silver Wolf, which was exactly why no JIA investigation had ever been initiated. The only evidence that Ryker had found that he could relate to the mysterious character was a vague reference to a yacht named *Il Lupo Grigio*. The Grey Wolf. Not a million miles away from what he was looking for. The relevance of the yacht was unclear, even within the data he'd seen. From what Ryker had gathered, it had belonged to an English businessman who'd lived in Sicily, who at one time had been on the Italian authorities' radar for tax evasion, but had since died of a heart attack.

It looked like a dead end to Ryker, but he'd downloaded the files he needed relating to the boat, and kept a mental note of the name of the dead Englishman, Nicholas Andrews, for future reference. He'd not yet told Winter about the find, but had instead used his own contacts to check on the fate of *Il Lupo Grigio,* and also to do some more digging on Andrews. Apparently the boat had been renamed *Natasha* by its subsequent owner, but not long after, had found its way to a scrapyard for dismantling. Ryker hadn't been able to find out the full story behind that one, but *Il Lupo Grigio* was no more. As for Andrews there was little to tell. He'd made millions in property and on stock markets but really seemed to have led a quiet life – certainly no indication that he was an organised criminal. His death too, according to official records, hadn't been deemed in any way suspicious. Ryker could have dug further but had no reason to. Andrews and that boat was something he could follow up on further if he came away from the Hive with nothing else.

There had to be something else.

Ryker pushed the keyboard tray and it slid out of sight, then he got up and moved along to bay twelve. He pressed the button and the tray whizzed out and he typed away, pulling up the directories for each of the servers located in that bay.

It didn't take Ryker long to figure that something was off. He frowned and stared at the screen for a few seconds, then rifled through the directory list in his hand. No, there was no doubt. He quickly logged off then pushed the keyboard away and strode over to the door.

Moments later, he emerged from the darkness and entered the white screening room. The female security guard there, who had been introduced to Ryker as Fran Black – was sitting behind her desk, reading a newspaper. She looked up, surprised by Ryker's reappearance so soon in the day.

'Finished already?' She quickly folded away the newspaper.

'No,' Ryker said, moving toward the X-ray machine, 'I need to make a phone call. Can you get my jacket?'

'Sounds urgent.'

'I think it might be.'

'You can use my landline if that helps?'

Ryker stopped. He didn't really want to have to go through the whole booking out, booking in process again. 'Okay.'

'Over here.'

Ryker moved over and Fran pulled a wireless handset off its cradle. Ryker took it from her and dialled Winter's number. He looked at Fran as the rings buzzed in his ear. She stared at him, unmoving. He realised he wasn't going to get any privacy for this conversation. He turned away from her but the call went unanswered anyway.

'No one there,' he said, handing the handset back to her, his brain whirring with thoughts as to what he should do next.

'Is it something I can help you with?' she asked.

'Who holds the CCTV records for this place?' He looked up to the camera above the desk.

'They're held right here.' She frowned. 'Why?'

'Good. And you keep those for how long?'

'Long enough.'

'And logs of people who've come in? Which servers they accessed?'

'Of course. It's all here.'

'I'm going to need to see those records.'

'Mr Ryker, that's a highly unusual request. Under whose authority are you asking?'

'My authority. I've been given unrestricted access to the records in this place. You know that.'

'To the servers yes, but not...' She trailed off and her expression changed from formal and just slightly hostile, to concerned. 'Is there a problem I should know about?'

'Yes. I think there is.'

Almost time, Ffion realised, staring at the clock in the corner of her monitor. She'd been next to useless the whole morning, her brain not able to compute even simple tasks. Not that it would matter soon enough. Ffion's eyes remained fixed on the clock.

'You must really like Blu Tack.'

Ffion turned to see her colleague, Heather, hovering over her shoulder. Her eyes were on the box by Ffion's side. Ffion reached out with her foot and pushed the box further under her desk.

'You planning on starting a side business in stationery or something?'

Ffion laughed. 'Yeah, you know me, always looking for my next venture.'

Heather's soft features hardened just slightly.

'Seriously, though, what's with all that Blu Tack?'

Ffion shrugged. 'Beats me. Boss asked me to order it. Maybe adhesive putty is part of her new diet. But only the blue stuff.' Ffion smiled at her quip.

Heather looked unsure but she still half-smiled. 'Do you want a drink?'

'Yeah, tea please,' Ffion said, without really thinking. She wasn't going to get a chance to drink it.

Heather walked away to the vending area and Ffion looked back to the screen and saw the minutes had clicked on to fifty-nine. Shit, she couldn't be late. She stood up from her chair and kept her head low, not making eye contact with any of her colleagues as she moved through the small open-plan office space where she and five other analysts worked.

Out in the main corridor, she looked around but saw no one. She walked to the door for the stairwell and pushed it open then climbed three flights of stairs to the eighth floor. She exited onto the main corridor, again checking around her. She was all alone still.

She took her security card in her hand and held it up against the pad by the door at the end of the corridor. The pad flashed green and she heard the click as the lock released. She pushed the door open and headed on into the space.

This part of the eighth floor had been empty for several months, and Ffion's footsteps echoed around the large space as she walked over to the windows at the far end. She jumped in shock when there was a bang on the window and she caught a movement off to her left. She looked over, and saw the small window cleaning platform swaying about on the outside. Two men in blue jumpsuits were standing on it, yellow buckets by their feet.

Ffion stared as muddled thoughts fired in her brain. The plan had been put together very precisely. So why was the platform on the other side of the building to where she'd been told? There was no way for her to access it there. She caught the eye of one of the men and pointed off to her right. He just looked at her blankly. Could he even see her behind the tinted glass?

Ffion pushed the growing doubts aside and strode over to the far end of the office space where a door led on to a large wraparound balcony that stretched across about a third of the building. It was the only floor that had the balcony. The only conclusion she had was that it was needed for maintenance of some sort.

She looked over as she walked and noticed the platform outside was following her. She reached the door, turned the lock and pressed the handle down, then pushed the door open, half-expecting an alarm system to suddenly start blaring. It didn't.

She stepped out and a shiver ran through her as cool air blasted into her face. She folded her arms, her flesh coming up in goose-pimples. She was already shaking – as much through fear as cold – a few seconds later when the platform nudged up alongside the balcony.

'Ffion?' one of the two men said.

She nodded. Who were they, she wondered? Were they just the regular window cleaners who'd been given a few pounds to perform their part in the plan, or were they Henderson's men?

The man who'd spoken bent down and lifted the lid on a cool box. Inside were sandwiches and drinks and crisps but also a somewhat out-of-place leather satchel. He picked the satchel out and lifted it over the top rail of the platform. Ffion stretched and grabbed it off him.

No other words were said. Ffion took the satchel back inside, shut and locked the door, then kneeled down on the floor. She lifted the flap on the satchel and peeked inside, aware that the two men were still there just behind her. Did they know what this was?

The quick glance inside was all she needed. She clasped the flap shut and straightened up. Then, gripping the satchel's handle, she headed for the door to the stairwell, not once looking back to the men who'd just handed her all the components she needed to complete the bomb.

CHAPTER 28

'Stop. Right there,' Ryker said, pointing to the screen.

Fran Black pressed a key on the keyboard and the image on the monitor froze. Ryker turned and looked at her. They were sitting at one of two computer terminals in a back room – a bland windowless office that was spotlessly tidy, not a piece of paper out of place. The room had three doors; one out onto each of the two desks for the Hive's security zones, and the third which connected directly into the server area. Fran's colleague, Graham Sutton, was still stationed out at his desk. They'd not given him the full details of what they were so urgently looking at. Ryker didn't want word getting out of what the problem was until he had a better idea himself. That said, they'd had Dylan, the guy in the shop upstairs, lock the front door and hang up the closed sign.

'You see it?' Ryker asked.

Fran was staring goggle-eyed at the screen. She looked angry more than surprised.

'It's... I just... '

Ryker focused back to the screen, where a young woman was frozen in the act: hunched down in front of the security desk, her hand a blur as it flicked a small object forward through the gap between the desk and the X-ray scanner.

'A thumb drive,' Ryker said. 'Probably loaded with software to clear that server. Clever enough to do so without tripping any alert.'

'That's impossible,' Fran said, shaking her head.

'Clearly not.'

'But... ' Fran trailed off.

But what? Ryker wondered, but didn't ask. But how? But why? But it's not my fault? 'Who is she?'

'I told you already. Ffion Brady. She's just an analyst.'

'What do you know about her?'

'I don't know *anything* about her. I just monitor people coming and going. I don't get their life story, I don't even know what their roles are. I'm just a security guard.'

Clearly not a very good one, Ryker thought.

'I need you to show me every other visit she's ever made here.'

'Ever?'

'That's what I said. I need to see every log sheet, who authorised her being here, which servers she accessed. I need to see the data logs to cross match what she *actually* did. I need the videos of her coming and going. We have to know whether or not this is an isolated incident.'

Fran gulped as though the potential ramifications of what they were uncovering was now hitting home. Neither she nor Ryker knew anything of Ffion Brady, but Ryker's mind was already whirring with possibilities. What was Brady's objective? Was this a single case of sabotage? Or was Ffion Brady a long-standing rogue operative, a double agent working for someone else, not just destroying data but probably stealing it too?

'I need to use the phone again,' Ryker said.

'Sure.' Fran pushed on her heels and wheeled her chair back then grabbed the phone from its cradle. She flung it to Ryker who caught it one-handed.

'I'll pull the paper authorisations first,' Fran said. 'We'll take it from there.'

She stood up from her chair, moved to a filing cabinet, and rifled through a drawer as Ryker punched in the numbers on the phone. He put the handset to his ear and listened to the rings. The call went unanswered again. He heard a beep and left a message.

'Winter, it's me. There's a problem at the Hive. We need to speak urgently.' He pulled the phone away from his ear and called over to Fran for the phone number. She recited it and Ryker repeated it down the line before ending the call.

'Do you have access to the JIA systems here?' Ryker asked.

'Of course not,' Fran said, like it was a stupid question.

That was a shame. Ryker had to find out more about Ffion Brady. There was one other person he could call to help him with that. Ryker dialled the number and once again waited, his eyes flicking from the computer screen to Fran who was still leafing through files.

'Hello?' came the female voice when the call was answered.

'Willoughby. It's me.'

'Ryker? What—'

'Sorry, did I wake you?' he asked, his brain computing what time it was in Mexico.

'Wake me? No. I'm in London.'

'London?'

Willoughby sighed. 'It's a long story.'

Ryker didn't have time for long stories, though he was certainly intrigued as to why she was no longer in Central America. 'I need your help. It's urgent. But also *very* sensitive. Can you do it?'

'Do what?'

'Ffion Brady, do you know her?'

'Should I?'

'Yes or no.'

'No.'

'She's a JIA analyst. And maybe a big problem. I need you to access the agency's databases, pull everything you can on her background for me. Family history, education, marriages, boyfriends, whatever. You know what I mean.'

'I do. But can I ask why?'

'Not yet.'

Willoughby sighed.

'Just trust me,' Ryker said. 'This isn't for me, it's not going to get you in trouble. It's for the agency.'

Silence.

'Please?'

'I'll call you back as soon as I can,' Willoughby said. The line went dead.

Ffion was sweating profusely by the time she made it back to her desk. She wiped the film of perspiration from her forehead with her arm then sat down in her chair, her twitchy eyes scanning the office space around her. No one was paying her any attention, but she couldn't shake the nerves.

Pull yourself together. She noticed the cup of tea on the desk; a thin skin had formed over the top, it having sat there so long. She picked up the mug and took a glug of lukewarm tea. Why had she done it? It tasted bloody awful and nearly made her gag.

She set the cup down then reached for the box under the desk, lifted up the top five packs of Blu Tack and took out the next five. She quickly opened the flap on the satchel and stuffed the Blu Tack inside. When she straightened up, her heart lurched as she realised Ed, another of her colleagues, was standing in front of her desk.

'You okay?' His face screwed in concern. Or was it suspicion?

'What do you mean?' Ffion sounded way more defensive than she'd intended.

Ed frowned and looked like he was going to say something, before having a change of heart. 'Nothing,' he said. 'I wanted to ask you about the Harlowe report. You said you wanted me to proof it for you?'

'Oh, that. Sorry, Ed. I've just not had time to finish it yet. I'll let you know as soon as I do though. That okay?'

Ed shrugged. 'Yeah, give me a shout. I'm should have time if it's this week.'

'Thanks.'

There was an awkward silence and Ffion could tell he was mulling over something. In the end he just gave a meek smile and wandered off back to his desk. Ffion let out a long but quiet sigh, trying to compose herself. Then she picked up the satchel and headed for the toilet.

She passed two more colleagues on the way, and smiled and greeted them before carrying on, hoping they wouldn't try to engage in conversation. The one time she just wanted to get on without distraction and it seemed every man and his dog was there waiting to chat.

She pushed open the door to the toilet and nearly slammed it into the face of a woman she didn't recognise who was just coming out. Ffion apologised, her voice as shaky as her body. By that point, her head was all over the place. She just wanted to get the whole thing over and done with, get Andre, get out of London – out of England – before she had a bloody heart attack.

Ffion locked herself in a cubicle and pulled the lid on the toilet down then took a seat, clutching the satchel in both hands. She looked at her watch. She didn't have much time left. She flipped open the satchel and first took out the packs of Blu Tack. Well, they weren't really tack were they? They were plastic explosive – C4. Security at the JIA was tight, but the metal detectors and X-ray machines had no way of distinguishing regular sticky putty from C4, it seemed. She had to admit, the paper packaging looked spot on too. Nothing that would have aroused suspicion, other than why a data analyst was receiving a box full of office supplies. The fact the box made it to her desk suggested any suspicion had been light.

Then she had a sudden moment of doubt. What if this really was just regular Blu Tack? What if she was being set up? Or perhaps she'd pulled the wrong packets out of the box – the rest of them were genuine after all. She'd known the C4 ones would be a slightly paler colour, but had she checked properly?

No, she hadn't. She was feeling flustered and had rushed, and she couldn't be sure if she had the right packs or not.

She could go back and check. But did she have time? She lifted a pack up to her face and sniffed. It smelled of nothing really. She removed the packaging and squashed the sheet together into a block. What the hell did C4 feel like anyway? This really did just feel like regular Blu Tack. Maybe a bit softer, a bit warmer.

It didn't matter. She had to do this. She quickly shaped the sheets from the other packets to form two blocks then placed the packaging into an empty plastic bag that was in the satchel. She'd dispose of that in the bin in the toilet.

She put the blocks of C4 inside the satchel then took out the tablet computer and the wires – the items that had been handed to her by the window cleaner. Ffion could have tried to smuggle those into the building herself, but Henderson had determined it wasn't worth the risk. The tablet looked innocuous enough but it actually contained the small blasting caps needed to detonate the bomb. C4 was a high explosive, but also quite steady because of the stabiliser elements included in the mix. A considerable shock was needed to set off the chemical reaction for an explosion to take place; lighting the C4 with a match, for example, would just make it burn slowly, like a piece of wood. The blasting caps were therefore essential for the bomb to detonate. The high explosive caps packed inside the tablet, however, would have looked seriously suspicious in the X-ray machine.

Ffion flipped the tablet over and used the tiny-head of the screwdriver from the satchel to carefully remove the back panel. Next to the battery a small space had been carved out for the two blasting caps which looked like elongated fuses. She pulled out the caps, a short, thin wire sticking out of each of them, then replaced the back cover. The wires were connected at one end to what resembled a regular phone charger, and she plugged that end into the tablet's charging point. Then she placed the tablet into the satchel next to the C4, and with shaky hands, she gently eased each of the blasting caps into one of the blocks of explosive.

When she was done, Ffion let out a long sigh, trying to get her heart and her breathing under control. Her hands were shaking viciously, but the bomb was ready. All she had to do was to put it in place and set the timer using her regular phone, and then get out of there.

She was about to get up when she heard the door to the toilet bang open.

CHAPTER 29

Ffion held her breath and listened to the sounds coming from outside her cubicle. Who the hell had just come in? Of course, it could be nothing, most likely was, but that didn't stop the feeling of panic growing inside her with every second.

After the initial sound of the door opening, she'd expected – hoped – to hear footsteps. The sound of a cubicle door being closed and locked. She'd heard nothing more, though, except the thud, thud, thud of her own heartbeat.

Then someone breathing.

Ffion was close to all-out meltdown. Who was out there? Achingly slowly, she got up from the toilet, holding the satchel with the bomb close to her chest. She took a step to the cubicle door and pushed her face closer to the crack between the door and the frame. The gap was too narrow to get a clear view outside, but was enough for Ffion to spot movement. She quickly stepped back again.

She looked at her watch. She didn't know who was out there, but she couldn't just stay inside the toilet all day. And if whoever was out there was on to her, then what would staying inside the cubicle achieve? Was she planning on enacting the world's most bizarrely located stand off?

No. She couldn't stay inside. Before she could talk herself out of it, Ffion turned and flushed the toilet then unlocked and opened the door. She stepped out.

There, by the sinks, was a woman. She looked surprised by Ffion's sudden appearance. Ffion noticed she was upset, tears welling in her eyes.

'I didn't realise anyone was there,' the woman said, looking at Ffion in the mirror, trying to compose herself. She dabbed at her eyes with a tissue.

Ffion said nothing, just gave a gentle smile then moved to the bin and placed the plastic bag inside. She stepped over to the sink to wash her hands and put the satchel down between her legs.

'You okay?' Ffion asked the woman. She wasn't sure why. They didn't know each other, and Ffion really didn't care why she was upset. It felt like the courteous thing to do. As if in a few minutes she wasn't planning to detonate a bomb in the damn building. Maybe this woman would even die in the blast, collateral damage.

'Just one of those days,' the woman said, shaking her head, and looking slightly put out that Ffion had asked.

Whatever. That was her good deed for the day done. Ffion turned off the tap and dried her hands on a paper towel then picked up the satchel and headed out, her arms and legs feeling heavy and unusually awkward.

She took the stairs down to the third floor, then used her ID card to enter the corridor. She passed closed doors that led to various open-plan spaces for different departments and sub-teams she'd never met, before finally coming to the open door she was looking for.

Ffion walked casually – at least as casually as she could – through into the anteroom. The desk in front of her, that she knew belonged to Rod Flowers, was empty as expected. The door to the office beyond was closed. The silver plaque in the middle of the door showed that the office belonged to Peter Winter, one of the JIA's commanders. Ffion glanced behind her, then moved up to the door and knocked twice. She expected the office to be empty, but wanted to be sure.

After a few seconds of silence, she put her hand to the handle and pushed it down. She wondered only then whether the door would be locked. If it were, what would she do? She could leave the bomb right there, by the door. In the anteroom, the C4 would still cause considerable damage, but would it be enough?

She needn't have worried. The door opened and Ffion found herself staring into the space beyond. There was no one inside. She was surprised at how large and luxurious Winter's office was. How differently the other half lived.

Without further hesitation, she moved forward and around the mahogany desk and pushed the satchel underneath, then she quickly retreated to the door. When she exited onto the corridor, she turned left and headed back the way she'd come.

A man and a woman were coming her way. They both locked eyes with Ffion for a second, but neither said anything as they walked past. She glanced behind her after a few seconds but they'd both simply carried on their way.

Ffion took out her phone and navigated to the app that would start the timer. She held her finger over the button, but didn't press. She had to be sure Winter would be there.

She could hang around outside the office and wait for him to come back, but that might draw attention. Instead she continued to move along the corridor, aiming to head into one of the open-plan spaces, which she had noticed were set up almost identically to her own floor, with a small kitchenette area near to the corridor with coffee and vending machines and water cooler. She could busy herself there for a few minutes without arousing suspicion.

She glanced at her watch again. He should return any minute anyway.

Ffion looked back up from her watch to see the doors at the end of the corridor open. Two smartly dressed men stepped through.

It was them. Rod Flowers and Peter Winter.

The commander was on his phone. His face was hard; a look of concern, or agitation? Despite the turmoil going on inside her, Ffion didn't break stride, just kept on walking toward them. At least she didn't need to hang about now. She pulled up her phone and her finger hesitated over the button again. But only for a second.

She pressed down onto the touchscreen and the timer started.

Three minutes. Enough for her to get away, but hopefully not so long that Winter would spot the satchel, figure out what was in it, and get himself and everyone else to safety.

When she looked up from the phone she realised both Flowers and Winter – just three yards in front – were looking at her. Did they have any idea what she'd just done?

No, how could they?

Yet the look on Winter's face... what was that look?

'Morning,' Ffion said as she passed them, her greeting more to Flowers than to Winter who was engrossed in his phone conversation.

'Morning,' Flowers said in return, giving a warm smile.

Ffion picked up her pace slightly and soon reached the double doors at the end of the corridor. Not looking back, she pushed the exit button to unlock the door and stepped out. She moved over to the stairwell door, pushed that open, then bounded down the stairs.

'Ryker, you're making no sense,' Winter said, stepping to the side slightly to let the woman past. Her eye caught Winter's for a brief moment before she quickly looked away and Winter carried on toward his office.

'Ffion Brady,' Ryker said, 'She's an analyst–'

'You said that already, but I don't know her.'

'You need to find her, now. There's been a serious security breach at the Hive. We're still trying to figure out exactly what happened, but she smuggled a device in here. She's deleted the data from an entire server.'

'What data?'

'It's deleted, Winter, how the hell am I supposed to tell you the answer to that?'

Winter put his free hand to his head, which was pounding. This was another problem he really didn't need. Why did Ryker always bring problems?

'When was this?'

'Six days ago.'

'And she was acting under whose authority?'

'You tell me. Her authorisation was signed by her line manager but who knows the real story.'

'She does, I imagine.'

'Hence why you need to find her. Now.'

'I'll put a message out,' Winter said. 'And if you find anything else down there, tell me.'

Winter ended the call just as he and Flowers turned off the corridor. Flowers went over to his desk as Winter moved through the anteroom and up to his office door, typing the number for the security switchboard as he moved. He didn't recognise the voice of the guard who answered.

'Yes, sir. How can I help?' the man asked after Winter had given him his ID code.

'Is Ffion Brady swiped in?' Winter asked and headed for his desk.

'Yes, sir, she is. Is there something I can help you with?'

'Find her and bring her to my office.' Winter ended the call, went around to his chair and sat down. He hit the space bar on the keyboard. The processor and hard drive whirred to life, and the screen came on. Winter navigated to the JIA's personnel records. It took him less than a minute to pull up the profile for Ffion Brady.

'Shit.'

The woman. From out in the corridor. Which meant...

'Flowers!'

Winter shot up from his chair. As he did so, his foot kicked soft material beneath the desk. He frowned. He looked down, under the desk, and spotted the leather satchel neatly nestled against the wood.

Flowers came into the doorway. 'Sir?'

Winter bent down and pulled out the bag. Flowers came over to his side.

'This yours?' Winter asked, as he undid the clasp.

'Nope. Not mine.'

Winter open the flap and looked inside.

'Sir?'

'Get out,' Winter said, looking to Flowers. 'Get everybody out!'

Ffion passed no one on the way down and slowed her pace as she reached the ground floor. Before exiting the stairwell, she tried her best to compose herself but it didn't really work. Her heart was pounding, she was sweating, her legs felt like jelly. Regardless, she had to keep moving. She pushed open the door and walked out, heading right, toward the main security checkpoint. Luckily she didn't have to go through the same rigmarole as on the way in. The X-ray scanners were only for people coming, not going. On the way out, she simply had to swipe her card for the electronic gates in the main foyer. Beyond that was freedom. Perhaps not freedom exactly. Not after what she'd done.

As Ffion passed by the scanners and the guards who were busy checking people entering the building, there was an unusual hubbub. Guards had their radio handsets pressed to their ears. Some were talking hurriedly. All seemed to be preoccupied – a message or an instruction being relayed to them.

Ffion picked up her pace. Just a few more steps and she'd be able to see the gates in the foyer. She had her security card ready in her hand.

'Mrs Brady!' came a man's voice from behind.

She didn't recognise the voice. She daren't look behind to find out who it was. She just needed to get out of there. She picked up her pace further.

'Ffion Brady!' came the voice again. 'Stop there, please.'

Still Ffion didn't stop. She could feel eyes on her from all around. Other workers and the guards in front of her had stopped to take notice too. Then a guard, just ten yards ahead, locked eyes with her and moved with purpose in her direction.

What was going on? Surely Winter couldn't have found the bomb and figured out it was her who had planted it already? So what had happened?

She couldn't hang around to find out. By her calculation, she had less than sixty seconds before the blast.

'Mrs Brady, please stop right there,' the guard in front said, holding up his hand, edging forward.

Ffion did stop this time, but she wasn't quite sure what to do next. She should have been out of the building and heading safely away already. However it was they'd found out, she couldn't be in the building when the blast came.

So should she just run?

'Mrs Brady, please come with us,' the guard said, taking another cautious step toward her, as though he was expecting her to do something stupid. Pull a weapon. Try to attack him.

'Is there a problem?' she asked, surprising herself at just how calm she sounded.

'Not a problem. But we can't let you leave just now.'

Ffion did her best to hide her confusion. Those didn't sound much like the words of a man who was expecting a bomb blast any second.

'We just need to ask a few questions, that's all.' The guard stopped a couple of yards away from Ffion.

She looked around. Three, four, five other guards were all edging closer.

Ffion dashed off to her right. The guard in front tried to reach out and grab her but she just managed to brush him off. The other guards shouted. At her? At each other?

Ffion lifted up her elbow, ready to smash it into the little red box on the wall – the fire alarm. The commotion might give her the chance she needed to escape. But before she'd even made contact, a piercing alarm blared. Did that mean Winter had found the bomb? If so he would surely get himself to safety in time. So all her effort was for nothing.

It didn't matter. She just had to get out. By her calculation there could only be ten, maybe twenty seconds remaining.

As she sprinted forward, some of the guards had already turned their attention from her, initiating the building's evacuation procedure. Within seconds there would be two hundred people from the upper floors descending on the exits. For just a brief moment, she really thought she would make it...

The next second she was rugby-tackled to the ground from behind. She smacked down onto the tiled floor, her shoulder taking the brunt of the fall. The weight of the guard slammed down on top of her, knocking her breath from her lungs. Her ID card scooted away out of one hand, the phone slid from the grip of her other and skidded along the surface. The phone's screen lit up, and she saw the timer, ticking down. Ten... nine... eight...

Her bleary eyes focused up ahead on the security gates, just a few yards away, which all opened at once. Ffion could only assume because of the alarm.

'Get off me!' Ffion shouted. 'There's a bomb!'

The guard didn't say anything. Just pushed himself up and dug a knee into the back of her neck.

'Did you hear me?' she screamed. 'We're all going to die!' She bucked, writhed and squirmed, trying to free herself. 'We have to get out!'

'You're not going anywhere,' another guard said, as his boots came into view by her face.

The next moment, two men hauled her up to her feet, one holding on to each of her arms.

She looked down at the phone again.

Three... two... one...

CHAPTER 30

Ffion tried to open her eyes. Or were they already open? She wasn't sure. Everything was so dark. She tried to move, but her body felt distant. Or was she trapped? Her brain was a muddled mess. Where was she? There was heat. There was noise. Lots of noise. Hissing. What was that? Water gushing. Gas? There was roaring too.

Yet the dominant noise, that Ffion's mind focused on, was the voices. Shouting. Screaming. Crying.

Ffion tried again. This time her eyes did open, though her eyelids flickered for several seconds as the blurred scene in front of her came into view and as she worked out the grit that filled her eyes.

She realised she was holding her breath. She exhaled, then took a sharp intake of air that tasted of smoke and was filled with dust. It made her cough and splutter. With her focus improving, she saw two black boots moving into her field of vision. She didn't have the strength to move her eyes to see the rest of the man they belonged to.

'Miss, are you okay?' an authoritative voice asked.

Ffion tried to respond but she wasn't sure if she managed it or not. Her senses were slowly returning to normal and with it her memory. Of where she was, and what she'd done.

'Miss?'

A large hand wrapped under her armpit and yanked on her. As she was pulled upright she felt pressure release off her midriff and her legs and there was a clatter as wooden and metal debris slid off her body and to the floor, sending a plume of dust into the air that once again filled her lungs. She coughed and hunched down to her knees to clear her throat and calm her breathing.

'Can you walk?' The man spoke hurriedly, his attention half on her and half on the chaos around, as he scanned for other casualties. 'We need to get you out of here.'

Ffion tilted her head to look up at him. His clothes, like hers, were covered in dust and ash. His face was smeared equally with black dirt and red blood, which was dripping from his hairline. Despite the injury, the state of his clothes, she quickly realised who she was looking at. One of the security guards.

Did he not know who she was?

'I think I'm okay,' Ffion said, grimacing as she straightened up.

She pushed her weight from her left leg to her right, tensing and relaxing the muscles in each limb to test them out. She was stiff as hell, pain was running up her right side. Her left leg felt numb and leaden. But she didn't think she was seriously hurt.

For the first time, Ffion properly took in the scene of carnage in front of her. The blast had been bigger than she'd expected, or at least the damage greater. The ceiling above the ground floor had collapsed into the foyer. Perhaps the ceiling above the first and second floors too. There was a gaping hole above her that was filled with smoke and fire. In front, metal girders and wood and partitioning and insulation and pipes and all other manners of the buildings fixtures and fittings were crumpled and broken and spread across the floor. There were people, walking wounded, hobbling for the exit, some on their own, some pulling fallen colleagues along. Others were busy heaving wreckage aside, searching for people who were trapped.

Ffion spotted another of the guards, across the way. She thought she recognised him. The one who moments earlier – how long ago was it? – had shouted out to her, probably the one who'd tackled her to the ground. He gazed across at Ffion and she suddenly felt faint with panic. But then he just looked away.

Did he not recognise her either? Perhaps he was concussed?

'Miss, please, you really need to get out of here. Can you manage?'

Ffion looked at the guard standing next to her. 'Thank you. Yes, I'm fine. Go help the others.'

He rushed off and Ffion pulled her battered body through the mess, to what was left of the front entrance of the building. She walked out into the sunshine, the bright light sending a stabbing pain through her brain. There were fifty, a hundred people on the outside looking like zombies – their faces white and lifeless, except for the blood and dust that covered them. Ffion wondered if that was how she looked to others. It was certainly how she felt. Several ambulances, police cars and fire engines were already on the scene. Paramedics and firemen and police dashed about in all directions it seemed, and she assumed they'd only been there for seconds. Ffion turned and looked up and saw the blazing inferno bursting out of the wreckage of the building, reaching several floors up.

'This way, please,' a uniformed policewoman said to Ffion, waving her arms to show her where to go. 'It's not safe here.'

Ffion carried on walking, her eyes taking in the scene but her brain too numb to process much. She noticed police tape marking a safe perimeter around the front of the JIA building. On the other side, numerous pedestrians watched as events unfolded, many with their smartphones held aloft. Ffion put her head down and moved for the tape, aiming for the point that seemed the quietest where the voyeurs' views were restricted by the L-shape of the adjacent building.

'Ffion!' someone called. A man.

Ffion looked over – Ed was ten yards away, a paramedic checking him over. Ffion just smiled at him. She wasn't sure why.

'Ffion, wait!' Ed said.

Ffion didn't. She just put her head down and kept on walking.

Soon she was at the tape. She ducked under it and then carried on her way, moving her banged-up body along as quickly as she could.

CHAPTER 31

Ryker was keeping a careful eye on Fran Black when the door off to his right opened. Thirty seconds earlier, the lights in the back room had flicked off, before emergency lighting kicked in. There'd been loud clunking all around them as – Fran Black explained – steel barriers came down outside to close off the server areas. When Graham Sutton poked his head through the doorway, neither Fran nor Ryker knew why the emergency security measures had kicked in. Ignoring Ryker, Sutton indicated to Fran with his head. She looked at him quizzically then scooted over and Sutton whispered to her. Ryker frowned as he watched them. He got to his feet when he saw the colour draining from Fran's face.

'Problem?' Ryker asked.

Sutton looked over at him. His face was hard and hostile. Fran, on the other hand, looked shocked, scared almost.

'What happened?' Ryker asked, already expecting the worst.

Thirty minutes later, Ryker was striding through the streets of London, heading toward the JIA offices in Vauxhall. He'd had to be at his persuasive best to get Sutton to let him out of the Hive. The explosion at JIA Headquarters had triggered an automatic lockdown at the underground sanctum. With the server area secured, Sutton did at least have discretion as to whether or not to open the doors to the outside world, and Ryker knew he could do much more to help on the outside than in. Plus he'd never been a fan of being locked away in windowless underground spaces. He'd spent too long in grimy, dark jail cells in his time, and claustrophobia was a natural consequence.

For that reason, and the obvious worry that perhaps there were secondary devices yet to explode, Ryker chose against taking the tube or a bus. That the streets around Vauxhall were crowded suggested most people who were busy trying to escape the area had made the same choice. The risk of terrorist attacks in London remained real, and in the immediate aftermath people were always especially cautious. The people around Ryker had likely never heard a bomb exploding in real life. Yet when that blast came, when news of what had happened cascaded through the streets, the natural instinct of many was to get away from the area as quickly as possible, even though in reality that might mean they were actually heading *closer* to a secondary attack.

As Ryker got nearer to the JIA offices, he spotted the trail of wispy black smoke ahead, weaving up into the air, over the top of the buildings in front. The sound of sirens had been ever present since Ryker emerged from the Hive, but was now getting denser and louder.

Despite the myriad thoughts going through his mind, Ryker walked calmly, though with vigilance, passing by the ultra-conspicuous Vauxhall Cross building – ironically the headquarters of the Secret Intelligence Service. At least someone had the good sense to house the JIA somewhere a bit more off the map. He turned a corner and came out into a large square, each of the buildings modern and built by companies who must have held shares in glassmakers. One side of the square was taken over by an impressive modern water feature. Usually water leaped from the ground, and in hot weather, young kids in their underwear ran through in delight.

The scene was more than a bit different.

The other three sides of the square were lined with modern, high-rise office blocks. The one that housed the JIA now had a gaping hole in its front, stretching several floors up. A heavy presence of paramedics, fire crews and police – including armed response units – were still on site, though everything seemed organised and under control. Multiple hoses were pouring water into the blast area, and the fire appeared to be almost out, just a few small pockets of flames still visible in the sizzling mess. Beyond the smoke and water and the remaining flames, the full extent of carnage inside the building was visible. Ryker wasn't a bomb expert, but it was clear enough this had been a big explosion.

Ryker headed toward the crowd of bystanders who were milling about near the police cordon, some thirty yards from what was left of the entrance of the building. What was going through the heads of these people, Ryker wondered? Most members of the public wanted to run away to safety, so what made these stragglers want to hang around and gawk at the chaos? Were they disorientated or confused, or just voyeurs? Perhaps they wanted to help but weren't being given the opportunity.

As he approached the cordon, Ryker took out his phone and dialled Winter for the umpteenth time since he'd left the Hive. The call wasn't even ringing through. Ryker might not have admitted it, but now that he was on site he could feel a lump in his throat at the thought that the JIA commander might be dead. Winter wasn't a close friend – Ryker didn't have any – but he was a good guy, and he'd looked out for Ryker plenty of times recently. It wasn't just sentiment, though, that was causing Ryker to feel that way. He was concerned about what it meant for *him* if Winter was lying dead somewhere in the wreckage. And then there was Willoughby. Had she been in the building?

Ryker tried calling her. She didn't answer either, but the call did at least ring through. He left a brief message then put the phone away and scanned the people on the other side of the cordon, looking for any faces he recognised.

There were still numerous walking wounded that Ryker could see, their faces and clothes covered in blood. One or two others on gurneys were quite obviously much more seriously injured. There was no sign of Winter though. No sign of anyone that Ryker recognised.

He looked to his side and noticed the man next to him, rather than watching the scene, had his eyes glued to the screen of his smartphone. He was watching a live news broadcast from the BBC. A reporter was stationed outside the JIA building, and

Ryker looked up and over to his left and spotted the camera and the smartly dressed but sober looking reporter in mid-take. Ryker looked back down to the screen, reading the scrolling news bulletin.

Explosion in Vauxhall, at Johnson & Irvine Associates, an insurance company. Over one hundred people injured, several critically. No confirmed fatalities.

With the reporter busily speculating as to what had happened – a gas explosion? Islamist terrorists? – the newsroom crew suddenly cut in, announcing that an urgent press briefing from the Metropolitan Police was due to start. Ryker frowned as he thought through the implications. The bomb had gone off less than an hour earlier. That was a hell of a response to have arranged a press briefing already.

The man with the phone groaned, perhaps annoyed that the live footage from where he was standing had been hastily cut, and he closed the browser. He glanced over at Ryker and gave an unfriendly glare. Ryker barely noticed. The man might not be interested in what the Met had to say, but Ryker certainly was. It was standard protocol for them to be involved, how could they not be when there'd been an explosion in broad daylight in the centre of London? But the JIA – a clandestine intelligence agency – was the target, and that almost certainly would not be made public, if anyone in the Met even knew. So Ryker was intrigued about what exactly was going to be said at their urgent press briefing.

Ryker whipped out his own phone and quickly navigated to the BBC website, then scrolled through menus to find the link for the live broadcast. The 4G signal on his phone meant it took a few seconds for the stream to open up and for the buffering to sort itself out and the image to become clear. By the time it did, the briefing was already in full swing.

A uniformed officer with a pockmarked face was centre stage, his hands clasped together on the table in front of him as he spoke. Despite the apparent urgency, though, Ryker quickly realised from the officer's vague words that the briefing was nothing more than a publicity stunt. Perhaps trying to allay the fears of the public. The key takeaway was that the police believed the blast to be from an explosive device, rather than an accident. Who had carried out the bombing, and why, was still unknown, though the police were treating it as terror-related. Which meant little really. There was no distinction there between race or ethnicity, religion or political purpose behind the bombing. Basically the police knew nothing. Or if they did know something, they weren't telling.

Ryker put away his phone and looked back across to the people beyond the cordon.

Over the next few minutes, he tried calling both Winter and Willoughby again with no success. He was about ready to just head through the cordon and blag his way to someone who knew what was going on when two paramedics came rushing out of the front entrance of the building with a gurney. The man on the gurney looked in a bad way. His face was a pulpy, bloody mess. But Ryker had no doubt who it was.

Peter Winter.

The first thing Ryker felt was relief. He was alive at least. The feeling didn't stick around for long though.

Ryker ducked under the police tape and dashed forward. Two police officers spotted his movement and quickly headed over to intercept. Ryker didn't stop.

'Sir! Please stay behind the perimeter line.'

'I need to speak to him,' Ryker said, indicating Winter, who was being swiftly wheeled toward the back doors of a waiting ambulance.

'I need you to step back behind the perimeter tape,' the officer reiterated, his hard tone causing other people around to take notice.

'Or what?' Ryker stopped and glared at the officer, though he realised this was hardly the place to make a scene.

'Or we'll have to arrest you,' the other officer said, sounding more balanced than his colleague. 'Please, sir. This is a very delicate situation here.'

Ryker looked around again. Reluctantly, he was about to step back and let the officers get on with their jobs when another man approached, hobbling along.

'It's okay, he's with me,' the man said.

It took Ryker a few beats to place the face. Maybe because of the thick soot that caked his features. The two men had only met a few times, but Ryker realised it was Rod Flowers, Winter's assistant.

'He still needs to step back behind the line,' the first officer said.

'I think you'll find he doesn't,' Flowers said. 'If you want to know why then I suggest you go and ask the Commissioner and see what she says?'

The look on the officer's face changed to a sour pout. He likely didn't understand what the hell Flowers was talking about, but the authority with which the young man had spoken, and the mention of the Met's big boss, was enough to get him to comply. He muttered something that Ryker didn't quite catch, then he and his colleague moved back toward the cordon.

'I'm Rod Flowers,' Flowers said, holding out his hand to Ryker.

'I know,' Ryker said, giving it a brief shake.

He moved past Flowers and over to the ambulance where the medics were in the process of loading Winter.

'Is he conscious?' Ryker asked them.

'Just about,' the female paramedic answered. 'He's got several broken bones. Some bad burns. We've given him some heavy painkillers so he's not overly lucid.'

Flowers limped up to Ryker's side. Somehow, he'd come off a lot better than his boss, with only superficial cuts and bruises.

Ryker looked at Winter. The commander's eyelids were open only slightly, but he could see Winter was looking at him.

'You okay?' Ryker felt quite lame that those were the best words he could come up with.

Winter murmured. His mouth opened and closed, but nothing intelligible came out.

'Sorry, we really need to get him to the hospital,' the paramedic said, putting her hand onto Ryker's shoulder and trying to push him to the side so she could shut the ambulance doors.

Ryker brushed her off and jumped up into the back of the ambulance.

'Sir!'

'Just a minute.' Ryker heard Flowers talking to the paramedic, trying to explain, but didn't pay attention to the words. He was too focused on Winter, on straining to hear what the commander was trying to tell him. He thought he'd heard the first time, but had to be sure.

'Say that again.' Ryker moved closer to Winter so their faces were inches apart.

Winter wheezed and when the words came out, his voice was hoarse and croaky. 'Ffion Brady. You have to find her.'

CHAPTER 32

Ryker had come to London in search of answers related to the Silver Wolf, an ex-JIA agent who was somehow directly involved in Lisa's murder. Instead he'd stumbled upon a rogue JIA employee who had deleted, and possibly stolen, data from a heavily secured underground compound – and also, potentially, set a bomb at the JIA's offices. Surely that's what Winter's words had meant?

Why else would he have said that to Ryker?

Ryker had no chance to question his ex-boss. The paramedic had insisted Ryker leave the ambulance and let them tend to Winter. Ryker didn't argue. He just wished Winter well then climbed out the back of the ambulance and walked away. He didn't repeat what Winter had said to Flowers or to anyone else. There was a chance Winter had told him in confidence. Why, he didn't know.

All he knew was that on the face of it – from the intelligence Willoughby had already gathered for him when he was in the hive – Ffion Brady was a routine data analyst for a government agency, not a crazed fanatic. Selling secret data for profit? Okay, Ryker could understand how someone in her position could be swayed under certain circumstances. Smuggling a bomb into an intelligence agency's offices and setting it off was something else altogether. Ryker was sure that Ffion Brady wasn't the mastermind behind that, even if she was the person who had planted the device.

He was determined to find out who was pulling the strings, and why. He had to find Ffion Brady.

Was there even a link to the Silver Wolf, or was that just wishful thinking?

In the time it took Ryker to travel across London to Islington, the news reports had updated to confirm four people had died in the blast, with ten still unaccounted for. Ryker had finally managed to get hold of Willoughby again. She was fine, she had been in a hotel when the bomb exploded. They'd spoken twice on the phone since he'd left the scene at the office. He didn't know who exactly was calling the shots at the JIA, but while she awaited further instruction, she was still eagerly beavering away pulling any data she could on Ffion Brady, anything that might give a clue as to why she'd gone rogue.

Willoughby had given him a brief but bland history of the analyst, and also Ffion's home address, which was the building he was now eyeing as he walked up a trendy residential street lined with Georgian terraced townhouses. Peter Winter lived somewhere around there too, Ryker knew. Was that ironic?

There was no sign of any police presence outside Ffion Brady's home, which said a lot. If she really was the suspected bomber, it seemed neither Winter nor anyone else at the JIA had yet informed the Met. Ryker knew their sheer numbers alone would be invaluable if the situation turned into an all-out manhunt, but informing the police wasn't his choice to make. He was pleased to have some breathing space to try and find some answers himself.

Keeping his eyes busy, Ryker turned from the pavement and headed up the path to the front door of the townhouse. He'd not spotted anything untoward on the streets. No lurkers. He pressed the buzzer for Ffion Brady's apartment then stepped back to survey the building. It was one of the more modestly presented in the row of terraces, yet each of the apartments inside undoubtedly would sell for an eye-watering amount, given the area.

'Hello,' came a grainy female voice through the intercom speaker.

Ryker couldn't imagine the voice belonging to Ffion. It was too deep and guttural. He noticed there was no camera connected to the intercom.

'My name's James Ryker, from the Department for Work and Pensions. I'm here for my appointment with Mr and Mrs Brady.'

The backstory Willoughby had given Ryker had included the fact that Ffion's husband was a quadriplegic, following a motorbike accident. Ryker's ruse of being from the DWP was therefore straightforward and plausible enough.

There was silence for a few seconds. 'Sorry, I wasn't told about that. Mrs Brady isn't in right now.'

'Oh. That's strange. I should be able to conclude what I need to with Mr Brady though. As I discussed with Mrs Brady on the phone, we need the paperwork completed today otherwise Mr Brady's disability payments will stop by the end of the week.'

Further silence.

'No, sorry,' the lady said. 'Mr Brady knows nothing about this either. I'm afraid you'll have to rearrange and come back another time.'

There was a click and then nothing more.

Ryker wasn't taking no for an answer though. He assumed the woman he'd just spoken to was Clarissa Weir, the main carer for Andre Brady during the week, and her response had aroused his suspicions. Either Ffion Brady was home, or Clarissa knew something was wrong. That Ffion was in trouble. Possibly knew where she was if she'd run.

One thing that could be said for pleasant Georgian townhouses was that the ageing fixtures were generally not the most secure. He could tell from the style and age that the lock on the door was about as standard as they came with no extra security features. The small gap between the door and frame was easily big enough to slip a card into. Then it was just a case of finding the right spot and leveraging the card so that it pushed back the latch.

Ryker had his hand in his pocket, digging for his wallet.

Then the door opened. Ryker jolted in surprise. He looked the guy on the other side in the eye. He was in his twenties, maybe, with straggly hair and messy clothes. The guy jumped in surprise, much the same way Ryker had, but he said nothing, just walked on past and down the path. Ryker stuck out his foot, catching the door just before it closed. He glanced around and saw the man was sticking some headphones over his ears. He turned left onto the street and was out of sight behind a bush a moment later.

Ryker shook his head. Complacency was the only word to describe that run-in. Perhaps that guy lived on the top floor and his apartment had never been broken into before. Not yet, but with that attitude to security...

Ryker moved in and shut the entrance door behind him, then headed for the front door to the ground floor apartment. He knocked then waited.

A few seconds later, the door opened a couple of inches until it caught on the chain. A weathered face, almost a foot below Ryker's eye line, appeared in the crack.

'Yes?' the woman asked.

Ryker couldn't see her fully, but he could see the look of fear in her eyes. Was that because of him being there or something else? He wondered why she'd opened the door at all. Had she thought he was a neighbour? Was she expecting someone?

'It's me again. James Ryker.'

Clarissa went to snap the door shut but Ryker's shoe was already in the way.

'If you don't move your foot in the next three seconds I'm calling the police.'

'Clarissa,' Ryker said, seeing her eyes twitch when he said her name. 'I'll drop the bullshit if you do the same. Ffion is in big trouble. I'm thinking maybe you know that already. I can help her. Help Andre and you. The police really can't.'

He saw the woman's resolve melting away. She was petrified, and it wasn't of Ryker.

'I can't take the chain off with your foot there.'

Ryker edged his foot back a few inches, leaving the tip just over the threshold should Clarissa try to slam the door shut again. She didn't. She nudged it forward an inch and Ryker heard the chain slip off then the door was opened fully. Ryker took in the lady standing in front of him. She was middle-aged, short and plump, wearing a blue and white dress. Her rounded faced looked weary.

'Please, come into the kitchen,' Clarissa said.

She turned and Ryker followed.

The front door of the apartment opened onto a small corridor that had five doorways off it. Kitchen, lounge, bathroom and two bedrooms was Ryker's guess. The doors to the three rooms at the far end were all ajar. The one to Ryker's right was open halfway and he did his best to peep in. He couldn't see the whole of the room but it appeared quiet. No signs of life.

She guided him off to the left, into the narrow L-shaped kitchen that had a small two-seat dining table in the corner.

'I don't see you carrying any paperwork,' Clarissa said, her back to Ryker as she pulled two mugs from a cupboard. 'And don't DWP workers get ID?'

Ryker frowned. He thought the bullshit had already been dropped, so why was she saying that? Ryker didn't ask. He was too busy working over the clues in his mind.

'Tea? Coffee?' Clarissa asked.

'Coffee, please. Black. Strong.'

Clarissa flipped on the kettle then fetched a spoon and a jar of coffee..

'Have you seen the news this morning, Mrs Weir?'

'Call me Clarissa. Yes, I've seen the news.'

'Four people are dead so far. Ten still missing. You know that's the building Ffion works at, right?'

Clarissa turned and the look on her face suggested maybe she didn't. Ryker had no clue what lies Ffion had told her husband and Clarissa about who she worked for, but he could sense that Clarissa knew something. And if she hadn't connected that explosion to Ffion, then just what exactly was Clarissa so worked up about?

'Nobody knows where she is,' Ryker said. 'I need to find her.'

Clarissa still didn't say anything, just turned away from him. Ryker saw her hand was shaking as she spooned out some coffee into the mugs.

'Everything okay there?' Ryker asked.

'How do you mean?'

'You seem a little on edge.'

'Just been a long day.'

'You sure about that?'

'Mr Ryker, I'm trying to be nice to you, but I really wish you'd say what you've come here to say.'

'Where's Ffion?'

'I don't know.' Clarissa turned to face him again. 'She left for work this morning. I haven't seen or heard from her since then. But I wouldn't expect to. I can call her, if you like?'

'You don't seem overly concerned about what I just said.'

'What did you just say?'

'That Ffion's place of work exploded this morning. A bomb. Perhaps she's one of the victims. Her body barbecued.'

He saw Clarissa cringe.

'I know you said that, Mr Ryker, but I'm not sure what to make of it. Ffion doesn't work for an insurance company. That's where the bomb went off, didn't it? Johnson and Alcock or something.'

'Johnson and Irvine Associates. JIA.'

'Never heard of it until this morning.'

The kettle clicked at the end of its boil, and Clarissa turned and poured steaming water into the two mugs. She picked up one of the mugs and handed it to Ryker, then moved to the fridge and took out a plastic carton of milk.

'Perhaps you could tell me who *you* really work for, Mr Ryker?' She dropped a splash of milk into her mug.

'Perhaps I should. Do you think I could just use the toilet first though?'

Clarissa put the milk back into the fridge then stared at him for a few seconds.

'Down the hall on the left,' she said eventually.

'Thanks.'

Ryker put down the mug then headed out. He passed the door to the lounge, again peering in, but saw nothing suspect.

He came to the doors at the far end. One straight ahead and one either side. He turned to the one on the right.

'Not that one, Mr Ryker,' he heard Clarissa call from behind.

He couldn't help but smile at her wiliness.

'Andre's sleeping,' she added.

Fair enough, Ryker thought. He was about to move away to the bathroom door when his attention was caught. The door to Andre's bedroom was ajar maybe ten inches, but the door was hinged on the left meaning all he could see was the near wall. Yet it was something on the wall that had grabbed his attention. A shadow, that he was sure flickered slightly. A person? Someone standing just out of view, behind the door?

Ryker stared for a few seconds. The shadow moved again – barely, but the tiny twitch Ryker saw was enough. There was definitely someone standing there, behind the door.

And it certainly wasn't the bedridden Andre.

CHAPTER 33

Ryker looked back to Clarissa who was still standing outside the kitchen doorway, as his mind played out possibilities. Was it Ffion in there, hiding with her husband? Or was it someone who was a threat? To Andre, to Clarissa, and to him.

The pleading look, the shaking and twitchiness – signals of fear – he was getting from Clarissa told him the latter was most likely. She wasn't just scared of getting found out for harbouring Ffion, she believed she was in imminent danger.

As though reading his mind, Clarissa gave a slight shake of her head, but said nothing. Ryker took a half step to the bathroom, reached out and grabbed the door handle. He pulled the door shut then moved silently back to a position outside the bedroom. The panicked look on Clarissa's face was intensifying by the second. Ryker stared at the shadow on the wall again. He saw movement. His gaze flicked to the edge of the door as a hand came into view. Thick, gnarled fingers. Definitely not Ffion Brady.

As if sensing what was coming, Clarissa darted back toward the kitchen. She was halfway through the doorway when Ryker burst forward.

He slammed his left forearm into the bedroom door, pushing it open with force. There was a loud *thunk* as the wood panels smashed against whoever was on the other side. With his right hand, Ryker reached out and grabbed the man's wrist. He twisted it around and pulled then smashed his free forearm down just above the man's elbow joint. He heard the crack as the man's arm snapped. He shouted out in pain and crumpled to the floor in front of Ryker. A split-second thought flitted through Ryker's mind. He'd possibly just broken the arm of an entirely innocent person. It was a risk worth taking, though, a conclusion that was firmly backed up a moment later when Ryker saw the man pulling up a handgun.

Ryker darted to the side. A shot rang out. The bullet whizzed past Ryker's ear, missing him by inches, and lodged in the wall behind him. Splinters of plaster burst into the air. Ryker kicked out, making solid contact with the gun hand, but the man's grip remained firm. Ryker pounced on top and grabbed for the man's good wrist. Despite one broken arm, the man had plenty of strength in him still, and he pushed against Ryker's resistance, trying to pull the gun into a firing position. Ryker heaved, wrestling for control.

A second shot boomed. Once again, the bullet was wayward, but the blast, so close to Ryker's ears, sent his brain swirling, disturbing his focus. He couldn't afford to let a third shot go off. Even if the bullet didn't hit him, the disorientation could well swing the balance of the fight too far away from Ryker.

He threw down his elbow, pushing his body weight behind the blow to maximise the impact. The bone crashed into the man's face, a spray of blood erupted from his nose and his mouth, and Ryker felt some of the strength in his arms fade. Ryker let go of the man's wrist and swung a ferocious hook into the side of his head, then flung his forehead down onto the bridge of the man's nose.

As Ryker looked down, preparing to deliver another blow, he saw the man's bloodied head loll to the side and his body go limp. Ryker pulled the gun from his now weak grip and, chest heaving, he stood up and looked down at the man he'd just felled.

Dressed casually, he was quite unassuming in his build – neither particularly tall nor short, nor broad, nor thin, His face... it was hard to tell much about his face because his nose was squashed, one of his eyes was swelling shut, and his whole face was glistening with blood. But those hands... they were big and strong and well used. Certainly not an office worker. A labourer would be an option, were it not for the situation they'd met in.

No, this was someone who was used to fighting and hand-to-hand combat. Ryker guessed at ex-army or Special Forces. A mercenary. Quite what that meant, he wasn't sure.

Ryker heard a gasp and looked over his shoulder to see Clarissa standing behind him. She had her hand over her mouth in shock. He followed her gaze. She wasn't looking at the bloodied man on the floor. She was looking across the room, to the single bed by the far wall, to the man lying beneath white sheets, propped up by several thick pillows.

Andre Brady, Ryker presumed. Ryker hadn't paid any attention to Andre until now, his prime focus being on subduing the armed man. Yes, he'd scoped out for other threats in the room the second he'd stormed in, but his eyes had glanced over Andre.

Staring at the helpless form in the bed, Ryker could see why Clarissa was so in shock. Andre Brady hadn't let out a shout, a cry, even a murmur since Ryker had been in the room. Not once since Ryker had been in the apartment in fact. Clarissa had said he was sleeping. Not anymore.

CHAPTER 34

'You need to talk to me,' Ryker said to Clarissa, his tone unsympathetic.

It wasn't that he didn't care that a defenceless man – who Ryker assumed was an innocent bystander in whatever the hell was happening – was now lying dead in front of him. It was just that Ryker needed answers. He needed to know who the man lying on the floor was. He needed to know if there were more of them. Most of all, he needed to know how this all connected to Ffion Brady and the bomb that had exploded at JIA headquarters that morning.

But Clarissa said nothing. She was too in shock. Ryker looked around the room. He wasn't sure how Andre had been killed. There was no evidence of injury, no blood. Had he been poisoned? Smothered with a pillow?

'Why?' was all Clarissa said, her gaze still fixed on Andre. She broke down, sobbing, and Ryker saw her legs wobbling.

He stashed the handgun in his jeans and moved over to her and she fell into him as her legs gave way.

'Come on, come and sit down,' Ryker said, edging her sideways to where there was a fabric armchair.

When she was seated she put her head in her hands, but Ryker wasn't about to give her the time to grieve. 'Are there more of them?'

Clarissa shook her head.

'Are you sure?'

'Yes!' Clarissa shouted, glaring at Ryker.

Ryker said nothing to that. He headed over to the fallen man, grabbing at the dressing gown behind the door as he went, pulling out the cord. He used his foot to turn the guy over onto his front then quickly tied the man's hands together before dragging him over to the bed.

Out into the hallway, Ryker moved confidently but with vigilance. He opened the adjacent door and moved into the second bedroom. As well as a double bed and wardrobe, the room had a desk and swivel chair. It was clear from the master bedroom – the single bed, the lack of anything feminine – that the married couple were no longer sharing a bedroom. The guest room stroke office was now Ffion's space. Ryker did a quick check over the small room, making sure no one was hiding, then found what he was looking for; another dressing gown cord, three pairs of tights.

He moved back into Andre's room. Clarissa had a phone in her hand. Ryker dashed over and grabbed it from her, and saw she'd punched in two nines already. 'No.'

'We have to call the police,' she said. 'They killed him!'

Ryker noted her use of the plural. He'd get to the bottom of what she meant by that. 'Not yet.'

She returned her gaze to the dead man on the bed.

'Perhaps you should go and wait in the kitchen, or the lounge,' Ryker said.

Clarissa nodded and got up from her chair, swaying on weak legs out of the room. Ryker wondered whether she might take the opportunity to try to run. He really hoped she wouldn't.

Seconds later, he was relieved to hear the kettle go on the boil again. No problem in the world that a cup of steaming coffee couldn't make slightly better.

Ryker spent the next couple of minutes securing the man's wrists and ankles to the legs of the bed with the cord and tights. It wasn't an unbreakable bond, but he'd make noise trying to get out of it, and Ryker wouldn't be far away. Satisfied with his handiwork, Ryker headed back out and quickly checked over the rest of the apartment. He was certain any other intruders who were hiding would have sprung out into the open, but he had to be sure.

Other than Clarissa, though, who was sitting somewhat spaced out in the kitchen, there was no one else there, and nothing to indicate anything untoward other than the dead man in the bed and the unconscious man by his side.

When he was satisfied with his search, Ryker went back to the bedroom and rifled through the pockets of the man on the floor. He found a wallet, some keys and a phone. He took them all. Then he spotted the suitcase underneath Andre's bed. Ryker moved over and pulled the case out. It was heavy. He unzipped the lid and opened it. The case was packed full of clothes – men's and women's. There was a carry case under the bed too. Ryker pulled that out. More clothes, shoes, medicines. He checked the pockets of the carry case. Found two passports. The pictures were of Andre and Ffion Brady, but the names he didn't recognise. Ryker understood what that meant.

Taking the passports with him, he went back to the kitchen as he flipped through the contents of the man's wallet. Ryker sat down opposite Clarissa. She was clutching a mug, steam rising from it. The coffee she'd made for him earlier was still on the table, a layer of scum on the top. He didn't bother to ask for a fresh one, and Clarissa didn't offer.

'Who *are* you?' she asked.

'One of the good guys,' Ryker said.

She just humphed. Ryker found a driving licence in the wallet and slipped it out.

'Kristian Schmidt.' Ryker held the licence up for Clarissa to see. 'You know him?'

She shook her head. Ryker looked through the rest of the wallet. The contents were pretty sparse. Some notes, one debit card, one credit card. Both were in the name of John Ingram.

'John Ingram?' Ryker held up one of the cards.

Again Clarissa simply shook her head.

Next he slapped the two passports for the Connors on the table. Clarissa looked at him quizzically. Ryker indicated to the passports and Clarissa opened them up in turn, her frown growing.

'Can you tell me about these?' Ryker said. 'And the packed cases in Andre's room?'

She looked genuinely confused. 'I don't know what you're talking about. What are you saying?'

'What *do* you know then? Where's Ffion?'

'I don't know.'

'You said *they* earlier.'

'They?'

'In the bedroom. You said *they* killed Andre. But there's only one man in here. One man with more than one name, but still just one man. Tell me what you meant.'

Clarissa didn't answer immediately, and before she did finally speak, she let out a long sigh. 'I've no idea who they are. A couple of days ago, Ffion was leaving the house. She said she was going on holiday with Andre.'

'To where?'

'I... I think it was Wales.'

'But they didn't go?'

'I knew something was up with Ffion.'

'Up how?'

'She was so distant, and scared. I didn't know why, and I had tried to ask, but she wouldn't talk to me. I thought maybe she was just struggling with Andre. I get paid... I *got* paid to help here, to look after him, it's a job for me. But Andre was her husband. I could see she struggled to deal with what happened. With looking after him.'

Ryker didn't know the full story of their lives, though he could well imagine how Andre's absolute dependency on others would cause problems for a marriage. But those problems alone didn't come close to explaining any of the recent events. 'Had something changed?'

'I don't know. Like I said, she seemed very uptight all of a sudden. Then the other day they were all packed to go on this trip. An impromptu trip, something I've never known them do before.'

'To Wales?' Ryker again looked at the passports. 'Fake IDs seems a bit OTT for Wales.'

'I'm just telling you what I know,' Clarissa said, her tone hard. 'But that was a few days ago. Then out on the street they bumped into these two men. I saw them from the lounge window. I knew they were up to no good.'

'How?'

'They just looked... off. Ffion said they were from her work–'

'And what do you know of her work exactly?'

'Not much. She doesn't talk about it. Just that she works for a government department. Administration or analysis of some sort. But those men, they didn't look much like office workers to me.'

Which was exactly what Ryker thought about the man he'd disarmed.

'I didn't stick around though. Ffion and Andre were going away so I wasn't needed here. I've no idea what happened with the two men, but the next thing I know Ffion calls me and tells me that they had to cancel their trip. Something urgent at work.'

'And that man in the bedroom, he was one of the men you saw that day?'

'Yes.'

'And the other man?'

'I've not seen him since.'

'What happened today?'

'He came to the door this morning. I knew something was wrong the moment I saw him. He told me Ffion was in trouble and he had to speak to Andre urgently.'

'Did he say why she was in trouble?'

'No. I let him in. As soon as he was in here, he pulled out that gun and hauled me into the bedroom. Andre was awake. God, imagine how scared he was. He had no way of helping.'

Tears rolled down Clarissa's face. Ryker had to admit he felt sympathy for her. She was just a civilian, had probably never seen a gun before in her life up until that point when the SIG Pro that was now stashed in his waistband had been pointed at her. And Andre Brady was defenceless in the whole thing, his killing unnecessary as far as Ryker could see. Why had Schmidt, or whatever his real name was, done that? A message to Ffion, or punishment? Or was it simply a spur of the moment action, because of Ryker's unexpected presence in the apartment?

'What did Schmidt tell you?' Ryker asked.

'Nothing. He only said if I didn't do exactly what he said that he'd kill both me and Andre. I... I've never been in a situation like that. I didn't know what to do.'

'You didn't do anything wrong, Clarissa. This wasn't your fault.'

'No. It wasn't. Until you arrived, Andre and I were both fine.'

Her words were tinged with bitterness, as though she were blaming Ryker for Andre's death. He didn't argue against that. He knew he wasn't to blame, and Clarissa was simply experiencing a whole host of reactionary emotions. It would take her a long time to come to terms with what had happened.

'He said we were waiting for Ffion. That she'd done something terrible and that his colleagues were looking for her. He was staying here until either she turned up or they found her.'

'Which I'm guessing didn't happen.'

'No. You're the first person to come here since.'

'How did he react to that?'

'He had the gun to my head when I answered the intercom.' The memory caused her eyes to well up and Ryker could see her fighting for control of her emotions.

'He told me to get rid of you, to not let you in, whoever you were and whatever you said. That I'd only be putting more lives at risk if I didn't do what he said. By which I took to mean your life.'

'Then when I came to the apartment door?'

'He was angry. He told me again to try to get rid of you, but to let you in if I had to, to not make you suspicious. Perhaps he really thought you were with the DWP, and you'd cry foul if you were sent away. He told me he'd hide with Andre and that if there was any hint of trouble... but I can't believe he actually did it.'

She closed her eyes, and began to shake. Ryker knew he should say something to try to comfort her, but his mind was too busy whirring with activity as he tried to process what was happening and why.

'Is there anything else?' Ryker asked.

Clarissa shook her head.

'Do you know where Ffion would run to?'

Another shake.

'You sure? You must have noticed those cases?'

'I did, but thought nothing of it. I thought perhaps they were just going on the trip they'd already planned to Wales. And I've never seen those before.' She tapped a finger on the passports.

'You know her and Andre better than most people. Where would she hide?'

Ryker picked up the mug of coffee, giving Clarissa time to think. He took a gulp of the barely lukewarm liquid. It tasted like crap but the caffeine would still do its job.

'I just don't know,' Clarissa said. 'It was Aberdovey in Wales I think they were going to go away to.' She paused. Ryker gave her the time to think. 'Her parents live in Telford. She has a brother in Scotland. Dunblane. Andre's an only child, his father's dead and his mother lives in South Africa.'

Clarissa went quiet again. Ryker didn't prompt her for anything more. He could see she was still working ideas over in her mind. Ryker thought she was about to say something else when he heard noises coming from across the apartment. A bang. Shuffling.

It was Schmidt.

Ryker jumped up from his seat. 'Wait there. Don't do anything until I come back.'

She nodded and Ryker turned and walked quickly back through the apartment to the bedroom. Sure enough, when he walked in he saw that Schmidt was conscious and he'd already managed to loosen the restraints on his wrists enough to give him space to work with. He was busy trying to untie himself from the leg of the bed. Or was he trying to push the bed up so he could slip the cord underneath? Perhaps that's what the bang had been.

It didn't matter. He hadn't been successful. Ryker stared down and Schmidt stopped moving and glared up in defiance.

'Maybe we should have a little talk,' Ryker said.

Clarissa had given him what she could, but this man likely had a whole lot more. Ryker saw just the slightest hint of panic behind Schmidt's one open eye as if he could understand exactly what lengths Ryker was prepared to go to, to extract information.

'Whatever you do to me, you're a dead man now,' Schmidt said, his voice gravelly and hoarse.

'Whatever I do to you?' Ryker smirked, amused by the bravado. His eyes narrowed. 'You couldn't possibly imagine.'

Ryker stepped closer to Schmidt and saw him squirm. Then a noise outside the apartment caught Ryker's attention and he stopped and listened. A siren. No, not one, but multiple. Getting louder by the second. Ryker held Schmidt's eye as he listened.

They were in a busy district in central London, so it was hardly unusual to hear sirens of the emergency services. Yet Ryker had a strong idea that they were headed directly to where he was. Perhaps Winter had now informed the Met that Ffion Brady was the suspected bomber. The apartment would be their first port of call. Or had Clarissa managed to phone the police after all?

Schmidt's face remained deadpan as the sirens got louder. It looked like he wasn't about to be interrogated by Ryker, but he wasn't going to be let off. He'd soon be locked in a cell for a long, long time. Perhaps the men and women in blue would get some answers out of him in a more conventional manner.

Ryker decided it was time to make himself scarce, but he wasn't leaving Schmidt there like that. It wasn't worth the risk of him somehow making an unlikely escape before the police found him. Ryker stepped forward and the look on Schmidt's face changed.

'No, please!'

Too late. Ryker drove the heel of his shoe into Schmidt's face, centred in on his one good eye. Just like that, he was out cold again. Ryker spun and walked quickly out into the corridor. Clarissa was standing in the doorway to the kitchen.

'It wasn't me,' she said without being prompted.

Ryker believed her. 'Is there a way out other than the front?'

'There's a shared garden. But it leads onto the other properties.'

That was better than meeting the police head on in the street.

Ryker said nothing more, just dashed forward to the apartment door. He opened it and headed out. To his left, beyond the building's entrance, out on the street, he could hear screeching tyres as the police cars came to a stop. Ryker moved the opposite way, going down steps to reach a fire door at the back of the property. He pushed down on the bar in the middle of the door and swung it open. He never made it out.

'Armed police!' came the shout from one of the three geared-up officers standing yards away from Ryker. 'Stop right there. Hands above your head.'

For once in his life, Ryker did exactly as he was told.

CHAPTER 35

Behind him, Ryker heard the front door of the building smash open. He didn't turn around, and could only assume the police had used a battering ram to obliterate the lock and latch. He didn't know how many police were coming in the front but this was certainly more than just a first response to a 999 call, it was a full-on raid.

'Down on your knees, hands behind your head,' said the officer on the left of the three. A woman, probably only five-seven or so. With all her gear on – utility belt, ballistic vest – she was almost as wide as she was tall. She spoke with authority and confidence. Nothing like a submachine gun to make you feel confident about yourself.

Ryker gave her a determined stare but did as she asked. Her two colleagues rushed past and into the building. They didn't bother to cuff or to check Ryker. Maybe they didn't have the manpower or time to do so immediately, and were happy enough that the remaining armed officer could handle whatever Ryker threw at her. It was Ffion they were after.

Lucky for them, Ryker had no intention of pulling out the SIG handgun that was stashed in his waistband to test that theory.

Behind him, there were a series of shouts from the officers as they stormed through the building. Not just the Connors' apartment, but those on the upper floors too. There was more than one scream of panic and surprise from the tenants and other occupants. Ryker recognised Clarissa's voice as one of them.

The officer in front of him kept the barrel of her Heckler & Koch MP5 hovering over Ryker's centre mass.

Ryker saw her eyes flicking back and forth from him to somewhere behind. 'Disappointed you're not getting in on the action?'

She said nothing.

'She's not here, you know.' Still no response. 'Did you hear what I said?'

'Who's not here?' She gave Ryker a cold stare.

'Ffion Brady. That's who you're looking for.'

'Do you know where she is?'

'No.'

'And who exactly are you?'

'I was about to come to that,' Ryker said, with a wry smile. The officer remained deadpan. 'I really could do with getting out of here.'

'Why's that?'

'I'm a busy man. Things to do, people to see.'

'Why don't you just pipe down. You can go when we've cleared you.'

Again her eyes flicked from Ryker to behind him. He felt she was becoming increasingly edgy, perhaps it was Ryker's overly calm manner. But he wasn't trying to heckle or rile her. He really did want to get away.

'Can you do me a favour?' Ryker asked.

'Probably not.'

'Call your commanding officer. Tell him, or her, you've got an ID you need to run. The ID is three, four, eight, a, nine, four, k, e.'

The woman just stared at Ryker. 'What kind of an ID is that?'

'Why don't you find out?'

She huffed and mulled over the request. Perhaps it was the confidence and command of Ryker's delivery that eventually made her succumb. He'd only given himself a fifty-fifty chance. It had been just as likely that once satisfied that everyone inside was under control, they'd haul Ryker into a waiting van and take him to the station to process. He had no ID on him, was carrying a gun in his jeans, which they'd surely find if they were doing their job properly, and among his other possessions were two fake passports and a phone, keys and wallet that he'd just taken from a heavily beaten unconscious man.

'I need an ID check,' the woman called into her radio after first identifying herself. She repeated the code Ryker had given her.

There was silence for a few seconds. At least silence from the officer and her radio. Behind Ryker there was the racket as officers thudded around and escorted the residents out onto the street. Ryker needed this resolved quickly. Before they tried to search him, and before they made a connection to him and the unconscious man in the ground floor apartment.

The code he'd just given the officer would identify him as an intelligence agent with top-level security clearance. It should, in theory, be enough to allow him to walk away without the need for him first being questioned down at the local police station. He'd always had such a code when working for the JIA, and Winter had been kind enough, at Ryker's request, to set up a new one following his return to England. Even though he was no longer an official JIA agent, Ryker had bet it wouldn't be long before he rubbed shoulders with the police, one way or another. Winter had obviously felt the same as he'd agreed to the request.

'Okay,' the officer said into the radio when she had her response. She focused back on Ryker and dropped the barrel of her weapon. 'Looks like you're good.'

'Thanks.' Ryker lowered his hands and getting to his feet. 'Do you think you could show me out the front? I'm not really in the mood for jumping fences.'

'Follow me.'

The officer walked past and Ryker moved in line behind. He looked off to his left as he passed the open door of the Connors' apartment. He saw at least three officers in there. No sign of Clarissa or Schmidt.

Ryker and the officer headed out through what was left of the building's entrance door. Outside the streets were teaming with police cars and vans with police officers scuttling about. A number of the residents of the apartments were outside as well, mostly looking bewildered at what was happening, one or two looking angry. The police were already in the process of checking IDs and stories.

Ryker spotted Clarissa. A policeman was holding on to her under her armpit, as though she was unable to stand on her own. It had certainly been one hell of a day for her. She locked eyes with Ryker, but there was no reaction on her face. She was probably wondering what was happening to him. Was he being taken into custody? Was he in fact working with the police? Ryker just gave her a slight nod then carried on with the officer until they were past the last of the police cars.

'You have a good day,' she said to him, then stopped moving.

Ryker turned to face her. 'Thanks.' With that, he turned and walked away down the street.

'Damn spooks,' he heard the woman mutter.

He didn't react, just kept on going.

When he hit a crossroads, he turned left and fished in his pocket for Schmidt's phone. It was time to turn detective.

CHAPTER 36

Lake Maggiore, Italy

I t had been another glorious day by the lake. Or on the lake, to be more precise. The sun was just dipping behind the far away mountains, turning the blue sky above a patchwork of orange and purple and pink. Draper, manning the wheel on the top deck of the *Angelica*, looked over his shoulder at Falah. Champagne glass in hand, the Sheik was looking out over the darkening water, running his fingers through his wiry beard.

'I'm thinking of staying a few more days,' Falah said.

Draper's hands gripped the wheel that little bit harder. Staying to enjoy the hospitality was one thing, but did Falah actually mean he was staying longer because he was delaying the deal?

'Italy's gotten under your skin?' Draper asked.

'And then some. I've been to a lot of places, but this...' Falah waved his arm around with true wonder on his face. 'I'll never forget it.'

'Perhaps it's best to leave while it's still so magical in your mind. After all, familiarity ultimately breeds contempt.'

'You're saying I'd end up hating this place?'

'Maybe not hating it, but that honeymoon feeling of something new and different never lasts.'

'Perhaps you're right. I guess the same can also be said of business relationships.'

'How do you mean?'

'I mean look at us. We're getting along so well, and we haven't even completed one deal yet...'

Damn right we haven't, Draper thought.

'But I've often found in business the more you deal with someone, the more you see their weaknesses. The more the cracks appear and the more they just begin to...' Falah screwed up his face as he tried to think of the word.

'Grate on your nerves,' Draper said.

'Exactly.'

'What's your point?'

'No point. Just wondering if perhaps that's why your history is so chequered and disparate. You never seem to stay long in any venture, or with any partner.'

Draper pulled the throttle, the yacht slowing, then let go of the wheel and turned to face Falah. This wasn't the first time the Sheik had questioned Draper's past. He was beginning to think there was an ulterior motive.

'Is there something you're trying to tell me?' Draper did a bad job of hiding his annoyance. 'Something you want to ask me?'

Falah pursed his lips. He was looking pleased with himself. Was that because of what he was about to say or just because he could see he had riled his host? Draper was beginning to seriously dislike the man. He couldn't wait to wave him off back to the hellhole country he lived in. As long as he had the money in by then. If not, Draper was increasingly thinking he might yet extend the Sheik's stay in Italy indefinitely. He clearly liked the place so much.

Draper's phone danced on the polished wood coffee table.

Falah gave a slight shrug then looked away. 'I'll go and see where the party's at,' he said before walking to the steps leading off the top deck.

'Don't choke on the oysters,' Draper said, quietly enough that only he would hear. He picked up the phone, his irritation growing when he saw who was calling. 'What is it?'

'You've heard?' Henderson asked.

Draper let out a long sigh. 'How could I not.'

'I know it's fucked up, but I'm sorting it.'

'Just come back here. We'll think about how to solve this together.'

There was a pause. What, did Henderson not trust him? Did he think Draper was about to string him up and skin him alive? Why was that?

'I'm sorting it,' Henderson repeated.

'And the cripple?'

'We did what was necessary. Damage limitation.'

'But you still haven't found *her*.'

'It's only a matter of time.'

'Time you don't have. Come back here, as soon as you can. I've a feeling we may have even bigger problems quite soon.'

'Problems? How?'

'Just do it.'

Draper put down the phone. The muscles in his arm twitched. Then spasmed. He balled his fist, trying to contain it. Within seconds, vibrations coursed through his whole body.

'Aaaaargghhh!' Draper screamed and lashed out at the yacht's control panel, again and again and again, punching it with venom. The toughened plastic didn't even take a scratch, but was left with smears of skin and blood from Draper's knuckle.

'Everything okay there?'

Chest heaving, snarling, Draper turned to see Clyde at the top of the steps. The young man, calm and composed as ever, brought some clarity and sense into Draper's mind. He didn't lose it often, but when he did...

'No, it's not okay,' Draper growled.

'Henderson?'

'Who else.'

'You know his *friend* suffocated that poor—'

'Yes, you told me already. I don't know what the fuck is happening over there. He told me it would be simple. That this would put an end to any problems Maddison's past could cause us. He told me the asset—'

'Asset? She's just a data analyst!'

Draper gritted his teeth. 'Yeah, well, Henderson told me she was someone on the inside at the security services, who could get the job done quickly and quietly.'

'And how did that work out? More explosions. More innocent people killed.'

'You think he lied to me? That this is what he wanted?'

'Yes. And I think he's still lying to you. I don't know what his goal is, but it's certainly not doing what you tell him.'

'You know I've always expected my men to be more than just arse-licking lapdogs.' Draper saw offence in Clyde's eyes, though he hadn't meant to tarnish his most trusted employee with those words, even if Clyde was more loyal than a pet. 'But now I'm thinking maybe not everyone can handle being given freedom of thought.'

'Not when they're intent on working at cross purposes with you.'

Draper snorted. He could sense Clyde was enjoying that Draper was so pissed off with Henderson. Clyde hadn't liked the newcomer from the start, was probably always waiting for him to cock up just so he could say I told you so. It looked more and more like Clyde was about to get his moment of glory.

'I told him to come back immediately,' Draper said. 'Let's see whether he does.'

'If he does?'

'Then we start over. Figure a way to clean up the mess in London.'

'And if he doesn't?'

'Then we start over. Figure a way to clean up the mess in London. Henderson included.'

'Got it,' Clyde said with a wicked smile.

CHAPTER 37

Ryker headed back to the hotel he'd been staying at for the last few nights, a three-star business hotel located near St Paul's Cathedral. From his window, he could just see the top of the main dome, though he'd hardly call it a room with a view. The overcrowded streets outside his window were a mishmash of office blocks, mostly ugly grey structures from the seventies and eighties. The hotel too was several decades old and the room was tired and worn. It was warm and dry, though, and Ryker wasn't paying so he couldn't really complain.

Surprisingly for its standard, the hotel offered room service. A club sandwich, fries, chocolate cake, diet Pepsi. Over thirty pounds for what turned out to be worse food than he'd get at the most basic of fast food outlets. It was still food though. It did its job.

In between mouthfuls, Ryker put a call in to Eleanor Willoughby. He'd already done what he could looking through Schmidt's phone. That had taken all of two minutes, as there was virtually nothing on there. No texts, no pictures, no browsing history. Two missed calls, one received call, and three made. All that day, all to the same number. Ryker had to find out who that number belonged to, but he wasn't just going to call it. Not yet anyway.

'Ryker, you know I've been calling you for the last two hours?' Willoughby said when she picked up.

'I know. I'm calling you back, aren't I?'

'Have you seen the news?'

'Yeah.' How could he not? Every single TV channel, every news website, was running the same story. Nationwide manhunt for Ffion Brady, suspected bomber of Johnson & Irvine Associates.

'She won't get far.' Ryker looked over at the passports on the table next to him.

'You would know about running, wouldn't you?'

Ryker wasn't sure if she was being facetious or not. 'Have you got any update?'

'I've been assigned to this case officially.'

He could tell, wherever she was, that she was walking quickly because of her footsteps and her breathing. 'I didn't mean an update on your career.'

'Yeah, well, right now the JIA are operating with a skeleton crew. You saw the damage that was done to HQ. Half the admin staff are in hospital, as is more than one commander. Anyone who's on the ground in the UK is on this case. Trying to figure out who planted that bomb and why.'

'Ffion Brady planted it.'

'Okay. Then who recruited her and why?'

'What can you tell me?'

'We're—'

'Where are you anyway? We should meet up to do this.'

Her footsteps stopped. 'Actually that's why I was calling. I'm right outside your hotel.'

Ryker shook his head and got up from the bed. He headed to the window and pulled across the curtains. He could just about see the front entrance of the hotel. Sure enough, Willoughby was standing there on the pavement, phone pressed to her ear.

'Can I come up?'

'How did you know I was staying here?'

'I'm a spy, Ryker.'

'Flowers told you.'

'Yeah. That too. Can I come up?'

'No. I'll come down. We'll get a drink somewhere.'

Ryker ended the call.

Ten minutes later, they were sitting in the back of a traditional style pub that was near empty. Describing it as traditional style was kind, really it was just down at heel. Ryker wasn't sure if the lack of patrons was due to the time and location or the state of the place.

After the day he'd had, he really wanted a beer. Actually, whisky would have been a preferred choice, though he opted for coffee. He wished he hadn't. Pubs were hardly renowned for making good coffee, and this place was no different. Willoughby had a diet coke. Clearly neither of them were finished for the day just yet.

'So what have you got then? Where's Ffion Brady?' Ryker asked.

'We're tracking her movements. The police think Scotland.'

'She's not gone to Scotland.'

'How do you know that?'

'It's too rainy.'

'Very funny. But she has family there. It's an obvious choice. She hasn't got many options right now.'

'No, she hasn't.'

Ryker pulled out the two passports and put them on the table.

Willoughby checked them over then looked back up at him. 'She was planning on leaving the country?'

'Looks like it, doesn't it.'

'So what went wrong?'

'She never expected the police to be on to her so quickly. She had an escape route, for both her and Andre, but she never even made it back to her apartment. Something went wrong for her, and she's being forced to run on the fly.'

'It's possible. I'll get the names passed through the databases, we may find out what their travel plans were.'

'Yeah. Though I'm betting she hasn't left the UK. She won't know how.'

'Maybe. Maybe not.'

'Those are good fakes,' Ryker said. 'Not many people can do a job like that. I'm not sure a data analyst like Ffion Brady would have the contacts. So who was pulling the strings?'

Willoughby sighed in response. Neither of them knew the answer.

'Tell me what the lead to Scotland is,' Ryker said.

Willoughby took a sip of coke and looked around the bar. She'd done so several times already but no one was in earshot. Just habit, Ryker assumed.

'She's not been too careful. Like you said, something went wrong this morning, with the explosion. She was there, in the middle of it. Security guards were trying to tackle her the second it went off.'

'Seriously?'

'Seriously. Flowers managed to trigger the alarm just a few seconds before the explosion, when Ffion was still in the foyer. I'm guessing she wasn't expecting to be caught up in that blast.'

'Instead, she was hunted from the beginning, and to start with she was walking around central London covered in soot and blood, no doubt.'

'Which explains some of her movements. Her credit card was first used at a Boots pharmacy just a mile from HQ. Then at a clothes store on Oxford Street not long after. Like I said, not very planned.'

'Why use cards and not cash?' Ryker asked.

'Because she didn't have cash. She hadn't planned on needing new clothes.'

'You can get cash out using cards, you know.'

'Which she did. But there's also a limit. Do you have a different theory about all this?'

'I do. But carry on.'

'Next we have a transaction at Marylebone Station. A return ticket to Birmingham Moor Street. An hour later, the same card was used to purchase two one-way tickets at London Euston, heading to Edinburgh. There's then a further transaction at Leeds station two hours later, a ticket to Manchester.'

Ryker shook his head. 'And you're actually buying this?'

Willoughby frowned. She looked offended by Ryker's tone. 'Not at all. She's sending us on a wild goose chase. Maybe she made one or two of those transactions but she's by now passed her card on to someone else, probably given them a hundred pounds and asked them to keep using the card all day, or maybe she gave them to a couple of homeless bums who are now off seeing the sights of the UK.'

'I'm glad you said that, not me. It's a pretty cheap trick. So why Scotland then?'

'The police still think she's heading there.'

'Based on what?'

'Based on the theory that she's running, and she's trying to get far away from London, and without smuggling herself out of the country, Scotland's as far as she can get while she figures out a better plan.'

'Wow, that's some solid evidence right there.'

'Did I forget to mention the phone call she made to her brother in Dunblane? And his unusual actions this afternoon? Look, Ryker, not everyone is like you. Normal people don't know how to just disappear. Especially not when they have every police force in the country looking for them. Given her original plans were scuppered, heading to somewhere she knows is a sensible course of action to take.'

'Fair point. But I still think you're wrong.'

'Then where do you think she is?'

'Like you said, somewhere she knows. I'd bet she's in London.'

'Why would she still be here?'

'Because she's too scared to get out. She knows everyone is hunting her. She's not going to jump on a train to anywhere. She can't rent a car or take a bus. She steals a car and she's on the radar too. Unless she's very close to contacts in the criminal underworld – which judging by the fact that her husband was murdered today I'd suggest isn't the case – then I'd bet you anything she's not more than a few miles from home.'

Willoughby said nothing to that.

Ryker realised his words had brought him back full circle to the purpose of their conversation. 'I need another favour.'

Willoughby rolled her eyes. 'Seriously?'

'The last time you and I were in a bar together we were on the good stuff in New Orleans.'

Willoughby smiled. 'Not quite the same here, is it?'

'Maybe in a few days we can find somewhere decent and have a proper drink?'

'Okay, Ryker. Thanks for the sweet-talking. Now what's the favour?'

Ryker smiled; it was not lost on him just how relaxed he felt with Willoughby. There was a familiarity to their relationship, even though they'd known each other for only a short period of time. Perhaps that was because more than once they'd been in life-threatening situations together. Nothing brought two people closer together quite like abject danger.

'I have a decent lead,' Ryker said. 'I think I found one of the people who hired Ffion Brady.'

'I heard about that. The man the SCO19 officers arrested at the Connors' house. His real name is Evan Tate. Former captain in the army.'

Ryker didn't respond, just took the information in. Willoughby was certainly well informed. Where was she getting all her intel from?

'Strange, though,' Willoughby added. 'Tate had nothing on him. Except for his clothes that is. No wallet, phone, or anything like that. I can only presume they were taken by the mystery guest who broke Tate's nose and tied him to a bed. The one that gave the SCO19 officers a JIA ID code before scarpering.'

Ryker laughed. 'Bloody hell, Willoughby. Have you any idea how much you sound like Peter Winter? Are you sure you're a field agent and not a desk-jockey commander?'

Willoughby looked put out by his quip. 'I'm not meaning to give you a hard time. This is nothing more than I've come to expect with you.'

'I think you mean that in a positive way.' Another eye roll. Though he sensed she was struggling to hide a smile. 'So what do you know about Tate?'

'Not much. Dropped out of the army nearly ten years ago. He's had odds and sods as a security consultant since then, but a lot of his time has been spent overseas, pretty much unaccounted for.'

Which, given his history in the army, likely meant he'd either been working as a spook for the British government or as a gun for hire in some war-torn country in Africa or the Middle East.

What had brought him back to London?

'There's only one number on his phone,' Ryker said. 'That's my lead. I need to find out whose it is. It'll be an unregistered burner, so we need to get a trace on it. How long will it take?'

'Half an hour. An hour maybe. But you should really hand in that phone. It's evidence, Ryker.' Willoughby paused. Her expression changed to a mix of worry and exasperation. 'You're not planning on using the phone to call that number, are you?'

Ryker shrugged. 'Quickest way to keep this moving, if you ask me.'

Willoughby sighed and Ryker gave her the time to think through the proposition. He could tell she didn't like it, but she also couldn't think of a better way. Of course it wasn't the way to handle evidence in a police investigation, but the JIA didn't abide by the same rules as regular law enforcement. That was their whole purpose.

'I should really run this by my boss first,' Willoughby said.

'If you feel you need to. Under the circumstances, I think they're going to agree.'

Ryker picked up his cup and drained the last of the coffee from it. He got to his feet.

'Where are you going?' Willoughby asked.

'To find Ffion Brady.'

CHAPTER 38

An hour later, Ryker was sitting in a Lexus GS, a cumbersome luxury saloon car that he'd already concluded was highly impractical for central London's roads and parking spaces. Beggars couldn't be choosers though. He'd found the car as he was walking down the street where the Connors lived, clicking the fob attached to the keys he'd taken from Tate. The Lexus was parked a few cars down the road from the Connors' apartment. He'd jumped in and left Islington without any fuss. The armed police had long since left the area, it seemed, with just a single patrol car parked directly outside the townhouse. No lights had been on in the Connors' apartment, Ryker noticed.

He'd driven the car the short distance north to Crouch End and parked up on a street of Victorian semis, most of which had seen better days. As in Islington, there was a single police patrol car parked on the road.

The journey from Islington was only three or four miles, he hadn't really needed to take the car, but it was there at his disposal so he'd thought why not. He'd wanted to check the vehicle out anyway, in case there were any further clues as to what Tate and his accomplices were up to.

There weren't.

Ryker hadn't long come off the phone with Rod Flowers for an update on Winter. The commander was stable, and conscious, but wasn't in any fit state to be commanding. Flowers didn't exactly seem too on the ball either, but then he had been in the heart of the blast too. If nothing else, he was mentally shaken by the experience, as most people would be. He had at least given Ryker the authority to carry on his work.

Or, to put it more accurately, he hadn't told Ryker to stop.

Ryker had also heard back from Willoughby. The trace had been put onto the number from Tate's phone, but so far there'd been no luck in triangulating the position of the device. The process of remote tracking only worked if the phone was emitting a roaming signal to its local base towers. The device didn't need to be on an active call for that to happen, but it did need to be powered on and in a location to receive a signal. Ryker had since tried calling the number but it hadn't rung through. The phone was off or out of reception.

Or maybe it was lying in pieces somewhere.

Ryker looked up the street, toward the building where apartment 161c was located. Despite the police car across the street, before long he'd be heading inside. That was the plan at least. But then the phone rang. Not his phone but Tate's, the call connected to the Lexus through Bluetooth and coming through the car's speakers. Ryker pushed the button on the steering wheel to reduce the volume while he built himself up to answering. He took a deep breath, trying to recall what Tate, or Schmidt as he'd then believed him to be called, had sounded like. A gravelly, hoarse voice. But then was that just the injuries? Ryker knew he wouldn't get far pretending to be Tate, he just wanted to hear the voice on the other end of the phone, get a chance to speak to whoever the number belonged to. Most importantly he wanted the chance for the trace to pick up the phone's location.

He accepted the call. 'Yeah.'

'Yeah?' came the voice on the other end. 'Is that it? What the hell is happening? We've been waiting two hours for you.'

Ryker froze. That voice. He knew it.

No, it wasn't possible. Yet it sounded just like... no. It couldn't be.

'I got caught up,' Ryker said, trying to sound calm.

Silence on the other end. Ryker could feel his heart racing. The last thing he'd expected was to recognise the voice. And *him*? No. It was just his mind playing a trick, surely. After all, the voice was distorted by the wireless transmission and through being played out of the Lexus's speakers. What Ryker was hearing was probably not even what the guy really sounded like.

So why was Ryker feeling so shaken?

'Had a problem,' Ryker said. He didn't know what else to say. He just wanted to keep the conversation going. He wanted to hear the man speak again so he could place the sound with the face that was now so clear and vivid in his mind.

That face.

Ryker felt himself tense up as anger took hold. 'Did you hear what I said?'

The line went dead.

'Shit!'

Ryker thumped the steering wheel. His brain fired in all directions.

Had the call dropped because of a lost signal? Should he call back? Would the man call back? The man. Could it really be *him*?

Ryker's mind started to take him back to those fateful days, but he wouldn't let it.

The phone in his pocket vibrated. The noise was exactly what Ryker needed to refocus. He took it out and answered.

'You got it?' Ryker asked.

'Yeah,' Willoughby said. 'The phone came on five minutes ago. At least we're presuming that's what happened. Its position was static the whole time until it went dark again just now.'

'And?'

'Not far outside central London. Looks to be at a hotel near Staines.'

Ryker didn't know the area well, but he knew roughly where it was. He looked at his watch. It would take maybe an hour, less if he was lucky with traffic, to drive over there. But then what? He'd just be stuck outside that hotel on a stakeout. And if the man was already spooked because of Ryker answering that call, he could be long gone before Ryker even got close. 'You need to get someone down there right now. Police, JIA, MI5, it doesn't matter. We can't let him get away.'

'Can't let who get away? Ryker, do you know who it is?'

Yes, I do, Ryker thought, but didn't say. 'Just do it. I'll call you back.'

Ryker heard Willoughby protesting as he pulled the phone from his ear and ended the call. He dialled Rod Flowers. The call seemed to ring for an age before it was answered.

'Where are you?' Ryker asked.

'At the hospital still,' Flowers said.

'With Winter?'

'Yeah. What's going on, Ryker? You sound harried.'

'I need to speak to him.'

'Winter? He's sleeping.'

'I don't care. Wake him. He needs to hear this.'

'Is it something you can tell me?'

'I will. But first Winter. Please?'

Flowers sighed but then Ryker heard footsteps followed by muffled voices. Flowers talking to a doctor or a nurse, or perhaps even Winter's wife, explaining why he needed to wake the injured commander so urgently. The voices grew louder and angrier but then after a few moments everything quietened down again.

'Flowers, you still there?' No answer. But then Ryker heard faint breathing coming down the line. 'Winter? Is that you?'

'Fuck's sake, Ryker. Can't I get a bit of peace from you even after being blown up?'

His voice was weak and croaky. Ryker heard Flowers muttering in the background, probably keenly emphasising that he'd been against letting Ryker wake him.

'Sorry, but you have to hear this,' Ryker said.

Winter let out a long sigh. 'What?'

'Flowers updated you on what happened today, right?'

'You mean about Andre Brady? And Evan Tate? Yes, he did.'

'Good. Saves me a job. I've found who Tate is working with. Or for, more likely.'

'Who?'

'That's the thing. It's insane. But I know it's him. I heard his voice.'

'Who, Ryker!'

'The last time I saw him he was lying on the frozen steppes of Kazakhstan, his body riddled with bullets,' Ryker said, though it was to his time training for the JIA, in the Highlands of Scotland, that his mind took him.

'Ryker, what the hell–'

'Winter, it's Captain Fleming. I'm certain of it.'

CHAPTER 39

Ryker felt his leg twinge, the way it did whenever he recalled that day. Ryker had been a young man, barely out of his teens, thrown in with the sharks as part of his gruelling training with the JIA. Captain Fleming and his SAS crew were supposed to help Ryker. Instead they'd bullied and belittled him. Then on their final task – an escape and evasion exercise – Ryker had finally snapped. That night he'd fought with anger and hatred. Fleming was too experienced and too wily. The result was a broken leg for Ryker, and Fleming and the other men had left him out in the frozen Highlands to die.

But Ryker hadn't died. For days, he'd crawled back toward safety, until eventually he was found by a tracking team. As well as the leg break, he'd suffered severe hypothermia. It had taken him months to recover.

Recover? Physically he'd come back stronger than ever. Mentally, that day still felt like a dark cloud hanging over him. He'd never gotten his own back on the captain.

Years later, Fleming, long after leaving the army in disgrace, had crossed paths with Ryker again. On that occasion, with Ryker being hunted across Eastern Europe and Central Asia after a botched JIA mission, Fleming had nearly become an unlikely ally for Ryker, their differences put aside because of a shared foe. Except Ryker should have known better than to trust a snake like Fleming. Instead of helping him, the ex-SAS man had tried to sell Ryker out to the highest bidder.

But he hadn't reckoned on being deceived himself. Rather than receiving the ten million dollars he'd been promised for handing Ryker to the authorities, Fleming's big payday had turned into his day of reckoning. He and his colleagues were gunned down at the exchange in the frozen steppes of Kazakhstan by the rogue agents who were hunting Ryker.

Ryker was one of the few people still alive from that day. He'd always believed that Fleming had died out there.

Could he really have survived against the odds?

Raw anger was building inside Ryker, and a need for revenge. His instincts were screaming at him to pull away from the kerb and head to Staines and storm through that hotel until he found Fleming – and put a bullet in the captain's skull.

As tempting as that was, Ryker had to keep his head. There was a bigger game at play. It wasn't just about Ryker ending a decades-old feud. This was about finding the people responsible for bombing the JIA. Finding the Silver Wolf. Finding Lisa's killers.

Ryker cringed at the stabbing in his brain. Just how were all of the elements connected?

Snapping himself out of his thoughts, Ryker looked at the clock on the Lexus's dashboard. Nearly midnight. Enough contemplation. First briefly touching the olive branch pendant under his shirt – for good luck or comfort? – he put his hand to the door and got out.

The temperature outside had dropped several degrees in the time Ryker had been in the car, and a shiver ran through him as he shut the door and walked. He put his hands in his pockets and sank his head down. The tree-lined residential street was quiet, not a pedestrian in sight. Some of the houses had lights on, but just as many were in darkness. The sporadic street lighting gave everything a dull orange tinge.

Ryker kept alert as he went, his eyes moving between number 161 in the near distance and the police car that was still parked across the road from it. Ryker walked past both and kept on going.

When he was several houses further down, he turned off the pavement and went up the front path of one of the houses.

He'd seen earlier that this one had an open-sided passage to the back. Most other houses had blocked the access off with a wooden or metal gate or a lean-to. Ryker was thankful that, on any given street, there were always some people who were less security conscious than they ought to be. There were also no security lights on the house, and Ryker was soon moving out into the back garden of the property.

He walked to the far end of the lawn without pause, before turning and scaling the fence to the next-door property, heading back the way he'd come. He kept on going, moving with fluidity, barely breaking stride as he hurdled several more fences of varying heights and quality, before he reached the back garden of 161 not much more than a minute later.

Moving more cautiously, Ryker crept closer to the house, alert for any signs of movement either in the garden or beyond the windows of the property. The semi-detached house was no longer a single family home, but three smaller apartments, one on each floor. He assumed 161c was on the top floor. There were lights on in one of the ground floor windows, but nowhere else on the back of the property. Ryker knew someone was home at 161c though. More than one person, he was betting.

When he was five yards from the back wall, a spotlight came on, bathing the area in bright white light. Ryker dashed for the back wall of the house and pushed himself up against it. He waited a minute. Heard and saw nothing. So close to the wall he should be out of view from the windows, unless someone stuck their head out.

He didn't know how long the light would stay on for. Maybe only a minute. Better to keep moving while it was on than to trigger it over and over. Ryker grabbed hold of the metal drainpipe next to him, and using the brackets that attached it to the wall, he quickly climbed up, past the infra-red security sensor and beyond its range, and across to the sloping roof of the small two-storey extension. He came to one of the windows of 161c. It was dark inside and the curtains were drawn, so he had no idea what room this was.

He tapped on the window, just loud enough to get the attention of anyone in there who was awake. He put his ear closer to the glass, but couldn't hear anything on the other side. He tapped again and waited. Still nothing.

It looked like he'd have to try plan B. The windows were wood-framed sashes. With decent jammers, they could be locked tight to prevent what Ryker was about to do. Perhaps, though, because this was the top floor, neither the landlord nor the tenant had felt it necessary to take such measures: Ryker could see there was nothing holding the window shut other than a basic clasp. He dug in his pocket for his tools. It wouldn't be easy jimmying the window, pressed up close to the glass while standing on a sloping tiled roof that was never designed to take anywhere near as much as Ryker weighed. But it was doable with patience and skill.

Ryker had both.

He still had his hand in his pocket when the curtain twitched. The sudden movement made Ryker jerk and he had to grab the ledge of the window frame to keep himself from toppling backward. A hand came around the edge of the curtain and peeled it back. He saw two startled eyes.

Then came a scream and the face disappeared.

Had she recognised him? Either way, Ryker bet that she wasn't about to call the police. She couldn't.

Moments later, the hand again appeared on the curtain and pulled it to the side. The woman's face came back into view. She was shaking, but looked more angry more fearful.

'What do you want?' Clarissa asked, her voice raised.

'Do you think you could let me in?' Ryker kept his own voice quiet.

'What the hell are you doing at my window?'

'Just let me in. I think you know why I'm here.'

He saw the cracks beginning to appear in her face. As much as she wanted to, she couldn't really say no. And if she did, he wasn't going away. He was getting inside one way or another.

Her head down, avoiding eye contact, Clarissa undid the clasp on the window. Ryker helped her to haul it upward. He ducked inside and jumped down, landing on the carpeted floor with a faint thud.

Behind him, Clarissa closed the window, then turned around, arms folded. She was wearing slippers and a long nightgown, but she seemed alert and Ryker didn't get the feeling she'd just been woken. The room they were standing in was an open-plan kitchen, diner and lounge. The only light in the room was coming from out in the hallway.

'So where is she?' Ryker asked.

'Who?'

'Come on, Clarissa, I'm not an idiot. Why didn't you call the police just now, when you saw a strange man outside your window in the middle of the night?'

'How do you know I haven't?'

'Because there's a patrol car on the street just yards away. How long would it take them to get over here? Do you hear any sirens? Any shouts from the police? Any knocks on the front door?'

'Just who *are* you?' she asked, her voice not hiding her disgust, though Ryker wasn't sure what exactly she was disgusted about. 'I thought earlier, when you left the apartment, that maybe *you* were police. Undercover. But now, turning up in the night like this–'

'I know you're scared, Clarissa. But I'm not here to hurt you. I think you know that. I'm just looking for answers. Let's drop the act. I know she's here. So where?'

'I'm right here.'

Ryker's gaze flicked over to the figure moving into the doorway, wearing jeans and a hooded top. With the light behind her, her front in shadow, it was hard to make out her features clearly, but Ryker could see enough to know exactly who he was looking at. Ffion Brady.

CHAPTER 40

Was Ryker surprised Ffion Brady gave her up presence so easily? Yes and no. What was clear was that she'd found herself in a situation that was way out of her comfort zone. Quite how she'd gotten dragged so far in, Ryker didn't know. Yet it was apparent that even after just a few hours on the run she was close to caving and giving herself up. Her husband was dead, and she had nowhere to go and no one to help her. Ryker intended to play on that as much as he could.

'I can't believe they killed him,' Ffion said, sobbing into her hands.

Ryker said nothing to that, but he thought, how had she really expected the situation to pan out? She'd got in with a group of people who were prepared to kill in order to achieve their aims – whatever those aims were – and she was acting like it had never crossed her mind that there could be grave consequences.

'I need to know who they are,' Ryker said. They were sitting in the lounge area of Clarissa's home; Ryker in an armchair, Ffion on a sofa. Clarissa was at the dining table, within earshot but not taking part in the conversation.

'I honestly don't know much about them.'

'Names?'

Ffion shook her head. 'Henderson was the main guy.'

'Henderson? First name?'

'I don't know.'

'You don't know?'

'No! Look, I don't... It's hard to explain.'

'Is it? Or is it hard for you to say it out loud. You're in denial. It's time for you to step up and take responsibility here. What made you do it? Money?'

Ryker realised his tone was hardly going to get her on side, but he wasn't there to comfort her.

'No.' Ffion looked up, giving him a steely glare. At least the sobbing mess was gone for now. 'It wasn't just about money.'

'Not *just* money. So what else.'

'I *hate* the JIA,' she said with genuine anger. '*They* ruined our lives. It's because of them that Andre wound up paralysed. And they washed their hands of it, pretended it never happened, expected me to carry on working for them like everything was the same. It wasn't the fucking same. Have you any idea what Andre's injuries did to *us*?'

How were the JIA responsible? Ryker didn't know, but he didn't question it. He wanted her to rant. He wanted her to vent all of that frustration and anger, because in doing so, she might well tell all.

Apparently Clarissa didn't get that. 'What are you talking about?'

Ffion looked over to her.

Ryker didn't. He just carried on studying Ffion. 'Andre was hurt in a motorbike accident.'

Ffion scoffed. 'An accident? Yeah, that's the story they made us tell. There was no accident. We were attacked, because of my job. In our own home. Two men broke in and they tried to kidnap me. Andre... why... I don't know why he did it. He wanted to protect me, but look where it got him. They beat him, they stabbed him in the back. It was a miracle he survived, the doctors said. A miracle? It's been more like a curse.'

The room fell silent. Ryker gave Ffion the time to say more but she didn't. He turned to Clarissa. 'Could you leave us? I've a feeling we're going to cover territory here that you really don't want to know about. For your own sake.'

Clarissa seemed to come to that conclusion pretty quickly too and got up from the table. 'I'll be in my room.' As she walked over, she put her hand onto Ffion's shoulder, before moving on out of the room.

'She's so kind,' Ffion said, with just the faintest of smiles. 'She's been the glue that kept me and Andre together.'

'It's why I knew you'd come here,' Ryker said. 'But it wasn't the plan, was it? So where were you headed?'

'It doesn't matter now.' She hung her head. 'I wanted to see him. Even though I knew he was dead, I just wanted to see him, to be near him. I can't believe I'll never be able to do that again.'

No, this wasn't good. He could see the guilt and the hurt building in her eyes. He didn't want Ffion the emotional wreck back, he wanted Ffion the vengeful wife.

'You're just a data analyst,' Ryker said. 'Why did someone want to kidnap you?'

'I don't know! But the JIA washed their hands of it. They gave us a token pay-out and made us sign all sorts of agreements about what we could and couldn't say, and what would happen to us if we did talk. Then they left us to it, just carried on like nothing had happened. Our lives were devastated.'

Ryker could well imagine the hatred she was feeling. It was an all-too-familiar feeling for him. Someone had exploited that vulnerability in her, but how had that someone even known the truth?

The answer was simple. The same people who had originally attacked Ffion – who had attacked the JIA by trying to kidnap her – were probably the same people who later came back to offer her a means of revenge. The JIA was the target, not Ffion. She was just a pawn.

'What were you investigating?' Ryker asked. 'Before the attack.'

Ffion stared at Ryker but in the end she said nothing.

'You can tell me,' Ryker said. 'I'm with the JIA. You can trust me.'

'Trust you? I never trusted anyone in that organisation. Not even before I was attacked, and certainly not now.'

'Was it the Silver Wolf? Was that who you were investigating?'

Ffion said nothing but he saw the look in her eyes. A look that suggested a painful connection to that name.

'I'm looking for the Silver Wolf too,' Ryker said. 'If there's anything you can tell me about him, now's the time.'

'I've no idea what you're talking about.'

Did she really expect him to buy that?

'What do you know about Thomas Maddison?' Ryker asked. 'He was a JIA agent.'

Ffion simply shrugged. Was that a genuine reaction? The Silver Wolf had seemed to mean something to her, so why not Maddison? But then she hadn't known about Ryker either, and he'd been a JIA agent for nearly twenty years.

'The data you deleted at the Hive, what was it?'

He saw surprise on her face. So far they'd only talked about the bomb. Perhaps she'd not realised her antics at the Hive had also been uncovered.

'I don't know.'

Once again, Ryker sensed she was holding back.

'Did you take any data with you? Hand it over to Henderson or anyone else?'

'I took some files, but not for them. Just some random files so as to not raise suspicion in the staff at the Hive.'

'And you don't know what data was deleted or why.'

'That's what I said.'

'I know that's what you said, but I also know it's not the truth.'

Ffion said nothing but he could sense he was losing her. She wasn't far from closing up altogether and Ryker knew he had little leverage, unless he was prepared to step up the interrogation.

'Let me make this simple for you. There're only three potential outcomes for you now, and one of those isn't that you escape and live a life of freedom, so get any notion of that out of your head. One, the JIA catch up with you and they simply execute you. In the middle of the night like they've had me do countless times...' He saw her squirm at that. 'Most likely, because of the public nature of what happened today, they'll hang you out to dry and you'll spend the rest of your life in jail. But, the third outcome is that Henderson, or whoever he works for, catches up with you first. And you must know they'll kill you. Maybe it will be quick, but very possibly it won't be. And don't think just because you're in jail that they'll stop looking for you. These are people who are ballsy enough to take on an organisation like the JIA. High walls and barbed wire won't stop them coming for you.'

'Thanks for the stark reminder.'

'I can't stop the JIA or the police. But I can stop the bad guys.'

'Who says the JIA aren't the bad guys?'

Ffion locked eyes with Ryker and neither blinked for a good few seconds.

'Tell me everything you can, and I promise I'll find Henderson and anyone working with him. I'll stop them.'

Ffion didn't say anything. Ryker took his phone out of his pocket. He went into the internet browser and pulled up the image he'd earlier found of Fleming, taken from a press story not long after he'd been booted out of the army. The picture was more than ten years old, he was no doubt even more gnarled now, but he should still be recognisable if she knew him.

Ryker stood up and took the phone over to Ffion and held it out so she could see the screen. 'Do you know this man?'

Ffion's eyes narrowed, and he saw both anger and loathing there. 'Yes. That's Henderson.'

CHAPTER 41

Ryker pulled shut the front door of the building and walked down the path to the street. His eyes focused in on the dark interior of the police patrol car across the street. With the illumination from the streetlights, he could just about make out their faces, the white of their teeth and their wide-open eyes. He smiled to himself.

One of the officers was speaking into her handset radio, the other thrust open his door and got out of the car, glaring over to Ryker, who just kept on walking. He wondered what they would do. Would they confront him?

The dilemma that Ryker knew was running through the police officers' heads was neatly solved for them just a few seconds later when Ryker heard the clunk of a lock releasing and then the wheeze as the front door opened a second time. He slowed and looked over his shoulder to see Ffion Brady emerging from the house. By the defeated look on her face and her slumped posture she wasn't about to wage a stand-off, she'd simply realised she had no other sensible option but to hand herself in.

The woman police officer jumped from the car too, and both of them shouted instructions to Ffion as they edged forward, Ryker eliminated from their thoughts in an instant. That was fine by him. He picked up his pace and kept on going to the Lexus. No doubt half the Met would soon be descending on Clarissa's apartment. Ryker wanted to be well away by then. He hit the ignition button and pulled out into the road, then headed away, into the night.

Although he was satisfied that the JIA bomber had been found so quickly, Ryker was still left with plenty to ponder following his encounter with Ffion Brady. Her attempted kidnapping years before. The data deletion at the Hive, the bombing. Was there a connection between those events and the disappearance of JIA asset Maddison, aka the Silver Wolf? Ryker felt sure there was. He was far from having the full picture, but the Silver Wolf, if only in name, was the one thing connecting everything that was happening.

After five minutes of working the ideas through his mind as he headed west out of London toward Staines, Ryker put a call in to Willoughby. She sounded harried.

'What's up?' Ryker asked.

'Shit, Ryker, it's all going off tonight.'

'Yeah?'

'The police lines are on fire. I just heard Ffion Brady gave herself up. And I'm guessing the mysterious man seen exiting the house where she was hiding, just moments before she did, is you?'

'I told you I was going to find her.'

'You did.'

'So why do you sound so surprised?'

'I know, I shouldn't really. Not when you're involved.'

'I think that's a compliment. So what's got you all excited then?'

'Not excited. Anxious. There was no one else available, the police weren't interested given the little I was prepared to tell them, so I've had to stake out for this Henderson guy myself.'

That wasn't necessarily a bad thing, Ryker decided. He knew Willoughby was good, and in his experience the fewer field operatives involved in JIA matters the better. Less chance for crossed wires, less chance of stepping on toes and really just less chance of mistakes.

'I know him,' Ryker said.

'Henderson?'

'Ex-army. SAS to be precise. His real name is Chris Fleming. Except he's been presumed dead for the best part of two years.

Ryker pulled the car to a stop at a set of traffic lights. A police car pulled up alongside. Ryker glanced over. The driver caught his eye for a second, and Ryker was busy preparing himself for a problem when the officer turned his focus back to the road. No, the police weren't after him. They had their catch.

'Last time I saw Fleming he had several bullet holes in him.' The lights turned green and Ryker pulled away.

'Which might explain why I've had so much trouble identifying him based on his name and his description. I was just going to blame the fact that all our best analysts are in hospital right now. Or, in Ffion Brady's case, in police custody.'

'No. This is a guy who knows about how we operate. He worked with us and the other intelligence agencies for years. He knows how to avoid being on our radar. I also now firmly believe there was a specific target.'

'Who?'

'Peter Winter. Henderson – Fleming – wants him dead. Probably because he blames Winter and the JIA for what happened to him. Me too for that matter.'

Which made Ryker step back from the puzzle again for a second. If Fleming were alive and intent on seeking vengeance, he would surely have Ryker on his target list too.

And there again was the connection to the Silver Wolf, and Lisa's death. He'd first come across the Silver Wolf through hunting for Lisa's killers. Was it all Fleming? Had *he* killed Lisa?

Ryker had to fight hard to keep his rage bottled inside him. He had to keep his focus. Then the sound of sirens caught his attention. He saw flashing blue lights up ahead. Two cars. Actually, no it was three, hurtling toward him. Ryker held his breath. Like moments before, he didn't believe the cars were coming for him, but he had to at least prepare for the possibility.

But they went speeding past. Ryker watched in his rear view mirror for a couple of seconds. No sign of brake lights. Soon the blue flashes were fading into the night. Okay, so maybe those cars weren't after him, but given the day's events – his presence both at the Connors' house and at Clarissa's, and the fact he'd stolen the vehicle he was driving in – he couldn't presume he was in the clear just yet. He'd have to remain vigilant.

'Ryker, are you still there?'

'Yeah.' Ryker picked up on the road noise in the background. 'Are you driving somewhere? I thought you were staking out.'

'That's what I was trying to tell you. This Henderson guy, or Fleming or whatever he's called, he left the hotel almost as soon as he finished that call with you. Luckily a patrol car already had him in their sights and I've now taken up tailing him.'

'You're still following?'

'I am.'

Ryker sighed. That wasn't ideal. A simple tail, particularly in the middle of the night, would be very hard to keep up without alerting him. 'Where are you headed?'

'At first I thought it was Heathrow, if he's behind the bombing then it would make sense that he's now scarpering.'

'I'm sensing a but?'

'But we just kept going on the M25. We're still on the motorway, south of London.'

'Gatwick?'

'That'd be my next best guess.'

Ryker wasn't letting Fleming get away. Not again. He hit the brakes and the Lexus's tyres crunched as it jolted to a stop. He swung the car around a hundred and eighty degrees.

'I'm on my way.'

CHAPTER 42

The night-time – or was it now early morning? – traffic was kind to Ryker, and less than an hour and a half later, he pulled the Lexus into the multi-storey car park outside Gatwick's North Terminal building. He'd had the radio on the whole way there. Every news broadcast he'd heard was playing the same story – about the capture of the Vauxhall Bomber, as Ffion Brady had been dubbed.

Ryker wound the car around the car park until he found a space on the third floor. He left the keys inside then stepped out and walked to the stairwell. He wasn't sure how long the car would be staying, but it was Henderson and his cronies who'd be picking up the likely exorbitant bill, should they ever come back for the vehicle.

Ryker phoned Willoughby again as he headed through the glass doors of the terminal building. 'I'm here,' he said.

'I see you. Look left.'

Ryker did so and spotted Willoughby fifty yards away, sitting at a high stool in a coffee bar, a tiny espresso cup in her hand. She was casually dressed in jeans and sweatshirt. Her hair was loose, closely framing her face, and she had a cap on her head. A pretty basic attempt at being incognito, but then she hadn't had time to prepare anything more elaborate. She was at least trying to keep a low profile. The last thing they wanted was for Henderson to be further spooked. Which was why Ryker also bought a cap from a stall in the airport, then walked over to Willoughby with his head down. Fleming knew Ryker after all. If the two locked eyes, there would be no doubt and no chase, it would be battle. Ryker wasn't completely against that, but it wouldn't get him all the answers he needed.

'You look like you need some sleep,' Willoughby said as Ryker took a seat on the stool next to her.

'I'm sure I'll get the chance eventually. Did you get the equipment yet?'

'No.' She looked at her watch. 'He's five minutes late. Boarding isn't for another forty-five though.'

Not satisfied with simply tailing Fleming to wherever he was headed, Ryker had requested Willoughby put an urgent call in to her colleagues for some tracking equipment. Micro-trackers just a few millimetres wide and paper-thin that could be stuck onto a target's clothing or belongings. In the end, the request had to be passed on to MI5 due to the lack of available resource at the JIA. The situation wasn't ideal. MI5 would no doubt be taking a long, hard look at what Willoughby was up to and may well try to scupper the plan, particularly given the disarray the JIA was in.

Willoughby's phone buzzed on the table. 'This should be him.' She picked up the phone and looked at the screen, then without saying a word she got up from the table and walked purposefully back toward the doors Ryker had moments earlier come through.

He spied on her as she went, keeping a keen eye not just on her but the people all around. She walked outside. Through the glass walls, Ryker still had a good view of her from where he was sitting. She turned right and walked another fifty yards along the pavement, then turned and came back into the terminal building through the next set of doors. She turned again and walked back to Ryker. He smiled as she approached. She was quite the mover. Ninety-nine per cent of people wouldn't have spotted the exchange even if they were looking closely. But Ryker had.

With Willoughby still walking toward him, Ryker turned his attention back outside to the man who'd slipped the equipment into Willoughby's hand. He wanted to make sure the guy was alone, and wasn't lurking.

A moment later, he was pleased to see the man step into a taxi which promptly pulled away and headed out of sight.

Willoughby reached Ryker and picked up her espresso cup, draining the last remaining drops of her drink. 'Four stickies.'

'What's the plan?'

'MI5 helped me to figure out which flight he's on.'

'We're on his flight?'

'No. There was no space, and knowing we were getting the trackers I didn't think it was worth calling in favours with the airline to get us onto that plane.'

'He's headed to Milan?'

'If we let him.'

'If?'

Ryker saw the look of unease on her face. 'We could just haul him in.'

'No' Ryker said, hoping his bluntness would cut off the prospect. It didn't.

'If you think he's the mastermind behind the bombing then why take the chance that we lose him?' She sounded exasperated. 'Even if he doesn't know we're onto him, once he's out of the country all bets are off. You must know that.'

Ryker sighed. He'd expected her sense of reason to take her down this road sooner or later. It was good that she was prepared to question him. He couldn't claim to be infallible. But he really wasn't going to be swayed.

'No,' Ryker said. 'Unless we're planning on kidnapping and torturing him, the only other option is to hand him to the police. He's not going to give them anything. We need to follow him, find who he's working with ourselves.'

'Is that really what you want? Or do you want to follow him until you spot the opportunity to take him out?'

Ryker didn't like the way she said that, as though he was simply a bloodthirsty mercenary. As though killing Fleming, if that became an option, was the wrong thing to do.

'You're a JIA field agent,' he said. 'You know how this works.'

'Yes, and I'm more than willing to get my hands dirty under direct orders. But that's not what's happening here, is it? This is just a personal mission for you.'

'You're saying we don't have authority for this? That's your problem?'

'I'm really not sure. I've been told that Peter Winter has given *you* authority to track Henderson and do whatever's necessary.'

'Then what's the issue? The word of a JIA commander isn't good enough for you?'

He could see Willoughby was getting angered by his tone and his push back, but what did she expect? It felt like she wasn't just questioning his motives but his whole drive for being there.

'I didn't say it wasn't good enough,' she said. 'I'm just questioning whether your approach is the right one. It would be remiss of me to say nothing when I see a viable alternative.'

'Okay, got it. Thanks for alerting me, but your alternative isn't actually viable.'

Willoughby tutted. 'I can see why you worked so many missions solo in the past.'

Ryker winked at her. 'That's because no one else gets the job done quite like me.'

Ryker saw her holding back a smile.

After a moment, it broke through. 'Nobody does it better,' she half said, half sang.

'Makes you feel sad for the rest.'

Willoughby held up her hand. 'Okay, that's enough. No need for a full rendition.'

'No, you really don't want that. I'm a terrible singer.' Ryker looked at his watch. 'How much time have we got?'

'Not long before he'll be boarding. Our flight is a couple of hours later.'

'Okay. Got passport, will travel. So let's do this.'

CHAPTER 43

Lake Maggiore, Italy

Draper was sitting with Angelica in the main living room at the front of Villa Mariangela. Facing north, the room was one of the coolest in the house, with a few hours of morning sun but shaded in the afternoon and evening. Which was exactly why Draper was in there. Like any other youngster, Angelica was biochemically predisposed to tantrums. Having blazed around outside in the heat for the best part of an hour, she was sweating buckets and weary, but had insisted she was fine and wanted to stay outdoors. Draper put his foot down about that. Cue theatrics; screaming, shouting, stomping, for the best part of thirty minutes, until he'd finally persuaded her to come into the lounge for a milkshake and a story with Daddy.

She was on his lap, slurping away at the frothy pink liquid, still red-faced and bleary-eyed and damp with sweat, while he read her a book about a young dragon who strangely seemed to carry many traits of Draper's daughter. Was that just because all kids were fire-breathing tyrants?

They never got to finish the book. Draper heard the double set of footsteps on the tiles out in the hallway and he guessed who it was. His irritation peaked. Not at the knowledge that his time with Angelica was once again about to be interrupted – he was well used to that – but at the conversation he knew was about to take place once his daughter left the room.

A knock came at the closed double doors. Draper stopped reading. Angelica looked up at him, that familiar look of disappointment on her face.

'We'll finish it later,' he said.

'Promise?'

'Absolutely.'

The knock came again. He heard muffled voices on the other side of the door.

'Come in,' he shouted as Angelica jumped off his lap.

The doors swung open and sure enough there were Clyde and Henderson. Both men looked seriously irritated, though Clyde did a much better job of hiding it. In fact a casual observer would probably think his face was entirely impassive, but Draper knew Clyde better than anyone and could read even the tiniest changes in the stoic man's features.

Behind them, Draper spotted Estella scurrying over. She too had well-honed senses and seemed to know exactly when she was needed. She scooted past the two men and Angelica, milkshake in hand, walked over to her, appearing oblivious to the heightened tension in the room.

'Come on, dear, let's go finish that milkshake in the kitchen,' Estella said, taking the girl by her hand.

Clyde closed the doors behind them. Draper got to his feet.

Henderson opened his mouth to speak. 'Let me explain–' was all he had the chance to say.

Draper's eye caught Clyde's, a fraction of a second before Clyde whipped his hands behind him, and they came back out holding a cheese wire. He reached up and behind Henderson and wound the wire around and tugged on the wooden handles. Henderson, caught unawares, had just enough time to thrust his hand up and wedge his wrist between his neck and the thin piece of metal. Clyde jerked back and Henderson's face screwed up in both pain and determination as he fought to keep the wire from slicing into his neck and garrotting him.

Both men were soon grunting and panting as each tugged and pulled. Draper could see the wire digging further and further into the skin on Henderson's wrist, blood dripping out and down his arm.

'You fucked up,' Draper said, locking eyes with him.

'No!' Henderson said. 'I can explain.'

With a burst of strength Henderson bent forward, taking Clyde off his feet, leaving him dangling on Henderson's back. He then surged backward and slammed Clyde against the doors. But Clyde was made of tougher stuff than that. He barely even seemed to notice. Just concentrated on pulling the wire tighter and tighter.

Henderson was far from finished either though. With Clyde still struggling to get his feet back on the floor, Henderson lurched forward, ducking further down and twisting, and Clyde went straight over the top of him. Clyde still didn't let go of the wire, and he took Henderson with him as he headed for the floor. The impact as he smacked onto the tiles caused his grip to loosen just slightly and Henderson, on top of Clyde on the floor but with his back to the younger man, quickly pulled his arm free from the wire. He used both his elbows to pummel Clyde, whose grip faltered further after just a few seconds.

Draper just stood there, watching it all. He hadn't expected Henderson to go down easily. Far from it. He was actually intrigued to see where the fight would go. Clyde was nothing short of a machine, but Henderson was well-trained, former SAS, and fought with animal instinct.

Moments later, Henderson had somehow worked the wire from around his neck, and he was on his feet and had one of Clyde's arms twisted into a lock. He pulled back his fist, ready to deliver to a blow that would snap the arm in two.

'Enough!' Draper shouted.

Henderson's arm twitched. He was snarling as he looked down at Clyde. Despite the precarious position, Clyde was looking back at him almost untroubled, as though it didn't matter one bit that his arm was about to be shattered. He was probably planning his next move.

'What the fuck is this?' Henderson snarled. He still gripped Clyde's arm and the younger man lay there and took it, waiting for his boss to speak.

'You thought you could just walk back in here and everything would be fine?' Draper asked. 'After what happened in London?'

'No. But I didn't expect your little bitch to try and kill me!'

'So dramatic.' Draper frowned. 'Who said I want to kill you?'

'Then what the fuck is this?'

'A message.' Draper nodded to Clyde who twisted his whole body around on the floor, like a break-dancer, in order to untwist his arm. He bounced up onto his feet, swivelled, and a second later, the position was an exact reverse of what it had been moments earlier. Henderson, looking dazed and confused, was now on the floor, his arm in the air, twisted to bursting point by Clyde who stood over him. One of Clyde's shoulders protruded awkwardly out of the back of his shirt where he'd dislocated the joint in order to pull off the move, though his features still remained calm – in fact popping his arms out of their sockets was nothing more than a gruesome party trick of his.

'You said you could explain,' Draper said. 'Now would be the time to do that.'

'London was a fuck-up,' Henderson said, grimacing. 'I admit it. I didn't plan for it to go down like that.'

'Wow, seriously? I'd never have guessed.'

Henderson huffed. 'There's no link from the explosion back to you,' he said. 'Brady won't talk, and if the police have anything it'll only lead them to me. But, like you, I don't exist either, remember?'

'No link back to me?' Draper scoffed. 'Except you're in my house. So if anyone is now looking for you, they're going to find me, aren't they, you bloody imbecile.'

'It won't come to that.'

'I admire your confidence but you're talking out of your arsehole.'

'No, I'm not. The explosion will divert attention. All of the data, that was the target. It's all gone. The UK security services have nothing on you now.'

'Nothing except an unexplained bombing.'

'We have to get that bitch Ffion Brady. She's the one who screwed up. And she's the only one who can pin this on me. I can still sort this.'

'How exactly?'

'I'll go back to London. I'll kill her.'

'Haven't you heard? The police have her! How on earth are you going to do that now?'

'I'll get it done. Trust me.'

'Trust you?' Draper's words hung uncomfortably in the air. 'So once again you swan off to do your own thing, your own way? I'm beginning to wonder exactly what your agenda is here.'

Draper saw a flicker of unease on Henderson's face at that statement.

'There's no agenda. I'm trying to help you.'

Draper thought about that one for a few moments. 'No. You're not going back to England.'

'But–'

'No buts. We need to get the deal with the Sheik done, because I'm starting to worry he's playing me along. When that's sorted, we'll discuss how to properly clean up your mess.'

Henderson didn't say anything, though Draper could tell he was pissed off. Draper's eyes flicked up to Clyde. 'Let him go.'

Clyde did so and Henderson pulled himself back to his feet, clutching at his arm that had been twisted to bursting and was covered in blood from the wire. There was a line of bright red around his neck too.

Draper's eyes narrowed as he stared at his man. Yes, he was fast losing patience with Henderson, and the small element of doubt in his mind that maybe Henderson was playing him was growing by the day. But the fact remained that Henderson knew far more about the intelligence community than Draper. Henderson had assured Draper he would help to keep the police and spooks away from their operations. His style was unorthodox to say the least, but with his knowledge and connections, he remained an asset, as long as Draper could keep him reined in – not an easy task.

'Get yourself cleaned up,' Draper said to both men. 'Then come back here and we'll figure out exactly what we need to do next.'

At that, Henderson gave a smarmy grin, as though he felt he was still in command of the situation. Draper felt his muscles clench.

Or maybe the best course was to just get rid of the prick after all? Because if Henderson looked at him like that one more time, it would surely be the last.

CHAPTER 44

Ryker was lying in long grass on a cliff top overlooking the glorious Lake Maggiore. The sun was high up in the azure sky, its warm rays only elevating the impressive scenery further. Fleming, or Henderson as he now called himself, had certainly stepped up in the world since Ryker had last crossed paths with him in the frozen wastelands of Kazakhstan. The Italian setting was simply... breath-taking.

Planting the trackers on Fleming had been simple. Or so Willoughby had said. Ryker had hung well back in the airport, not even heading through security until Fleming was already on his flight. There was no point in jeopardising the chase so early. Willoughby had moved through to departures alone, and had placed two of the four trackers on Fleming; one on his shirt and one on a rucksack he was carrying.

Once Ryker and Willoughby had landed in Milan several hours later, they'd been able to easily follow the signals from the two trackers to Lake Maggiore.

Ryker took his gaze from the lake and the rolling hills and the white lavish villas and expensive yachts, and put his eye to the telephoto lens of the camera he was holding.

Villa Mariangela was several hundred yards away, and Ryker had been lying in the grass spying for over two hours. When he'd first arrived in Italy he'd felt fresh and somewhat revitalised, both from the few hours' sleep he'd managed to get before and during the flight from Gatwick, but also because of the setting he found himself in. But lying still in the grass in the heat for so long was making him feel sleepy. He needed some action to wake up.

Ryker twisted the scope to the right and focused on the *Angelica*. The yacht had been moored at the bottom of the cliff above Villa Mariangela before its owner had taken it out for a spin just over an hour earlier, and now it was slowly approaching its berth once more. Ryker focused in on the man on the top deck, the yacht's wheel in his hand. Ryker clicked on the camera twice more.

'Have you got anything for me yet?' Ryker asked.

'Just a minute,' Willoughby answered, her voice playing through the bud in Ryker's right ear.

She was back in a hotel in the small city of Varese, just a few miles south of the lake. They didn't need two of them out there, exposed. A dongle attached to Ryker's camera instantly transmitted the pictures he took to Willoughby. She was better employed being in the hotel with her laptop and her internet and telephone connections, able to quickly ping the numerous pictures Ryker was taking to her contacts to try and identify the various parties at play.

She was missing out, though, because lying on the cliff top was one of the best jobs Ryker had had in a long time.

'Okay, I'm starting to get some results coming through now,' Willoughby said. 'The house is registered in the name of a Jonathan Andrews, English national, but there are no records on him in any official database.'

Ryker's eye was still on the man on the top deck of the *Angelica*. He already had an inkling this was the man in charge by the body language of those around him. So was he Andrews?

'Ah, but here's something,' Willoughby continued. 'The young girl you spotted playing outside, her name is Angelica Primoli. Her mother was Natasha Primoli; she passed away two years ago. Father is recorded as unknown at birth, but according to school records her next of kin is a Lawrence Draper.'

Ryker was impressed. Where the hell was Willoughby pulling all this data? He thought about the girl. When he had first seen her playing on the grass outside the villa, his heart had sunk. He wouldn't launch an attack on the villa lightly, knowing a child was there not just as a witness but potential collateral damage.

He worked the other information over in his mind. Were Andrews and Draper the same or different men? Then he remembered.

'It all fits,' Ryker said. 'Remember the English businessman from Sicily I told you about? Nicholas Andrews?'

'Yeah, you said he's dead.'

'Here we have Jonathan Andrews. You said the girl is Angelica? The same name as the boat?'

'Yeah.'

'Mother Natasha?'

'Yeah.

'Natasha, which is the same name as the boat I told you about. The one that used to be called *Il Lupo Grigio*. The one that belonged to Nicholas Andrews in Sicily before he died.'

'Except he's not dead, is he?' Willoughby said. 'And the boat is still going strong too by the sound of it. They've both just got different names.'

But where was the connection to Maddison and the Silver Wolf?

There was silence on the line for a few seconds. The *Angelica* came to rest at the jetty underneath Villa Mariangela. Ryker watched as the three men on board climbed off and walked along the jetty toward the building there. It looked like it had once been a simple boathouse, but it was now a modern glass-fronted villa in its own right.

Ryker clicked away on the camera. Along with the boss, there was one man whose identity Ryker didn't yet know. The third man was Fleming. He looked less confident than he had done at Gatwick, and had a red ring around his neck. What the hell was that all about?

'Okay,' Willoughby said. 'I've got something else here, just give me a second.'

The three men disappeared into the boathouse, and Ryker swivelled the camera up and along the grounds of the property.

He couldn't see anyone else in sight, though earlier had spotted two females who he guessed were housemaids, judging by their uniforms, as well as several casually dressed men. Security, he presumed. Though they weren't particularly overt. No assault rifles slung over their shoulders, no anti-stab or bulletproof vests. They didn't wear earpieces or have any visible equipment, except for the small bulges under their shirts that showed they were armed. It was discreet security. The villa wasn't an armed fort. It was a home.

'Right, the owner, the guy on the boat,' Willoughby said, 'facial recognition suggests he really is Nicholas Andrews. According to official records, he's been dead for five years. He was under investigation for tax evasion in Sicily but there's nothing in the system linking him to any other illegal activity, nor is his face associated with any other profiles, so he's kept himself pretty much under the radar since he died.'

Ryker scoffed. 'So what's his name now then?'

'Judging by the records I'm finding, I'd say he has several. Andrews. Henderson. Draper. Maddison. Montana.'

'All the same names, just recycled between him and his closest allies.'

'It creates a hell of a lot of unconnected trails, that's for sure.'

'Let's call him Draper. I'd say he's definitely the father of the girl, and therefore I'd say he's the owner of the property too. He's our leader.'

'Agreed. He's in charge here.'

'What about the others?'

'Not much else yet. A lot of the security guys are mercenaries. Mostly UK citizens, a couple Irish. One Italian. One South African.'

'How does Fleming figure in this picture?' Ryker asked, more to himself than to Willoughby. She must have sensed that too, because she didn't attempt an answer.

'The younger man,' Willoughby said, and Ryker knew which one she was talking about. He was tall, slim and smartly dressed in suit trousers and a tight-fitting dress shirt with tie. His manner was so rigid it looked like he walked with a plank of wood strapped to his back. He was clean-shaven with glasses and an almost inexpressive face. He certainly looked a world away from Fleming and the other mercenaries.

'You mean the stiff?'

Willoughby laughed. 'He does look kind of stiff, doesn't he? In a Clark Kent, ultra geeky sort of way.'

'Clark Kent. You nailed it.'

'I've found nothing on him.'

'Come again?'

'Nothing. I've found nothing. His face doesn't match any profile in any database we've access to.'

'Odd. You don't think–'

'It's possible he's undercover. An asset of another agency.'

'Try to find out. If that's what he is, then he's our way in.'

'And if he's not?'

'Then he's one to be wary of. I don't like dealing with people I can't size up in a few seconds, but I can't get a reading on that guy... Hang on, we've got action.'

Ryker took the lens away from his eye for a second and stared over to the villa. The blurry image slowly came into focus as he gave his eyes a rest from staring into the lens. Even without the glass to his face, he could see the grounds were buzzing with activity all of a sudden. The three men emerged from the boathouse and traipsed up the steps.

Above them, four security guards came out of the main house, two milling about in the garden, and two walking around to the front of the property. From where he was, Ryker couldn't see the front of the house, but he could see the gates to the property that lay beyond, and most of the large turning circle of the driveway.

That was where Fleming and Draper and the mystery man all headed, walking side by side with Draper, the boss, in the middle.

'What is it?' Willoughby asked.

Ryker put his eye back to the lens and was once again clicking away on the camera as the gates began to swing open in the distance.

'Visitors,' Ryker said. 'And someone important, I'd say, given the welcoming party.'

As the gates continued to open, Ryker spotted the vehicles on the other side. First was a long, black limousine. All its windows were heavily tinted and Ryker could see nothing of who was inside. Following the limo in was a bright yellow soft-top Ferrari. That was handy. With the vehicle nearside on to Ryker he had a perfectly clear view of the two men inside, both wearing traditional Arab headdress.

'Okay, these two you're about to see, I'm going to need IDs ASAP.'

Ryker continued to click away as the two vehicles came to a stop. The doors to the limo opened and four men emerged, though Ryker didn't spend much time on them. It was the driver of the Ferrari he was most focused on – he was already out of the car and was walking up to Draper, his hand held out in greeting.

'Bloody hell, Ryker, I know him,' Willoughby said.

'You know him?'

'I'm still running the picture to be sure but yeah, I'm know him. Sheik Falah, hails from Qatar. He's worth something like ten billion dollars.'

'And you know him how?'

'Before I was sent to Mexico, one of my first assignments was in the Middle East. He's been a known player in weapons smuggling for years.'

'Years? The JIA has had a known weapons smuggler on their radar for years? So why is he still swanning around in a Ferrari in Italy then?'

'Because we turned him. Last thing I knew, Sheik Falah was a JIA asset.'

CHAPTER 45

Monte Carlo, Monaco

Ryker checked his watch. Nearly two a.m.

'Just be patient,' Willoughby said.

Ryker looked over at her, sitting on the stool next to him at the bar. With her long sequinned black dress, high heels and her silky hair neatly coifed, she looked every bit the wealthy and glamorous socialite she was pretending to be. Ryker wore a black suit with open-necked white shirt. Willoughby had complimented him on the look though he felt oafish and clumsy in it.

They'd been inside the grand Casino de Monte Carlo for over three hours. Willoughby had pulled out all the stops to try to get them full access to the facilities but the security was tight, and it was clear the private rooms were an absolute no-go. They'd settled for the Salle Médecin, jumping between the roulette and blackjack tables and the bar, keeping an eye on the closed double doors that led into the most private of private rooms the casino had, where Sheik Falah and his entourage were enjoying the entertainment on offer.

'How much are you down?' Ryker sipped on a glass of beer that had cost a small fortune.

'Actually I'm up,' she said, giving him a cheeky smile. 'Two hundred euros. Beginner's luck perhaps.'

'Looks like you're paying for the drinks then.'

'Looks like it, yeah.'

Ryker glanced across the floor that was only just beginning to quieten down now that the night was edging closer to an end. It was the first time he'd been to the casino, but his time in other high-end establishments around the world meant everything felt familiar, from its striking façade to its bohemian chandeliers, rococo ceilings and the columned gold-and-marble main atrium. The room they were in was no less impressive, with lashings of gold and crystal and polished wood everywhere.

'I wonder how much the Sheik has gambled tonight?' Ryker glanced again over to the double doors that were flanked by beefy but smartly dressed security guards.

'More than we could afford in a lifetime, I'm sure.'

'Does he know you personally?'

'No. I was only in training when I first came across him. I wasn't the lead agent. I know he was being investigated by the JIA and several other agencies for weapons smuggling. The lead agent was Thomas Maddison.'

'Seriously? Our missing agent who may or may not be the Silver Wolf? So another piece of the jigsaw falls into place.'

'Maybe.'

'But how did Falah become an asset?'

'To save his own skin probably. He's a money man. His wealth was all inherited from his father who made his fortune when oil production exploded in the region in the thirties and forties. The family isn't part of that anymore though. The Sheik sees himself as a businessman, but he's not a squeaky clean businessman.'

'No, he's got too much money to need to do things by the book.'

'He buys weapons from whoever and sells them to whoever. He's not picky, it seems. He keeps far enough removed from the end players, though, which is why he's still in the game.'

'End players? You mean terrorist cells, basically.'

Willoughby shrugged. 'It was long suspected the weapons he smuggles were ending up in the hands of rebels and insurgents—'

'In that part of the world they're often the good guys.'

'Well, yes. And therein lies another problem. At some points, Falah was seen as a friend of the West, at others he was a terrorist sympathiser, depending on the state of play of relations at any given time. We know he's been broker to countless deals, but he was never a primary target of the JIA. Which is why he's still alive and free.'

'But he was an asset?'

'He *was*. I know that because I know Maddison used him and got some useful leads from him. Exactly what the payoff was and whether Falah was given immunity or protection in return, I just don't know. I'm trying to find out, but you saw what happened to the JIA yesterday.'

Ryker raised an eyebrow. 'So you're saying you've no idea what the situation is with him now?'

'That's exactly what I'm saying. As you've seen, Maddison's movements in the months before he went missing were all off the books. On top of that, a good chunk of data related to his previous missions at the Hive has been deleted. His old commander is dead, so there aren't many people left who would know about Falah.'

'So really we have no idea what Falah is up to these days.'

'No. We don't.'

'But we know he is most definitely alive. And he's right over there.' Ryker indicated over her shoulder with a slight nod.

The double doors were open and Falah and his crew of eight men were just emerging, the Sheik in the centre.

'Follow or confront?' Willoughby asked, not looking in the slightest bit fazed by the mark's sudden appearance.

Follow or confront. They'd mulled over both options. They'd already kept their distance as they followed the Sheik to the casino, some four hours' drive from where they'd first spotted him by Lake Maggiore. They could continue trailing him, but they were surely only delaying the inevitable if they did that.

The only question remaining was *when* to confront. In a public space with lots of eyes and ears was safer, in some respects, but it also limited the playing field somewhat. The other choice was to get the Sheik somewhere more private. That was the plan they'd both agreed earlier.

'Ryker?'

'Stick to the plan. I think he's just made it even easier for us.'

Willoughby turned and looked over. Falah, along with two other men, were hovering over a roulette table. Then Falah took a seat, followed by one of his friends. The rest of the crew spaced themselves out.

'What the—'

'Looks like he got bored of betting on his own,' Ryker said. 'Maybe he likes an audience.'

'Come on then.' Without waiting for confirmation, Willoughby got up from her stool and grabbed her cocktail glass and sauntered to Falah's table. As she headed over, Ryker spotted another couple also making a move in that direction. Willoughby picked up her pace to head them off, her high heels causing her hips to sway seductively inside the tight dress.

Her movement caught Falah's attention. He looked up at Willoughby and gave her a hungry smile. Ryker couldn't see what look she was giving him in return, but Falah certainly seemed pleased with himself. Ryker got up and moved cautiously toward them – he didn't want to spoil Willoughby's intro.

Willoughby and Falah exchanged words, then the Sheik indicated to the chair next to him and she took it. She looked over her shoulder and winked, and Ryker moved with more purpose up behind her. As he approached, he noticed Falah's men turn their eyes from their boss's new companion to him. A couple of them took a half-step forward, as if they were about to ward Ryker off, but then Willoughby spun around and held out her arm.

'This is my friend, James,' she said, with a wide smile.

Falah didn't object as Ryker came up behind Willoughby. He held his hand out and Falah shook it. He'd noted Falah's eyes widen when Willoughby had said friend, and not boyfriend or husband.

'Pleasure to meet you,' Ryker said. 'Mind if we join you?'

'Why would I mind? I often find luck in strangers.' Falah stared at Willoughby.

'James, have you seen the chips he's got?' Willoughby indicated the vast swathe of casino chips in front of Falah. Probably a couple of hundred thousand euros at least. And that was just what was on display, never mind what was in the briefcase Ryker had seen one of the men carrying. She turned back to Falah. 'I think if anything you're going to be the one bringing some luck to us.'

Willoughby reached out and put her hand onto Falah's, and Ryker noticed him flinch just a little, before his confident smile grew further.

'The night is young,' Falah said. 'So let's just see about that.'

CHAPTER 46

Ryker quite quickly decided that he despised the Sheik, and everything that he was and represented. He had a certain arrogance and confidence that only extreme wealth brings to a human being. His world was a cocoon where he was forever the centre of attention.

After two hours of playing and mostly losing big money, Falah was nonetheless still going strong with plenty of chips left on the table. Willoughby was all out of her two hundred euros. Ryker, sitting next to her, was out too. Falah had already given her a one thousand euro chip to keep her going, but that had lasted barely ten minutes as she wilfully frittered it away. Ryker had to admit, she was playing the role well. So well that he had to stop and ask himself every so often how much of it was play and how much of it was real.

Falah had been plying Willoughby with drinks – champagne, cocktails. More than once she'd clumsily spilled a good deal of drink – to avoid consuming it, Ryker assumed – but it was clear she was still becoming drunker with each sip, and with it, more flirty and touchy with the Sheik. Much to Falah's amusement. He was drinking too, albeit more slowly, and less noxious concoctions, Ryker decided.

Regardless, the evening was playing out nicely. He was sure Falah would do whatever he could to spend some more time with the alluring and inebriated Willoughby, and Ryker had been playing his part as the slightly disgruntled friend with aplomb, probably only further adding to Falah's sense of masculinity and importance.

'What brings you to Monte Carlo, anyway?' Ryker looked over at Falah, his tone more hard-edged than he'd intended.

The Sheik glanced up from his chips, seeming slightly put out by the question.

Willoughby turned and gave Ryker a look that said, *Just keep playing along.*

'I come here often, James,' Falah said. 'This is a place where you really can get everything you need.'

'Yeah, I guess. If you have enough money.'

'Enough money? The way I see it, there can never be enough.'

Ryker just about managed to avoid an eye roll.

'Are you familiar with the rest of the region?' Ryker asked. 'You're so close to some spectacular areas here. The Alps are just a short drive away. The Italian Lakes too.'

Falah looked more alert now. 'As it so happens I've visited the Lakes on this trip. My first time ever.'

'Yeah? Which Lake?'

'Lake Maggiore. Do you know it?'

'I was there very recently,' Ryker said, his eyes narrowing.

Willoughby shot him another look. Gave a slight shake of her head.

'Where did you stay?' Ryker asked.

'More than one place, actually. I like to try different things. New places, new people. Variety is the–'

'Yeah, yeah,' Ryker said. 'Heard that one before.'

The Sheik glowered at Ryker, clearly not liking his tone, and for a few seconds the table fell silent.

Then Ryker thumped his hand down, causing everyone to jump.

'Blimey, would you look at the time,' he said. 'I think I'm done for the night.' He stood up from his chair and held his hand out to Willoughby. 'Are you coming?'

She looked back to Falah who smiled at her and shrugged.

'Don't you want to stay just a bit longer?' she asked Ryker.

'I can have one of my men drive you back,' Falah said, ever the gentleman. 'I'll bring Eleanor later. Where are you both staying?'

'Hotel Marina,' Ryker said.

'Ah! There you go. I'm staying at the Grimaldi, it's not even two minutes away. This is a tiny place, remember. I can take you back later, Eleanor. What do you say?'

She turned to Ryker. 'I'll be fine. I'll see you in the morning, yeah?'

'Yeah. Don't do anything I wouldn't do.'

'I can have someone drive you back,' Falah said.

'No, that's fine.' Ryker bent down to kiss Willoughby on the cheek. 'Enjoy the rest of the night.'

When he pulled up, he stepped forward to shake the Sheik's hand but accidentally-on-purpose tripped over Willoughby's chair leg and went stumbling into the suited man stationed behind Falah. There was a brief commotion as two other men jumped forward to protect the Sheik, while others descended on Ryker, who was quickly on his feet, backing away, hands in the air in apology.

'Sorry, sorry. Looks like that beer went to my head more than I thought.'

He looked over at Falah who was still seated, calm and collected. In fact, he looked amused now that Ryker had made a fool of himself.

'Not a problem,' Falah said. 'You take it easy.'

Ryker said nothing. Just turned and walked away, heading for the exit. He heard Willoughby saying something to Falah. Ryker didn't look around, just kept on going.

Moments later, he heard her call out.

'James! Wait.'

Ryker took a couple more steps before she called again and he turned to see her, heels off, shimmying over to him.

'What?' Ryker said, a hard edge still in his tone.

'I told him we needed to arrange a time to meet tomorrow,' she said, quiet enough that no one but Ryker would hear.

Ryker realised now her voice was clear, her words not slurred at all. It made him feel that little bit more sure of what they were doing.

'How far are we taking this?' Ryker asked.

'As far as we can.'

'You're putting yourself at risk, you realise.'

'This was the plan. And you'll be there to back me up?'

'You know I will,' Ryker said. 'You've got the microphone still?'

'On my thigh.'

'Okay. I'll be listening. I won't be far.'

'Did you get anything? When you fell?'

'I think it's a room key. I'll know for sure when I get out of this place.'

'Okay, I'll see you soon. Good luck.'

'You too. Knock him dead.'

Ryker kissed her on the cheek then turned and walked away, not looking back to the likely gloating face of the Sheik.

When he was outside, Ryker gazed around. The lush gardens in front of the casino – deep green grass, multi-coloured flowerbeds, palm trees, and grand central fountain – were lit up spectacularly by a series of floodlights, but at that time of night the area was almost deserted, except for a few security personnel.

In front of him, parked directly by the front entrance, Ryker saw several ridiculously expensive cars, including Falah's gleaming yellow Ferrari. He wondered what the valet staff did with the cars worth less than a quarter of a million? Probably they were shepherded around the back to a grotty unlit yard.

'Do you have a parking ticket, sir?' a keen valet asked, striding up to Ryker.

'No. Not tonight.'

The valet nodded and skulked off. Ryker looked around again then took out his phone and navigated to the app that would connect to the tiny microphone Willoughby had earlier taped to her inner thigh. He switched on the receiver then fished in his pocket for the wireless earbud. He put the bud in his ear and after a short crackle the voices from the roulette table came through loud and clear.

Next, Ryker pulled out the card he'd just pilfered from Falah's security guy. Or was he just a friend? It was hard to tell with the Sheik. Did he have friends or just people he paid to be with him?

Ryker smiled. Not only did he have the guy's room key, he also had the paper wallet the hotel reception had given him. Hotel Grimaldi. Room 603.

That was exactly where Ryker headed.

CHAPTER 47

It didn't take Ryker long to arrive at Hotel Grimaldi, even with the detour he first took to his own hotel to change out of his formal garb. Falah was right, Monte Carlo wasn't a big place. The hotel wasn't big either, but what it lacked in size it more than made up for in luxury and exclusiveness. The building, with its ornate façade, could well have been a smaller version of the casino Ryker had just come from, although at the hotel, as well as the ornate, there was a much more liberal use of modern floor-to-ceiling glazing to provide spectacular views of the Mediterranean sea.

Dressed in casual clothes and with his baseball cap on, Ryker was far from the playboy he'd earlier appeared to be, but at least this way he looked like an average guy, and with his head down and cap on, his face wouldn't be captured on the many CCTV cameras dotted about the place. He stood across the street from the hotel and paused a second as he listened to the voices still in his ear from the casino.

It seemed Willoughby, with another thousand-euro chip, had hit a lucky streak, and the build-up of background noise and chatter suggested the table had a mini audience to whoop and holler every favourable spin of the wheel. He could tell Willoughby still had the Sheik enthralled, though his murmurings suggested he was losing interest in the game and would rather be back at his hotel suite where he could entertain his new companion more privately.

'I told you I often find luck in strangers,' Falah said after what Ryker guessed was another winning bet.

'I can't believe it!' Willoughby cooed.

'I tell you what, we should quit while you're ahead. You could buy yourself something really fancy with all that.'

Willoughby said something in return but Ryker didn't catch the words clearly. Perhaps she'd accidentally covered the microphone as she spoke.

'Okay, that's it then,' Falah said to the rattling of casino chips. 'All or nothing.'

Ryker heard expectant murmurs. He could only assume, with the Sheik now keen to get out of there, both Willoughby and Falah had put everything on the next roll.

A few seconds later, the earbud fizzed and crackled with raucous shouts and calls, forcing Ryker to pull the bud from his ear.

After a few seconds, when the noise had died down, he put it back in place.

'That's never happened for me before,' Falah said.

'Not for me either,' Willoughby said.

'You must be my lucky charm.'

'Wow, look at the time, I really should get going. Here–'

'No. That's all yours. You won it.'

'You think you can buy me?' Willoughby said playfully.

'That wouldn't even come close to what you're worth,' Falah said, and Ryker had no need to hide his eye roll this time. What a slimy prick the Sheik was. 'Come on, I'll take you to your hotel.'

'You're such a gentleman.'

Ryker looked at his watch. He probably only had ten or fifteen minutes until the party arrived. Time to get moving. He walked up to the large glass doors that had the hotel's fancy logo emblazoned in shiny gold. The doors slid open silently and Ryker walked into the spacious atrium. Several yards in front of him, the sole male receptionist was stationed at a polished-wood desk. Key card on clear display in his hand, Ryker gave the guy a slight nod and a smile then kept his head down as he walked toward the lifts, hoping the receptionist wouldn't try to engage in conversation. He didn't.

Inside the lift, Ryker hit button six, and moments later, he arrived on the second top floor of the hotel. He noted that the next floor up didn't have a number seven button, but simply a small plaque next to the button that said Presidential Suite. That would be where Falah was staying then.

Ryker walked out of the lift and along the corridor to room 603. A quick recce of the floor suggested there were only ten rooms. Ryker wondered how many were taken up by Falah's entourage. He reached the door for 603 then did another quick glance up and down the corridor before pushing the card against the keypad on the door. The lock released and Ryker edged the door open, preparing himself in case one of Falah's cronies was already inside – perhaps the dayshift security, taking a nap.

No, the room was dark and quiet. Ryker flipped on the lights then closed the door softly and rummaged around. In his ear he heard the roar of a high-revving car engine starting up. The yellow Ferrari no doubt. Was Falah really in a fit state to be driving?

'The sun will be coming up soon,' Ryker heard Falah say over the engine noise. 'My hotel suite has a private roof terrace. We could watch the sunrise together, if you like.'

A short pause. 'How could a girl refuse an invitation like that?' Willoughby said.

The night was turning out exactly how Ryker and Willoughby had intended. Within minutes, Willoughby would be inside the Sheik's hotel room. It was as good a place as any to turn the tables on him. The only issue now was how Ryker himself would get in there.

He took just a couple of minutes to look through room 603. It was exceptionally tidy, and Ryker guessed from the belongings that it was being shared by two men. Apparently the Sheik's gratitude didn't spread as far as providing individual rooms for his workers. As well as clothes and toiletries, Ryker found a tablet computer and some 9mm magazines. No handgun. Ryker tried to power on the tablet but he needed either a thumbprint ID or a six-digit code to get inside. He wasn't breaking into that before the room's occupants arrived, and there was little point lugging it around with him.

He left it in place then looked at his watch. Falah and Willoughby would be back any minute. Somewhat dissatisfied with his findings – or lack thereof – Ryker left the room and headed back to the lift. He hit the button for the next floor up.

When the lift arrived, the doors opened and Ryker walked out onto a small hallway. In front of him was a wide set of double doors that led into the suite, which by the looks of it took up the whole of the top floor of the hotel. Off to his left was another door that Ryker assumed was for maintenance staff – a cleaning cupboard or access to the air conditioning system.

Ryker moved up to that door. It was locked. Across the other side of the hall was another plain-looking door with two narrow windows in it. The green sign above it showed it provided access to the stairs – a fire exit. Ryker walked over and pushed the door open and moved out into a carpeted stairwell. He peered over the banister, looking down the seven storeys to ground level. Within two floors, the plush carpet and ornamental light fittings were replaced with bare concrete and plain white lights for the plebs.

In his ear the grumbling whine of the Ferrari cut out and Ryker heard car doors opening.

'Wow, this is so beautiful,' Willoughby said.

'Wait until you see inside.'

'But no funny business. Not on a first date.'

'Who said this was a date?'

'Oh, I er–'

'I'm joking with you.'

Ryker heard their footsteps. The sharp tapping of Willoughby's heels as they came inside the hotel and traipsed across the marble. There was giggling too. He could imagine Willoughby walking clumsily, needing the Sheik's trusty arm for support.

Ryker moved down the stairs. He came to a stop when he reached the door to the sixth floor. From there he was out of view if any of Falah's men did a quick sweep of the stairwell from the top floor. If they did a full sweep of the entire staircase from top to bottom, he'd have to make himself scarce somewhere else, but unless they were particularly paranoid he couldn't see why they'd do that.

Through the walls next to him, Ryker heard mechanical whirring as pulleys hoisted the lift car upward.

A few seconds later, he heard the lift doors opening above him.

When Falah next spoke, there was a noticeable echo, his muffled voice from upstairs coming a split second before his much clearer voice through the earbud. 'We'll just wait here a minute. I always let my security team check first, just in case.'

'Why? Who are you expecting to be in there?' Willoughby slurred. 'The bogeyman?'

'You'd be surprised.'

'Ooooh. I've always enjoyed living dangerously.'

A few seconds later, Ryker heard Falah's man confirm the room was as they'd left it.

'After you,' Falah said, presumably to Willoughby. 'And I'll see you ugly lot in the morning.'

'Night night, boys,' Willoughby said.

Ryker heard the doors to the suite close both in his ear, and also up above. He stayed in position for a few moments, listening to the increasingly grating chatter of Falah and Willoughby. Soon they were heading up the staircase within the suite to the roof terrace. It was time for Ryker to move. It was clear what the Sheik intended, and Ryker wanted to head that off before Willoughby got herself into a position of no return.

He moved away from the door and cautiously walked up the stairs, his footfalls on the soft carpet silent. When he was five steps from the top, he caught a glimpse, through the narrow glass of the stairwell door, of the entrance to the presidential suite. He spotted a suited man standing outside, arms folded. Then another. Two men to contend with to get inside. That wasn't a problem. The Sheik had earlier had a much bigger detail, only reaffirming that this longer game was worth it.

Ryker carried on creeping up the stairs, alert for anyone behind him, but also increasingly aware that he was moving further and further into the field of view of the two security guards in front of him. If they looked his way, they'd spot him, and he'd have no choice but to spring into attack.

Either they just weren't that on the ball or they were tired, because they didn't once glance in Ryker's direction, and he made it to the top of the stairs without being spotted, then pulled up against the wall, out of sight of the stairwell door. He let out a long, slow exhale as he prepared himself for the next part.

'Come and take a seat over here,' Ryker heard Falah say.

'Is that a bed? On a roof terrace?' Willoughby said. 'Now that's something you don't see every day.'

'I have plenty more than that to show you.'

Ryker heard shuffling, creaking. The two of them sitting, or lying down. Then a gasp from Willoughby.

'There it is,' she said. 'It's beautiful.'

Ryker assumed she was talking about the sunrise and not Falah's manhood.

'Perfect timing,' she added.

Perfect timing. A message to Ryker to get on with it?

No point hanging around. He stepped to the door and pushed it open then giddily and drunkenly stumbled out into the hallway.

'That bastard!' Ryker slurred. 'Is she in there with him?'

Ryker swayed toward the suite's doors. One of the guards moved across to block his path, his face hard and no-nonsense.

'Get out of here!' he said.

The other guy looked faintly amused by the whole thing.

'I want to see her,' Ryker said, reaching out and shoving the guard blocking his path. Not too hard. But hard enough.

Both of the men drew their handguns. Colts, Ryker noticed. He tried his best to appear shocked and suddenly sober.

'Whoa, whoa!' Ryker said, reeling backward.

The amused guy held his gun pointed downward, casually at the ready, but the hard-faced guard was pointing the barrel at Ryker's head. He stepped forward.

'I said get out of here.'

Ryker dropped to his knees. Held his hands out in front of him, as if in prayer. He quivered. 'Please. Don't shoot me. I just—'

Ryker reached forward with his hands. His right arm smacked onto the man's wrist, his left hand whipped in the opposite direction, his fingers taking hold of the Colt's barrel as it came free from the man's hand. Ryker launched his whole body upward and crashed the butt of the gun into the guy's chin before he even knew he'd lost his weapon.

Ryker's momentum – the force of two hundred pounds of fast-moving bone and muscle – sent the guy up into the air. Ryker spun and kicked out as the not-so-amused second guard pulled his gun up. The top of Ryker's foot connected with the barrel and the Colt went clattering away. Without pause, Ryker spun again, and this time his elbow smashed into the side of the not-at-all-amused guy's head. Somehow he seemed to land on the floor at the exact same time as his colleague.

Ryker looked over the two men. Both were grounded. At least for now. He grabbed the fallen gun and stuffed that in his waistband – two guns were always better than one – then quickly checked the guys' pockets. He had to hope at least one of them had a key for the suite, to get inside in an emergency. They had no radios, Ryker noticed, which was good. The rest of the team were hopefully tucked up in bed and wouldn't be coming up to check on the boss anytime soon.

It was only then that Ryker reconnected with the sounds that were still coming into his earbud. Not talking. Not just breathing either. Heavy breathing. Murmuring?

Were they kissing?

'No, not so fast,' he heard Willoughby pant.

For fuck's sake, Ryker thought. It was time to put a stop to this.

He found two key cards in the angry guy's pocket. He took them both and held them up to the keypad in unison. The light flicked green and, gun held out, Ryker pushed open the door.

'No, please, stop,' Willoughby said, more strongly this time.

After that, there was a grating sound. Rustling. Falah's hand running over the mic?

'What the–' Falah said. 'What the fuck is this!'

Silence. At least from Ryker's earbud. Up above though, he could hear shouting, screaming, banging.

Ryker raced forward, through the opulent room. Room? It was more like a luxury apartment, with several doorways off the main corridor. Ryker headed directly for the far end, where he could see a winding staircase, not really taking in much about the lavish surroundings, other than looking for any signs of movement – Falah or other security personnel who might get in his way. There were none.

He reached the stairs and bounded up them two at a time before crashing open the door at the top. Knowing he was coming up on the far side of the building, he quickly spun around, looking back across the expansive terrace, gun held out and at the ready.

Ryker let out a long sigh, feeling his heavy, fast breaths calming. His eyes fixed on the mattress of the oversized poolside lounger that Willoughby had referred to as a bed, on the other side of a tastefully lit-up plunge pool. Willoughby and Falah were both there, though the mood wasn't quite so intimate as it had been moments before.

Falah was lying down, on his back, a dribble of blood coming from his nose. He was looking seriously pissed off. Straddling him, her dress hitched up over her thighs, was Willoughby. She had a gun in her hand, the barrel inches from Falah's eyeball. Where the hell she'd got that from, Ryker had no idea.

'You okay?' Ryker asked her.

'You took your bloody time,' she said, without taking her eye off Falah. 'He pulled this damn gun on me. Found the microphone when he couldn't control his wandering hands.'

Ryker huffed.

'Who the hell are you two?' Falah asked with a look of disbelief. It was the first time Ryker had seen or heard him without his cocky confidence.

'I think we're just about to get to that,' Willoughby said, her smile lit up orange and red by the rising sun.

CHAPTER 48

With Falah subdued, they'd moved back into the suite. Being on the roof felt too exposed, particularly as daylight had arrived. Ryker had hauled the two lumps from the hallway into the suite, taken off their clothes down to their underwear, hog-tied and gagged them with rags and towels and dressing gown cords, then stuck them in a corner of the main living room, still in sight.

Falah was sitting in the middle of an enormous cream leather sofa. Willoughby, gun in hand on her lap, was sitting on the edge of a glass coffee table in front of him. Ryker was standing behind, the Colt in his hand but by his side.

'We're not here to hurt you,' Ryker said to the Sheik, still trying to break through to the guy after nearly thirty minutes of trying. 'If we wanted you dead, you'd be dead. If we wanted to torture you, we'd have started cutting off your fingers already.' Ryker saw Falah gulp. 'We want to talk, and for you to answer our questions. We need your help.'

'Help? This is how you ask for my help?'

'I've found it to be a persuasive method.'

'I'm sure you have. You say you work for the JIA?'

'That's right.'

'Not for long, my friend. You're finished, both of you.'

Ryker was slightly surprised by Falah's words, and his assuredness. Did that mean he still had contact with the JIA? Was still an asset?

'I know you were an asset of Thomas Maddison's,' Ryker said, fishing for either a confirmation or rebuttal. None came. 'Which is why we're prepared to be hospitable with you.'

Falah humphed. 'I have ten more men in this hotel. I can't wait to show you *my* hospitable side.'

'Let me make this really clear for you,' Ryker said. 'It's not going to come to that. No one is coming to your door for at least the next three hours. Eleanor already told me that. She heard the instruction you gave your men.'

Falah looked angrily to Willoughby, who didn't show any reaction.

'Three hours is a long time,' she said. 'Or it can be shorter, if you just do what we ask.'

'Which is what?'

'Tell us what you were doing at Lake Maggiore,' Ryker said.

'Fishing.'

'No. You were meeting with Lawrence Draper.' Falah's face looked blank. 'Or should I say Nicholas Andrews.'

This time Ryker saw a flash of recognition.

'We need to know why,' Ryker said.

Falah said nothing.

'Okay, let me backtrack. Who did you used to work with at the JIA?'

'*Used* to?' Falah said. 'You really don't know much about me, do you?'

'Thomas Maddison? He's been missing for nearly two years, you know.'

Falah humphed again. 'If only you knew.'

'What's that supposed to mean?'

'It means I know so much more than you do. You haven't seen your colleague Maddison for more than two years?' Falah let out a mock laugh. 'Do you know when I last saw him?'

'When?'

Falah snorted.

'What do you know of the Silver Wolf?' Willoughby asked.

'What?'

'The Silver Wolf. Is that a name Maddison went by?'

'Or perhaps you've heard of Silver Wolf Investments,' Ryker said. 'We have evidence of money coming from you going to that business. I wonder what that was all about.'

It was a lie. Ryker had no such evidence. But the unease on Falah's face suggested Ryker had hit on a truth.

'We know there's a weapons deal in place between you and Andrews,' Ryker said, reading further between the lines. 'We're not interested in that. Not directly. What we're interested in is Andrews, and his sidekick Henderson.'

'Henderson?'

Ryker pulled out his phone and found the picture of Fleming taken the day before, Falah shaking his hand outside Villa Mariangela. He showed Falah the picture. The Sheik tried his best to show no reaction, but Ryker could see he was getting increasingly rattled.

'We were spying on you,' Ryker said. 'We know a lot more about this deal than you think.'

'I don't know anything about him,' Falah said. 'Henderson, you say he's called? I've only met him once. I don't think I even talked to him. He's just security, a muscleman. Like those two.'

Falah looked over to the two sorry lumps on the floor. One of the men was still unconscious. The other was awake and staring into space. He knew whatever happened here, he was done representing the Sheik. Ryker wondered what the severance package would be like.

'Security? No, Henderson's more than that,' Ryker said. 'He's one of our main targets. This is simple. I want you to get me inside.'

'Inside where?'

'Inside Villa Mariangela.'

'Can't you just go and knock?'

Ryker glared at Falah but said nothing.

'Okay, okay. That's it? I get you inside, and then what?'

'And then I do what I need to do. When I'm finished, you go home. I'm guessing you might need to look for a new business partner though.'

Falah scoffed. 'Have you any idea how much money I'll lose if that deal falls through?'

'No. But I'm sure you've plenty more. And maybe what Eleanor won for you tonight can go toward your losses.'

'You seriously think you can just swan into my life, knock out two of my team, break into my hotel room and scupper something I've been working on for months, probably costing me tens of millions of dollars, and then expect me to help you? What do I get out of it?'

'Maybe you get to live. Maybe you get to stay out of jail.'

'Jail? Which jail are you planning to send me to? And for what exactly? Do you even have any kind of jurisdiction here?'

Ryker was beginning to tire of Falah's obstinacy. 'Let me try one more time. And I'm serious, this is the last time. You can help, or you can not help. Either way, your deal with Andrews is finished, because Andrews is finished. So you can tell me what you know about him, and what you know about the Silver Wolf, and get me inside his home so I can close this matter down once and for all. Or you can continue to be a dickhead with your head in the sand, and see where that gets you when the shit hits the fan. Which is going to be very soon, whichever path you choose.'

'Who do you work for at the JIA?' Falah asked after a few seconds of silence. Ryker groaned, tired of Falah not getting the position he was in. 'I ask because I wonder just whose authority you're acting under. Do Cameron and Sanderson know what you're doing here?'

And there it was. The game changer. Cameron was Maddison's ex-commander. She'd died under suspicious circumstances not long before Maddison's disappearance. Sanderson was an MI6 stalwart who'd previously been part of the JIA's Committee – the panel of four who oversaw everything. But Sanderson had had his throat slit in his London home by a rogue operative well over a year earlier. Life in the JIA was anything but safe, even for those in the upper echelons.

Falah had likely thought he was being clever naming the big dogs, thinking it might scare Ryker off. But Falah had played the odds and lost. He didn't know about either of their deaths, otherwise he wouldn't have brought up their names. Which meant he wasn't anywhere near the inside of the JIA anymore.

'They're both dead,' Ryker said. 'It looks like you're all out of luck.'

Falah looked stunned. He really did have nowhere to go. Ryker felt he'd pushed enough. Falah wasn't an idiot, and he had previous dealings with the JIA. He knew what the organisation was capable of, and with no clear ally remaining for him, he had little choice left.

'I need to go to the toilet,' Falah said.

'I don't think so,' Ryker said.

'I'm serious! You want me to piss right here?'

'Not really.'

'Come with me, whatever. You can watch if it'll make you happier.'

Willoughby turned to look at Ryker.

'An offer I can't refuse,' he said. 'Come on then.'

Falah and Willoughby both got to their feet. Ryker indicated down to the two guards on the floor. Willoughby nodded. Falah led the way along the corridor to the main bathroom, Ryker a step behind while Willoughby stayed watch. Ryker had already swept the suite for hidden weapons, panic buttons, and had found nothing, but if Falah was particularly prepared there could still be something, somewhere.

Twice, the Sheik looked over his shoulder as they walked along. Ryker felt sure he was up to something, but the Sheik wouldn't get far. Ryker was well prepared to shoot him at the first sign of indiscretion, though he'd certainly not want to kill Falah, just like that. The Sheik was more valuable alive, and Ryker didn't want the repercussions of killing the billionaire – the police and the Sheik's security team on his case – before he'd gotten what he needed from Andrews and Henderson.

Falah headed into the bathroom and Ryker stood in the doorway as the Sheik relieved himself. When he was finished, he washed and dried his hands.

'All good?' Falah asked with a look of disdain.

'Never better,' Ryker said. 'Can you give me a yes or a no now?'

Falah snorted. He edged past Ryker who followed the Sheik back into the living room. Willoughby was still standing just a couple of yards from the guards, ready to pounce should they suddenly spring to life. They didn't.

But Falah did, when he was right next to her, almost in position to take his seat once again. He reached out and grabbed at Willoughby's wrist – the one holding the gun – and although she tried to counter, the Sheik was surprisingly quick. He twisted her arm around and pulled it up behind her back. He thrust a knee up into the small of her back, then wrapped his other arm around her neck, squeezing hard.

As soon as Ryker saw the move, he pulled up his Colt, looking for a shot, but Falah was covered too well behind Willoughby.

'Don't be stupid,' Ryker shouted. He edged around, to get a better view of Falah, but the Sheik matched Ryker's moves, shifting around in an arc.

'Just shoot him!' Willoughby shouted.

Ryker's finger twitched on the trigger. The position was reminiscent of the one in Orrantía's mansion. That time Ryker hadn't thought twice about firing. But this time... the risk was too big.

Perhaps what happened next was because Willoughby sensed his hesitation, or perhaps, with her hand up behind her back, she lost control of the gun and that forced her into action. She wormed out of the hold, ducked and turned as she and the Sheik grappled and writhed with each other.

The gun went off.

The boom of the shot echoed through the suite and sent a shudder through Ryker.

Whose finger had been on the trigger, Ryker didn't know. For just a split second, he wasn't even sure who the bullet had hit, because blood covered both Falah and Willoughby.

Then the Sheik's body slumped to the floor, and with his head turned, Ryker saw the gaping wound in his neck. Ryker looked up at Willoughby, her face and neck covered with blood spatters. She began to shake. Just like Ryker, she knew what this meant.

'I didn't mean to... I–'

Ryker held up a hand to stop her. It didn't matter what she had or hadn't intended. The fact was that Falah was dead. And because of that, he and Willoughby were well and truly screwed.

CHAPTER 49

'What do we do?' Willoughby asked.

She shakily picked up a length of towel from the floor, a leftover from the ties they'd used on the two guards, and wiped at the blood on her face.

'We go. Now.'

Willoughby looked down to the two security men on the floor. They were awake, wide-eyed, and staring at the corpse of their boss. Willoughby turned her gaze back to Ryker. She didn't need to ask the question; he knew what she was thinking. There were two witnesses in the room. Could they afford the risk of leaving them alive? No, they couldn't, not really, but then Ryker didn't believe they deserved to die.

'No,' Ryker said, quashing the idea.

Willoughby looked slightly relieved at that. They both quickly checked their weapons then rushed for the suite door.

'That gunshot won't go unnoticed,' Ryker said. 'We have to expect the rest of the crew to be on our case any second. Not to mention the local police.'

'I know,' Willoughby said.

Ryker put his hand to the door handle. 'You ready?'

Willoughby nodded. Ryker looked deep into her anxious eyes for a brief moment. He reached out and used his sleeve to wipe at the smudged red still on her cheek.

'I'm sorry,' she said.

Ryker shook his head, turned and opened the door. Gun at the ready, he burst forward into the hallway, shifting the barrel this way and that. There was no one there.

'Follow me,' Ryker said, heading for the stairs. He pushed the door open and walked quickly across to the banister to peer over. All was quiet down there too.

'Is it just me or does this feel wrong?' Ryker whispered.

He looked at Willoughby. She shrugged. 'Everyone's asleep. Maybe no one heard the shot and no one will be alerted until those goons figure a way out of their ties and then raise the alarm.'

Ryker said nothing. He could well imagine the two men squirming and writhing at that moment. They'd be up on their feet in minutes and as soon as they made the call...

It might mean that he and Willoughby would get a chance to make it out of the hotel though. Taking one last look over the banister first, Ryker headed down, Willoughby a couple of steps behind. They made it past the sixth floor no problems. Then the fifth. Then the fourth.

That was when the fire alarm began blaring. A shrill, piercing alarm that made Ryker's insides curdle. The brightness of the lights in the stairwell ramped up several notches. Ryker and Willoughby didn't break stride.

'This'll help us.' Ryker could only assume the guards in the suite had managed to free themselves enough to set off the alarm to alert their friends. 'Within seconds there'll be people teeming down these stairs and in the foyer. Put the guns away. Move with the crowds.'

Willoughby didn't say anything. Ryker realised it was a bit harder for her to lose her gun in a dress, but she managed to tuck it away underneath. The bulge on her side was clear, but at least the weapon wasn't in open sight.

Sure enough, by the time they reached the third floor the most alert of the hotel's guests were already coming out. Some were dressed, some were in their hotel gowns. Most looked sleepy and slightly put out by their lie-in having been ruined.

A uniformed hotel worker came out into the stairwell and barked instructions in French.

'It's a bit early for a drill. Is there a fire?' Ryker asked, fishing for whether the hotel staff knew the cause of the emergency.

'It doesn't matter,' the man said. 'We need everyone out. Get yourselves safe.'

That didn't help much.

By the time they were approaching the ground floor, the numbers of people in the stairwell had swelled, and progress slowed. Ryker looked upward every now and then, canvassing the stairs of the floors above. He thought he could see the outline of two of Falah's suited men, rushing down, pushing and shoving past other people. Or were they just over-eager guests?

Ryker walked out into the hotel lobby and the bottleneck eased, giving space to move again. There were several hotel workers there, going through the motions of their well-drilled evacuation procedure. Ryker also spotted two uniformed security guards belonging to the hotel – where they'd come from he didn't know – but they didn't appear to be on high alert.

No chance for complacency though. When they were just five yards from the wide-open glass doors, Ryker heard the police siren above the din of the fire alarm. Then he saw the car, crunching to a halt right outside the entrance, sending the escaping hotel guests scampering. Two officers jumped from the patrol car, both pulling out pistols.

Not two seconds later, another car screeched to a halt alongside, and two more officers – a man and a woman – got out.

'Now there's a helluva response time,' Willoughby muttered.

'The largest police force in the world, per capita.'

'Lucky us.'

'Let's split up. Just keep your head down and get away. We'll meet back at the car.'

With that, Ryker held back slightly as Willoughby took her high heels off and moved forward with them in her hand. She made it as far as the doors before one of the policemen clocked her. Was it the smears of blood on her? Or did the police already have their descriptions?

'*Arrêtez!*' the man shouted. Stop. He crouched down and pulled up his gun.

Maybe he thought shouting and training his gun was a good move, with his target so close and in sight. But with the other guests all around him, it was really quite dumb. Willoughby stopped, just as she'd been told, but hotel guests shouted and screamed at the sight of the drawn weapon. Some ran. Some froze. Some dropped to the floor and covered their heads with their arms. A good start for Ryker and Willoughby, but Ryker wanted to ramp up the panic.

He pulled out his gun and shot into the air. Now everyone moved. There was chaos. One policeman ran for cover behind his car. The policewoman and her colleague both trained their guns on Ryker, but in the melee there was no way they could shoot. Willoughby dropped the shoes and launched herself at the officer in front of her and, using the identical move Ryker had earlier used to take the gun from Falah's guard, she disarmed the officer with ease and sent an open-palmed strike up into his face that caused his head to snap back and sent him to the ground.

Willoughby continued to rush forward, ducking in and out behind scampering guests. She was soon on the policewoman who suffered a similar fate to her friend. Willoughby wouldn't get so lucky with the next officer though. He'd had plenty of time to react.

Ryker, already bursting forward, took aim and fired, but at the last split second a guest darted in front and the bullet tore out of the gun and sank into the thigh of the middle-aged woman. She screamed and fell to the ground and, still rushing forward, Ryker fired another shot. This one hit home, and just in time. The bullet hit the officer in the lower leg and he shouted out and stumbled back.

Ryker could see the dilemma sweeping across his face. Could he stand and fight still? Or was he done for? He was still caught in that quandary when Willoughby swivelled and sent a roundhouse kick to the side of his face.

Just one policeman left. But now that Ryker was outside, he could hear the sirens of more fast-approaching vehicles.

'Go!' Ryker shouted to Willoughby.

Without hesitation, she darted off, moving with the still-escaping crowd. The remaining officer, who was hunkered down behind his car, bobbed up and lifted his gun but Ryker fired two warning shots that made him think twice.

Ryker looked off to his left. Willoughby was already several yards away. He edged in that direction, still facing the officer by the car. He again bobbed up but Ryker fired another shot that smacked into the metal of the car just two inches from the policeman's face. He disappeared from view again and Ryker took the chance to make himself scarce.

He turned and ran. Willoughby was still in sight, but after a few yards she took a left. The sirens behind Ryker were getting closer. A gunshot rang out and Ryker instinctively ducked, but there was no indication where the bullet went. Another two shots. Again, no hits, no ricochets.

Who was shooting? The policeman? Falah's men? Ryker didn't turn to find out. He was almost at the entrance to the street Willoughby had taken. Ryker headed straight for it, only looking back to the hotel at the last second before he moved out of view. He spotted two more police cars at the hotel entrance, a van too. Several officers were giving chase on foot. That wasn't good. He needed a vehicle.

He turned his focus back in front. Despite running barefoot and in her long black dress, Willoughby had managed to pull further ahead of Ryker, whose path was being impeded by petrified pedestrians. He pushed his limbs harder, trying to close the gap. He thought about shouting out to her, giving her an instruction of where to go, but he didn't. She was good enough at this, she knew what she was doing.

At least he thought she did, but there was really nothing she could do about what happened next. Up ahead, two police mopeds hurtled into the street. The drivers spotted Willoughby straight away and raced toward her. Maybe if it was just those two she could have gotten away. Kicked them off their bikes or fired non-fatal shots, but within seconds a police van appeared too.

Barely a second later, officers swarmed out, moving in on Willoughby with guns raised, as the two mopeds weaved around her like a hunting pack circling its prey.

Ryker moved for cover, the entrance to an alley. Just before he reached it, he saw Willoughby do the only sensible thing she could. She flung her gun to the ground and sank to her knees.

Her game was up.

CHAPTER 50

Ryker wormed his way back to the car, using every bit of guile he had, but also using a good amount of luck to evade the police. Once he was in the car, it felt like he was home free. The one saving grace of the situation was that Ryker was being hunted for murder in the second smallest country in the world. Monaco, a tiny principality, had its own police force, independent of neighbouring France. There were no official border crossings to contend with as Ryker made his escape, and the Monaco police had no authority to leave their jurisdiction.

Within a couple of minutes, Ryker had safely driven out of Monaco and was back in France, allowing him to leave the Monaco police far behind. Ryker knew the French police would soon be on his case, but he had plenty enough breathing space to get himself clear.

Three hours later, he'd hit no stumbling blocks since leaving Monaco. With new clothes, clipped hair, and having removed his blue coloured contact lenses, Ryker was soon back in Italy in a different car – the Fiat that he and Willoughby had left just beyond the border in France the previous day.

He wound the Fiat along the twisting roads of northern Italy that hugged the contours of the land, passing jagged rocky mountains, deep blue lakes encircled by thick green forests, valleys and gullies.

The scene was spectacular, but Ryker was far from enjoying it. The trip to Monaco had been a disaster. More than just a waste of time, it had jeopardised everything. Willoughby was in police custody for the murder of Sheik Falah, and sooner or later the

Italian police, or Interpol perhaps, would come looking for Ryker too.

But really that was the least of Ryker's worries. The JIA would surely get Willoughby out of jail as soon as they could. The more immediate concern for Ryker was the ramifications that would occur because of the Sheik's death. As soon as Fleming and Draper got wind of the death of their business partner, they would react. Ryker worried that by the time he made it back to Villa Mariangela the place might be deserted and he'd have to start his search all over again.

He had to hit them quickly. Hope that the message hadn't got through to them, or that if it had, they were still debating what to do next. He'd had no sleep for well over twenty-four hours but Ryker had to push on and get back to Villa Mariangela before it was too late.

Ryker looked at the clock on the dashboard. Eleven a.m. He'd wanted to call Winter sooner, but had been too busy with his cross-border evasion. Driving one-handed, he punched the numbers into the phone and put on the loudspeaker. Flowers answered.

'I need to speak to Winter,' Ryker said.

'He already knows,' Flowers said.

Ryker didn't bother to ask what or how.

Seconds later, Winter's weak voice piped up. 'Another day, another shit-storm, eh?'

'I'll get this sorted,' Ryker said.

'Get what sorted exactly? You're going to get Eleanor Willoughby out of police custody?'

'No. Not that.'

'How on earth did you go from chasing down Ffion Brady in London, to you and Willoughby shooting dead a billionaire Arab sheik in Monte Carlo!'

'Does it help if I tell you it was an accident?'

'Do you think this is a game? Willoughby is in police custody in Monaco charged with murder. There are alerts out in several southern European countries for your arrest.'

'I didn't call you to get a hard time.'

'What, you were expecting me to congratulate you?'

'What's happening in London?' Ryker asked, hoping for a way out of the berating.

'Ffion Brady isn't talking, but then that's not much of a surprise, is it? The press are happy though. They're loving dissecting her life.'

'She talked to me.'

'Talked about what?'

'Talked about how her husband wasn't injured in a motorbike accident, but when kidnappers turned up at their house one night.'

Silence on the other end.

'Did you know about that?'

'No,' was all Winter said.

'She said she thinks it was because of what she was working on at the JIA. But that the JIA – she didn't mention names – washed their hands of what happened to her and her husband. That's why she hated the JIA so much, and why someone – Fleming – was able to turn her.'

More silence. 'What are you expecting me to say to this?' Winter asked eventually.

'I'm just explaining why I'm here. Sheik Falah was a JIA asset. Did you know that?'

'Not until a couple of hours ago. He *was* an asset, but it's been impossible to track down exactly how that came about and what happened.'

'What, you mean because Ffion Brady managed to delete the records?'

'You're saying this is all connected? Andre Brady's injuries? The data breach, the bombing, Falah?'

'All connected by one man. The Silver Wolf.'

'A missing, presumed dead JIA agent.'

Was the Silver Wolf really Maddison? Or was it Draper, the mega-rich businessman?

Was it even Fleming? He seemed to have his dirty hands all over every facet of the puzzle.

'I'm not so sure about that,' Ryker said.

'About which part?'

Ryker didn't answer that question.

'Where are you now?'

'I'm going to finish this.'

'*This?* Do you even know what this is?'

'I know enough. The Silver Wolf is central to everything that's happened over the last few days, may even be the reason Lisa is dead. I'm going to find out which of these bastards he is and kill him.'

'Really? And if I tell you to stand down?'

Ryker thought about that. 'I'll call you when it's over,' he said, then hung up the phone.

Ryker had planned to explain more to Winter, to outline his proposal, to hopefully receive some advice, some support even, but it was clear that Winter was anything but fully behind Ryker. The more Ryker told, the more he risked his own position.

Yes, Ryker and Willoughby had messed up with Falah, but was that the only reason Winter was now so cagey? Did the JIA commander know more than he was telling about Falah, Maddison, the Silver Wolf, or was he simply uncomfortable because he didn't know enough?

Ryker was left swimming in those thoughts as he continued his journey along the twisting roads of northern Italy. The conclusion he kept coming to was that he had to go on the attack. When he'd first arrived in Italy, he'd been reluctant to simply launch an assault on Villa Mariangela, instead taking time to surveil the villa before concocting the plan to use Falah as his way in. Now he was back to square one, and with no help and the feeling that he didn't have any more time for planning on his side, an all-out attack was the best option he could see.

Such an approach wouldn't be easy though. The villa was secure from the road with high walls and CCTV, not to mention the many men on the inside. As much as he didn't want to wait another minute, Ryker would at least wait a few hours, until the sun had gone down, before springing the assault. He just had to hope the delay wouldn't prove fatal.

After setting up his spotting position across the lake, he would stake out the villa for a few hours, confirming who was home, before heading across the water and attacking from there. The water side was by far the most straightforward way onto the property.

That was the plan, at least. But recently his plans had had a tendency of going badly wrong. It seemed like this time would be no different.

Finding himself on an unusually straight piece of road, Ryker had clear sight in his rear view mirror going back about a quarter of a mile. There was no mistaking the flashing blue lights behind. Then, when he came around the next corner, he spotted the same up ahead, only two hundred yards away. The lights were attached to a large, black SUV that was parked across the road, blocking both of the lanes.

Ryker didn't know how, but the police had found him, and with them blocking both his front and his rear, he couldn't see a way out this time.

CHAPTER 51

Ryker shook his head as he looked in his mirror again. He'd been travelling at a steady speed, not wanting to attract attention, but the vehicle behind him was going much faster, and was quickly closing the distance. He looked up ahead again and studied the vehicle there as he slowed the Fiat. There were no police markings denoting it as belonging to any of the many police forces in Italy, and he questioned exactly who was trapping him. An undercover team? Perhaps even Special Forces? Ryker had some experience with the elite divisions of both the Carabinieri and the Polizia di Stato, Italy's national police force. Neither were organisations that Ryker fancied going up against solo.

He slowed the Fiat further. He was just fifty yards from the vehicle in front. Two men, dressed head to toe in blue and black fatigues and Kevlar vests, their faces covered with balaclavas, stepped from the vehicle and pulled assault rifles up to their chests. Even if Ryker was minded to make a run for it, turn the Fiat around and try to blaze out of there, those guns would cut his car up in seconds. It would be suicide. As much as he hated to admit defeat, the only option he saw was to play safe, and look for a way out further down the line. Winter would help get him out, wouldn't he?

Ryker rolled the Fiat to a stop twenty yards from the men in front and pulled on the handbrake. He left the engine idling for a few seconds but then shut that down too. He pulled the gun out of his waistband and looked at it. He could jump from the car and deliver a head shot to each of the men in front, who were now inching closer. The move would take Ryker barely two seconds. How many more men were there in the vehicles though? And he couldn't just start killing policemen, if that's who they really were. Ryker was prepared to do many things to save his own skin, but killing innocent people was not one of them.

Ryker put the gun down on the passenger seat then opened the door. He got out, making sure his empty hands were in plain sight, and took two steps away from the vehicle.

The men in front barked at him in Italian, and Ryker dropped onto his knees as they moved with more purpose up to him. Ryker heard the vehicle behind come to a stop, doors opening, heavy boots on the ground, but he didn't turn around to look. No sirens, Ryker noticed.

One of the men in front of Ryker came right up to him, grabbed his wrists and pulled them behind his body, securing them together with two sets of plastic cable ties. Then he kicked Ryker hard in the kidney and Ryker keeled over onto the tarmac. Lying on his side, he could now see two more figures behind him, each dressed and armed identically to the first two men. Ryker did his best to haul himself back up onto his knees, and was soon aided by one of the men, who swivelled him around so he was facing the vehicle that had approached from behind Ryker.

Nobody said a word. Ryker felt a stabbing in the back of his neck and realised it was the barrel of one of the assault rifles. He was deeply suspicious now. That no one had identified themselves – who they worked for – was worrying, and Ryker was already regretting not going for the all guns blazing approach when he'd had the chance.

He wondered if this really was the end for him. He'd been in situations that were seemingly impossible to escape from before, and had always come out on top. But this time?

The rear door of the SUV opened and one of the armed men spun around and went over. He reached inside and pulled something... no, someone, out. Ryker showed no reaction when he realised it was Willoughby.

Somewhere along the line, someone had had the decency to let her slip into more comfortable clothing. She was now dressed in jeans and a white T-shirt. Her hands were tied behind her back and the armed man tugged on her restraints to get her to move along. Ryker noticed her right cheek was bruised, her lip was split. Her eyes were bloodshot and weary. Neither she nor Ryker said a word. Ryker was too busy trying to figure out what was happening. Were these Falah's men?

No, he soon realised, when the last man to join the party finally revealed himself, stepping out of the car after Willoughby. He was dressed more casually than the others, and he didn't appear to be armed. He had a horrible smirk on his face.

It was Fleming.

'Surprised?' he asked.

Ryker didn't say anything.

'They were watching the Sheik the whole time,' Willoughby blurted, talking quickly as though she knew she'd be shut up if she said too much. She was right. Fleming swivelled and sent a punch to her gut. She doubled over. It looked like she might well have fallen down if it weren't for the man holding her.

'Please don't spoil my moment,' Fleming said, before turning back to Ryker. 'Yes, like she said, we were watching Falah. Not me personally, otherwise we wouldn't have waited so long to reveal ourselves. If I'd known the infamous Carl Logan was hot on our tails... let's not go into ifs and buts, there really isn't any point now.'

'You set up that bomb in London?' Ryker asked. 'Why?'

'Why? The JIA destroyed my life!'

'You killed Lisa,' Ryker said, shaking with rage.

Fleming said nothing. Just smiled.

'You're not the Silver Wolf though. Draper is. What, did you get onto his crew by giving him some shit about how you're an expert on the UK's intelligence agencies? Did you expose Thomas Maddison? Is that what happened to him? But really it was all just so you could get to the JIA. And to me.'

Fleming looked pissed off with Ryker's deductions, as though he'd wanted to do the big reveal all by himself.

'Except you're no expert,' Ryker said. 'I found you. I followed a trail from Mexico to London to here. You thought you'd destroyed everything that connected Maddison to Draper and to you. But you're wrong. Whatever you to do me, and to Willoughby, the trail is still there.'

'You let me worry about that.'

'Who said I'm worried?'

'You really should be, Logan. Do you realise how much money you've cost my employer now?'

Ryker said nothing.

'Luckily the Sheik had friends in high places down in Monaco, and they were amenable to my request to have your friend here brought to me. On one condition. Two actually. Yes, money had to change hands, so you've gotten me further into the red. Do you want to know the other condition?'

Ryker remained silent, defiant. He didn't even want to look at Fleming, instead keeping his focus on Willoughby. She was looking straight back at Ryker, and the look she was giving suggested she had no idea of how they would get out of this mess either.

'I asked you a question. Do you know what the second condition was?'

Ryker gave no response.

Fleming sighed. 'Let me show you, then.'

Fleming pulled a handgun out from behind him, lifted the weapon up and fired. Ryker jumped as the bullet tore out of the barrel and smashed through Willoughby's forehead. Her body crumpled to the ground, her deathly eyes still staring at Ryker who was frozen in shock. He didn't know how to react, how to feel to see Willoughby gunned down so suddenly, and so viciously. It brought back too many painful memories. Jane Westwood, aka Mary White, who'd been gunned down by his side in Russia as they raced to save Lisa. Lisa, whose bones were now buried in the grounds of their secluded home by the ocean. Now Willoughby. Ryker felt responsible for the deaths of them all.

'That's better,' Fleming said, turning and moving toward Ryker. 'I always feel relieved when I've paid my debts. Now, it's time for you to pay yours.'

Fleming swiped his arm forward and the barrel of his gun smacked Ryker in the side of his head. He squinted, opened and closed his eyes as the world in front of him spun.

Seconds later, with Fleming standing over him, still smirking, Ryker collapsed down to his side, out cold.

CHAPTER 52

During his unconsciousness, Ryker's mind played images of all those people who'd lost their lives because of him. Not those whose lives had ended at his hands, but those he'd simply failed to save. Each of them haunted him, blaming him for what happened and asking one simple question: *Why?*

Ryker's eyes shot open and he stared at the space around him as ice cold water dripped through his hair and down his face and onto his naked torso.

'Why what?' Fleming looked pleased with himself.

He was standing a few yards in front of Ryker, over the other side of a large oak dining table. Ryker didn't answer. He took in his surroundings. There were three men Ryker could see in front of him in the modern open-plan space. Fleming was at the head of the three, with Draper and the thin man with glasses standing behind. Given the surroundings and his company, Ryker hazarded a guess that they were in the boathouse next to Draper's villa.

Ryker tried to move but couldn't. Each of his limbs was securely tied to the chair he was on with thick rope.

'Last time I tried this I had to get a new dining table,' Draper said with disgust. 'So we're going to try it a little differently today. A chair is much easier to replace.'

Ryker frowned. He had no clue what Draper was going on about, and he realised he was also groggy and light-headed, like they'd slipped him some sedatives or other drugs while he was out.

Draper moved forward, around the table and toward Ryker. He went out of sight behind Ryker, who heard a clunking sound – Draper picking up something hard and metallic?

The next moment, Draper came back into view, right by Ryker's side, holding a metal rod, about a foot long, and a claw hammer.

Draper paused, looking down at the lumpy scar in the centre of the back of Ryker's hand.

Ryker laughed harshly, though doing so made his head pound. 'Do you ever get the feeling you've been here before?' He looked up at Draper, whose eyes had narrowed in suspicion. 'Last time it was a drill,' Ryker added.

'Just because you've been tortured before, Logan,' Fleming said, 'doesn't mean it's going to be any less painful.'

'What do you think?' Ryker stared at Draper, who was looking a little less confident. 'Have you been tortured before? Do you know what it does to a man?'

'No, and yes.'

'Ah, so you're just a giver. You *think* you know what torturing a man does to him. But you don't *really* know. How could you?'

'So tell me then.'

'You're the Silver Wolf, aren't you,' Ryker said.

Draper snorted. 'Am I now?'

'You go by many names, but that's the one that sticks.'

Draper raised an eyebrow.

'There's one thing I can't figure out though.'

'And what's that?'

'Thomas Maddison. He was a JIA agent, he went missing two years ago.' Ryker saw the reaction on Draper's face to the name. He definitely knew him. 'Was he bent, or did you just find out who he really was and kill him?'

'Just do this for fuck's sake,' Fleming said. 'Don't let this prick get into your head.'

'You should listen to him,' Ryker said. 'You want something from me?'

No answer.

'You want something from me otherwise I wouldn't be sitting here. I'd have a hole in my head, like my friend... Eleanor

Willoughby.' He struggled to get her name out and doing so caused his focus to wobble for a few seconds.

'What if we just want to skin you alive for the fun of it,' Fleming said.

'But you don't, do you?' Ryker said to Draper, though when his eyes flicked to the thin man with glasses standing by Draper, a shiver ran right through him.

'You didn't need to kill her,' Ryker said, turning his attention to Draper again.

'She cost me one hundred million dollars,' Draper said.

'So did I.'

'And you'll get what's coming to you.'

'Which is what?'

No answer again.

'You know who she works for?' Ryker's gaze flicked from Draper to Fleming, to the man with glasses who so far had taken a back seat, but who Ryker had to admit he was most wary of. There was just something about the look in his eyes.

'Yes, I know who she *worked* for,' Draper said.

'Then you should know how much shit you're in now.'

'Is that so? Seems to me that you're the one in the shit.'

'Pretty soon I'm going to be the least of your problems. Has Fleming even told you how I came to be here? He told you he'd clear up the trail for you, didn't he? But he's been playing you. He only ever cared about hurting the JIA, and hurting me.'

Draper now looked seriously pissed off. 'Why are you here?'

'Because Dumbo over there had someone whack me over the head with a pistol grip and then I guess they drove me in their car.'

'Very cute.'

'He's here because of his girlfriend,' Fleming said, smiling.

Ryker felt a burning rage building up inside of him.

'The woman from Monaco?'

'No. Not her,' Fleming said. 'Angela Grainger. Or should I say Lisa Ryker.'

Draper shook his head. 'And who the hell is she?'

'Exactly,' Fleming said. 'She was nothing, Logan.'

The rage in Ryker was growing still. He knew that was exactly what Fleming wanted to see, yet Ryker couldn't stop it. He pulled his eyes from Fleming and focused back on Draper. He couldn't let Fleming dictate the situation.

'I've no fucking idea who you're even talking about,' Draper said, cementing Ryker's deductions.

'The trail of her death led me here. To the Silver Wolf,' Ryker said to Draper. 'But it's clear she wasn't killed under your orders. Fleming's been lying to you. Somehow he managed to convince you he was helping by tackling the JIA, by blowing up their offices in London.' Ryker saw a look of unease on Draper's face, and noticed the anger lines on Fleming's face deepening.

'I just want to know why,' Ryker said to Fleming.

'No,' Draper said. 'No more questions from you. Whatever the story between you two, that's not why you're here now. You're here to answer *my* questions.'

Draper moved behind Ryker again, coming up on his left side. He dropped the hammer onto the table and used his free hand to grab Ryker's hand. Ryker tensed and bucked and squirmed, but he wasn't going anywhere. Draper pulled Ryker's hand flat.

'I can see your right hand's taken quite some punishment in the past. Time to even you up a bit,' he said with malice.

Draper thrust the metal rod down and it plunged into Ryker's hand. He gritted his teeth, doing as much as he could to channel away the pain and show no weakness, but the growing pleasure on Draper's face suggested he could see right through the façade.

Draper picked up the hammer and turned it over in his hand for a moment before suddenly spinning and slamming it down onto the top of the rod and sending another two inches of the metal through Ryker's hand. The tip of the rod poked out underneath the chair arm and Draper hit the rod again and again until there was little more than an inch of metal sticking out above Ryker's hand.

Draper was breathing heavily from the force of the blows he'd delivered. Ryker gasped for breath and squirmed in his seat, but he didn't let out a single shout or scream.

'Is that enough scene setting for you?' Draper asked. 'Whatever you *think* is happening here, you need to know only one thing. *I'm* in charge. Not Henderson or Fleming or whatever you want to call him, not my good friend Clyde here, and not you or anyone else.'

'I'm going to kill anyone who had anything to do with Lisa's death,' Ryker snarled, channelling the pain into anger as best he could.

Draper kneeled down and brought his face close to Ryker's and when he spoke his voice was little more than a whisper.

'You said you came here looking for the Silver Wolf.' Ryker said nothing. 'Then perhaps it's about time you met him.'

Draper nodded behind Ryker and he felt a stabbing in his neck and cold liquid surged into his bloodstream. He hadn't even known there was someone else back there. Within seconds, he could feel himself drifting, but not before Draper came back with another rod, and drove it through Ryker's other hand. With his focus and consciousness on the wane, Ryker's eyes fixed on Fleming at the other end of the table. His wicked smile was the last thing Ryker saw before he closed his eyes.

CHAPTER 53

Ryker didn't know how long he was out for. In fact, he wasn't sure whether he'd been unconscious, or just so heavily drugged that his mind felt detached. Wherever he was, it was cold and dank and dark. He'd been in plenty of prison cells in his life and that was his first thought as to where he found himself. Solitary confinement in some shithole jail in some shithole country.

But as Ryker slowly became more lucid, he put the pieces back together. He could vaguely remember being dragged out of the boathouse and along the jetty, and then into the darkness where he now lay. He wasn't in some third world country, he was still in Italy. And it wasn't a jail. Although the room was almost black, there was a sliver of light seeping through the gaps between the door and its frame. Enough light to make out that it wasn't a room with straight lines, but a small cave with misshapen and overhanging walls of bare rock.

Ryker, lying on his side on the cold floor, reached out and touched the rock wall next to him. A shock of pain coursed through him, from his injured hand and all the way through his body. The wall felt clammy to the touch. Water? Or was it simply the blood that likely covered Ryker's hand and arm?

A shuffling noise in the opposite corner of the space caused Ryker to jump. He held his breath and remained still, listening for other sounds. Was it a rat? Maybe even just an insect?

In the darkness, Ryker sat up and lifted his hands, tentatively feeling around his wounds. He didn't remember when, but someone had bandaged both of his hands. Ryker felt he understood why. They didn't want him bleeding profusely, or the wounds to get infected. They wanted him there for the long haul.

The sound came again, louder this time, and Ryker was sure he saw a large, dark shape moving in the far corner. He realised his heart was racing in his chest. He'd never been one to be afraid of the dark, but he'd forgive himself for feeling fear under these circumstances.

'Is someone there?' Ryker asked.

He shuffled forward. The noise came again. Ryker reached out with his hand, slowly and cautiously. He touched something soft, but warm. Definitely not rock. Ryker whipped his hand back.

'Who are you?' a raspy and weak voice asked. A man, Ryker thought, though the words were mumbled and almost unintelligible, like whoever had spoken them had a mouth full of marbles.

'I could ask the same thing of you,' Ryker said.

Another noise. Was that an attempt at a laugh?

'My name's Thomas Maddison,' the man said.

At least that's what Ryker thought he heard. Draper's words suddenly reverberated in his mind. *Then perhaps it's about time you met him.*

So Maddison really was the Silver Wolf? A rogue JIA agent? Then why had he ended up in here?

'Everyone thinks you're dead,' Ryker said, trying to speak calmly, in contrast to the sloshing of his mind as he tried to work out what Maddison being alive but incarcerated meant.

A whimpering sound. Ryker shuffled further forward.

'What have they done to you?' He reached out again with his hand.

'Don't,' Maddison said with more clarity. Ryker stopped. 'You don't want to know.'

'I'll get us out of here.'

'No. You won't. Not *us.*'

'Tell me what happened.'

'It doesn't matter. What's your name?'

'Ja... Carl Logan.'

Silence. Ryker had never known Maddison at the JIA, but perhaps Maddison had known of Ryker, or Logan as he'd been called then.

'I'm sorry,' Maddison said, sniffling. 'There was nothing I could do.'

'Sorry? For what?'

'They made me. They made me tell everything.'

By now, Ryker had worked out the roles of Draper and Fleming and Falah in the whole mess, but one thing he hadn't figured was how Fleming was getting all of his intel on the JIA. Now the source was in front of him.

'You killed her,' Ryker said, surprised at how little feeling there was in his words. 'You killed Lisa. Angela Grainger.'

'Not my hand, but my actions.'

'She was everything to me.'

Ryker reached forward again. He was trembling with pure anger and hatred. He didn't know what was left of Maddison, but he was ready to choke the life out of him.

'I can help you,' Maddison said, and Ryker, shaking hand stretched out to within an inch of where he believed Maddison's neck was, stopped still. 'I'll help you get out of here.'

'Why?' Ryker asked.

'So you can kill them. I want you to kill them all.'

CHAPTER 54

'They took my eyes first,' Maddison said. Ryker was staring into the darkness, about where he thought Maddison's face was. He was imagining what Maddison had looked like on those grainy CCTV shots back in Mexico, and what he now looked like as a captive at Draper's mercy. 'I thought then that I still had a chance of escaping. I went through the same training you went through at the JIA. You know what it's like. You never give in. I wasn't going to give in.'

Even though it was dark, Ryker found himself closing his eyes as he relived some of his worst days of torment, the numerous times he'd been tortured. Whatever he'd been through, it seemed to pale in comparison to what Draper had done to Maddison.

'You said you know how to get out of here?' Ryker said.

A short pause. 'It was just a tiny screwdriver,' Maddison said. 'Like you'd get in Christmas crackers. It was the only thing I had stashed that they didn't find. It took weeks but I managed to scrape away at the rock where I found a seam. Once the chunk came out, I blocked it back in with slime and grit from the walls and floor.'

Ryker felt around on the wall, prodding and poking about until he found the unnatural edge. He picked at it with his fingers and felt the debris crumble away.

After a few minutes a large chunk of rock came loose, four, maybe five inches thick. The rock fell into Ryker's hand and he clenched his fist to catch it, sending another shock of pain right through him. He really didn't know how he could do anything useful with his hands in the state they were in.

'What's left of the screwdriver is behind there too,' Maddison said.

Ryker fished for it and found the inch-long piece of metal.

'You never tried to attack them?'

Ryker heard a sharp intake of breath, as though Maddison was struggling to hold himself together. 'I never got the chance. They took my hands. Then my arms. Then—'

'I'm sorry,' Ryker said, bowing his head.

He didn't want to hear any more. Yes, he'd been subjected to brutal torture, but Maddison had been savagely mutilated. He couldn't even begin to imagine Maddison's suffering. And what was all the more striking was how deliberate his torture was. For him to have suffered like that and not died of blood loss or shock or infection required skill. Surgical skill. Was Draper really capable of that?

No, not Draper, Ryker realised. Clyde. Ryker shivered at the thought.

'I'll get them for you,' Ryker said.

'No, not for me. Do it for you, and for Angela, and for all the other people who got hurt because of me.'

Ryker put his hand to his chest, feeling the form of the olive branch underneath his shirt. The symbol of peace. That's all he and Lisa had both wanted. Peace. He hoped Lisa would forgive him for what he was planning to do next. He was doing it to honour her, after all.

'Someone's coming,' Maddison whispered.

Ryker frowned. He hadn't heard anyone. But then Maddison had been in the cave for many months, alone in the dark, his senses heightened.

'They'll take you on the boat, or to the boathouse. That's where Clyde does his handiwork.'

Ryker gritted his teeth. He held the rock as firmly as he could and lay down on his side, facing away from the door, with the rock nestled into his abdomen.

A few seconds later, he heard footsteps, getting closer. They stopped, and a key turned in the lock. Ryker's eyes were wide, and when the door opened and the bright sunlight from outside burst into the cramped space, Ryker was at first blinded and had to blink several times before he realised he was staring right at Thomas Maddison, aka the Silver Wolf.

At least what was left of him.

Ryker had seen some terrible things in his time, but he'd never before seen brutality and savagery like that. Maddison was nothing more than a head, neck and torso, each of his limbs gone. There were two black holes where his eyes used to be. Another where his nose had been removed. His ears too were missing, as were his teeth. Not much could genuinely shock Ryker, but in that moment he felt frozen.

At least until Maddison spoke.

'Hello, Clyde,' Maddison said. How did Maddison know who was there? 'I think he's unconscious. Either the drugs you fed him or what you already did to him. Draper get a bit too hungry too soon?'

Ryker heard shuffling behind him as Clyde came closer. An arm reached out to Ryker to pull him onto his back. Ryker channelled as much strength as he could into his muscles, into his throbbing and devastated hands. He swung around, his hand and the rock hurtling for Clyde's face.

The move was born of desperation as much as anything. Ryker was already seriously injured, and there was little skill in what he was trying. He paid the price.

Clyde flung out his forearm, blocking Ryker's ambush attempt with ease. His weakened grip meant he could do nothing as the rock tumbled away. Ryker had so far seen little of who or what Clyde was. Maybe if he'd known more he would have thought through his attack for longer.

Clyde, still hunched down, swung an elbow at Ryker's face then quickly sprang back upright. He lifted a heel and got set to drive it into Ryker's face, but Ryker turned over at the last second and pulled himself up as the heel smashed onto the stone floor.

Ryker wasn't given a second's respite though. A flurry of fists and knees and feet came his way in the cramped space, and he had to pull out everything he could to block the attacks. But he was too drained to defend properly, and he didn't have enough energy or focus to thwart the lightning fast barrage for long.

Moments later, Ryker was caught in the head for the umpteenth time and then a strike to the solar plexus made his heart dance and he sank to the ground, dazed and confused.

Before he knew it, a panting Clyde had grabbed hold of Ryker's hands and squeezed the pulpy holes in his palms. Ryker shouted out this time as an unimaginable pain swept through him. Together with the beating he'd just taken, it made him feel delirious.

Clyde stood over him, his face creased with anger, spittle dripping down his chin – such a stark contrast to his usual squeaky-clean look. He grabbed Ryker and dragged him out of the cave by his hands.

Ryker's head was lolling and he pulled it up, trying to stay awake and alert. Seconds later they were out in the bright sunshine which only made the stabbing pain in Ryker's brain worse. He squeezed his eyes shut, hoping the sensation would pass. It didn't. The pain was immense, but Ryker knew he had to do something. He'd seen what Clyde was capable of. He couldn't let that happen. He'd rather die than suffer like Maddison.

Ryker's hands were next to useless now. His arms too, because of the numbing pain that was sweeping up them. But there was still fight left in him. He would fight to the end.

Clyde was snarling and panting as he dragged Ryker across the wooden planks of the jetty. The *Angelica* bobbed up and down on the water just a few yards away. Ryker shook his head, trying to find clarity. Through his blurred vision, he spotted four thick ropes tied around metal cleats, holding the yacht tightly against the pier – one rope at the bow, one at the stern, and a forward and aft spring line.

As they neared the yacht's bow, Clyde twice glanced over to the deck. Ryker guessed that was their intended destination. Were Draper and Fleming already aboard?

Ryker shook his head once more, and tensed the muscles all across his body as he summoned every ounce of strength he had. He took two big lungfuls of air as he readied himself. His legs twitched with anticipation and then, when Clyde next glanced over to the boat, Ryker made his move. One last final attempt.

Ryker used his stomach muscles to haul his legs into the air, right over his head, a classic Jujitsu move. He swivelled his hips, spinning his torso a hundred and eighty degrees, causing Clyde's arms to twist over each other and forcing him to release Ryker's hands. Ryker thrust the heel of one foot into Clyde's groin, quickly planted his feet either side of Clyde's left leg, then swivelled again to bring Clyde crashing to the ground.

More through luck rather than judgment, the back of Clyde's head smashed off one of the metal cleats, a blow that was certainly hard enough to crack his skull. Ryker, his vision blurring again from the sudden exertion, hauled himself back to his feet and – eyes squinting – glanced up at the gardens above. No sign of Fleming and Draper.

Ryker looked down at Clyde. He was still breathing – murmuring, in fact. He went to get up. Ryker was surprised he had any fight left in him, given the smack to the head. He couldn't afford any chance of Clyde returning for a second round. Ryker launched his foot into Clyde's gut, then kneeled down next to the cleat where there was several feet of rope that hadn't been tidied up.

Grimacing in pain, Ryker quickly tied both of Clyde's ankles together with the slack, then unwound the rest of the rope from the cleat. He looked at Clyde. He opened his eyes, looked like he was about to say something.

Ryker used his foot to heave Clyde into the water.

The yacht, now with no rope holding its bow in place, edged away from the pier a few yards. Ryker looked over the side. Sure enough, Clyde was on top of the water, splashing around, trying to pull himself up the rope. But the next second, as the bow pushed away from the pier, the other three ropes holding the boat were stretched to their limit, causing the mass to snap back toward the jetty. There was a crunching sound as the bow knocked up against the wooden struts of the pier.

Looked like it wasn't Clyde's lucky day.

Voices from somewhere up above caught Ryker's attention. He achingly turned and moved as quickly as he could back for the cave entrance, trying to get out of sight. He was unarmed and badly injured, and his only hope of fighting was by using stealth and surprise.

Moments later, Ryker caught sight of both Draper and Fleming coming down the steps from the main house. They were talking loudly, jovially. Like two nutcases would on their way to witness the torture of another human being. Ryker stuck his head back into cover and listened as the two men came closer.

They reached the jetty. There was no sign of anyone else joining this party. That was good. Ryker wanted his revenge on both of those scumbags, though he'd fight anyone else who got in his way.

Then a high-pitched voice cut through the air and Ryker froze. He risked a peek and saw the young girl in a flowing yellow dress, at the top of the steps. She was shouting down to Draper who, together with Fleming, had his back to Ryker as he looked up to the girl.

Ryker willed her not to come down the steps. She was one of the reasons he'd been reluctant to launch an all-out assault on the villa in the first place. He really didn't want her getting caught up in the melee.

'Daddy, come and say goodbye to me properly!' the girl shouted, sounding more excited than annoyed or upset.

Draper turned to Fleming, who shrugged.

'Okay, I'm coming to get you!' Draper said, in a pretend monster voice. He rushed off back up the steps and the girl squealed and disappeared out of sight into the garden above.

Fleming shook his head and turned to the boat. He looked at the ropes then along the pier, smiling as he followed the trail of blood that led from the cave from when Ryker had been dragged out.

Ryker pulled his head back in. He wondered whether Fleming would guess something was up given neither Clyde nor Ryker were in sight. But moments later, Ryker heard the whizzing sound of ropes being uncoiled, and he stuck his head out again to see Fleming untying the remaining three ropes from their cleats. He moved over to the final one, at the stern.

Ryker looked back up to the steps.

Having done his fatherly duty, Draper was just starting to make his way back down again. 'Okay, we're good to go,' he called to Fleming.

Fleming gave him the thumbs up and unwound the last rope, then remained there on the pier, holding the rope tightly in his hand while he waited for the boss to embark. Ryker wasn't going to let that happen.

Once again summoning an inner strength, he darted forward. Draper spotted him first, and shouted out to Fleming who spun around. Ryker was only two yards from him by that point and he launched himself forward, both feet off the ground. He flew through the air as Fleming tried to get into a defensive position. He didn't have a chance.

Ryker smashed into him, and both men shot off the pier and landed in a tangled heap on the yacht's bottom deck. With all the ropes untied, and the momentum created by four hundred pounds of flesh and bone scuttling across the deck, the boat drifted from the pier.

Ryker heard shouting. From Draper. Possibly from his guards too. He could only hope anyone on shore who was armed wouldn't shoot with Fleming right there.

The rope had come out of Fleming's hand when he fell, and was lying just inches from Ryker on the deck. But with Ryker dazed not just from the fall but from his debilitating injuries, it was Fleming who moved first.

He grabbed the rope, wound it around Ryker's neck and pulled. Ryker grimaced and spluttered for breath as his neck was crushed, the thick ligature pushing down hard against his windpipe. He bucked, trying to kick out at Fleming who was positioned behind him, both men on their sides, but he couldn't get an angle for any of the shots to make a difference. He threw his elbow out behind him, several times in quick succession. He couldn't tell where exactly the blows hit, but eventually Fleming released his grip just enough for Ryker to force his forearm through the gap between the rope and his neck, and he used the strength in his shoulder and upper arm to pull the rope over his head.

Running on nothing but adrenaline and survival instinct, Ryker spun and jumped back to his feet, just as Fleming did the same. Ryker glanced back to the shore. They were already a good twenty yards from the pier. Draper and an armed guard were there, staring over to them. The guard lifted his weapon.

Then sirens cut through the air. Police?

Ryker looked at Fleming. They hunched over, snarling, as they squared off.

Back on shore, Ryker heard shouting, and he glanced across and saw Draper and the guard shoot back toward the steps.

Seconds later, the boom of helicopter rotors roared in Ryker's ears as a chopper hurtled over a nearby hill.

This was a full-on police assault. Ryker wondered whether Winter had somehow initiated it.

'Looks like it's game over for you,' Ryker said to Fleming as they circled on the deck, both wary of making the next move.

'No. This is right where I want to be.'

Ryker felt he knew what Fleming meant by that. They both wanted the other dead. Yet Ryker knew to be wary with Fleming, even if he'd been at full strength. The ex-SAS man was a dirty brawler. Ryker's injuries only made the fight all the more uneven.

One thing Ryker did have on his side though, was pure hatred, and an absolute need for revenge. He couldn't let Fleming get away from him again, police or no police.

'*You* killed Lisa.'

Fleming snorted. 'How else was I supposed to get you out into the open?'

Ryker shook his head. 'That's not why you did it.'

'No?'

'You did it because you're a hateful piece of scum.'

'Fuck, you're always so tense.'

There was a blast of wind as the helicopter swooped over the top of them. Fleming momentarily glanced up and Ryker lurched forward. His aim was clear. Get Fleming on the deck and use his uninjured legs to choke him. But Fleming was no amateur, and he blocked Ryker's leg swipe with ease, then spun and delivered a roundhouse kick that caught Ryker in his kidney and sent him down onto one knee.

Fleming hauled up his knee, aiming for Ryker's chin, but Ryker had just enough time to shift his head back. In a reflexive move, he grabbed hold of Fleming's dangling leg, aiming to use it to topple him, but instead he screamed from the pain in his hands, and was forced to let go.

As Fleming righted himself, Ryker clambered back to his feet, cradling his hands close to his chest, hoping the shock of pain would pass. It was so bad his sight was once again blurred and jittery.

He noticed Fleming rushing forward, but this time could make only a half-hearted attempt at blocking the hook. Ryker tried in vain to counter, but Fleming grabbed his arm, twisted and smacked down just above the elbow. Ryker's arm popped as it dislocated from the shoulder, and he screamed in pain again.

Through sheer agony, Ryker found himself down on one knee, and he was struggling to muster any fight. Fleming seemed to get that. He wound up for a killer blow.

Then the yacht struck something. Ryker had no idea what, but the sudden jolt sent Fleming stumbling off course.

Ryker saw one last desperate hope.

He didn't know where he found the strength but he sprang to his feet and rushed for Fleming, barrelled into him and kept on going. His legs taking the weight of both men, Ryker powered forward and slammed Fleming into a metal column that connected to the upper deck. There was a cracking and a squelching sound, and Ryker wondered if he'd just snapped several of Fleming's ribs. As he stepped back, he realised it was worse than that. Worse for Fleming at least. Fleming half stepped forward, half fell, his eyes distant. Ryker saw the metal hook on the column, just below neck height. Blood dripped from it.

Fleming collapsed onto the deck.

Ryker, snarling, stared into Fleming's drifting eyes. There was another blast of air as the helicopter once again swooped over the boat. Ryker glanced up and saw it turn and hover, just a few yards away. Then, across the water, he saw a fast approaching police boat. A man hanging out of the helicopter barked orders at Ryker, but he wasn't really listening. He was too busy staring at Fleming.

He was still breathing. Still moving. Ryker couldn't have that. He'd made the mistake before of believing Fleming was finished, and it had cost Lisa her life, and Willoughby. He couldn't risk him leaving the boat alive.

Ryker looked over the deck. A toolbox had spilled its contents when the yacht had banged into something just moments before. Ryker kneeled down and grabbed a screwdriver. He turned Fleming over. He was grimacing and wheezing, no strength left in him, but he appeared lucid. Ryker caught Fleming's gaze... then drove the screwdriver into his neck. Fleming's eyes bulged.

'This is for Lisa,' Ryker said through gritted teeth as he pulled the tool out and sank it into Fleming's neck a second time.

Above him, the barked orders from the man in the helicopter got louder and sterner.

Ryker paid no attention to the warning. He pulled the screwdriver out again and a spray of blood erupted from the wound. Fleming's body shook. His head lolled but Ryker reached out and moved it back centre so they were still looking at one another. Ryker wanted his face to be the last thing Fleming ever saw.

After a few seconds more, Fleming went still.

Ryker heard another warning from above, though he wasn't really paying attention. He went to stand up.

A single gunshot rang out, and Ryker keeled over onto the deck.

CHAPTER 55

London, England

Ryker sat on the bench and looked across the field at Regent's Park. Everything felt calm and relaxed, and with the thick tree line surrounding the grass, there was no hint that this was the middle of one of the world's busiest cities. Joggers, walkers, cyclists were all out and about doing their own thing. A group of young men and women played touch rugby. There were countless people just sitting on the grass chatting and laughing. A man in a wheelchair was rolling himself along a winding path.

Not just any man. Peter Winter.

'I guess it was about time you built up some muscle in those scrawny arms of yours,' Ryker said when Winter had come to a stop next to him. His cheeks were red and he was out of breath.

'Don't you worry,' Winter said. 'I'll be out of this thing in no time. And you shouldn't joke. By the time you get out of that sling, your right arm will be a twig.'

Ryker laughed. Doing so sent a shock of pain through his shoulder, across his back and down his arms into his hands. He'd been injured before, been shot before, but these most recent wounds were more than just superficial. Even two months later he was still far from full strength, and he wondered if he ever would be again. His body was too old and battered to keep going through hell.

'So where do we go from here?' Winter asked.

It was a question Ryker had asked himself countless times in the last few weeks, following the events in Italy. He really didn't have a clear answer yet. 'Fleming's dead. I mean really dead, this time,' Ryker said. 'Isn't he?'

'He is. I can assure you of that. Flowers saw the body.'

In a twisted way, Ryker wished he'd seen that too, yet after the Italian police had shot him in the shoulder on that boat he'd fallen unconscious and had woken up in a hospital bed where he'd spent the next month. He'd only returned to London less than forty-eight hours earlier.

'In answer to your question, then,' Ryker said. 'I've done what I needed to do. I found who killed Lisa. I made him pay.'

'You did. You also managed to bring down a powerful weapons smuggler in the process. Lawrence Draper, aka Nicholas Andrews, is going to spend the rest of his life in jail.'

'He got off likely if you ask me.'

'We'll see about that.'

'What about the kid?' Ryker asked, a vision of the happy little girl he'd seen rushing through his mind. She was the real victim from the whole sorry saga.

'That's down to the Italian authorities, I'm afraid. Her mother is dead, her father will never be a free man. If there aren't any grandparents around then who knows.'

Ryker felt little comfort from that answer. He'd find out what her fate was, try to help if he could.

'And my actions also saw one of your agents get killed,' Ryker said soberly. He truly felt grief over what had happened to Willoughby. He'd miss her.

'It's not your fault,' Winter said.

'Did you ever find the full story on Maddison?'

'We've had *his* version of events,' Winter said. 'That he was put deep undercover by Victoria Cameron. That's why there was nothing in the official files. He was working for the Silver Wolf, aka Draper, aka Andrews, for close to two years.'

Ryker wasn't so sure about that. The way Maddison had spoken made it sound like he was a rogue. That *he* was the Silver Wolf, and Ryker had assumed that most likely Draper had simply taken on that title after turning on the ex-JIA man. Perhaps that wasn't the case though. In many ways it didn't matter. Whoever the Silver Wolf really was, he was finished.

'Then dear old Captain Fleming turned up and he rumbled Maddison as a JIA agent,' Winter continued. 'And we all know how that turned out for Maddison. They milked him, got everything he knew about the JIA out of him for their own benefit.'

Which was certainly true. Whether Maddison had been clean or dirty before Fleming showed up, there was no doubt he had suffered horribly.

'Fleming only ever wanted his revenge,' Ryker said. 'Against me. Against you. Against the agency. Draper was just in it for the money. Fleming is the reason so many people are dead, why Ffion Brady will spend the rest of her life in prison too. He did it all to get back at us.'

'He can't do any more damage now, though, can he?'

'No. He can't.'

They both fell silent for a short while, Ryker still lost in his thoughts about what had happened and how he could have done things differently. Did he make mistakes along the way? Or had he done his best battling against the unknown?

'Every time you get knocked down, you come back stronger,' Winter said, gazing at Ryker with admiration.

'It doesn't feel like that right now.'

'I'm not kidding. You're like a damn Stretch Armstrong or something. Nothing breaks you. In a few weeks you'll be back raring to go.'

Winter paused and Ryker felt he knew where the commander was headed. He didn't say anything, just waited for Winter to go ahead and spit it out.

'I can still use you, Ryker. The JIA can always use a man like you.'

Ryker sighed. The fact was he really had no idea what he wanted from life anymore. He'd had Lisa. She had been his one shining light. But his past had got her killed. In fact, every person he got close to – Lisa, Willoughby, Mackie, Winter – got hurt eventually. He'd be better off heading away into the sunset and going to live in solitude, if only to avoid causing pain for others.

Or should he just take a bottle of whisky and a packet of pills to bed one night? He'd certainly contemplated that enough times recently.

But what kind of a selfish action was that? So maybe he would never be happy, maybe he'd never find love again or get the chance to settle down, have a family, enjoy life like other people did. That didn't mean he couldn't still do good for others.

'Can I count on you?' Winter asked. 'You can have your old identity back. Or keep Ryker. Or a have new one. Whatever suits you. But come and work for me again. What do you say?'

'I don't need a new identity,' Ryker said. 'James Ryker fits just fine. It reminds me of what I wanted to be. What me and Lisa could have been.'

He put his hand to his chest. Felt the comforting form of the olive branch through the fabric of his cotton shirt.

'But you'll come and work for me again?'

Ryker got up from the bench, grimacing in pain as he did so. 'Why don't you give me a call when you've got a case. We'll talk about it then.'

'There's the thing.' Winter reached out behind him, to the satchel that was strapped over the back of the wheelchair. He fumbled around and came back out with a brown paper envelope. 'Take a look.'

Ryker frowned and took the envelope off him, ignoring the pain in his still-bandaged hands. He slid the papers half out and scanned through. He flicked to the next page, then the one after, taking the information into his head in snippets.

After a few seconds, he slid the papers back inside.

'So are you in?' Winter asked.

Ryker just smiled, then walked away.

ACKNOWLEDGEMENTS

The Silver Wolf feels like a landmark book for me, not just in terms of where it leaves James Ryker as a character, but for it marking the end of an incredible year in my life. In the space of just twelve short months I've had four releases with Bloodhound Books, and with each one I have hit greater heights. Who'd have thought all of this came about from a chance encounter with the owners of Bloodhound over a beer in the bar of a Bristol hotel?! I am filled with gratitude to Bloodhound Books, and especially to Fred and Betsy, for showing faith in me. A special mention must also go to the growing team behind the scenes, particularly Sumaira, Alexina and Sarah.

As ever I am also incredibly grateful and humbled by my readers, and all of the reviewers and bloggers who have done so much for me, many of whom have now stuck with me loyally through seven books. It's been a whirlwind few years since Dance with the Enemy was first released, and I can only hope that those of you reading this will stick with me through the next seven books too.

Thank you all so much, and here's to the future...

21869918R00190

Printed in Poland
by Amazon Fulfillment
Poland Sp. z o.o., Wrocław